Lucy McCarraher

Kindred Spirits

To Mark ·

Lots of love —

Lucy x

23 · iii · 2009 ·

Kindred Spirits

Published in 2008 by YouWriteOn.com

MORE BOOKS BY THE SAME AUTHOR:

Blood and Water

Mr Mikey's Ladies

The Book of Balanced Living

Acknowledgements

I discovered much about the detail of life in a South Norfolk village in the Second World War, not only from the normal research sources (in particular those listed at the back), but from the memories and memorabilia of Maureen Blake, Jane Cannell, Pat Ramm, Sue Reynolds, Bryan Taylor and Margaret Thorburn. My mother, Gillian Wagner and parents-in-law Gill and Neil McCarraher also contributed their recollections of wartime childhoods.

My thanks to friends in Bunwell who allowed me to use parts of their lives as the basis for present day Haddeston, especially Kathy Parkins and Barbara Boyer; and to the Bunwell Book Group who gave me useful feedback on the first draft, including Ros Ali, Cate Harper, Sue Jordan, Shaun Parsons, Marian Rout, Tamara Rowe and Rachael Seaward.

Stuart Davidson patiently answered my medical questions about asthma and the process that a doctor accused of misconduct would undergo; Peter North also gave useful input on the latter. Liv O'Hanlon and Bruna Gushurst supplied information on herbal cures for asthma, past and present.

Mark Wagner explained how a company takeover would work and Mary Brehony gave legal advice on intestacy and wills.

Much support during the writing process came from Verity Ridgman, Cate Sweeney and Patrick Tilley, all of whose input was salutary and perceptive; as were comments from my sons James Page and Chris Page – who also created the enigmatic cover image – and Peter Bourne.

Mike Elliston was responsible for introducing me to the character of Henry Tinker, whose apparent wish to have his story told inspired this book.

Without the generosity and hard work of Jo and Andrew Holloway of Sunberry Books (Sunpenny Publishing), this book would not have achieved publication.

Thanks, as ever, to Richard McCarraher.

"Kindred spirits are not so scarce as I used to think. It's splendid to find out there are so many of them in the world."

LUCY MAUD MONTGOMERY
Anne of Green Gables

Chapter One

And then, finally, it was time.

Time to leave the set on which the past decade of my life had been played out.

To my surprise I found the mounting trepidation of the last few weeks had made its departure ahead of mine. The house, stripped bare of everything that made it ours, had already lost what I had most dreaded leaving. Like an empty theatre after the play has ended, the bare walls contained only silent echoes and empty memories.

It was time to move on.

My older children had cleared out their attic bedrooms weeks before, but as I checked them for the last time the empty rooms flashed images of their teenage lives at me: I closed one door on the abiding memory of Mark playing 'Tears from Heaven' on his guitar; the other on Jess watching back-to-back episodes of *Friends* with her two real life best friends. On the first floor, Lily's ceiling retained the luminous stars which had watched over the days and lit all the nights of her seven years;

whilst the indentations of Felix's cot legs remained indelibly in the lino floor of his room.

The pervasive intimacy of the bedroom I had shared with Jack seemed to have been removed with the furniture and the room felt as impersonal as the day we'd moved in. I hoped the particles that had absorbed nine years of marriage had crammed themselves into the van with the rest of our household goods and were at this moment bumping their way eastward amongst the packing cases. Perhaps they would unfurl the other end with the sheets and quilts, clothes and cushions, paintings and photos, and envelop us in the aura of contented family life I envisaged at our new home.

After a final mug of coffee, I swabbed the last stains from the kitchen surfaces, mopped the tiles and hauled the final bin bag out to the pile by the pavement. I unwound the door keys from my key ring and left them in the hall with a welcome note and the local take away menus. Jack had left earlier, to stop in at his surgery round the corner for the final time and load the boxed-up contents of his office into his new Landrover, already stacked with all our computer gear and his precious sound system.

Mel, my next door neighbour, saw me closing the car boot on the last bag of over night necessities the removal men had left us and came out to say goodbye. We exchanged fierce hugs, me smiling through tears and saying that they must all come and stay very soon; Mel saying yes, of course they would, though we both knew they wouldn't. I got into the car and drove away without looking back until I had almost rounded the bend. Mel was still on the pavement her arm raised in a final farewell.

But I was OK.

I was on the way and feeling good.

If I'd known then what lay ahead of us, I might have had second thoughts about moving out of my city comfort zone to a new life in the country.

Not that I had been a willing convert to Jack's plan to leave London. Having spent my childhood in Pimlico and lived most of my adult years around the eccentricities of Crystal Palace, I could hardly conceive of a life outside the capital. But Jack's suburban roots had long sought deeper soil and Felix's asthma, serious and intractable since his birth two years ago, provided him with the ultimate justification.

We had argued the case at length, with me pitting my friends, work and access to the city's arts and heritage I rarely took advantage of these days but thought our children should have; against Jack's implacable belief that our quality of life, health, stress levels, and the children's education would all be vastly improved in a rural setting.

Unspoken between us remained what I suspected was his hidden agenda: the desire to be closer to his birth mother, with whom we had made contact before Felix was born.

Our increasingly regular trips to stay with Kathleen and her politician husband, Maxwell, in their Norfolk constituency home had exposed a new side of Jack: a man who worked out by walking dogs rather than running laps; relaxed by digging vegetables instead of watching football; and chopped wood and built fires of an evening in preference to writing research papers. I enjoyed this relaxed, weekend version of my husband, delighted in the children's occasional countryside freedom and kept my less positive feelings to myself. How could I resent Jack's boyish happiness in the company of his newly found parent?

Yet insecurity sometimes gnawed at me when I watched him with Kathleen who, still beautiful, looked younger than her sixty years and sometimes a near mirror image of her adult son. She showed little of the mother and still less of the grandmother she had recently discovered herself to be in her attitude towards him. Six years his senior, I was the older woman in Jack's life, but had the long term demands of motherhood robbed me of the appeal that Kathleen's belated assumption of the role conferred on her?

"Don't even think like that," Ros reassured me when I had finally confided these uncharitable thoughts to my four best friends at one of our regular meetings at the Café St Germain on Crystal Palace Parade.

"You and Jack have a really robust relationship with all the resilience it takes to surmount even serious problems."

Ros was a child psychotherapist and talking with her professional hat on.

"I understand why you're worrying, but you'd be better off concentrating on the positive. I know when I'm working with my most severe cases, it's parents with relationships like yours and affirmative attitudes who come through best."

"Thanks for the vote of confidence, Ros," I replied, "but we're going to be almost on Kathleen's doorstep, and in her territory too."

"And don't you think that sort of familiarity might not breed a little more contempt in Jack?" she asked, stretching her long legs as she took a sip of her decaf latte. "A bit of everyday contact is bound to put a few dents in his shiny, happy image of her."

"And by contrast, your sacrifice in moving to the country for him will make you shine more brightly in Jack's eyes. You are the light of his life – don't ever forget that, Mo," broke in our American friend, Miranda. "And of course it is critical for children to identify with their genetic heritage, however late in life that happens."

Suzy had listened silently to both of them while scooping up remnants of froth from her large, full-strength cappuccino. Carefully blotting her mouth with a paper serviette, she had put her head on one side and looked at me affectionately.

"Do you know what, Mo?" she asked, smiling. "Much as I'll miss you, I just know that village life is going to suit you all the way down to the muddy ground. The children are at exactly the right age to act as an entrée to the community and you'll make new friends easily enough. It's Jack who's going to find it harder to make the transition, whatever he thinks now. Being a GP in deepest Norfolk will be a very different experience to South London, and Kathleen can't help him with that."

I took enough comfort from Suzy's opinion, knowing how accurate her perceptions usually were, to ignore Venetia, my oldest friend and perennially perverse, when she warned me against Kathleen and capitulating to Jack.

"He's only a man, he can't help thinking he's the head of the family and you should all do what he wants. But Kathleen's an unknown quantity – you don't know what she might be planning!"

I had taken this melodramatic advice to be her unsentimental way of saying she too would miss me, and our weekly coffee mornings. I was shattering a twenty-year tradition through which we five had supported each other as our children grew from babies to adults, our relationships ebbed and flowed and our careers bloomed and branched.

Slowly, though, I had allowed myself to see Jack's point of view, to imagine a different life and savour the possibility of change. For the first time I had permitted myself to recognise that my London had become increasingly dirty, aggressive, unsympathetic and claustrophobic. I admitted that the traffic, the inescapable quantities of people, the polluted air and extremes of both poverty and affluence oppressed me.

Perhaps it was middle age setting in, maybe I was influenced by Jack's desire for *lebensraum*, but from somewhere deep inside myself I became aware of a yearning for views of open fields and distant horizons, for the sound of birdsong and wind through branches, for pure silence and clear skies at night, and for a greater connection with un-manicured nature and her seasons in the raw.

———

The rain petered out as I paid my toll to get out of London through the Dartford Tunnel and the clouds began to pull apart over the Essex landscape on the other side.

Somewhere on this stretch of motorway, the fumes of London gave way to fresh country air, and I breathed in the damp, grassy smell like the elixir of life. The sun came out and, by the time I turned off to Norfolk the low East Anglian scenery was bathed in luminous spring light.

I felt I had really made the transition from our old life to what was now my home strait.

As I drove through forest green Scots pines and flat fields patchworked in russet ploughed earth, silver green wheat, acid yellow rape and ice white poly-tunnels, I went over yet again the way in which, once I had opened my mind to the possibility of change, the means to make it a reality had instantly appeared.

After dinner on one of our weekend visits some six months ago, we had told Kathleen and Maxwell that we were seriously considering moving out of London. Her response had been quietly ecstatic.

"I hope that means you'll be looking for something in our neck of the woods, now you've got to know this part of Norfolk," she said in a light tone, turning her radiant smile and amber-coloured eyes intently on Jack.

"We haven't decided on anywhere specific," I responded before Jack could agree. "Though we wouldn't want to take the children too far from Colin and Betty."

I felt the need to remind her of Jack's solid relationship with his adoptive parents and their status as 'real' grandparents to Lily and Felix.

"And it just depends where a partnership in a good surgery comes up. We'll go where Jack's work takes us."

"Oh, but you'd get so much more for your money in terms of a house and land here, than in Surrey, Mo." Kathleen smiled sweetly at me and took another sip of the excellent Chablis

Maxwell had opened. "And it's not so far for them to drive."

"Well, let us know if there's anything we can do to help," cut in Maxwell, before Kathleen started to assert the parental rights that she had renounced forty-two years ago. She had always stated her intention never to come between her twins, Jack and Julia, and the parents who had raised them, but perhaps the alcohol we had consumed that early autumn evening had allowed deep-rooted feelings to break cover and made her less careful of how she exposed them.

As Maxwell got up to collect our plates, scraped clean of the poached rainbow trout he and Jack had caught earlier in the day, he caught his wife's eye and a look I couldn't then interpret passed between them. With hindsight he must have been reassuring her that her desires would be met. Maxwell was a fixer par excellence, and within a week had called Jack with the news that a friend of his was looking for a new doctor for her health centre and would he like to come and meet Dr Elizabeth Gidney for an initial discussion.

When Jack returned from the meeting, he had brought with him the opportunity to buy not only a partnership in a small rural GP practice, but also a seventeenth century farmhouse with just under an acre of land, set in a village whose amenities included a primary school, playgroup and broadband connection – instantly disarming all my first lines of resistance.

Dr Gidney and her late husband had been the main partners in the Haddeston Health Centre until he had died unexpectedly last year. Now Elizabeth was working with a part-time doctor and locum support, but seeking to reduce her own hours as she moved closer to retirement. They had been planning to advertise for a full-time partner, but had heard of Jack's interest in moving to Norfolk following a 'chance' conversation with Maxwell the day after our visit. What was more, her recent widowhood meant Elizabeth Gidney wanted to downsize domestically and had just found her ideal cottage in the village. If Jack became her partner and a price could be agreed, her spacious family home would be ready to move into as soon as we were able.

"You'll love it, hon," Jack had enthused after his tour of the rural community, surgery and house. "It's a good sized village and I had a quick look at the school. It's got a new headmaster who Elizabeth says is well-respected and raising standards all round. The Health Centre is just what I've been looking for, and I know Elizabeth and I could work well together."

"OK, that sounds good," I had replied non-committally.

"And look at this – " Jack pulled out his mobile phone and clicked through the photos he had taken of Stargate Farm. "You're going to love the house. Isn't that just perfect for us as a family? Here's one of the garden."

I had peered curiously at the little screen's images of a long, creamy yellow farmhouse with a steep pantiled roof and tall chimneys. The garden, with its lawns, trees and flowerbeds, looked massive compared with our strip of grass and decking, though the perspective could have been deceptive.

"This is it, isn't it, Mo? Our ideal house in the country with all the trimmings. Doesn't it make you want to move in this minute?"

If Jack, who always took decisions based on rationality and practicality, could be so enthusiastic, surely I, with my faith in intuition and synchronicity, would agree with him. But I had been torn between irritation at the speed and success of Maxwell and Kathleen's machinations, interest in the apparently idyllic life that might await us and alarm at the magnitude of the decision I was being asked to make. This was about my family's future and possibly the rest of my life.

"It all looks and sounds wonderful," I had told him, truthfully. "But I don't want to feel pushed into buying a house that isn't absolutely right for all of us, in a location I don't feel entirely committed to. You'll have to let me get my head round it in my own way."

So I had postponed an exploratory trip to Great Haddeston

until I had done my own investigations. As a professional researcher I had used my expertise to gather the hard evidence I might need to oppose unwanted aspects of the plans that were forming inexorably around me.

Great Haddeston boasted all five of the local facilities – a pub, village hall, shop, primary school and church – which were highly rated by rural communities. Its Community Primary School had a very reasonable Ofsted report, even if not quite as glowing of that of Haddeston Rode, second largest of the three Haddeston villages. Haddeston St Michael appeared to be not so much a village as a straggling collection of farms and dwellings with no discernible centre other than a large pub, but it was part of the surgery's catchment area.

I had trawled the websites of Norfolk estate agents, got to grips with what was on offer in our price range and requested details of several other properties I liked the look of. I had to admit that Stargate Farm held its own in price, size and location, but I insisted we view a couple of other houses, if only for comparison.

Leaving Lily and Felix with Jack's parents, he and I had set off early one Saturday morning and reached our destination before midday. I made Jack drive slowly around the three villages, past the well designed, eco-friendly Health Centre complex at one end of Great Haddeston, then Stargate Farm at the other. In reality, the well-proportioned farmhouse with its own small barn was even more attractive than in Jack's photos. The sun beamed through the autumnal trees and bathed the surrounding fields in a genial glow. My cool attitude to the potential life that awaited us here had started to warm.

———

Neither of the properties I had requested viewings of had been remotely tempting alternatives. Cherry Tree Farm in Haddeston End belied its pretty name and the estate agent hype; it was a rundown sixties house with admittedly stunning views, set in four acres, but too remote for me. Ashbrook House, on the other hand, was situated on a busy road called the Turnpike from which the traffic noise was intrusive, and the house's traditional oak beams held up ceilings so low that Jack had to stoop the entire time we were indoors.

We decided to have a pub lunch in Great Haddeston's Trowel and Hammer before meeting Elizabeth at Stargate Farm.

Looking back, the indefinable sense of familiarity had started as we entered the traditional hostelry and I breathed in the first whiff of local ale, pipe smoke and steak-and-kidney pudding. Jack had looked surprised when I ordered a completely untypical half of Adnams bitter. I was surprised myself, but for a moment I had felt a pleasant anticipation of tangy beer in my mouth and my hands warming at a blazing fire. It passed almost instantly as I saw the dried flower arrangement in the barren fireplace and I smiled to Jack in explanation:

"Just getting into the local spirit. Isn't that what you wanted?"

While he bought the drinks and ordered lunch, I had peered at the framed black-and-white photos of late nineteenth and early twentieth century Haddeston that decorated the walls. I recognised one of Stargate Farm with a classic car on the road outside and smiled with recognition, not of the house I had recently glimpsed, but the face of the young man in uniform standing with evident pride beside a military 4.1 litre Humber Snipe.

"What kind of car is that?" I asked Jack as he handed me the half pint glass. I took a sip of the bitter and tried to pretend I liked it. He peered into the picture, saw it was of Stargate Farm and grinned.

"Is that what you want to park in the drive when we take possession? I'd say that was one of the big Humber Snipes the Rootes Group was building during the war. The military used them as staff cars for the top brass. Monty had one called 'Old Faithful'. Not exactly what I had in mind for us, I was thinking of a Landrover..."

But I was more intrigued by how my mind had thrown up with such accuracy the make and model of a historic car which I had no recollection of ever seeing before, and why I should have thought I recognised the man beside it. There was no rational answer and I had missed the thrust of Jack's rationale for owning the ultimate country vehicle.

"...perfect for camping expeditions and fishing trips with Felix when he's a bit older. What do you think?" he finished. "Mo?"

I refocused.

"Why is Lily excluded from fishing trips – because she's a girl?" I asked irrelevantly and with unnecessary asperity, particularly as I had a girly antipathy to fishing myself. Jack started to deny a sexist attitude to the children then stopped, looked searchingly at me and put his hand on mine.

"Are you nervous about meeting Elizabeth and seeing the house, hon? Don't be. We don't have to take the house or the job if you're not happy with this place."

It was true, I was nervous.

But mainly because I was unaccountably starting to feel I'd come home.

———

April 1941

I am beginning this journal to record my life as a member of the Women's Land Army. I wish I had a nicely bound leather diary to write it in, but with the shortage of paper nowadays, I am lucky to have even this shorthand notebook. What I have to say may not be so exciting as if I had joined the WRENS or the WRAFS, but coming to Norfolk to work on a farm is something I should never have done had it not been for the war. Perhaps the details of my life here will interest my children or grandchildren whose futures I hope I am helping to secure by working to feed the nation.

The other girls at Mayfield Secretarial College were dismayed by the Government's new Registration for Employment Order for all women between eighteen and forty five, but they were a dull lot with no sense of adventure. Compulsory war work beckoned as the road to freedom for me, and my chance to get away from Raynes Park and Mother's plans. She would not allow me to train as a teacher because a school could not provide me with a suitable milieu in which to meet a husband, while as a well-trained secretary she envisaged me working for a wealthy businessman or the upper echelons of the armed forces or civil service. She will not accept that such people find wives within their own social circle rather than amongst their minions and Father, who knows this from his experience in the War Office, never stands up to her even on my behalf. So I had to make the most of this opportunity and present my plan of escape in a way they could not refuse.

I began by telling them I had taken the decision to follow in Douglas' footsteps and volunteer for the WRENS; it put them in a fluster just as I had anticipated. With Douglas defending convoys in the Mediterranean on the Ark Royal, the idea of her other child 'in peril on the sea' gave Mother one of her turns. I had to administer sal volatile, while Father finished his brandy in one gulp, tut-tutted and said I was only just eighteen and too young for such work. Then I pretended to back down and said I supposed that if they really did not want me to join the Navy I could sign up for the Women's Land Army instead. As I had hoped, they were so relieved as to be almost enthusiastic.

Father kissed me on the forehead and said, "Dearest Dottie, you are my brave girl! You will still be doing your bit for King and Country and at least you will be away from the air raids." Mother wrote straight away to Aunt Phyllis to ask if she could help find "a 'suitable' position for Dorothea amongst your Norfolk neighbours." This might seem a calculating way to treat one's parents, but when you have a mother who will not let you take the smallest decision about your own life and a father who will not say boo to a goose, the effect is too frightfully suffocating and even in wartime you will do anything to get away.

A week later they saw me off (Mother in tears, but she will not think of coming to visit even though I am hardly going far) at Liverpool Street Station, where I boarded the Norwich train along with RAF crews and families of children evacuating from London. Aunt Phyllis met me at Attleborough Station with her friend Miss Pringle and we walked the short distance into the centre of Attleborough, an old and pretty little market town. As we turned into Surrogate Street my eye was caught by a memorial to the peace after the Crimean War, with 'Sebastopol', 'Inkerman', 'Balaklava' and 'Alma' inscribed on each of its four sides. I commented on its age – nearly ninety years – and said that in another ninety years, there would doubtless be a memorial to peace at the end of this war.

Miss Pringle did not seem to appreciate this sentiment as she aimed a kick at the crumbling stonework and muttered something like, "Look on my works ye mighty and despair".

They treated me to tea at the Doric Restaurant in Queen Square. The sandwiches were filled with real eggs and cress, which are not to be had for love nor money in London. Afterwards, as it was market day, we walked down to where the stalls spread out in an open area between two ancient hostelries - the Angel Hotel and the Griffin Inn. Most of the town's money, though, is made from turkey breeding and Gaymers' cider works and there is plenty of amusement, for as well as the half dozen hotels, the old Corn Hall has become a cinema which is showing 'Road to Zanzibar' with Bing Crosby, Bob Hope and Dorothy Lamour.

It is hard to believe Aunt Philly is Mother's sister, she is so gay and amusing. She and Miss Pringle, who is a little more intimidating, both teach at the local school and share a cottage in Haddeston Rode. Miss Pringle keeps bees at the bottom of their garden and produces delicious clover honey, which we had later on Aunt Philly's homemade bread. They exchange witty banter the whole time and have intellectual discussions about art, history, literature and politics. They go about a great deal, meet friends and, despite their rural existence, lead a far more stimulating life than Mother and Father. Last night we talked about Rommel's attack on Tobruk, whether Greece would surrender to the Germans and the tragedy of Virginia Woolf's recent suicide.

Miss Pringle is good friends with Mrs Charlotte Jackson, whose husband owns the biggest farm in the H. villages and was happy to take me on as a farm hand. First, though, I had officially to 'join up'. Anne, as Miss Pringle asked me to call her (and I told her I preferred Dottie to Dorothea, though Mother would not approve), took me into Norwich to the Women's Land Army Headquarters on Castle Street. The Norfolk County Secretary was delighted that I had a job and lodgings already arranged, so all she had to do was enrol me and give me my new uniform. Mother would be mortified to see me in my corduroy breeches which lace up under my knees, long socks and gaiters above stout lace-up boots.

"Most unlady-like," she would say in disgust, "you will never find a husband looking like that."

I do not care if I never find a husband. I am warm, comfortable in my Aertex shirt and khaki green jumper and overjoyed to exchange my typewriter for a tractor. Aunt Philly and Anne seem much happier without husbands than Mother does with Father.

I borrowed Aunt Philly's bicycle and rode over to present myself to my new employers. I wore my uniform in case they expected me to start work immediately, but Mr and Mrs Jackson were very kind and said it would be enough for me to familiarise myself with the farm today, ready for an early start in the morning.

Mr Elijah Jackson showed me round the farmyard where they keep chickens, turkeys, geese and ducks. A small herd of cows was being milked in the milking parlour, and a number of pigs in pens lived up to their reputation for odour. There are stables for the horses, barns of hay, sheds for the tractors, workshops and the farm offices. An orchard of apple, pear and plum trees stands at the back of the house and the rest of the farm is arable. I shall learn to milk and see to the pigs and poultry, but my main employment will be working in the fields, where they grow mostly sugar beet, potatoes and wheat for the war effort.

Since the war started, they have had to plough up every inch of land to increase production, whereas before they left 'scutes', which Mr J explained meant irregular shaped pieces of land, and small fields he called 'pightles', uncultivated. I tried not to look as excited as I felt when Mr J said I would be trained to drive the tractors. I am a little nervous, but looking forward to handling the big machines. I hope someone will take a photograph of me so I can send it home to Mother.

When we got back to the farmhouse, it was teatime. This did not mean a pot of China tea and sandwiches, but a hearty cooked dinner. Mr and Mrs J, their daughter Emma, who is about my age, her older brother Archie, their much younger sister, Maudie, two farm hands and a simple, but nice-looking fellow they called Billy Stonepicker, all sat down at the big kitchen table to eat. Emma and her mother produced a huge meal of roast chicken, roast potatoes and a quantity of vegetables, of which we have not seen the like in London since rationing started. There was fresh, home-baked bread – the Js also own the mill down the road. We even had apple pie and cream for dessert and I wished I could wrap up a portion for Father and post it to Raynes Park, as he so misses his puddings. Thinking about this gave me a pang of homesickness and perhaps it showed, as Mrs J chose that moment to say my parents would be very welcome if they wanted to come and visit me.

Emma is tall with blue eyes and long dark hair that is always escaping from its pins. She is friendly in a distant way and seems quite a dreamy kind of girl. Her mother spoke sharply to her first for letting the gravy boil over and then not giving Maudie her spoonful of Radium Malt before the meal. The little girl can only be about three years old and must have been a 'late surprise' for Mrs J, who I estimate to be in her late forties. When we were washing up together, Emma was quite amusing about her brother and his activities with the Home Guard and told me I would have to watch him as he can be an awkward so and so. I sensed there was no love lost between them. Emma used to work for a solicitors' firm in Norwich, but was not happy there. Now she is in charge of baking and gardening, though she says she would rather sit all day with a book.

Archie is dark too, only a little taller than his sister and as thickset as she is willowy. At tea, he argued with his father and the farm hands about investing in new machinery, which Mr J said was too much of a gamble, but twice I glanced up and Archie was looking at me from under his dark brows. I will not mention this in my letters home, as Mother will urge me to set my cap at an heir to a country estate. She might even find his Norfolk accent respectable if she thinks him wealthy enough! After tea, Archie changed into uniform, which made him look far more handsome than his labouring clothes, and went out on patrol with the Haddeston Home Guard Unit. He is second in command of the platoon and had more words with the farm hands about their refusal to join up. They only laughed, but I would not like to get on the wrong side of him.

When we had washed up, Mrs J asked Emma to show me round the house. The front door opens into a tiled porch where everyone leaves their muddy boots and walks around the house in socks or slippers. From the porch, you enter a small hall, on the right of which is the kitchen, which seems to be the heart of the house. It has a red-tiled floor, dark beams in the walls and ceiling, an old-fashioned range and a bread oven set into the wall. The big pine table and chairs take up most of the room, but Mrs J has a rocking chair by the range. The kitchen has a confusing number of doors opening out of it: at the back, one leads to a dairy and an apple store – which is just a slatted cupboard under the stairs; another is the larder and yet another the wash house with a copper built into one corner and airing racks full of damp working clothes hoisted up to the ceiling.

On the other side of the hall is the drawing room, which has a comfortable, worn leather sofa and chairs and seems to be used mostly by the men for smoking and listening to the wireless. Emma turned it on and we listened to a few minutes of Tommy Handley as the Minister of Aggravation and Mysteries in 'I.T.M.A.'. It broke the ice between us when we both split our sides at a joke about the German newspaper called the 'Damandblaster Biterbittern'.

The drawing room has a door out to the back garden, which used to be lawn and flowerbeds, Emma told me, but has been dug over to grow vegetables for the war effort. Mrs J's parlour opens straight out of the far side of the drawing room and is a nineteenth century addition to the original building. She has made it quite charming, with a sewing table in the large bow window, a chaise longue and a grandmother and grandfather chairs.

The stairs from the hall lead up to the family bedrooms and a fearfully old-fashioned bathroom with its small, claw-foot bath. The only thing I miss about home so far is our modern bathroom with Mother's big, powder blue bath and tiles up to the ceiling. There are also three big attic rooms under the roof, Emma said, but I did not care to climb up the ladder to them to see. Apparently temporary farm hands sleep there at harvest time. I am glad they have not put me up there.

My bedroom is one of two maids' rooms built over the dairy, which is also a more recent addition at the other end of the house. Yet another door in the kitchen conceals a little back staircase leading to these servants' quarters. The rooms are both freshly whitewashed with floral curtains and have beamed, sloping ceilings. I have a small electric fire and my room has a painted iron bedstead with plenty of blankets and a thick counterpane. I am writing at the table under the window with the hot water bottle Mrs J kindly lent me on my knees.

Another Land Girl, a friend of the family, is expected soon to occupy the other room, so I shall have company. Emma's bedroom has a door onto our little landing as well as one opening onto the main landing. Emma has said I can use her room as a passage to get to the bathroom, otherwise I have to go down the servants' stairs, through the kitchen and up the main staircase. I do have a chamber pot, or a 'guzunder', as Emma called it when pointing it out under my bed, and a pitcher and ewer on the washstand.

I wonder what my first day working in the Women's Land Army will bring.

————

I passed the exit signposted to The Haddestons and continued into Norwich.

Jack and I were meeting at Dr Gidney's solicitors to sign his contract, complete the house purchase and pick up the keys. The security officer at The Close waved me up the picturesque cul de sac to Newling and Wood's exclusive office nestled in the lee of the ancient cathedral. Jack had made good time; his Landrover was already parked outside and he jumped down from the cab when he saw me pull in behind him.

Alison Wood, the firm's intimidating Managing Partner, had handled the conveyancing of Stargate Farm and Jack's agreement herself. The Health Centre contract was settled, the links in the house purchase chain had held together and our solicitors had successfully transferred the money that morning, yet I felt she was scrutinising us for our suitability to take on both the property and the partnership.

Apparently, we met her criteria, as we walked out of Ms Wood's first floor office with Jack's agreement signed and sealed and a large bunch of keys labelled 'Gidney'.

"I helped David and Elizabeth open the Haddeston Health Centre," she had told us, with a frosty smile and wintry eyes, "and I take a personal interest in its continuing success."

"And I look forward to contributing to that success," Jack replied civilly. He put out his hand to shake hers, but received only a cool nod in response.

On the way down, I found myself shivering as we passed a portrait of Maurice Newling, founder of Newling and Wood, hanging in a place of honour on the impressive staircase. Outside in The Close, though, we hugged each other, grinning broadly, and might have jumped and whooped in the spring sunshine had we been in less imposing surroundings.

We drove home – home! – in convoy. As we left the main road, the peaceful pace of rural life was palpable. We waited for a branch line train to pass a level crossing and the railway man to walk leisurely down from the signal box and unhurriedly lock both gates back into place. Five minutes later we had driven past the assortment of cottages old and new, bungalows, semis and farmhouses on Great Haddeston's The Street, to open fields where cow parsley danced along the hedgerow.

Turning into the drive, we found brilliant yellow forsythia and variegated daffodils waving a welcome to our sun-lit house, along with the removal men who had already arrived and were waiting for us to let them in. Amazingly, there hadn't been a single breakage en route, and Stargate Farm embraced our eclectic and battered mix of furniture as if it had been made to measure.

Another sign, I felt, that we were swimming with the current of life.

I had just finished unpacking the children's rooms when, with more good timing, Colin and Betty arrived with an excited Lily and a sleepy Felix in the back of their car.

Jack proudly showed his parents around the house while I ran about the garden with the children, who needed to let off steam after their journey. Indoors Lily was thrilled with the bedroom I had chosen for her, even though the pretty pink and yellow sprigged wallpaper and faded curtains must have been decades old. We had already taken up the old carpet from Felix's room and thrown it out on the drive. I had washed the walls and scrubbed the floorboards, made the bed up with his allergy-free bedding. Even after twenty four hours away from London, Felix's breathing was easier and Betty assured me she hadn't had to use his inhaler once.

Colin went through the house hanging all our pictures on random hooks left by the Gidneys, which gave the place a lived-in, if eccentric, appearance; Betty organised my kitchen into the spacious pine cupboards with her typical orderliness. Why would I not be able to keep it this tidy, I wondered regretfully, and surreptitiously dropped the fridge magnet reading 'Dull women have immaculate houses' back into the empty packing case.

By the end of the day we had unpacked enough for the house to feel like home, and the inexplicable sense of familiarity I had felt on first viewing it had been over-ridden. The children ate, bathed in the charming old claw-footed enamel bath and fell comfortably asleep in their new bedrooms. I made my first meal in our new home and we toasted our future in Colin and Betty's house-warming gift of champagne, after which we slept like logs in the profound quiet of the countryside.

So far, I had no regrets for the life I had left behind.

———

The euphoria of being in the country still enveloped us the next morning.

After breakfast Colin fired up the lawn tractor we had bought off Elizabeth Gidney and trimmed the grass, while Jack went down to the Health Centre to unpack his surgery boxes.

Betty and I took the children on an exploratory trip to Wymondham, our nearest small town. We dragged Lily and Felix round the ancient Abbey and allowed them to jump on and off the ancient gravestones while we gazed across the gently sloping green fields of the Tiffey Valley. We browsed the stalls at the farmers' market set out beneath the hexagonal Market Cross building on its wooden stilts before heading for the real object of our expedition, the local supermarket.

It was a joy to find the car park expansive and only half occupied while the store offered wide aisles full of produce and empty of shoppers, ending in checkouts with genuinely friendly staff and no queues. This was as welcome a change from South London for me as the village recreation ground was for Lily and Felix. Unlike our old local parks, they were grassy and clean with few other children playing, so no queues for the swings, no rampaging older kids to be scared of and no teenagers lounging around smoking.

Simply driving home through the winding lanes and

variegated green landscape with its stands of trees and sprinkling of flowers soothed my soul and lifted my spirits. I waxed lyrical to Betty about the hedgerow bushes, so heavily laden with hanging white blossom that, with cow parsley frosting the banks, they looked like a floral parody of winter.

But she was more concerned about the balance of maternal bonds than Mother Nature's beauties.

"I suppose you'll be seeing a lot of Kathleen and Maxwell now you're so close to them," she asked in an offhand tone, which the tense anticipation in her face belied.

"With Jack's work, London friends coming to stay and becoming part of a new community, we won't have time to get together that regularly," I tried to allay her anxiety. "And you'll be coming up as often as you can, won't you? Lily and Felix want to see Nanny and Grandad as much as possible – and so do we."

Betty allowed a tiny sigh to escape her perfectly lipsticked lips.

"I was afraid of losing Julia when she wanted to find her birth mother, but that's not how it's turned out," she said quietly. Jack's twin sister had been the one most anxious to find their birth mother, but felt much less need to maintain the relationship once they had made contact.

I wanted to make the most of this rare admission to my mother-in-law's inner feelings, but I could sense Lily's ears pricking up in the back seat where her game with Felix had suddenly gone silent.

"Jack's dealing with what he has to, Betty," I tried to make my point elliptically. "I don't much like it either, but he'll come out the other side. You won't lose him either, trust me. Nurture will win over nature, though it's not even a contest."

"What is Daddy dealing with?" asked Lily. "Does he have to win a contest? And where have you lost him, anyway? I know where he is, he's in our new house with Grandad."

"So he is, dear," responded Betty in her talking-to-children voice, which she had failed to notice that Lily had outgrown. "Silly Nanny, of course Daddy's not lost."

"Is Kathleen coming to see us soon? I want to show her my new room," my daughter, unconsciously I hoped, twisted the knife. "I like Kathleen, do you Nanny?"

I gave her the task of keeping Felix awake to distract her till we got home.

"It's not the genetic thing that bothers me," Betty had resumed softly. "I don't mind that the twins don't look like me or Colin, or that they're cleverer than both of us put together. I just always so wanted to be pregnant, to have that time when you and your baby share a life. I mean emotions are just hormones in your blood stream, aren't they, so a baby must feel what you feel as well as eating what you eat and all that. I can't help worrying that those nine months that Kathleen had with the twins inside her meant more than all the years I've had with them since. What is pregnancy, Mo, nature or nurture?"

It was a surprisingly philosophical question and, despite having given birth to four children myself, I found I couldn't answer her. I reminded myself to maintain more respect for Betty's acumen and sense of loss, however well concealed beneath her meticulously suburban exterior, and felt a flash of anger on seeing Kathleen's sporty BMW parked in the drive when we arrived back home with the shopping and two sleeping children.

———

July 1941

If only Mother could see me now, I have thought to myself on many occasions in the last two months.

She would scarcely recognise me, nor want to, I think. My face and arms are brown and freckled from the sun and I only bother with a dab of lipstick when we go down to the pub. My permanent wave has grown out, but Anne has cut my hair shorter, so it curls naturally and I never need to set it. Life is harder work and more enjoyable here than it ever was in Raynes Park. I do worry about them in the air raids, which have been very heavy of late, but I get exasperated with Mother's frequent letters complaining about Father and rationing, and Father's occasional postcards that tell me nothing at all. I know he has signed the Official Secrets Act, but he could have written a little more about Douglas' triumph in sinking the Bismarck. I, at least, will record for my children and grandchildren that my own brother may have dropped the torpedo that hit the rudder and made the Jerries a sitting duck to the Ark Royal. Those old-fashioned Swordfish planes that he calls the Stringbags can cut the mustard, despite being partly made of wood and canvas!

I have learned more skills in the last few weeks than the whole time I attended Mayfield Secretarial College. It took me a few tries before I got the hang of milking, but now I can get a bucket filled as quickly as any of the farm hands. The sows have produced several litters of piglets and I enjoy my turns at taking in the heavy buckets of pigswill. Mucking out is not so frightful as you might think, and of the two I prefer the smell of pigs to that of chickens, which brings tears to my eyes.

My biggest adventure, though, has been learning to plough on the Fordson tractor. Old Tom, who is not old at all, but is the 'Hid Stifler' – or Foreman – of Jackson's Farm, showed me how to get on from the back and either sit on the round metal seat, or drive it standing on the footplates. When I thought I had got the hang of controlling it, Tom told me to drive the tractor out of the yard, but unfortunately I steered too close and my back wheel pulled the five-bar gate right off its hinges. On hearing the dreadful cracking noise, Mr J came out of the office to inspect the damage, and I expected an awful pi-jaw about looking where I was going. But he very kindly said it was all to the good as the wood was rotting and now he could get Billy Stonepicker to make a new gate.

After I had apologised profusely, Tom led me slowly down to one of the arable fields where he attached the plough to the back of my tractor and showed me how to drive it in a dead straight line towards a small white stick at the other side of the field. This is 'opening the first furrow' and was hard enough to manage, but when you go round on the 'headland' (the end of the field) and plough your way back, you have to turn the soil right up against the first furrow, still driving absolutely straight. The first ridge you make is the 'top', and you go round and round it until you have ploughed a 'rig'. Then you start again, with another top some distance away, and plough around until the two rigs join up. When you have ploughed the field into neat, straight pairs of rigs, then you go round the headlands and your field is done.

Needless to say, my first rigs were neither straight nor neat, but Tom was a great sport. "Tha's on the sosh but good tidy for a mawther's fuss time," he said, with a twinkle in his eye. Emma told me later he meant it was not bad for a girl's first attempt, even if it was skew whiff! Now I can get my rigs passably straight and even plough the pightles and scutes, which are more difficult than they look. I have written home about my achievements, but Mother is far from impressed and I do not know if Father even reads my letters, as all he says are things like "Keep up the good work, old girl!" and "Hope to be seeing you soon, dearest Dot!" when he will never get Mother on a train, even to see Aunt Philly.

We get up at five am and have an enormous cooked breakfast, take our packed lunches and work through the day. As we have Double Summer Time this year, it keeps light till quite late at night, so we are out until tea is on the table, then fall into bed, exhausted, soon after. Despite the amount I am eating, I am thinner and much stronger than I have ever been before.

I do not see much of Emma during the day, but we are becoming friends. She is an unusual girl, full of imagination and with an independent kind of personality which I admire and I feel we are kindred spirits. This is not the case with Heather Newling, who took up residence in the room next door to mine a month ago and works alongside me. I say 'alongside', but she does not enjoy the farm work as I do. She comes from Norwich, where her father runs a successful solicitors' practice. I do not like to pass judgement, but in my opinion she has been a spoiled only child and a Daddy's girl, and is not giving the Jacksons or the country her all. Emma, Heather and I are chums and get on well to all intents and purposes, but there are what Mother would call 'undercurrents'.

Emma was given a job by Mr Newling because she is clever and could make something of herself, but she left and there seems to be friction between them on that account. Heather also seems to believe that she and Archie have an understanding and she is welcome to him, but when he takes more notice of me than her she gets very out of sorts and makes cutting remarks. This endears her to no one, though Mr and Mrs J humour both her moods and her laziness.

Emma and I walk down The Street to the Trowel and Hammer on Saturday nights, and sometimes on a Thursday too. Archie goes there more often as this is where the Home Guard platoon hold their meetings. Since her arrival, Heather comes with us. Mother would never have let me go into a pub, but now I am a regular and have 'my usual', which is a half of cider. Emma, who is always cold, has her own seat by the fire and drinks beer like the men, but I find it too bitter. Aunt Philly and Anne are often in there, and a group of airmen from RAF Swanton Morley drop by regularly. They are from 105 Squadron and have been working so hard recently, keeping planes in the air. Sometimes a couple of the men from RAF Stoke Holy Cross come in, but they cannot tell us about their work, it is top secret. Loose lips sink ships – and also crash planes. I do not think I was giving away anything important when I told everyone that the Ark Royal has two cats aboard, called Oscar and Harry.

A chap called Henry Tinker has started coming to the T&H. He is a Londoner like me, but comes up to stay with his aunt and uncle at Lavender Farm further down The Street. He is a charmer, very handsome, with a moustache like Clark Gable in 'Gone With The Wind', and the life and soul of the pub when he is there. He is educated, but a wheeler-dealer (or a 'higgler' as they call it here) and at first some people thought he must be a Fifth Columnist. Archie was all for reporting him, but changed his mind when Henry told everyone about a dog that was running at Haringey called Toftwood

Manuss, which was sure to win. He offered to place bets for us all; I put on one shilling, but Archie gave him a £5 note to bet on the dog! Heather was livid with him and told him he was a fool and her father would disapprove, but Archie took no notice. She was mortified when Toftwood Manuss won at one hundred to eight and we all made twelve times what we put on. Now Archie is always muttering to Tink, as we have nicknamed him, and slipping him 10/- and £1 notes.

Tink started coming to visit his relations here because he realised there was money to be made selling chickens, eggs and vegetables to London restaurants and hotels. He has made other local contacts and collects as much produce as he can at weekends, takes it down to London and sells it during the week. Anne is selling him her clover honey. He says he could sell ten times what he can get his hands on and that I would be amazed at how much they charge for meals now. As Mother and Father never ate out, I do not know what restaurant prices used to be. I must try again to persuade them to visit me, as I am sure Mrs J would send them home with a basket of provisions they cannot get with their ration books.

Last night, Tink got me on my own and told me he comes to Gt H every weekend now for more than 'business' reasons. He asked me if Emma liked him. I said I thought she did, though she always denies having feelings for him when I tease her. He said he wanted to give her a gift for her birthday and asked what I thought she would appreciate. I told him her two great loves were reading and herbalism.

Unfortunately, Emma saw us talking intimately and I could see she was upset. Archie also thought Tink was making a pass at me and spent the rest of the evening 'guarding' me as if I was his property, which annoyed Heather, so I was in trouble with all three of them. I went to Emma's room and explained our conversation (though not Tink's plans for her birthday) when we got home. She looked pleased, but said I could not tell anyone else, so Archie remains possessive and Heather sulky. I hope it will become clear soon that Tink is keen on Emma, not me, and then we can go back to normal.

Although the Germans have moved into Russia, we have occupied Syria. I want us to win the war as quickly as possible, but I must admit I have never been so happy in my life, and could never go back to life in Raynes Park.

Chapter Two

"So, how's it all going out in the sticks? Have you only just managed to get one of those new fangled telephone connections, or are your friends in the big smoke just a distant memory?"

Venetia's typically acerbic tone rasped into my ear when I picked up my new state of the art, digital handset. It was the first hour of the first day of my new working life, in my bow-windowed study with its view of fields and the church tower. My PC with broadband internet and email connection, two printers, phone and fax were connected up and humming lightly in anticipation of a productive day.

"Oh, sorry, Vee," I replied guiltily. "We've just been so busy getting everything sorted out, I haven't been in touch with anyone yet."

"Hmmph," she snorted. "Since when was I 'anyone'? I've got a fifteen minute window before my next meeting, so start talking and don't leave anything out. I've been assigned to get the info and report back to the girls at coffee – and I'm taking notes."

I refocused on all our domestic issues of the last three weeks, having consciously just put them aside to concentrate fully on my new research project. I had started writing a punchy press release for *Time Crunch,* a topical reality TV show that I was organising in pre-production. It had to be sent out today to the voluntary organisations and support groups I hoped would help me find individuals and families wanting professional help with organising their time better. There were plenty of those around, no doubt, but the ones I needed had to be willing to let our cameras in and reveal the extent of their current failure to cope, as well as their expertly assisted rehabilitation.

"Well, where shall I start?" I wondered aloud, while my mind flashed back over the three weeks in which my life had changed so radically.

"House? Kids? Jack?" Venetia's voice at the other end of the phone jerked my mind back sharply. "Or how about you – have you gone all green wellies and Barbour coat, churning out home-grown veggie casseroles on the Aga?" Her confusion of country images made me smile.

"Well, the green wellies came from Homebase and the Barbour's a fake. We don't have an Aga, but I did find some leeks growing in what was obviously once the vegetable patch and I have to say, the soup I made was rather tasty. We've been watching all sorts of birds in the garden: a brace of pheasants – do you call them a brace when they're alive? Probably not – strut around the garden after a beautiful, fat male who obviously thinks it's his manor; a charming pair of collared doves bill and coo on the electricity wires; there are robins and tits, or maybe they're finches; even the pigeons are plump and pink and pretty unlike London ones..."

I stopped, sensing complete lack of interest at the other end.

"But otherwise I've been unpacking, exploring with the kids, sorting out phone lines, broadband, a child minder for Felix, school uniform for Lily – "

"Cut to the chase," she broke in. "What's it like? Are the locals inbred and half-witted? Are you bored? Do you miss London?" Through her crabbiness, Venetia sounded almost wistful.

"Oh, Vee, I'm sorry. Of course I miss you, and I haven't had time to make any new friends yet, but I'm loving it here. The house is, well, home, the countryside's beautiful, the kids are happy, Jack's relaxed – he started work last week and he's really enjoying the practice and the patients so far. None of the inner city problems to deal with and Elizabeth's ethos is to treat all patients as if they were family. Jess drops in when she can get a lift and needs a home-cooked meal, Felix started with his child-minder yesterday – she seems great – and it's Lily's first day of term today.

"The school's small and friendly, only about ninety children in total, and her class is one of the biggest, with fourteen of them – can you believe it? There are no statemented kids and they all have English as a first language, so hopefully she'll really get her reading sorted out now. It's not as if she's stupid after all."

"No, of course not, she's sharp as a tack." Venetia had a close bond with Lily, perhaps because they shared a certain contrary nature and an instinct for people's emotional Achilles heels. "She made any friends yet?"

"It's only her first day. She was assigned a 'buddy' called Kimberley to look after her this morning. She looked sweet enough, but no doubt I'll find out when I collect her this afternoon. Felix is going to keep the childminder on her toes, but she's got three other kids of his age and a lovely big garden for them to play in. His asthma's definitely improved since we've been out of town. So I'm sorry, we won't be selling up and moving back to London just yet. And what's the news from Crystal Palace?"

Venetia filled me in on Suzy's luxury holiday in Belize, Miranda's research breakthrough with a new cancer drug, and the sad demise of Ros' elderly dalmation.

"And how does it feel now your baby's finally left home?" I asked. "Are you rattling about the house without Aurora on the top floor? Or does Nick fill the gap nicely?"

Venetia's daughter had finally moved out of the house she had shared with her mother for all her twenty seven years and in with Denis, who was now designated her 'partner' rather than boyfriend. This coupled with a successful job running an art gallery meant Aurora had broken her financial and emotional dependency on Venetia in a way that I suspected her mother did not entirely relish.

Venetia sighed; I had jangled an unusually exposed emotional nerve.

"Yes, it's quiet without her. I miss the two of them popping in and out, and having to complain about the noise they made in her bedroom. I miss her oily paint brushes in the sink and gossip from the art world. And Nick? Nick's... busy. I suspect he'll be 'busy' till I agree to the church wedding he wants. And you're not here to moan to, so yep, I suppose I feel a little bit adrift."

Mindful of my fleeting, childfree minutes, I postponed a sympathy session by suggesting she and Nick came up for a therapeutic weekend in the near future. Reassuring her that the house was warm and in good repair, we had a working shower and she wouldn't be forced to go on any muddy walks, I sent my love to the girls and said I would be drinking my cappuccino with them in spirit tomorrow morning and expected to hear all the gossip in person very soon.

As I put the phone down, though, I felt a momentary twinge of loss.

There were some aspects of city life I was missing, though I wouldn't admit it to Venetia or anyone else just yet. At a personal level, my friends and my mother, in person rather than at the end of a phone or email; Mark and his girlfriend Zoe dropping in for Sunday lunch; my weekly yoga classes. From a wider viewpoint, the diversity of South East London – how long would it take before Lily stared at black or brown faces simply because she rarely saw them now? And most prosaically, the inability to get a takeaway delivered out to the Haddeston villages.

However, I had managed to end the conversation before Venetia could ask about Kathleen's role in our lives, and once more turned my thoughts away from her weekend outings with Jack and the children, which were always thoughtfully offered to give me some time out.

Time out from what,I wondered as I clicked my computer screen alight and returned to my press release. I didn't hanker after 'me' time while my family went off to have fun with someone else.

Time Crunch – it's crunch time, was all I had written. Drawing inspiration from the pair of wagtails hopping around on the lawn, I tapped on:

Balanced Living, Work-Life Balance, Time Sovereignty... Whatever the current buzz word, everyone's trying to have it or do it: earn a living, have a life, manage a home, raise a family, rise up the career ladder, stay fit, support older relatives, keep all the balls in the air, keep everybody else happy and keep themselves sane.

Some lucky people glide through life finding time for all their commitments and interests with serene good humour, but for most of us, staying balanced on the tightrope of twenty first century life is physically and mentally exhausting. Every now and then we take a fall and when we do, we usually take those around us down too.

Time Crunch is the in-depth, reality television series for, and about, those individuals who have too many balls in the air and are facing crunch time. For some of our subjects, the issues will be around family life – not making or having enough time for it, feeling pressured by it, getting stressed by it. Where do their priorities really lie? For others, their relationship with their partner is falling apart around them while they concentrate on their career. At work, many people can't say 'no' to ever increasing workloads, stand up to bullying tactics by managers or challenge selfish colleagues – while their stress levels rise and their health and lives outside work disintegrate.

Tamara Gordon, writer, coach and international expert in Life Balance is the presenter of *Time Crunch*. Working with a different person and their time crisis in each programme, she will use her experience to help them confront issues with their partners, families, colleagues or bosses, as well as face up to ways they need to change themselves.

If you are someone who could benefit from a time and life makeover with Tamara's help, please contact Mo Mozart at Generation Films for more information.

I emailed the draft to Tamara at The Balance Consultancy and to Jane, the series producer at Generation Films, for their comments. As I trotted through to the kitchen for another cup of coffee, I felt smug about the balanced life Jack and I had fashioned for our family without expert help. Perhaps I could draw on our experience to support Tamara and help some of the poor subjects our television series would put in the spotlight.

———

I left plenty of time to walk down to school, taking a shortcut along Buxton Lane, then a footpath my Ordnance Survey Map grandly called Old Wash Lane, though it was nothing more than a track bisecting a wheat field, which then divided the playing field and Victorian school building on the right from the graveyard and Norman flint church to my left.

Outside the school gates I felt somewhat conspicuous as the only, as well as probably the oldest, mother with no group of friends to join and chat to. But not for long. A tiny, bird-like woman in her seventies, I guessed, dressed in an elegant if dated suit and high heels, stood beside me and spoke as if we were old friends.

"Hello, my dear. It's hard when you're new to somewhere

and a working mother, isn't it? Don't worry, they're a friendly lot really. I must introduce you to my daughter, Laura; she's a working girl as well and it took her some time to fit in. She's always worrying that Gracie doesn't get enough of her time, but one can only do what one can, don't you agree?"

I nodded and smiled, pleased to be spoken to but somewhat nonplussed by her apparent knowledge of me, and took the small, veined, be-ringed hand she held out to me.

"Barbara Mayhew. Mother of Laura Goodall and grandmother of Grace. Most people call me Nanny Babs. So nice to see a new face in the village. We could do with some fresh blood once in a while, if you know what I mean!" She hissed the last sentence in a loud stage whisper. I looked around to see if the sentiments she was making me complicit in were offending anyone, but the other parents all appeared engrossed in their own conversations.

"You're familiar with the phrase 'Normal for Norfolk'?" She continued loudly. "Well, there's a few of them round here that applies to. Hello, dear!" Babs waved and smiled warmly to a new arrival then turned back to me. "She's one of them, Nina. Lovely girl, five children, three fathers, not all there, in my opinion," she enunciated behind her hand. I smiled again, trying to appear non-committal to anyone who might be watching. "And your name, my dear?"

I tried to summarise my life: "Mary Mozart, generally known as Mo, wife of Jack Patterson, the new doctor, and mother of Lily and Felix – also Mark and Jess, but they're grown up and not living at home."

Perhaps it was too short a précis, as Barbara raised her finely pencilled eyebrows and was clearly formulating a number of supplementary questions. To my relief, teachers leading classes of children started to appear from various doors at that moment, and lined them up at the school gates. I was pleased to see no younger children were allowed to leave without being matched to their collecting adults, and stepped up to take possession of Lily, who looked happy enough, chatting to a small, dark girl with a round, good natured face, while her 'buddy' of this morning stood disregarded beside her. Her teacher ushered Lily out of the gate, assuring me that she'd settled in well and done some good work.

"Alright, darling?" I took Lily by the hand. "Have you had a good day? Made some new friends? Hello Kimberley!" I smiled at the disgruntled-looking child who ignored me and walked off to engage her mother in a conversation which, from her tone and their glances towards us, focused on Lily's uncooperative attitude to the buddy system. I would have introduced myself and attempted to smooth things over, but Lily was demanding my attention.

"Mummy, this is Grace. She's my friend and I want her to come to our house. Now," she insisted in the shrill, edgy voice that signified over-excitement and could presage emotional meltdown. I had to make an instant evaluation on the lesser of two evils: refuse on the grounds that she needed to come home and chill out, but risk loud and public fallout; or agree and deal with over-tiredness and a possible falling out with her new friend, but in the privacy of our own home.

I went for the latter, to find Nanny Babs at my elbow, holding Grace's hand and assuring me that they would love to come and have a cup of tea, but only if it wasn't any trouble. I smiled and said that would be very nice, and yes, of course she could ring and let Laura know where to pick them up from on her way home from work, and that it would indeed be a great opportunity to meet her.

———

December 1941

What news we have been hearing on the wireless recently!

We all agreed with Mr Churchill that what the Japanese have done at Pearl Harbour was 'A day that will live in infamy', but Anne said that terrible though it was, they have done what no one else has been able to do and brought America into the war. At least we are not alone now, and everyone seems to feel confident that we will defeat the Nazis, however long it takes.

You would think from Mother's letters that she minded more about the new rationing restrictions than any of this, or even that the Ark Royal has been sunk. I know Douglas is safely back in Blighty for the moment, now he and his shipmates have been brought home from Gibraltar, but he has been in fearful danger and no doubt will be again when the Fleet Air Arm posts him to another aircraft carrier. Mr J has said I can go down to London when Douglas has his leave and Tink has offered to give me a lift to Raynes Park in his rackety old van, which means I can take milk, butter, apples, potatoes and carrots, bacon, a chicken, a Kilner jar of plum jam and some of Emma's bread and scones home with me. This will save Mother from a Christmas dinner of greasy cow's heart and, as Mrs J has offered one of her plum puddings, Christmas pudding made of swede and carrots coloured with cold tea.

We have such a quantity of fruit and vegetables carefully packed for winter at the farm; the apple store cupboard is full to bursting and there are more boxes stacked in the pantry where the hams, a side of venison and the rabbits and game Archie shoots hang from great hooks in the main beam. I am sure I would be given a pheasant for Mother, but she does not care for the gamey taste. I will be able to take her some of the extra eggs we keep preserved in ising glass. Mrs J dissolves the stuff in water, dips the eggs in to coat them and keep the air out, then carefully stacks them pointed end up in galvanised iron buckets. They do not taste as good as fresh eggs, but are a lot better than the powdered variety, which is all Mother can get in London over and above the ration of one per person per week .

Tink says he may be able to add some tobacco for Father's pipe and some nylons for Mother to the basket, which will make the best Christmas presents I could give them. I shall not ask where he has got them from, but in return he has asked me to help him with a gift for Emma – who is still refusing his advances although she moons around at home and talks about him all the time.

'The Complete Works of Shakespeare' I suggested for her birthday was a great success. She has been engrossed in it ever since and her shelves of other reading matter have languished untouched since Tink's beautiful leather-bound volume was taken out of its brown paper wrappings.

Tink is besotted with Emma, as he often declares to me. I am a little surprised that someone as worldly as he has fallen for her innocent charms, rather than a girl about town such as myself, or even Heather, who I admit is quite showy-looking with her thick, blonde hair and high cheekbones, and he must meet plenty more in London. I suppose Emma is pretty in a more uncommon way and there is an innocent side to her that makes one want to protect her, added to which, though she is whimsical she is no fool.

Her herbal experiments have had excellent results: Billy Stonepicker's skin complaint has been much improved by her marigold and speedwell lotion, Archie's sprained ankle seemed to heal unusually quickly when she applied a camomile fomentation and she has treated the cows' sore udders with some stinking garlic concoction that appears to relieve them instantly. In another age Emma might have been called a witch, but she is kind and amusing and, although I feel there are things she does not confide in me, has become my closest friend.

Archie is another kettle of fish entirely. He is as forceful as Emma is reflective and goes at everything he does with a fiery intensity. He tries to push all the farm hands to do as much, or more, than they are capable of and sometimes Mr J has to intervene. It is the same with the Home Guard and his platoon, which must be one of the most drilled in Norfolk. He, deputising for his CO, Lord Buxton, has them out almost every night of the week and on parade every Sunday. His troops have been depleted, though, as more of the younger men have been called up, and he has insisted that the Parish Council write to every remaining man in the Haddestons who has not volunteered to join the Home Guard asking them to do so. Archie says it will soon become compulsory and they might as well join up of their own accord now. As 2IC he has a Sten gun and seems to most enjoy *honing his skills at the range and taking part in the platoon's more dangerous exercises.*

Tink tells me Archie has got himself in with Lord B's very wealthy crowd up at H. Hall, which apparently includes Heather's father on occasions, and the evenings he passes up there are spent playing cards for high stakes as much as on Home Guard tactics. He says that if Archie is not careful he will get in over his head as he is not in the same league as the upper classes. I think Tink may be spreading these rumours to get back at Archie, as we suspect Archie has warned Emma off Tink and even she will not cross her brother. It seems to be the only explanation as to why she will not admit she loves him, when it is so clear she does and that her feelings are reciprocated.

Heather still has her cap set at him, but Archie pays me more attention than her, in his silent, smouldering way. He sometimes stands very close or sits next to me at the pub and I know there is a magnetism between us. I admit I find him not unattractive and when he has had a few drinks he can be quite animated, but there is something a little menacing about him too. Perhaps I shall try to tame him.

Heather has become an even less active member of the Women's Land Army. She has convinced the Js that she suffers badly from the cold, so since winter has arrived she has been given all the light duties such as feeding the poultry and collecting any eggs (of which there are not so many at this time of year), feeding and grooming (but not mucking out) the horses, and even churning butter in the pantry! It is a poor show. Old Tom calls her "a botty little mawther" when she does anything for him, which I take to mean a self-important fusspot. She sometimes goes home to Norwich at weekends, so we do not have the pleasure of her company so often in the T&H.

I hope Douglas gets his leave soon, and that it will not fall over Christmas itself. I feel more a part of the J family than my own and would rather enjoy the village celebrations with all the friends I have made here than sit it out in Raynes Park. Mother and Father have been invited to stay with Aunt Philly and Anne for Christmas, and I know they would all be invited to the farm for dinner, but I do not suppose for a minute that they will come. It is almost as if they enjoy having something to complain about, and to find a way of improving their lot would not suit their purposes at all. Sometimes I wonder if Douglas and I were adopted, as neither of us take after our parents in any respect.

I have discovered that Billy Stonepicker sleeps in the stables with the horses. One morning I woke even earlier than usual and saw him come out of the stable, go across to the outside 'petty', then wash his face at the pump. Emma explained that the Jacksons feed him and give him cast off clothing and in return he does odd jobs for them, not just stone-picking and woodwork (at which he is not at all simple), so the poor man is in effect little more than a beggar. Emma does not care for him as she says he watches her when she is working in the garden and steals some of her produce. But he has a sweet face and seems gentle enough to me. His new gate is now hung at the farm entrance, so I am no longer reminded by the old broken one of my first disastrous day on the Fordson. He has made a solid five bar gate with an unusual star pattern in the centre.

"Hallo Mary, or can I call you Mo?"

The woman standing on my doorstep leaned forward and planted a kiss on my cheek.

"Ever so nice to meet you! I'm sorry my mother and daughter have wormed their way into your house on the first day of term. I do apologise for my family's appalling behaviour!"

"Oh no, it's lovely to make new friends!" I warmed instantly to her broad smile and ushered her through our small hall into the sitting room.

"Oh, fabulous beams and fireplace," she enthused, peering round as she took off her tailored jacket and stilettos. "They would have had the kitchen range there in the old days, wouldn't they? I've never been into this house before, though I hear it has something of a history! Mother, you're very naughty!" She called into the kitchen where she could hear the sound of Babs raiding my cupboards for another mug. "You could have restrained your curiosity for a day or two!" And turning back to me: "In case you hadn't guessed I'm Laura. Ooh, fabulous haircut! London hairdresser? Thought so. Never mind. Hallo my gorgeous girl – " as Grace rushed into the room and launched herself at her mother.

I couldn't help laughing at Laura's unstoppable flow and infectious enthusiasm. During her entrance I had taken in an attractive, asymmetrical face with large grey eyes, topped by a head of glossy, dark, plum-rinsed hair. She wore a smart but fashionable skirt and top, lots of silver jewellery and more expertly applied make-up than she needed. Seeing my appraising glance, she grinned again.

"Clothes are uniform, the bling's cheap and cheerful – I have to look well turned-out, I'm in retail fashion, dahling, don't ya know? Manager of Ladies Clothing at Jarrolds. Big department store in Norwich? Not discovered the City yet? You will. We've got some great shops, lovely restaurants… pity I never have the time or money to try any of them myself!" And laughing, Laura allowed her daughter to drag her by the hand into the kitchen, where Babs was making a proper pot of tea with three cups and saucers and milk in a dainty china jug with roses on it that I didn't even know I possessed.

An hour or so later, after Grace and Lily had devoured egg and chips and were still playing companionably, I felt I as though I had known Nanny Babs and, especially, Laura all my life. They had heard about my first marriage; Mark's job and relationship with Zoe; Jess's studies at the University of East Anglia in experimental economics. I'd found myself telling them how Jack and I had met when I was a single mother and he our new GP; how we had had Lily within two years of getting married and been surprised by Felix's appearance some four years later.

Laura wanted to know all about my freelance research career and the surprising areas it had taken me into; and Babs was particularly sympathetic to the story of finding Jack and Julia's biological mother and her role in our move to Great Haddeston.

"Interfering relatives can cause so much trouble, can't they, my dear?" She patted me on the hand, and I tried not to smile while Laura, nodding vigorously, made comical faces and pointed at her mother out of Babs' line of sight.

In return I had understood that Laura and her brother had lived a rootless life as children, following the succession of more and less paternally-minded men that Babs had fallen in and out of love with around the country. I had empathised with Laura's resulting deep-seated desire for stability and 'normality', and been pleased to hear that she had found this in Pete, an engineer at the nearby Lotus car plant, and the miraculous birth of Grace, when she had believed herself to be infertile.

To lighten the tone, the two of them had then given me an invaluable thumbnail introduction to Haddeston families such as Lady Janet Morton's at Haddeston Hall, whose six children were named after Anglo-Saxon kings and queens: Edmund, Judith and Alfred; Agatha, Harold and Elfrida, the last two being twins and in Grace and Lily's class. Lady Janet was also Brown Owl to the Haddeston Guides and Brownies; I was advised to contact her and put Lily on the waiting list for Brownies, as all the village girls went on a Tuesday afternoon when they turned seven.

The juiciest piece of information was that Mr Morton – Janet's title was hereditary and her own – worked in London all week, during which time his place in the marital bed was filled by their Estate Manager and no one, apparently including Janet, knew which of the royally-named offspring issued from which father.

"No! A real life Lady Chatterley? It can't be true!"

"It is! It's all true," insisted Laura. "She'll even tell you if you ask her. Mother did once and got the whole story! She only married Arthur because the family needed the money or they'd have had to sell the Hall. He's a rich businessman, wanted the social standing and has a mistress down in London. Apparently they're both very happy with the arrangement. Janet's brother, St John – she pronounces it 'Sinjun' – who's Lord Buxton and the real heir, has been pensioned off to a bungalow in Haddeston Rode where he potters around and paints terrible watercolours. Isn't village life more fun than London?"

I agreed and begged for more. Laura was delighted to have got such a good reaction from me.

"If you talk to the girls at the school gate you'll soon find that every other marriage is in trouble, there's all sorts of affairs going on, and don't think you can keep a secret – everybody knows what everyone else is up to on the Haddeston grapevine. Charlotte who runs the Post Office – she moved here from Birmingham a few years ago – thinks she's the queen of the village because she knows everyone's business: pensions, registered letters, special deliveries, the lot. And discretion is not exactly her strong suit. She's very keen on alternative therapies, doesn't like proper doctors at all, so you'd better watch her." Laura looked at me with one raised eyebrow. "Seriously, she can take a real dislike to some people."

"Now, Laura," broke in Babs. "Let Mo make up her own mind about people. Charlotte's not all bad and she is paying for her old grandmother to live in Black Carr House, which costs a pretty penny. I shall expect the same from you when I finally lose my marbles."

"*When* you lose them? That happened some time ago, Mother. We're just too tactful to tell you!" And they went off into a riff of family banter that I sensed sounded one or two sharp notes amidst the light jingle of laughter. Craving a stronger caffeine hit than Babs' refined pot of tea had offered, I got out the cafetiere and went to refill the kettle, but Laura broke off from their repartee to ask whether it wasn't time for something a little stronger to drink.

"A glass of red would go down very nicely just now," she said. "When I'm at work everything's under control and I'm a model of efficiency. By the time I get home I'm totally stressed out, and I need a little boost to stay sane."

"Good idea!" I agreed, not quite sure how to react to this admission. "I'll just grab a bottle." I hurried out to the dining room on the other side of our little hall, where Jack had judged the most constant temperature to be for his small but cherished 'cellar'. I chose a bottle of Australian Shiraz as being very drinkable but not reserved for an occasion, while wondering whether Laura might be a suitable candidate for *Time Crunch*. Returning to the kitchen to ask her, I found Babs sitting with her hands folded in her lap, her eyes closed, and her daughter gazing intently at her.

"Talking of being off the wall," Laura turned to me, "did Nanny Babs tell you she's a bit of a witch? She gets contacted from the other side at the oddest times and it looks like someone's just come through. Well it's only to be expected in a house of this age. Bound to be lots of the dear departed hanging around." She turned back to Babs who, smiling gently, opened her eyes to locate the brimming glass I put on the table in front of her.

"Wait a minute, please," said Babs to nobody visible, and looked intently into my eyes. "Are you comfortable with the spirit world, my dear? I can tell you have psychic gifts yourself, so you may not want my interference, but I have someone here who wants to use me to speak to you."

"Umm, I don't know. Who?" I couldn't help being intrigued by this unexpected turn of events, whilst a rational voice in my head reminded me that I had left my unwanted, 'other-worldly' connections in Crystal Palace, that Jack was due home shortly, collecting Felix from the childminder on his way, and that Lily should really start winding down for bed.

Babs took a long sip of the smooth cabernet and a short shudder ran through her brittle body.

"Aah, that's better, always helps open up the channels of communication. Now, Mo, I have a gentleman standing beside you, he's a very nice man, very pleasant, attractive, an attractive personality. He's someone who would be accepted almost anywhere he went, he was that sort of person, very outgoing. I feel he's in the 1930s or 1940s... he's wearing a pin stripe suit, a little bit flashy, and a hat, a trilby – he's doffed it, my dear, and bowed to you, he's introducing himself! He's very good looking with a small moustache and I get the feeling he was a bit of a wheeler dealer, a bit of a ladies' man perhaps – I would almost say he's a likeable rogue. No, no. He's wagging his finger at me: I'm not to give you the wrong impression, he's a man of integrity!"

Babs seemed to be working hard to communicate this information, like a translator at an international conference struggling to convey with utmost accuracy the content of an esoteric lecture.

"He is connected with this house, though it was never *his* house," she resumed after another mouthful of red. "He was associated with it, people he loved lived here. What he wants you to know is that an injustice was done. To whom?" she asked the air, and cocked her head as if listening. "Aah, I see. Thank you." Babs addressed me again. "It was an injustice done to him and therefore to them, his loved ones. There is a wrong to be righted, and he is very pleased you've come to live here, tickled almost, I would say, because he feels you are the person who can do it, who will make things right at last."

"Me? Why? How?"

I had been enjoying the bravura of her performance without needing to decide whether I believed in it. With the best part of a glass of wine inside me an amiable, attractive male spirit seemed like an exotic bonus to our heavenly home, and in no way something to be unnerved by. But now, suddenly, I was implicated. I was being presented with a task, bequeathed a responsibility to some unknown, presumably dead, previous inhabitants of Stargate Farm. If he had been waiting for someone whose twin senses of destiny and duty were so overdeveloped that any challenge to seek out the truth or make things right for others had to be accepted, my ghost had indeed lighted on the right person.

"Give me some facts. Who is he? What was the problem and what does he want me to do about it?" I quizzed Babs, both the professional researcher and natural adventurer in me called up to active service.

She seemed to be listening again, but shook her head.

"He's fading. He says it's not the right time, he has to go. He's leaving you with a rhyme. I think it's a riddle: Find tinker and tailor, find soldier and sailor; of rich man, poor man and beggar man, which is the thief?"

"That's no use," I protested. "Tell him I need to know more, I've got to have a starting point!"

Babs shut her eyes, screwed up her face and held her head as though trying to catch a fleeting sound. "A car. He's showing me a car, a grand old car… He's proud as punch of it, even though it's not his. No, that's it. He's gone now. Perhaps he'll come back with more information when he's ready."

"Damn! How incredibly frustrating!" I almost shouted – then stopped short.

Jack stood in the doorway to the kitchen, holding Felix who was whimpering quietly, with Lily and Grace peering out from behind his legs, and a look on his face in which incomprehension, incredulity and irritation coalesced.

"Hello, darling," I struggled to my feet from behind the kitchen table. "Had a good day? Let me introduce you to my new friends, Babs and Laura."

January 1942

Douglas's leave fell in the week before Christmas, so I was able to cadge a lift down to London with Tink on the Monday, laden with parcels from the farm.

When Tink dropped me off in Raynes Park, I invited him to come in and meet Mother and Father. He utterly charmed them and promised he would find them some more tobacco and nylons in the New Year. I could see Mother sizing him up as husband material, but she said nothing, so perhaps he did not come up to scratch in that department!

It was wonderful to see my dear brother again; despite his adventures he looks well and fit and kept us all entertained with hair-raising stories of protecting the convoys against German U-boats. He did not tell the worst tales in front of Mother and Father, but when we were alone he admitted that sinking the Bismarck had been more death than glory, and a desperately tragic business for the Ark Royal crew as well as the Jerries. Only about a hundred members of the Bismarck's two thousand crew survived their attack. The wounded and the dead were just men, Douglas said, like him and his pals. Seeing them helpless in the water or trapped on the ship, he could only think about their families back in Germany who would feel no different from us if he had been killed.

But then the Bismarck had sunk The Hood and only three men from that fourteen hundred-strong crew survived. What a waste war is. Damn Hitler and his Nazi henchmen! I hope our children never have to endure this, as we have.

When the U-boat torpedoed the Ark Royal it opened a hole one hundred and thirty feet long. I cannot truly conceive how enormous an aircraft carrier must be. It carries more people than live in the three H villages put together. The ship whipped so violently with the explosion, Douglas said, that the torpedo-bombers on the flight deck were hurled into the air. He thinks the Captain and officers completely botched the rescue operation and with better tactics the upshot might have been different. If the Captain had not evacuated the ship straight away, but instead concentrated first on staunching the flood, the Ark could perhaps have been saved. He let the shipwrights and electrical staff leave the ship early on, so they were not on hand to help with the counter-flooding operation, which meant water came into the boiler room and killed the engines. Though the engineers left on board eventually managed to get the plant back on line, by the time they did so it was too late. The ship had taken on so much water that she was listing right over and so they watched the poor old Ark Royal capsize and sink.

Still, Douglas and all except one man are safe and sound, carried to Gibraltar by HMS Legion. And since Christmas he has returned to the Med on HMS Eagle, which I pray stays out of harm's, and the Hun's, way.

Mother was almost endearing in her pleasure at seeing us both, and tried to fill us with all the fresh produce I had brought with me. She would not understand that we eat such food all the time at the farm and Douglas is well fed in the mess. We made her keep back enough to provide a decent Christmas dinner for her and Father – for they will not come and stay with Aunt Philly, despite the renewed invitation in the letter I brought down from her. Father says she hardly leaves the house any more, as if she has become quite afraid of the outside world. He has to queue for their rations on a Saturday morning, and now even attends church on his own. The vicar has agreed to come and give her communion at home on Christmas Day, as if she is ill in some way.

Now Tink has met them, I think I shall ask him to pop in on them occasionally on his London trips, and bring regular supplies to supplement their rations.

I was able to help him once more with a present for Emma.

On my suggestion of buying her a book of herbal recipes, Tink found an edition of Nicholas Culpepper's 'The Complete Herbal'. He inscribed it with a quotation from Shakespeare, wrapped it in a length of exquisite amethyst coloured silk (who knows where he procured this!) and presented it to her on Christmas Eve at the Trowel and Hammer. At the pub Emma was blushing and disarmed by his charming gift and thanked him very prettily, but on the way home, she was quite distressed.

*"You might think yourself a dabster at match-making, Dottie,"
she told me. "But you have no call to be leading him on on my
account. There are things you do not know and he cannot know. If he
did he would soon change his tune about me. That is all I am saying
so do not ask me any more."*

*I said I had not realised she felt so strongly and that I was sorry
for interfering. I had thought that either she was being coy, or that
Archie was bullying her – neither a good reason for blocking the path
of true love, which I was sure was what Tink felt for her, and I
suspected she for him. "'Love conquers all things', as your beloved
Shakespeare said," I told her.*

*"That was Virgil, not Shakespeare," she retorted, "Shakespeare
knew better. Now let's forget Henry Tinker and have a Merry
Christmas." She took my arm to show there were no hard feelings and
we sang 'Silent Night' and 'The First Noel' as we walked home up
The Street, with the frost crunching under our feet. Of course I was
horribly curious as to what it was that Emma believed could change
Tink's feelings for her, but I could see that to press her on the matter
would make her clam up still more. I resolved to wait until she
trusted me enough to divulge her secret, however trivial, and sure
enough it did not take long.*

*Christmas Day was ever so jolly. Emma and Heather had
decorated the house with holly and ivy, and there was a great
Christmas tree in the corner of the drawing room, adorned with
ribbons and fruit, candles and little wooden animals that Billy
Stonepicker has whittled over the years. Twelve of us sat down to
dinner at the kitchen table: Aunt Philly and Anne were invited to join
the five Jacksons, Mrs J's elderly parents, Mr J's cousin Ned, Billy
Stonepicker and me. Mr J carved the most enormous turkey I have
ever seen and we all took a glass of port after the plum pudding and
brandy butter. Mr J proposed a toast "to absent friends, and Dottie's
family", which brought tears to my eyes. After the women had
washed up and the men smoked a pipe, Aunt Philly played the piano
and we all sang carols. The bare minimum chores, just to keep the*

animals fed and comfortable, were carried out with good heart, and we spent the evening playing card games and charades, made the more merry by some bottles of whisky and brandy that Archie produced – a present from Lord and Lady Buxton, he said.

Whilst he was giving me the title of my charade out in the hall ('Whispering Grass', not too tricky), Archie suddenly pulled me under the mistletoe and kissed me hard. I was taken aback for an instant, but under the influence of the brandy, found myself returning his kiss with some passion. It was not until the assembled company in the drawing room started calling for us to hurry up that he let me go and went back into the room without a word. I hope I did not appear too flushed and dishevelled when I entered to mime my charade.

I do not know whether Archie was simply inebriated or whether he has some feelings for me. He has not attempted to kiss me again since then, nor said anything of the incident. I feel his eyes burning into me, though, whenever we are in the same room. I cannot help thinking about him sometimes in bed, in my little maid's room, and wonder what I would do if he knocked on my door in the dead of night. I shall not be forward, nor flirt with him. Archie is my employer's son, and I do not wish to lose my job or make him think ill of me. And there is still something that alarms me about him.

We went back to work as normal on Boxing Day.

I and some of the other Land Army girls who live locally – but not Heather, of course – were on sprout-picking duty. The plants are close together and you have to straddle each one, holding the leaves back with your legs, and put the sprouts you have picked into a small sack. When we have filled two, we take them to the weighing machine at the edge of the field, trying to fill as many as quickly as possible. This January has been one of the coldest ever and on some days the plants have been frozen stiff, but we cannot wear gloves and our clothes get sodden with the melting ice.

On Old Year's Nyte, as they call New Year's Eve here, Mr and Mrs J were content to stay at home and sent Archie, Emma and I off to the Trowel and Hammer, where our RAF friends had planned a *celebration. Tink was there, courting Emma as usual, which had the extra benefit for him of aggravating Archie, whose earnestness he finds a great joke. Although I stuck to my promise not to encourage Tink in his attentions to her, I did draw Archie away from Emma's fireside corner and distract him from the pair of them. He was just beginning to let down his guard a little, and was, I think, about to put his arm around me when Billy Stonepicker ran into the pub all out of breath, with a message for Emma to go home as Maudie was taken ill with an asthma attack. Emma turned quite pale and rushed out. Tink said he would go with her, but I stopped him and ran after her myself.*

When we got to the farm we found Maudie in Mrs J's arms wheezing badly, hardly able to catch her breath and her lips quite purple. She had used her inhaler, but to little effect. Emma ran into the pantry for one of her herbal tinctures, which she poured into a bowl of boiling water with some Friar's Balsam and held the child's head in the steam, with a towel like a tent over the top. Mrs J explained that one of the cats had got into Maudie's room, where they are never allowed because of her allergy to them, and had been lying on her pillow. Mr J had gone for Doctor Coleman, but he and his wife had gone out to celebrate and their house was empty.

I do not know what Emma had put into her tincture, but as she inhaled the pungent steam, Maudie's rasping breaths started to quieten and when Emma eventually lifted the towel from her head, we saw some colour had come back into her face. Her mother went to pick up the little girl, but Emma took Maudie from her and said she should sleep with her tonight in case she had another attack; tomorrow her bedding would have to be boiled up in the copper. She carried her upstairs to her bedroom and I brought up the remaining tincture in the bowl in case it was needed. I was surprised to see tears rolling down Emma's face as she laid Maudie in her bed, and even more surprised when she said "If I was allowed to look after her myself, this would never happen."

Of course I asked her what she meant, and after making me promise never to tell a soul, Emma finally explained why she could not allow Tink to make love to her.

Maudie is not Emma's sister, but her daughter!!

While she was working at Heather's father's firm, she was taken advantage of and had the greatest bad luck to fall pregnant. Her parents decided that in order to protect her reputation they would bring up the child as their own, so she and Mrs J went away for the last months of her pregnancy and returned home with her new baby 'sister'. The only thing Emma was permitted to do was to name her, and she chose Maud for the writer, Lucy Maud Montgomery. I am now the only person outside the family who knows the truth. She thinks there was tittle-tattle in the village when they first came back, but because she was young and muscular she did not show until late and her figure returned directly after the birth. Mrs J, on the other hand, is round and plump, so no one could say for sure she was not pregnant when they left. And few people would question her parents as they are well liked and respected. They think they are shielding Emma by their actions, so she can marry and have 'her own' children. Emma loves Tink, but because of her honest nature has decided she will not lie to him, and she cannot tell him the truth because of her parents' 'sacrifice'. So she is stymied and Tink's love must remain unrequited.

This seems to me a terrible situation of star-crossed lovers. Since she told me, I think constantly about how I can help to resolve it, but the more I turn it over in my mind, the less I can see any solution. I cannot break Emma's trust and tell Tink, though I do not think he of all people would turn against her if he knew the truth. So far I have not been able to persuade her of this, for she believes she is 'damaged goods'. How cruel people can be.

———

Luckily Jack saw the funny side.

Laura and Babs, recognising the situation they had placed me in, ran a quick and effective charm offensive, which had Jack responding in kind to Laura's flirty flattery and agreeing to a family lunch at her place on Sunday. In a whirlwind of thanks, apologies and compliments, they whisked Grace out of the house into Laura's smart little car and off up The Street to whatever the rest of the evening held for them.

"So, Dr Patterson," I smiled at my husband, pouring a glass of the remaining red wine for him while Felix clung round my neck like a bush baby, "it looks like we've been accepted into village life by both the living and the dead. What did you make of the Haddeston coven? I really get on with Laura – just as well, seeing Lily and Grace have hit it off in a big way. In some ways she's as different from Venetia as you could get."

"Which is probably a compliment in itself," laughed Jack. "No, despite the Mystic Meg nonsense, they seemed very pleasant, hon, and it was nice of them to ask us round. So, Li'l Girl," he said, sitting Lily on his knee. "New school, new uniform, new friend. Has it been a good day for you?"

"Grace is nice. Nicer than Kimberley. I wish she'd been my buddy today. I want to go round her house, but I thought you and me were going to look at a riding school with Kathleen this Sunday, Daddy."

Jack and I exchanged a look, and before he could even attempt to dissolve it, I set the lunch date in stone.

"Well, it can't have been a firm arrangement with Kathleen as no one's mentioned it to me. We've accepted an invitation from some new friends and it would be very rude to change our plans now. We can all go and see the riding school another time."

"Promise, Mummy?" asked Lily, yawning.

"I promise, darling. Now you're tired, it's school again tomorrow, so up to bed."

———

"All quiet on the Western Front?" I asked, adding some final seasoning to the Great Haddeston butcher's succulent lamb chops, when Jack came down from reading the children's bedtime stories.

"Both out like lights," he answered, leaning over my

shoulder to inhale the aroma of the sauce I was stirring. "Hopefully it'll stop Lily sleep walking again. I got quite a shock last night when I opened my eyes and saw her standing next to the bed like a little ghost in her white nightie."

"Oh. I don't think I even heard her. Did you put her back to bed?" I asked, spooning rice out onto our plates.

"No, she just drifted off, must have gone back to bed on her own," replied Jack, as he drizzled dressing over the salad. "Mmm, looks great. I'm starving."

It was only when we had finished eating, and were discussing the events of our different days, that the thought occurred to me.

"Jack. Lily wasn't in a nightie last night. She was wearing those horrible, too tight, pink Barbie pyjamas."

"Oh. Right," he replied. "Perhaps I was dreaming, then."

But he looked puzzled as he pressed the button which sent the dishwasher whooshing into action.

Chapter Three

"So while we were all getting ready to leave, the phone rang and it was Tamara, the balance expert, wanting to go through the possible programme participants with me.

"And of course, being so concerned with everyone's family time – except mine, apparently – she had to do it there and then because she was flying off to the States in an hour to give a lecture on long hours working and parental stress and wouldn't be back before I had to start calling them up. So I had no option but to tell Jack and Kathleen to take the children and go off without me, and that I'd see the riding school another time," I related to my mother, who had driven up for the day.

I hesitated before continuing. Having been rescued by my parents emotionally, and to some degree financially, from the rubble of my first marriage, I hated to reveal any cracks in my relationship with Jack. Not only did I dislike admitting failure, but with my mother approaching eighty I didn't want to burden her with any more of my worries.

And yet, I couldn't stop myself.

"The way I saw it, the two of them tried hard not to look pleased, Lily was hopping up and down with joy because she knew Kathleen would book her riding lessons on the spot while I wanted to wait till she was more settled at school, and only Felix seemed remotely upset that I wasn't coming with them. And of course I can't blame Kathleen, or Jack, for Tamara's phone call, but it was as though they somehow got their own way by sheer force of will, because they simply didn't want me with them. Even though I like her, it feels as if Kathleen's trying to take my place with Jack, especially, and the children. Do you think I'm being totally paranoid?"

Athene Mozart had been Professor of Family Psychology and Sociology at the London School of Social Sciences and, though now retired, was still involved in research and considered an authority in her specialist areas.

"No, darling, not paranoid exactly," she replied, snipping vigorously at the dead branches of a Mermaid rose with my secateurs. "Possibly a little fixated on a natural bonding process, which is well documented and needs to run its course." She removed one gardening glove to retrieve a wisp of white hair from her still piercing blue eyes and replace it in her bun.

"Explain," I demanded, not sure whether what she was going to tell me would make me feel better or worse.

My mother closed the cutters, sat down on the ancient and somewhat rickety wooden bench we had inherited with the garden, and gave me a brief tutorial on genetic sexual attraction.

The bond between mother and child, in her view, was so primal and so physical as to be almost sexual in nature, though not in the same way as between two adults. These feelings were part of the natural experience of both boys and girls with their mother; creatures of sensation, the spontaneous holding, touching and above all breast feeding in the period following birth, aroused in all babies strong sensual or sexual type reactions. These were reciprocated by mothers, especially nursing mothers. In the normal course of events, this symbiotic relationship between mother and child gradually dissipated as the baby grew up and experienced separation.

This seemed a perfectly reasonable thesis and made sense in terms of my own mothering relationships. I probably wouldn't have described them as 'sexual', even while breast-feeding, but intense and sensual, certainly. But where did Kathleen and Jack fit into this model? She was well beyond breast feeding and he no baby. Here was the nub of the problem. I half closed my eyes against the early afternoon sunshine and braced myself.

"If these sensations weren't experienced and worked through in the typical post partum period, and if reunion takes place only when both parties are mature," my mother clarified carefully, watching my face as she went on, "these latent sexual feelings can emerge at that point and in a more adult way. There can be a real draw to express them, because it feels as if that is the only way to get close enough. I'm not saying many reunited people actually act on these instincts, but at a primal level the adult child is still a baby and undergoing those powerful emotions. The problem is, as a grown up, he or she can't achieve that symbiotic connection with the mother, nor go back into the womb. I don't want to upset you, Mary darling, but when the child is a man, he may subconsciously feel that the only way he is able to get back inside the mother is through sexual intercourse."

My head knew I was over reacting, but my body went ahead anyway, drawing the blood out of my guts and my extremities and into the essential fight-or-flight organs of heart, brain and running muscles. I felt sick and sweaty, my pulse raced and blood pumped behind my eyes.

"Are you alright? Put your head between your knees, darling," advised my mother impassively.

"Sorry," I gasped. "I'm being silly, I know." Then I remembered my yoga breathing and allowed my para-sympathetic nervous system to reassert itself over the primeval adrenalin surge, "Jack's not like that, Mum," I insisted. "He's the most rational man I know."

"I know," she agreed calmly. "And Kathleen is not 'like that' either. I'm not suggesting for one moment that either of them would act out these feelings, but understanding that one or both of them may be struggling with this unwanted attraction, which they have to work through in order to release themselves from it, might help you deal with the situation."

Yeah, right! I thought, but didn't say. Helps me like a kick in the crotch to know my husband wants to fuck his mother, my internal, rebellious teenager shouted crudely. Aloud, I said "But Mum, Kathleen's just had her sixtieth birthday, she's post post menopausal, let alone...."

"Mary, pull yourself together! I said that Jack and Kathleen might be experiencing these deep seated impulses, not that they were having an affair. In any case, the incest taboo is at least as strong in most adults as the primal urges. All you need to do is sit out this difficult period, which will pass, and try to be sympathetic. For Kathleen there's probably the added complication that Jack reminds her of the man she loved. It must be hard for her – though I do believe the parent should always be the one to take responsibility for managing the relationship sensibly."

"Granny!" shouted Lily across the garden. "Do you want to see my new riding clothes? Kathleen bought them for me. Come and see!"

Sympathetic – my arse! yelled my adolescent alter ego, stamping her foot. Why should I be? What's responsible about spoiling my daughter rotten when I've made it clear I'm not happy about her getting involved in a dangerous sport with horrible horsey girls?

"Oh go and have a look at the pink and purple jodhpurs – she's in seventh heaven with them," was my external response. "And she does seem to have taken to horse riding like a duck to water, if that's not too much of a mixed metaphor. Thanks, Mum. That's all useful information. I'm sure we'll get through this fine."

My mother raised herself creakily off the bench and followed Lily into the house as Jack rounded the corner on the lawn tractor with Felix on his knee. For a moment I saw him as a stranger might: a fit, good looking, early middle aged man with thick auburn hair greying at the temples; a strong, sensitive face and gentle, protective arm around his son. Then I tried to imagine that stranger grappling with the knowledge that this man had once been inside her body, as his son had grown inside me. It was a leap my imagination was not robust enough to take without causing internal injury. I stood up too quickly, knocking the old bench backwards with a sound of splintering timber, in my desire to escape.

"Just going to get some milk," I mouthed in Jack's direction, aware that I couldn't be heard over the growl of the tractor engine, and walked determinedly to the drive, ignoring his questioning shout of "Mo?" and Felix's cry of "Mummy!" I got into the car, started the engine, backed out of the gate and drove off in the opposite direction to the village shop.

After driving down the Turnpike for about ten minutes, I found myself in New Buckenham.

This small village, once moated and based on a still intact, medieval grid pattern, was considerably prettier and more 'desirable' than any of the Haddestons and I wondered for a moment whether I had not looked widely enough or done sufficient research to find us the right location. Then I recalled that while it might have two churches and the remains of a castle, New Buckenham had no primary school or playgroup, which was why I had discounted it early on in my searches. After ambling round the village green, noting the two pubs and beautifully preserved market house amongst the other sixteenth century dwellings, I bought a litre of milk and some home made cakes at the shop.

Only then, with my emotions in control once more, did it occur to me that I'd better get home and explain my absence. But driving slowly east out of the village, back towards the

Haddestons, I noticed that what I had assumed to be just another field was a wild area of common land, despite the dun-coloured cows grazing on it. I turned off the main road for a better look, and up a little lane, which appeared to circle the Common. Round the bend, though, a metal gate barred the way to cars. Frustrated, I was about to turn round when I felt an irresistible urge to explore the expanse of raw countryside before me. I turned off the engine and slipped through the wire fence.

As I strode across the uneven grass, pitted with rabbit holes and peppered with droppings and wild flowers, a feeling of deep peace settled about me. I realised that without the prompt of my yoga classes I hadn't once sat down for my daily fix of meditation since we had left London. True, I hadn't felt the same need to seek out the tranquillity I had craved in the hub of urban activity, but this altered state of mind, which I used to achieve deliberately and regularly, had never overcome me spontaneously in this way before. It didn't require me to stop, sit in position and work at maintaining the changed awareness, indeed the act of walking seemed to disseminate the effervescence that sparkled through my blood stream and intensify the feeling of airy expansion my mind had suddenly acquired. My persistent, low level buzz of anxiety about Kathleen lifted and a conviction of the rightness of my life, a sense of being in the flow, took its place.

I found I could not only walk and engage in this form of spiritual exercise, but that my senses were drawn to small sounds and sights I wouldn't normally take note of: the concentrated but lustrous green glow of a drake's head as he swam with his dappled mate across the gleaming grey lake; the melodic stream of what I knew must be a skylark filtered from the brew of birdsong flowing from the shimmering spring trees; distinct identities within the profusion of flowers blooming around my feet – sprinkles of delicate yellow stars, sprays of white blossoms with throats full of golden stamens, and swathes of sturdy green stems supporting exquisite, hot pink, hooded flower-heads. I slowed and bent to pick myself a little posy.

That was when I found myself not just sensing an altered state of mind, but seeing life from an altered view of time.

———

May 1942

Norwich is still recovering from the raids of last week, as are Canterbury, Exeter, Bath and York.

We heard the German planes fly over then the resulting explosions and saw the sky lit up with the fires. The bombs make a kind of 'whump' when they go off that you feel in the pit of your stomach as well as your ears. They are saying that this is Hitler's revenge for our bombing of Lubeck and that he chose these cities as the most beautiful and historic of Britain. Well, he may have succeeded in destroying some of our heritage, but a guardian angel must have been hovering over the Cathedral, the Town Hall and St Peter Mancroft Church, as they were not harmed at all. Anne says the saddest loss is little St Julian's on Kings Street as it was a Saxon church and one of the first to be built in the city. A high explosive bomb destroyed all except the north wall and porch.

I would not admit this to Anne and Aunt Philly, but I am more saddened by the bombing of Bonds Department Store. Tink has taken me and Emma to their Tea Rooms in the old thatched Assembly Rooms on All Saints Green on several occasions and it was very pleasant to sit near the elegant sofas and chairs in the Furniture Department and watch the people coming and going at the Bus Station. Although it was a smouldering ruin the day after the raid and the Tea Rooms are done for, Tink says Mr Ernest Bond has got the store open again and is selling off the damaged goods. He has found some good bargains there and has a big trip to London planned.

Since his lodgings in Earls Court were bombed out, Tink has spent even more time at Lavender Farm and only makes forays down to town when he has a full vanload to sell. It has proved a splendid idea of mine for Tink to lodge with Mother and Father at Raynes Park on those occasions. Now they get regular provisions from the farm, other titbits that Tink manages to pick up for them and a substitute son to fuss over. He has a free bed to sleep in, a lovely big bath to soak in and gets his shirts, collars and socks washed, ironed and darned by Mother, who adores him. She has even allowed him to escort her to Lyons Corner House in Wimbledon, which Father says is a break-through. He is pleased to have male company from time to time and it sounds as if they are getting through the brandy (which Tink procured from 'The Golden Can' on St George's Street, which was also bombed out) at quite a rate.

Thousands of houses in Norwich have been destroyed and many more damaged by the German incendiary bombs. Businesses are ruined and many people have nothing but the clothes they stand up in. Hundreds of them have gathered up what belongings they have left and trekked out of the city to sleep wherever they can find shelter in the countryside. The Government disapproves of this, but what are people to do? Mr and Mrs J have given shelter to some families made homeless by the bombing in a pair of labourers' cottages on Rectory Lane that were standing empty. They were in a bad state of repair, so Emma and I were dispatched to clean them out (Heather refused, saying the dust would set off her asthma) and Billy Stonepicker stopped some leaks in the roof and boarded up broken windows. Mrs J ran up some curtains on her Singer sewing machine from a bolt of dark red cloth Tink bought at Bonds and the wackerjees, as the locals call evacuees, are so grateful. The cottages have no plumbing or electricity, so they have to fetch water from the garden well, cook on paraffin stoves and use Aladdin lamps at night, but they are much better than the city shelters, or sleeping in fields.

Heather was truly distressed by the destruction of her home town, though her parents' house, which is a big Victorian Rectory on a hill behind the Station, is still standing and her father's office next to the Cathedral was not touched. They insist she stays at the farm now – where she is meant to be anyway, but her anguish is yet another reason why she can manage even less work than before. She claims now to be scared of the horses, which gets her out of helping me with horse-hoeing the sugar beet fields.

Actually it is a peaceful and pleasant enough activity and, unlike Heather, I love the two red-gold Suffolk Punch mares, Marnie and Goldie, who take it in turn to pull. Bob guides the hoe while I lead the horse and on a cold day they are lovely and warm to work with. I walk close to their heads to keep them straight down the row and we stride together for miles, up and down, in companionable silence. I can feel their hot breath and warm flanks next to me and if sometimes one of them treads on my toe with her hoof, I know she is sorry, the big gentle creature. Whilst I am still wearing my uniform greatcoat and boots in this cold spring weather, Bob wears only a 'slop and ganzer' – a blue linen smock over a dark wool jumper. When we stop and "ha' foive minutes" for a smoke, I always learn something new from him, about horses, crops, weather or the soil.

Despite the air raids, the Haddestons held their May Day celebrations on the green beside Gt H Village Hall. Children danced around a maypole, weaving their coloured ribbons in and out, back and forth, forming complicated plaits and cat's cradles, while a small band of two fiddlers, an accordionist and piper played jolly country tunes. One of the girls was crowned May Queen – Maudie was most impressed with her white dress, gay sash and coronet of flowers and said when she was bigger she would be Queen of the May. The women of the village had baked cakes and biscuits (Emma's Victoria sponge and fruit cake were the best) and there was home made apple juice, cider and ginger beer and some traditional games to play.

The next excitement will be Mrs J's fiftieth birthday next month. There is to be a garden party for the village folk if the weather is fine and an evening dance in the Village Hall for family and friends. Preparations have already started at the farm and Tink has been assigned to locate various items – a gramophone and records, champagne to drink Mrs J's health and I believe Mr J has taken my advice and enlisted his help with a birthday present.

Archie shows little interest in his mother's birthday, but is more than ever taken up with the Home Guard and meetings up at

H. Hall. It is now compulsory to enlist, as Archie predicted, and no one is allowed to leave unless on grounds of age or ill health, so he has got all the farm hands where he wants them – except, to his fury, they are often too busy on farm duties to attend drills and parades. He has arguments with his father over what the men are most needed for; Mr J's view is that producing food is the farm's contribution to the war effort. He quotes Sir William Beveridge, who said that the British people must be fed like an army.

I am swayed by both sides and listen avidly when they air their views at the kitchen table. Archie's dark eyes flash and a muscle twitches in his cheek, which makes me want to stroke his hair and soothe his furrowed brow. Of course I do nothing of the sort, just sit quietly listening. In any case, I should be afraid he would push me roughly away. He has threatened to report Tink for not joining up, and even Emma has told him he should, if only to keep Archie quiet; that there are people in the village who have regretted crossing her brother. But Tink simply smiles and says Archie will never report him as he has too much information (here he taps his nose and looks mysterious), and that he will do his bit for the war when the time is right. I believe he has something up his sleeve on that front, but I fear he may have given up on Emma.

———

The flowers I was bending to pick were no longer poking bright yellow, white and incandescent pink through an expanse of grassland, but little creeping, purple alehoof, drab yellow coughwort, ribwort plantain and common nettle mingling in the hedgerow bordering Buxton Lane. How I had arrived here from New Buckenham Common seemed not to matter as I added a handful of gleanings to those already neatly laid in the wooden trug I carried on my arm.

As I did so, I glanced down and saw I was wearing a worn tweed skirt, its box pleats ending just below my knees, over thick woollen stockings carefully darned in several places. I couldn't help being pleased at the long, shapely legs they covered, stretching down to a pair of sturdy but scuffed brown, laced brogues. A heavy strand of long black hair fell over my eyes and I pushed it back behind my ear, which I could feel was unpierced and without the silver hoop earring I had clipped in this morning.

I straightened up and walked on down Buxton Lane, past Primrose Cottage, which looked in considerably worse repair than when I had last seen it, along to the break in the hedge which was the entrance to Old Wash Lane.

I stepped onto the now not so narrow footpath and glanced down towards the church and school. The field was full of young sugar beet shoots rather than winter wheat, beyond which the graveyard seemed to have receded back towards the church; and the school playground was a grassy field devoid of the wooden play trail with its rings, ropes and ladders, and the mobile classroom where Lily was taught.

Who am I? When is this? demanded one part of my brain, while the person whose body I was inhabiting went methodically on with her task.

"Good, mallow's now out," I muttered, and moved forward to pluck some tall, coarse stalks sporting large pinkish-mauve flowers growing at the side of the footpath.

As I turned out of the field and back onto Buxton Lane, I caught sight of the distinctive high pitched gable and tall chimneys of Stargate Farm across the fields in front of me, but the pantiled roof had no spaces where ordinarily the velux windows of Jack's attic study reflected out sunlight between the pantiles.

The throaty growl of an approaching engine made me jump up onto the bank, and as the khaki green military vehicle approaching tooted at me, I felt a rush of pleasure pump blood into my cheeks. The canvas covered truck had the high, divided windscreen, blunt radiator, and small round headlights of a bygone era, and the man who stopped and wound down the window wore a blue uniform and side cap that I instinctively knew to be RAF ground crew.

"*The fair Ophelia! Nymph, in thy orisons be all my sins remember'd,*" he quoted, laughing, his cool grey eyes and warm wide smile melting my heart.

"*Good my lord, how does your honour for this many a day?*" I replied instantly, bobbing a jokey curtsey and trying not to give away too much of the happiness I felt at seeing him.

"Just heading back to base, old girl, thought I'd tootle down the lane in the hope of catching a glimpse of you. Will I see you in the 'Trowel and Hammer' tonight? A couple of the chaps want a lift over, having heard about the delightful company we keep there. They could do with a drink and a laugh after what they've been through. I thought we could have a bit of a sing song if Philly's in to tickle the old ivories. Say you'll be there."

He put his hand on his heart and made a comical, lovesick face. I nodded, a little reluctantly. He beeped the horn once more, winked and smiled, "Toodle pip!" before winding up his window.

As I watched him drive off up the lane and turn right towards The Turnpike, the familiar but unutterably foreign surroundings faded, along with my expansive state of mind. I found myself standing, clutching a small bunch of wild flowers on New Buckenham Common, feeling faintly nauseous and dizzy as if I had just been whirled too fast on the children's roundabout across the road. I rubbed my temples and walked back to the car, noticing gratefully as I got in that the digital clock showed my fantastical experience had stolen no appreciable minutes of real time.

My mother would understand why I had needed some time out to recover myself after our talk and hopefully cover for me. Perhaps Jack would overlook the two litre bottle of milk in the fridge which gave the lie to my feeble excuse for bolting.

But where had my mind taken me in those minutes of unpremeditated meditation?

To an escapist haven created at random from a kaleido-
scope of images and a stockpile of information secreted in the
back room of my brain? Or could it conceivably be that my
disturbance about Kathleen and Jack, channeled by the altered
consciousness of meditation, had actually shifted me to a
different time and another mind's experience?

———

My little posy sat on the kitchen table in the pretty milk jug
Nanny Babs had discovered until it began to wilt, but I resisted
throwing it away.

I wanted to know what the blossoms I had picked were, but
it wasn't until Jack brought Dr Gidney home for a drink after
their weekly late evening surgery that I learned their names
and discovered in so doing that I had committed a major faux
pas.

"I hope I'm not intruding," said Elizabeth, as Jack ushered
her into the kitchen where, luckily, I had just finished clearing
up the debris of the children's tea.

"Of course not, it's lovely to see you," I lied, knowing that
if I left their bath time for more than a few minutes, Lily's
invincible superiority at hide and seek would provoke Felix
into howls of frustration. "Have a seat, Elizabeth. I'm sure you
could do with a drink after a hard day's work – I know I could.
Jack?"

Elizabeth pulled out one of the mismatched Windsor chairs
around our pine table and smiled as she sat down.

"Oh, how sweet. Do you know I found that little jug in the
house when we moved in, and here it's stayed. I always had
wild flowers in the kitchen, too. What have you got here?
Lesser celandine, meadow saxifrage, and – oh dear, Mo, you've
been picking green winged orchids on New Buckenham
Common," she said disapprovingly, fingering the drooping
pink blossoms. "They're a protected species, did you not
know?"

I flushed at the memory of that day and apologised for my townie ignorance as she sipped the gin and tonic Jack had made for her.

"It's an amazing place. So peaceful – spiritual even," I ventured, trying to make amends. "I was captivated when I found it the other day, couldn't tear myself away," I added for Jack's benefit, who had not entirely accepted the explanation for my sudden disappearance on the afternoon of my mother's visit.

"Absolutely," Elizabeth agreed. "Of course there's no reason you would have known about the orchids, if you didn't stop to read the notice at the main gate. The Common is one of those rare pieces of land that has survived intact for over eight hundred years, never been ploughed, you know – although the ponds were originally dug out for clay and flint. Spittle Mere and the streams contain a cornucopia of water plants, there's a colony of crested newts, and all those hawthorn bushes are perfect nesting cover for songbirds like skylarks and black caps. The colony of orchids is one of the largest in Norfolk, so I'm sure a few won't be missed!"

They were still discussing Health Centre business when I came down from the bedtime run to send Jack up to read the children's stories, so I asked Elizabeth if she wanted to stay and have supper with us.

"Oh, thank you Mo, but no, I must get back to my little cottage," she responded quickly. "I'm sorry to have taken up Jack's time like this. He's such an asset, of course, the patients trust him implicitly, even though he's not a local. And it's marvelous for me to have someone to talk things over with, someone who's part of the Centre and the community on a long term basis. It's been difficult on the professional level as well, since David died."

"I'm so sorry, Elizabeth," I told her. "Do stay. It's only cottage pie, but there's plenty of it, and vegetables from the farm shop. I'd love to hear something about the history of the house – that is, if it's not too painful for you…" I tailed off, suddenly aware that her eyes were taking in my willow pattern plates on what had been her dresser, my cookbooks on what had been her shelves, photos of my husband and children on the pinboard where pictures of her family must once have hung.

"No, not at all," Elizabeth pulled her gaze back to me and smiled warmly. "It's wonderful to see happy family life in Stargate Farm again. That's what makes this house come alive. I was lucky enough to bring up my children here and I can tell you about all the changes David and I made over the thirty five years we were here. Starting with this kitchen. Did you know this used to be the dairy, where they hung all the meat and fowl and churned the butter? They added this room onto the kitchen – which used to be in your living room – in the 1830s, along with a couple of maids' rooms above, and we knocked them through into one big bedroom and the shower room."

"That's our bedroom now," I broke in. "It's got the best views in the house, over the fields to Haddeston St Michael and up The Street to Lavender Farm."

Elizabeth nodded. "Indeed it has. The family who owned the farm then must have been going up in the world, because that's also when they put in the central staircase – it would have just been ladders before that – and the little parlour with the bow window at the other end. The original farmhouse was just the two central rooms, two stories high plus the attic space because a thatched roof has to be steeply pitched. We put in the staircase to the attic – there was just the old ladder up to it when we bought the house."

"And who owned Stargate Farm before you and David?" I asked Elizabeth after we had finished off our meal with some Norfolk Dapple Cheese and oatcakes, washed down with local cider. There was a short silence as I pressed down the plunger of the cafetiere, and then Elizabeth replied, a trifle defensively I thought.

"Oh, it's a long story and I don't know the ins and outs. The Jackson family farmed the land successfully for years; they owned most of Great Haddeston at one time, then after the war things got more difficult. Farm land got parceled off until there wasn't enough left to make a decent living. Eventually they sold the house with an acre of land to us, then the barns next door to people who converted them into separate dwellings, and finally the land beyond them was bought by a developer who built the modern houses a few years ago. The Health Centre was built on the site of an old mill which they used to own, too."

"How the mighty are fallen. An example of social mobility in twentieth century rural England," I quipped. "I suppose that must have happened to lots of farming families after the war, with all the new mechanisation, then the European Union and agricultural subsidies."

"Yes, I'm sure that was all part of it. It's all water under the bridge now, though."

Elizabeth still looked a little uncomfortable as she stirred her coffee.

I wondered if she and David had encountered hostility when they moved into Great Haddeston as a young couple and started up their new Health Centre venture. Resistance to change must have been stronger in those days; Jack and I were lucky to have been so readily accepted by everyone we had met so far. I was reminded of Laura and Nanny Babs sitting at the kitchen table, and the handsome spirit she had conjured up whose request to right an ancient wrong I had not been able to completely forget, despite Jack's derision. Now he shook his head almost imperceptibly at me, but said nothing when, as if to relieve the tension, I lightly asked Elizabeth:

"And aren't there any local myths or ghost stories about a house of this age?"

Only for her to stiffen involuntarily and reach for her handbag under the table before pushing back her chair to stand.

"Oh dear, Mo. You haven't been listening to silly village talk, I hope? David and I never had any truck with that sort of thing – we were both scientists of course. I'm afraid I hold no hopes of an afterlife or a reuniting of souls. Our lives were dedicated to improving the lot of the Haddeston community in the here and now and helping them to reside in this world for as long as possible. David's memory lives on in the Health Centre, not in any kind of supernatural visitations to Stargate Farm!"

"Oh, Elizabeth, I'm so sorry, I didn't mean – "

Jack's look became a glare and I cursed myself inwardly for my lack of tact towards a recent widow as we both stood up to join her. As she shrugged on her long quilted coat and shrugged off my apologies, Elizabeth attempted a smile then kissed me goodbye on both cheeks.

"Sorry, my dear. Take no notice. It's been a strange experience sitting in this kitchen again now it's no longer mine. Delightful evening and I'm glad to have done it; next time will be easier. There were supposed to be goings on at Stargate in the distant past, but it's all nonsense and I've never felt anything but at ease here."

At the front door Elizabeth returned my hug with warmth and stepped out into the evening cool with Jack, who insisted on walking her back to her beautifully refurbished cottage on Rectory Lane. When he returned twenty minutes later all animosity had dispersed and he snuggled into bed beside me.

"Was she OK? I didn't mean to upset her," I mumbled in his ear as he warmed his cold hands on my body and buried his chilly face in my neck.

"Mmm, no problem," he replied indistinctly, disinclined to talk further.

As I stroked Jack's curly head which, some time later, lay pleasantly heavy on my chest, and heard his even breaths lengthen with sleep, I reflected with satisfaction that we seemed to be coming to the end of the beginning of our new life.

I couldn't know that only a few weeks later I would be feeling it was the beginning of the end.

———

August 1942

So much has happened since Mrs Jackson's birthday that once again I have found no time to keep this journal up to date.

Now it is Sunday evening and although it is late and I will be up early for the corn harvest in the morning, I feel I must record as much as I can of what has taken place in these heady weeks of summer.

First, and most important, Douglas has survived the sinking of HMS Eagle. My brother appears to have the nine lives of a cat, for which I thank God profoundly! In June he was flying Sea Hurricanes from the Eagle to provide cover for the convoy heading for Malta, when they came under attack from the Germans and Italians. Douglas and his boys did a splendid job of defending the convoy, backed up by Fulmars from HMS Argus, and he says they shot down a good few Italian planes. Then they joined another convoy in the Med, but they never made it to Malta as, nearly two weeks ago now, a U-boat torpedoed the Eagle and she sank near an island called Majorca. Two of their officers and over a hundred ratings were lost but the rest of the ship's company including Captain Mackintosh were picked up by HMS Laforey and HMS Lookout. Douglas and a few others were taken to shore in a tug called Jaunty. We think he is now based at RNAS Stretton awaiting posting to a new carrier.

This near miss for Douglas, and not seeing much of Tink any more, has set Mother back badly, Father writes. She has once more confined herself to the house and of course they are not even getting the extra food from the farm nor the treats that 'dear Henry' used to provide regularly. It is a sad situation and I worry that Father is now working his way through the remaining brandy alone at an excessively fast rate.

It was early June, I think, certainly before the birthday

celebrations, when an RAF Bedford truck pulled up at the Trowel and Hammer where we were sitting outside enjoying a drink in the warm summer evening. It took us a minute or two to realise that the tall, uniformed man who jumped out of the driving seat was none other than Tink. We had not seen him for a few days and assumed him to be on his travels, but he had finally signed up, and come to tell us he was now based at RAF Coltishall, a few miles north of Norwich, where he would be employed mostly as a driver.

I do not know whether Emma was more relieved that he had finally done the right thing, or upset that he was no longer going to be living in the village, but she flung herself into his arms in front of everyone. If Tink was surprised but pleased, Archie was shocked and furious to see his sister disporting herself with someone he so disapproves of. My first reaction was a selfish one – that I would worry about Mother and Father for the reasons I have outlined above – but this was quickly overtaken by pleasure at seeing Emma and Tink together, and looking so happy and well-suited to each other.

They sat close together on one of the benches outside the pub for some time, talking quietly and laughing occasionally. His arm was behind her shoulders on the back of the bench, but scarcely touching; her hands were folded demurely in her lap, though she stroked his arm occasionally during conversation. They made a charming couple – both dark haired, he looking quite the dashing airman in uniform and she in a pretty muslin blouse (darned quite invisibly by Mrs J) with her long hair pulled back off her face – apart from the heavy front lock which is always falling over her large blue eyes.

People went in and out of the bar, returning empty glasses and buying fresh pints, and all those who knew the pair looked pleased to see them together. Aunt Philly and Anne stopped and talked to them for a while, but mostly they were completely absorbed in each other's company. I tried to keep Archie distracted from them, demanding he fetch more halves of cider than I knew was good for me, which also had the effect of making me more daring and flirtatious with him than I usually consider appropriate. However, I knew I did not have his full attention and that below his impassive face, resentment seethed.

We were all four of us still outside when the landlord called last orders. Emma and Tink stood up and he offered her his arm and walked her to his truck. As he held the passenger door open for her, I could feel Archie about to intrude in some violent way, so I did the only thing to distract him that my somewhat befuddled brain could suggest. I took his face fiercely in my hands and kissed him hard on the mouth. I held him in this position until I heard the Bedford pull away onto The Street and then I loosened my grip, thinking he could do them no harm now. But I had acted without anticipating Archie's response, and when I dropped my hands from his face, he pulled me back against him and kissed me passionately, his hands feeling me all over. My body wanted to respond to his rough caresses, but even after four halves of cider my mind stopped me short and I pushed him away, saying "Archie, have a care. We are in full view of the world and his wife out here."

I was particularly anxious that Aunt Philly should not see me with him and make even some joking reference to my country beau in a letter to Mother. Luckily Heather was not with us that evening. He seemed to come to his senses and let me go, offered me his arm and we walked almost in silence back to the farm, where he joined Mr J for a pipe in the drawing room and I went up to my room. I knocked on Emma's door, but there was no answer.

After that night he treated me more or less as usual in public, but on occasions when we found ourselves alone together, or after a few drinks at the T & H, he took the opportunity to embrace me forcefully, kiss me and run his hands all over my body, sometimes so passionately that I feared he might tear my clothes. Although I cannot pretend I did not enjoy his attentions, I felt somewhat confused by the lack of affection he displayed, and always taken by surprise, for he never made any attempt at courtship or even flirtation. Whatever Archie felt for me, it was clearly nothing like Tink's emotions towards Emma. When I asked her what she planned to tell Tink about Maudie, she simply replied, "Henry knows that there can be nothing serious between us. He will be moving on when the war is over, and a good thing too." This made me guess that Tink was just humouring

Emma, as I am sure he has no intention of 'moving on' from her.

Archie's attitude toward me changed after Mrs J's fiftieth birthday party.

Saturday 27th June dawned fair and we were all given the day off to help with preparations for the afternoon garden party. As the 'garden' was no longer lawn, but full of Emma's abundant vegetable beds, the party was held in the orchard. We spent the morning carrying out all the chairs and tables that the farmhouse and neighbours could provide, arranging them under the trees and covering the tables with cloths and posies of flowers which Emma picked and arranged in vases, jugs and even jam jars. Her baking marathon of the last few days was a triumph and provided a mouthwatering array of cakes, biscuits and buttermilk scones, along with dainty sandwiches filled with egg and cress, cheese and cucumber, ham and mustard and jams for the children.

All afternoon villagers trooped up The Street to take part in the festivities and pay their respects to Mrs J. The same band who had played on May Day struck up and in between eating and drinking, adults and children danced under the apple trees – a very pretty sight. While Mrs J sat resplendent in the grandmother chair which had been moved from her parlour into the centre of the orchard, Emma, some of the other village girls who had come to help, and I ran in and out of the house carrying pots of tea, jugs of hot water, milk, ginger beer and apple juice, while the men ensured there were bottles of ale, stout and cider for those who wanted stronger refreshment.

The real fun for us young people, though, began at the village hall in the evening.

This was a more sophisticated event, to which Lord and Lady Buxton, other local dignitaries, and higher class family friends such as Heather's parents were invited. Mrs J, whom I now know to be a skilled tailor as well as seamstress, had spent many hours fashioning evening dresses for herself, Emma, Maudie and me. Tink had produced half a bolt of emerald green satin from Bonds' sale, an almost new pair of long voile curtains from an abandoned house and a set of linen sheets. Emma dyed the latter in various concoctions of gipsywort, ragwort and berry juice, I purchased a quantity of blackout material, as that is not rationed, and Mrs J cut out paper patterns from old newspapers. By the time she had finished sewing seams on her treadle machine and hemming and over-stitching by hand, we all looked most magnificent – quite as stylish as Mrs Newling and Heather, who had, of course, managed to purchase couture gowns.

Mrs J's ample, high-necked frock used most of the green satin and was trimmed with yellow; Emma, with her waist cinched in tight, appeared quite ethereal in sky blue linen trimmed with white voile, and my strapless bodice and full skirt were dark mulberry on black, and most flattering if I say so myself. Maudie looked very sweet in white and yellow voile with a green satin sash. Some of the older men wore evening dress, others day suits, but most were in their uniform. Tink, who appeared particularly debonair in his, had borrowed a magnificent wind-up gramophone for the evening and a pile of records which he had been loaned by all and sundry at Coltishall. Champagne seemed to flow, and after we had partaken of a light supper spread out on the trestle tables at one end of the village hall, the company danced the night away until past midnight – though I was not so lucky.

After he had partnered Mrs J and Emma, Mr J claimed me for a dance to 'We'll meet again', then Heather's father approached me and held me uncomfortably close while we waltzed to 'There'll always be an England'. I thought he did not realise that his hand was slipping down into the top of my bodice and I was too embarrassed to tell him. When the record ended, Emma beckoned to me as if she had something urgent to say, but she only asked if I was all right after my dance with Mr Newling. She told Tink to dance with me, and he whirled me round to 'Wish me luck as you wave me goodbye'. He is a splendid dancer and I felt almost envious of Emma while I was in his arms.

I think it may have been seeing me with Tink that finally made Archie step in to claim me. As the record finished, he tapped me on the shoulder and pulled me into his arms; someone put 'Fools Rush In' on the gramophone and we turned slowly around the dance floor, our eyes and bodies locked together, oblivious of everyone else. We danced like this to several more tunes before we could break away from each other, and then we went out for a stroll in the moonlight...

We re-entered the hall just in time for the birthday toast. Mr J made a brief but heart-felt speech in which he expressed his affection for Mrs J, "his better half", and presented her with the triple string of pearls that Tink had acquired for the purpose. Mrs J was obviously delighted; she thanked everyone, especially her husband, and asked Archie, Emma and Maudie to join them on the little platform. Archie tried to take me with him, saying something about an announcement, but I pulled my hand from his and stayed at the back of the hall. As he made his way forward alone, Heather walked purposefully past me, treading on my toe as she went, and hissed in my face, "Don't think you'll get away with this, he's mine, you know!"

Before I had fully taken this in, or could think of a suitable reply, there was some kerfuffle at the front and I looked up to see Emma pulling Maudie from the arms of Mr Newling, then she pushed through the crowd with her daughter in her arms until she reached me. I saw she had tears in her eyes and looked quite distraught. "Come home with me," she whispered, dragging at my arm and, though I did not at all want to leave the party, thinking Maudie must be having another attack, I went with them out of the door into the warm night air and up Church Lane back to the farm.

When we arrived home, I saw this was not the case at all and Maudie had fallen peacefully asleep on Emma's shoulder as she carried her home. I was annoyed, especially as Heather would doubtless see my departure as a victory and I did not like to think what she might be doing with Archie in my absence. So after she had tucked the little girl up in bed, I demanded an explanation from Emma as to why she had dragged me away from the party. To my dismay, she dissolved into tears and was quite inconsolable for some minutes, but when she could speak again I was deeply shocked by what she had to say.

Mr Maurice Newling, apparently the most respectable of men, is Maudie's father (making the child Heather's half sister!).

While Emma was working for him, he made unwelcome advances to her over several months, and when she finally had the courage to rebuff him, he violently raped her in his office, "to teach her a lesson". She felt unable to tell her parents, as they are long-standing friends with Mr and Mrs Newling, but confided in Archie. His response was chivalrous but hot-headed; he wanted to charge into Newling and Wood and fight his sister's attacker, but she persuaded him against this course of action. Then she found that she was pregnant and had to tell Mr and Mrs J of her condition, but she refused to disclose the name of the father and persuaded Archie to keep mum.

Mr Newling does not know that Maudie is his, or indeed Emma's, child, and to her horror was made a Godfather by Mr and Mrs J. At the party, Emma had seen him first holding me close with his hand down my bodice (which I then realised was no mistake on his part), later picking up Maudie for the birthday toast, and had felt unbearable revulsion towards him to the point that she had to leave.

I agreed that we would tell the rest of the family that Maudie had been taken ill with an asthma attack again and hope Mr Newling would not contradict this. He has said nothing to Emma since she left his employ, but treats her in a jovial manner at family occasions, quite as if nothing had happened between them. He would never, of course, admit to the rape, but Emma fears that if he suspected Maudie was his, he would abuse his role as Godfather and try to interfere in her life. It also explains why Archie is so protective of his sister – though I believe Tink to be a hundred times more honourable than Maurice Newling, despite his lower social position.

I should like to write to Mother about all this, and tell her quite forthrightly that I reject her social ambitions for me as I have discovered for myself that the upper classes have no better morals than the lower classes and in many cases considerably worse. Mr Newling is a rich man and a pillar of the community, but if I had become his secretary I would quite likely have suffered the same fate as Emma. Tink may be a poor man and wheel and deal for a living, and Archie labour on his father's farm, but I would trust either of them more than the Mr Newlings or Lord Buxtons of this world.

It is now nearly two months since the party and we have all (excepting Heather, of course) been consumed by the work of harvesting. Emma and Tink and Archie and I have settled into regarding ourselves as a pair of couples, and this seems quite acceptable to Mr and Mrs J, who continue to treat me as one of the family. I even feel a little sorry for Heather, who has retreated from her rivalry with me over Archie, and returns at weekends to the bosom of a family which is not so upright as she would like to think.

Archie is not a romantic type, unlike Tink, who showers Emma with little gifts and gestures to show his affection, but I am certain he cares for me in his rougher, farmer's way. He would rather argue with his father – who has been backed up by the Eastern Daily Press headline 'Harvest Must Come First' – or train with the Home Guard than whisper sweet nothings in my ear. But he can be very passionate in other ways. At present he is gone to an intensive training camp at a secret location somewhere in the county, along with some two thousand other Home Guarders and Lord Walsingham as the CO. Mr J is not best pleased to lose him, even for a couple of days, in the middle of harvesting!

While he is away I have spent more time with Aunt Philly and Anne, who has been promoted to Head Mistress of Haddeston School. We went for a bicycle ride this afternoon and rode down to Old Buckenham to see the new airfield that Taylor Woodrow are building there. They have brought in a great many Irish labourers to create three runways and all the buildings required to run an airbase and house the crews. We cycled down Abbey Road and suddenly found ourselves riding through wet concrete, leaving clear tyre tracks in what is probably to be the main runway! We pulled out our bikes and made our escape as quickly as possible, apparently getting away without being seen.

Word is that the Americans will be flying from Old Buckenham and Emma is hoping Tink can get himself transferred back here. It is not always easy for him to find reasons to drive the jeep all the way from Coltishall and they do not see as much of each other as before..

Chapter Four

I was in the middle of a conference call with Tamara and Jane about the subjects I had lined up for *Time Crunch*, when my mobile phone rang and I saw the word **School** illuminated on the screen.

Assuming that a life balance expert would understand the urgency of a possibly sick or hurt child, I quickly explained and took the call. The secretary's measured tone, though, didn't imply that there was anything physically wrong with Lily when she asked me to come in and see the Head Teacher at 12.30 today, and she carefully did not elaborate when I asked if something was wrong.

"Mr Chatham would just like to have a word with you about Lily. So I can tell him you'll be there? Ring the bell at the Office entrance and I'll sign you in. Goodbye, Mrs Patterson."

I returned to the conference call trying to sound as upbeat as I had been before the interruption, though I felt a prickling of anxiety and a slight sinking feeling in the pit of my stomach. This was reminiscent of when Jess had been at primary school and her uncompromising views on life, which had been apparent from an early age, had brought her into frequent conflict with the more inflexible teachers she had encountered. As a teenager, her hostility had been focused more on me, but since we had been domestically separated, first by her gap year and now nearly two years of university, she and I had grown emotionally close and far more appreciative of each other.

I used to blame the less easy aspects of Jess's personality on her father's genes, and his absence in her life, but if Lily was starting to display the same characteristics with Jack's steady presence and defining trait of stability in her DNA, perhaps the fault line lay in what they had both inherited from me. But then again, maybe there was nothing to worry about and Mr Chatham simply wanted to tell me himself how well Lily had settled in to Haddeston Primary.

"So, we have Edward the senior manager who works long hours, has a wife who resents this and he thinks might be having an affair, and two teenage children who have no respect for him," I recapped.

"That's right," agreed Tamara. "We have to look at why he is spending so much time at work – is he taking on too much, or working inefficiently or simply subconsciously escaping from home life? Then we must unpack the family situation, especially the relationship with his wife and whether in fact there is anything left between them to salvage. There might not be. Is everything alright with your daughter, Mo?"

"Fine, thanks. I'd just forgotten to sign a release form about a school trip," I lied. "The Edward situation could be potentially explosive, then. Family meltdown would make great viewing, of course."

"Tamara, we have to be sure we would have support systems in place for all four of them if that's a real possibility," broke in Jane, pragmatic through years of production experience. "We don't want to be accused of being exploitative here."

Tamara reassured us that her own life-coaching and relationship counselling skills could be augmented by child and family specialists in her consultancy, and I went on to describe the five other subjects I had got to agree to appear in the series.

"That's a great spread of talent – covers different age groups, a variety of time and balance issues and we've got a good range of locations to shoot in – well done, Mo," Jane congratulated me and Tamara concurred. "Just one problem. The broadcasters decided yesterday that they want seven episodes instead of six, so we've got to find one more subject to fill the slot. Do we have any also-rans we can get back to?"

I sighed.

It had been hard enough finding these six families who had sufficiently diverse problems and were willing to make themselves public property. Not all of them had yet signed the contract with Generation Films and it was often when potential subjects of reality TV series read the small print that they decided not to go ahead after all. I was just keeping my fingers crossed that I could keep all of them hanging in there until production started.

"And do you know what?" Tamara's eager tone alerted me to some further challenge she was about to set me. "There is one crucial contemporary issue we are missing amongst these families. We do not have a 'sandwich generation' woman."

"Sorry, I'm not familiar with that term," said Jane, while I tried to put away thoughts of tasty local bacon between wedges of the granary loaf baked by Nanny Babs that I was planning to have for lunch – and which I would now have to postpone until after my visit to the school.

"They are the women who, because of their careers, started a family late in life and are now juggling not only a senior position at work with the needs of possibly quite young children, but also care of elderly parents or relatives in poor health. Sandwiched between the two generations – do you see?" Tamara spelled it out for me and Jane. "One of those would be the perfect seventh subject. Do you think you can find someone in that position, Mo?"

My hesitation was only a fraction of a second. "I'll do my

best, give me a couple of days, ok?" But it was enough for Jane, who had worked with me for a long time, to pick up on.

"Are you sure, Mo? Don't restrict yourself if that's too hard to come up with in the timeframe. I have to start working on a production schedule by Wednesday so any definite is better than an ideal possible, right?"

As we rang off, my mind was already racing through suitable friends I might be able to persuade to take part in *Time Crunch*. Miranda and Simon in Crystal Palace: his parents were still hale and hearty and her sick mother lived in America, probably beyond the production's travel budget. Suzy and Duncan had fragile parents but the boys were more or less off their hands. Laura and Pete had already declined to take part – "No time to learn how to manage my time better!" – and in any case, Nanny Babs was rather too sprightly for the role of decrepit mother. But they had mentioned someone who was keeping their elderly grandmother in our local care home, Black Carr House? Might they have children as well?

I sent a quick text to Laura.

Her answer, when it came, added to my discomfort in the Head Teacher's office as my mobile sang out its arrival with the loud salsa beat I had inadvertently downloaded while fiddling with the web browser. I managed to speed read: **Charlotte @ PO. Yes kids - u no K from skule + 1. Lx,** before apologising for the intrusion and turning off my phone.

I was having trouble making sense of Mr Chatham's gently presented news that my daughter had been the subject of a complaint from the parent of another child in her class. Apparently Lily had been bullying this other child, whose name he was not allowed to give me because of their confidentiality policy, by excluding her from a group of friends, making up stories and insulting her family.

"But Lily doesn't know anything about anybody's family round here; we've only been in Haddeston a few weeks and the one strong friend she's made in class, as far as I know, is

Grace. I can't believe the two of them constitute a 'group' if they play together and it really doesn't sound like Lily to bully anyone – except her little brother occasionally," I smiled.

But Mr Chatham was not going to be amused by the pleasantry.

"I have, of course, spoken to Lily and – the other child in question, as well as Lily's teacher about this. Miss Oldroyd's view is that this is not a one-sided episode, but Lily has come into an established set of friends and has had, probably without realising it, an effect on existing relationships. We don't regard it as a major problem; please don't worry about it, Mrs Patterson. But I felt it best to make you aware of the complaint and that we will be keeping an eye on things. For the moment, Lily and – the other child will be kept apart in the classroom and all the playground staff have been told to monitor potential incidents at playtime. Do I have your agreement on this course of action?"

"Well, yes, of course," I stammered. "Though I can't help feeling it would be easier if I knew who the other child was so I could talk to Lily and perhaps have a word with the mother – or father."

Mr Chatham stood up as he reiterated that this was not appropriate and I shouldn't worry. It was probably just teething problems for Lily moving into a new school and new area and that girls in school years two and three were notoriously fickle in their friendships as they established a pecking order and relationships. He advised me not to make an issue of it with Lily as he felt it had been suitably dealt with at school. Her reading was coming on and he was most impressed that she could recite Wordsworth's 'Daffodils', as they were studying spring flowers in class this week.

I was impressed too, as I didn't recall ever reading the poem to Lily myself, was certain Jack would not have. Perhaps it was a favourite of Kathleen's, I mused as I walked out of the Head's office, down the narrow staircase and through the old wooden front door. It was only as I got back in the car that I felt a lump in my throat and wondered how many parents in Lily's class had discussed my daughter and found her wanting, a city misfit in the cosy little school community which I so wanted her, and us, to be a part of.

By the time I reached the Great Haddeston Post Office, I was calm once more, focused on the need to find a seventh subject for *Time Crunch* and reassured by Mr Chatham's words.

I stood behind two other people in the queue that constituted Haddeston's lunchtime rush hour and listened to the woman behind the barred counter whose face I couldn't see from my corner of the tiny shop, as she chatted extensively to her customers.

"Oh really?"

"Oh, how interesting!" and

"Oh, I know," were her favoured responses, delivered in a noticeably Birmingham accent and judiciously used to extract maximum information about themselves and other villagers.

Now I remembered Laura's description of Charlotte at the Post Office as a hub of local gossip and advocate of alternative healing methods. Perhaps I could use the latter as a point of contact despite Jack's position as a mainstream medical practitioner, I thought hopefully – until I moved up a place in the queue and shuffled round to face the counter.

Charlotte Tinker was not only Great Haddeston's Sub Postmaster, as I read on the badge attached to the bars in front of her, but the mother of Lily's rejected buddy, Kimberley. Hence Laura's cryptic text about me knowing K from school. If she bore any grudge on her daughter's behalf, though, she was professional enough not show it as I bought a large quantity of first class stamps and a couple of birthday cards painted by a local artist.

She smiled politely, if coolly, when I asked after her daughter and said I thought Lily was settling in at school now and getting on well with Miss Oldroyd. I realised as I spoke that she had probably heard gossip about the classroom dispute and might even know who the mystery complainant was, but she looked genuinely concerned when I told her Felix suffered from asthma.

"Oh, really?" she asked rhetorically once more. "Oh, I know!" as I explained how the late spring pollen count seemed to have affected him badly after his improvement away from London pollution.

Charlotte paused, the large blue eyes in her thin, careworn face appearing to size me up before continuing. She pushed a tress of black hair behind her ear, gave me my change and looked directly at me through the safety barrier.

"I know your husband's the new doctor and you might not be interested, but there's been asthma in my family and I have a herbal remedy that works very well for young children. I can give you some if you'd like to try it."

I told her I'd be very grateful for anything that would help and that I was really interested in alternative therapies in general. Charlotte gave no appreciable response to this intended olive branch, but pulled down the grille between us.

"I'll take a short lunch break while no one's here," she said, locking the till. "I only live round the back; come over to mine and I'll give you a bottle."

I followed her out of the shop into the bungalow behind, which sat in a garden divided equally into a children's play area and an immaculately tended vegetable patch. As we walked down the narrow central passage from the front door to Charlotte's kitchen at the rear of the house, I caught sight, in the lounge to the left, of a young woman, perhaps in her late teens, smoking in front of daytime tv, while two open doors on the right revealed one extremely tidy and one chaotically messy bedroom.

We passed through the kitchen and into the adjoining conservatory, which seemed to be a herb nursery and laboratory combined. All manner of common and exotic-looking plants grew in pots on the sunny windowsills and shelves, whilst jars, bottles and vats, which could have come from DIY beer and winemaking kits, containing liquids, jellies and creams stood on a table or the floor beneath it.

Charlotte picked up a large container of brownish liquid, uncorked it and poured some of its contents through a funnel into a clean, empty medicine bottle.

"You can take this orally as syrup, a teaspoonful three times a day works as a preventative, or to treat actual symptoms put three teaspoons in a bowl of just boiled water, keep the child's face over the steam and cover his head and the bowl with a towel. He should inhale for at least five minutes if possible. You can have that free of charge. If it works and you need more, I'll let you know my prices."

I thanked Charlotte profusely and considered quickly how I could introduce the subject of *Time Crunch* before my window of time with her closed and she had to return to the Post Office.

"Is that your other daughter watching the telly back there?" I asked, a little too bluntly. Charlotte bridled and gave me a suspicious look.

"Yes, that's Kylie. I don't know what you've heard, but she's a good girl. Helps me in the Post Office and looks after Kimberley. She might have been excluded from school, but she's still studying to take her A levels this term. She didn't do nothing bad, just doesn't get on with authority."

Been there, got the t-shirt and looks like I'm going for a return trip, I thought.

"I expect she helps you with your old grandmother, too," I ventured. "It must be hard for you juggling the needs of different generations with a full time job."

I had clearly hit a target. The taut lines on Charlotte's face softened so she looked almost vulnerable and as she sighed, her slim body visibly wilted. Encouraged, I plunged into a description of *Time Crunch*.

After a few sentences I heard the television go silent and

footsteps approach the conservatory, but only when I got to the bit about my search for a 'sandwich generation' woman and her family to take part, did I turn to include the lanky figure leaning against the doorframe. The younger, angrier looking version of Charlotte stared at me from beneath backcombed black hair and through similar deep blue eyes, accented to an alarming degree by her full on, white faced, black lipped and lidded Goth make up.

———

October 1942

Once again there have been alarms and excursions in Gt H and surrounding country since I last wrote my journal. Some of these have been of a military nature and others of a personal kind. Sometimes the two have been one and the same.

Douglas's squadron, 801, was reformed at Stretton after the sinking of the Eagle and they have now joined HMS Furious. He is flying Seafires this time and has hinted they are in the Med again. Neither Mother and Father nor I are receiving many letters from him, but we hear snippets of information from the radio and newspapers and, like everyone else in the same situation, have to assume that no news is good news.

Whilst my brother is involved in the realities of war, Archie and the H. Home Guard platoon have been playing war games – although he would be furious if he knew I had written of them like this, and of course it is serious work. The Germans could invade us at any time and then we would be relying on all the little platoons to save our towns and villages. If H. is anything to go by, they are getting smaller all the time, now conscription age has been lowered to eighteen. Archie is mainly training with boys and old men, along with a few who have protected jobs like him or are unfit for active service. Perhaps this is why he so enjoyed the Summer Camp, where they saw some real action, throwing actual grenades instead of the swedes they use for practice here, and firing real mortars. Archie managed to knock the wheels off a moving target with one shot from a

Spigot Mortar and wrecked a jeep with another – feats he was most proud of!

Last month he and the platoon took part in 'Harvest', an exercise to test the Wymondham Invasion Committee's defence plan. The Home Guard set up their HQ in the new Drill Hall in Pople Street, and Archie had a hand in organising this co-operative effort between the Home Guard, Civil Defence, Fire and Police services. Local troops played the part of the 'enemy', and Tink managed to involve himself here, so inevitably he and Archie were fighting on opposite sides of this 'war'.

It began on 17th September when the 'enemy' were said to have established a bridgehead on the north coast, then columns of 'Germans' passed through Dereham and were 'reported' to have reached Thetford by the 19th. They were supposed to have used gas against residents and bombed the telephone wires to destruction, so in the event communications were somewhat confused. However, on the 20th, the day Wymondham was finally 'invaded', the H. Home Guard patrol had a run-in on the Turnpike with 'enemy paratroopers', one of whom was none other than Henry Tinker.

I am afraid Archie and Tink had to be separated from hand to hand combat by Lord Buxton, who was for once fulfilling his role as Commanding Officer. It was lucky the 'enemy' had been provided with steel helmets, or else Tink might have come off the worse. Archie was near boiling when he discovered this 'Nazi' with one of the packets of sandwiches the Jacksons had agreed to provide for the Home Guard's lunch (this was thanks to Emma, of course). In the finish, Tink had the last laugh, for the chief umpire, Lt Col Back, declared that Wymondham had been successfully occupied by the 'enemy', and the town had to 'surrender'. Archie was, however, commended by the Invasion Committee for his leadership and commitment to protecting the Haddeston villages!

I do not know why Archie and Tink are at such loggerheads; neither of them will tell Emma or me and I do not believe it is simply Archie being protective of his sister. He tells me it is men's business and I should not worry my pretty head about such things – at least that is what he says when he is in a good mood. At other times he is more dismissive and even rude. Tink tells Emma that it is best for her not to know, then she will not have to divide her loyalties. We both think it is something to do with money and probably dog racing, but who owes money to whom we cannot tell.

Aunt Philly and Anne know now, of course, that Archie and I are courting and I have even written about it to Mother. She must be very down in the dumps, for she hardly mentioned it in her return letter and Father only wrote that he was pleased I had found a friend. I do not think Aunt Philly and Anne exactly approve of Archie, but they do not say so in as many words.

I do have some doubts about Archie, I must confess. I find him physically attractive and somehow fascinating, but he is hard to converse with other than about farm or Home Guard business. He does not flirt or act romantically and sometimes I wonder if he actually likes me, never mind loves me. I do not know whether I am in love with him. I have never been in love before so how should I know if this is the real thing? I can only say that we do not share interests or display the same depth of feeling that I see between Emma and Tink. I believe she has been holding much of herself back from him because of the situation with Maudie, but perhaps now there will be no need. Once again, Tink may have had the last laugh over Archie, which will not sweeten his temper at all.

Tonight we were in the Trowel and Hammer, when a heated discussion arose between Archie and the men he was playing cards with. Archie had had a few pints, as he is often prone to do these days, and started to threaten one of airmen from RAF Coltishall whom he claimed was cheating. He stood up to take a swing at him, but Tink quickly got his arm behind his back and manhandled him out through the front door.

Emma and I followed them, she shouting at Archie to stop acting like a silly ass and behave himself, whilst I did not know who to support. Both Tink and Archie told us to go inside and leave them to sort it out, so we did. When they had finished roaring at each other, Tink came back in and said Archie could do with my help to walk back home. I feared they had been fighting, but he was only drunk and in surprisingly good spirits. He said he had given old Tinker a piece of his mind and he didn't expect to see any more of that numb chance lummox around H. any more. He was so cheerful that, despite the chilly evening, he dragged me down the side of the field to the little spinney behind Buxton Lane that Emma and I have named 'Lovers' Leap'. We went further than I have let him before and although I had eventually to stop him, he quite made up for his bad behaviour at the pub.

When we got home I came up to my room and found Emma waiting for me here, pale and shivering, wrapped in my eiderdown. She told me, whispering so that Heather did not hear through the wall, that Archie had told Tink about Maudie being her daughter and that Mr Newling was the father. Worse, though, he had led Tink to believe that Emma had been a willing participant in the relationship and still had feelings for Mr Newling. "I'll not forgive my brother for this," she said, cold as ice, and I believed her. She shed no tears and said she would not let him win over this. I know Archie has done wrong, but tonight of all nights I cannot find it in me to be very angry with him.

Emma then told Tink the whole story, and how that had led to her sudden disappearance from Mrs J's birthday party, which she had never explained to him before. Emma said he had been more shaken than she had ever seen him and she did not think he was sure how to take it or what he felt about her. Instead of heading back to RAF Coltishall, he has feigned sickness, let one of the others drive the truck back to base, and gone to his aunt and uncle's at Lavender Farm for the night. Tink told Emma he needed time alone to think things over. If he came to a decision before midnight he would signal to her by lighting a candle in his bedroom window, despite the blackout, and if she returned his signal they would meet at Lovers' Leap to talk.

Mine and Heather's rooms have the only windows that face down The Street towards Lavender Farm, so she would have to wait here until midnight. I undressed and got into bed, exhausted by my own exertions of the evening, and would have slept had Emma not sat restlessly on my feet, fully dressed with my eiderdown around her, peering out of the window for signs of a light.

It was a quarter to twelve when Emma finally jumped up and made me get out of bed to look at the tiny flicker in the far darkness. She lit a candle and held it by the window. I could just about make out an answering flash from what must have been Tink's little dormer window under the thatch, as he held his hand in front of the light three times. Emma tiptoed out of my room and down the back stairs and I could distinguish her shadowy figure for a few minutes as she walked silently up The Street in the moonlit dark to discover her destiny.

Now I cannot sleep for worrying about her, so I have written this in my journal and do not know how long I will have to wait before she returns with news of Tink's resolve.

———

"Well you know who it must be," said Laura, as we sat facing each other at one of the pub-style picnic tables.

We had joined the drift of mothers and children who, on sunny days, wandered up the lane from school to the playground, where we could chat and the kids let off steam before heading home. It had brightened up since I left the Post Office and there was only a mild breeze blowing through the swings, around the village hall and across the wide expanse of football pitch. Lily and Grace were helping Felix up and down the slide and the other mums had congregated around the further table where they were out of earshot of our conversation. I had told Laura about my summons to school earlier in the day and she now leaned conspiratorially across the table to me.

"It must be Lady Janet," she whispered. "She thinks her children are all perfect little angels as well as academically gifted. That's a joke. Edmund and Judith are at Old Buckenham High now, but I've heard Edmund was a right tearaway when he was here. Alfred's dyslexic, though a nice boy. Agatha's bright but a bully, and of the twins, Harold's out of control and Elfrida's a spoiled baby. Anything that goes wrong for her is an earth shattering tragedy. She's always asking Grace to play up at the Hall, and I'm always having to find excuses because Gracie never wants to go. I expect Lily turning up from London and becoming best friends with Grace has put Elfrida's snotty little nose out of joint."

"Well, what could Lily possibly have said against the Buxton family? She doesn't know anything about them – we certainly haven't been invited to take tea at Haddeston Hall," I puzzled.

"Ah, but think about it. What was I shouting my mouth off about the first time I met you? Lady Janet and her harem. Little piglets have big ears and I'm sorry to say that wasn't the first time Grace has heard the story." Laura added the final corroboration to her theory.

At that moment the group of mums near the roundabout started recalling their children and loading them into cars and people carriers. One tall imposing woman in a well worn denim skirt and baggy fleece came towards us.

"Hello, Janet, my love," smiled Laura. "You're looking well. How is your beautiful brood? Hasn't Agatha got pretty lately? I don't know how you do it with six; one's more than I can manage!"

For an instant I thought Laura a total hypocrite after her judgmental remarks moments earlier, but then I read genuine affection and admiration in her face for Janet Morton. There was, after all, nothing contradictory in anything she had said: Agatha could be bright and pretty as well as a bully and Janet Morton a caring and competent mother of six despite seeing only the best in her offspring – and possibly logging a complaint against mine. Her weathered face devoid of makeup and badly dyed hair with an inch of grey roots made her look older than she probably was and an unlikely latter day Lady Chatterley.

"Mary Patterson?" she asked me. I nodded, smiled and took the large, rough hand she put out for me to shake. "Janet Morton, Brown Owl, First Haddeston Guides and Brownies. Got your phone message. Lily's on the list for Brownies. She can start after half term. I'll give you the information pack nearer the time."

"Oh, thank you, that's great! Lily will be thrilled about that," I replied ingratiatingly, but, business transacted, she had turned to go.

"Alfred! Agatha! Harold! Elfrida! Car *now!*" Lady Morton's stentorian tones rang out across the playground. Four children in diminishing sizes, two very dark, one mousey and one very blonde, but all with their mother's aristocratically prominent nose and chin, detached themselves from the mêlée and trailed behind her to the green landrover with attached horse box.

"See? She's not a bad old stick, but she'd think it was the right thing to do to put in a formal complaint rather than make it personal," said Laura.

"She wasn't exactly friendly," I admitted. "Though she has put Lily down for Brownies."

"She'd never be unfair in that way, and she probably sees this as the best way of dealing with a problem. She certainly wouldn't like anyone casting nasturtiums on her family, no matter how free she is with the information. Take no notice, it'll all blow over. Now tell me about the lovely Charlotte."

So I related my good news: that Charlotte seemed nice enough and had given me a herbal remedy for Felix' asthma, which I was going to try when we got home; that the Tinker family had almost agreed to be my subjects for the seventh *Time Crunch* programme; and that Kylie had been a bit bolshy, but her mother seemed sure she could talk her round.

"What happened to the girls' father?" I asked Laura. "From my point of view it's great that she's a single mother as well, but it's extra tough on her."

"I know nothing," she replied, gesturing extravagantly.

"Charlotte turned up to take over the Post Office a few years ago and she was on her own then. She was the only candidate for the job and, as the alternative was for it to close, everyone was very grateful and supportive. Her gran, who is completely gaga, went into Black Carr House without being on the waiting list and no one asked questions. I have heard her say that her family came from round here, but that might have been ages ago and I've never heard of anyone in the village being related to her."

We chatted on until the girls got bored. I told Laura that Venetia and her boyfriend Nick were coming to stay for the weekend and wondered if she and Pete would like to come over to dinner on the Saturday night. At first she was delighted and jumped at the idea of meeting some of my London friends. I tried to lower Laura's expectations.

"Venetia's quite high up in the Department of Information, but I've known her since we were at school. She can be a bit sharp at times, but she's got a heart of gold beneath the spikes. Nick's made a pile because he started this political lobbying business after being an MP's researcher and it just took off. But he got God a couple of years ago and only lobbies for good causes now. He wants Venetia to marry him, but she's so independent minded, and she won't do church."

I tailed off. Laura was looking daunted, her usual bubbling confidence suddenly evaporated.

"Oh, Mo, I don't know. They'll probably want to spend time with you and Jack and not have to meet your country bumpkin friends. Me and Pete, we don't do politics; I couldn't hold a conversation about things like that. I'd just embarrass you."

I felt quite upset that Laura should see herself in that light and insisted, to her and myself, that Venetia and Nick weren't snobbish, didn't talk politics outside work and would enjoy my new friends as much as I did. Anyway, Jess would be there, with whom Laura made friends and always enjoyed talking fashion with. In the end Laura agreed to come, but I could see she still had reservations. I'd have to warn Venetia to keep her barbed tongue in cheek, if not in check.

The girls were tiring of their game with Felix and he was starting to wheeze a little, so we began to make a move. As I bent down to retrieve Lily's school bag from under the bench, I felt a familiar and unwelcome lurch inside my head.

Sitting upright again, I found myself displaced once more and out of time.

I was in my dining room at Stargate Farm, except it was now a sitting room and, judging from the patterned wallpaper, worn leather sofa on which I sat and large Bakelite wireless set, sometime in the 1930s or '40s. Outside the window our lawn had turned into a massive allotment where all manner of vegetables flourished – I noticed sleek rows of leeks where I had earlier (or later, much later) found a surviving few.

The anxious feeling which Laura's reticence had triggered in me seemed to have magnified and I realised that I was shivering with fear and gripping my long fingered, work worn hands between my knees. A smaller, but equally roughened hand clutched my wrist and I turned to look at the young woman wearing corduroy breeches and a green sweater, who was sitting next to me on the sofa.

"What are they saying, Dottie, do you hear?" I asked, becoming aware of the indistinct sound of conversation behind the door of what I would normally have called my study. She cocked her head with its neat cap of curly chestnut hair towards the next room and listened intently. The rumbling of two male voices sounded antagonistic, rising in volume until a clear female voice interrupted them.

"Hush now, 'Lijah Jackson," it ordered, forcefully. "You hent no call to git titchy. We've kept things squat for our Emma's sake, but it's her and Maudie's happiness that do signify. Think on that afore you do make a wry you live to regret."

There was a silence and then a "Harrumph" from one of the men behind the wall. The discussion took on a quieter and more conciliatory tone and a spring of hope welled up in my breast, though for what I was unable to fathom.

"I told you so, old thing," said the girl with round brown eyes, ruddy cheeks and a sprinkling of freckles across her nose, as she squeezed my arm. "Mrs J will jolly well sort them out. And Mr J is an old pussycat beneath his gruff exterior. Chin up!"

As she finished, the door of the study opened.

I jumped to my feet, too fast it seemed, for the blood rushed from my head, my legs turned to jelly and the room swam before my eyes. I sat down again and held my head.

"Are you OK, Mo? You look a bit ghastly. Here, have a sip of this – I keep it for purely medicinal purposes," and Laura held a pink plastic drinking bottle to my lips. I gulped and gasped; a nip of gin and tonic was not what I'd expected from the childish container, but the kick was salutary and my nausea passed.

"What happened there?" Laura pressed me. "You don't usually go in for funny turns."

I took a deep breath and exhaled. "If I tell you something, promise you won't think I'm losing it?" I requested.

"*Me* think *you* were losing it? That would be pot and kettle! Tell me."

So I did.

December 1942

I have not had a chance to bring my journal up to date until now. And perhaps it is no bad thing that I do not write very often, for if I use up this old shorthand notebook, there is little chance of laying my hands on anything other than scrap paper.

I had fallen asleep by the time Emma crept back into the house some time in the early hours, and she was too thoughtful to wake me, though I was desperate to know what had taken place between her and Tink.

When they met at Lovers' Leap, Tink, far from rejecting Emma, told her he did not blame her or believe that she had led Mr Newling on; indeed he was relieved finally to know the true reason she had tried to keep him at arm's length and more protective of her than ever. Emma no longer had anything to hide and admitted that she was head over heels in love with Tink and could not bear the thought of him ever leaving her.

So a few days after all had been revealed to him, he drove up to the farm in his best blues and asked for an interview with Mr and Mrs J. He would not tell Emma what he was going to say to them, so she and I waited outside Mrs J's parlour, she practically shaking with fear and I trying to reassure her that all would be well. Archie walked in at one point to inform his sister that he had told their father 'the truth' about Henry Tinker, so he would be sure to send him packing and good riddance. Although I understand that he holds deep and sincere views about certain things, there are times when I think Archie can be most cruel in the way he expresses them.

He could not, in any case, have been more wrong.

The three of them came out of the parlour, after some heated discussion of which we could not hear the detail, and Emma nearly fainted. But they were all smiles and congratulations.

Mr J had been persuaded by Mrs J and Tink that it was best for all concerned that he should have Emma's hand in marriage and that since they were so fond of her (this would be the public story), the couple should adopt Maudie and bring her up as their own daughter. Emma and Maudie would remain living at the farm until the war ended, but the wedding would take place as soon as the sibbits, as the banns are called round here, could be read. Archie came back in to gloat and was speechless when Tink warmly shook his hand and thanked him for helping to make him the happiest man in the world. Emma poured him a glass of the apple cider we were toasting the happy couple with and asked him to drink her and her future husband's health.

He could hardly refuse, but I believe it nearly choked him.

And so yesterday, on Christmas Day itself, Emma and Henry Tinker became man and wife at St. Mary's Church, Gt H, and though it was not possible to have the bells rung, as this is still the signal of a German invasion, the Church was beautifully decorated with holly, ivy and mistletoe and other winter greenery. Emma asked for just villagers and family (of which she considers me to be a member) to be present, as that was the only way of not inviting the Newlings. I was her maid of honour and Maudie her bridesmaid. Archie reluctantly agreed to be Tink's best man, though he was not best pleased to stand in his Home Guard uniform next to Tink's two RAF pals.

Christmas dinner after the service doubled as the Wedding Jollifications, and we had turkey, pheasant, roast potatoes, sprouts, artichokes, peas, carrots and bread sauce followed by plum pudding and a two-layer fruit cake which combined Christmas and wedding iced decorations.

Archie, as best man, was required to make a short speech and propose a toast, which I feel he could have carried out with a little better grace. He made some reference to Emma joining the Tinkers and made it sound as though she had become a gipsy. The only sadness for me was that Mother and Father, who were warmly invited by Tink and the Js, chose not to attend as Mother was too 'unwell' to make the journey. If they could only have got themselves to Liverpool Street Station and boarded the train, everything would have been taken care of for them from the minute they arrived at Attleborough.

I believe that Mother, at least, prefers to suffer and let the world know she is suffering. She sent me the recipe for 'Mock Duck' which she is cooking for their Christmas dinner, made from bullock's heart, veal stuffing and dripping, as if to insinuate that I should miss my best friend's wedding in order to take provisions to them in Raynes Park. I was angry with this attempt to make me feel guilty, but Aunt Philly told me that I should try to be charitable as Mother has a condition called 'Agoraphobia' which makes her dreadfully anxious when she leaves home, and Father has to put up with a great deal because of it. Why they have told Aunt Philly this and not me, I cannot imagine, and I wonder if it is just a ruse to get her to prevail upon me to spend Christmas with them in London. Well, I have not, though I was a little mollified by the silk scarf of Mother's that they sent Emma for a wedding present. It was one of her best and Emma was very pleased with it.

As they cannot go away for a proper honeymoon, Tink and Emma have driven to Cromer today, Boxing Day, and will spend the night in a pub up there before he has to return to RAF Coltishall and she to the farm. It was lucky they were away, as the Newlings came over from Norwich this afternoon for an unexpected visit, bringing some gifts for the newly weds and Maudie, including an envelope in which Heather made sure to tell me was a very generous cheque. Mr N was very friendly towards me and gave me rather a wet kiss under the mistletoe. I was glad Archie was there, acting as possessively as ever, but Heather looked daggers at me when he put his arm around me. I hope Mr N has not given me his chesty cold, which was giving him some trouble with his breathing. Mrs J offered him some of Emma's tincture and said it worked a treat with Maudie's asthma, but he did not take any. I thought he looked queerly at Maudie after that; she was playing with Heather and for a moment the resemblance between them was quite striking. Their heads were together over a dolly they were dressing and you could not tell where one's blonde locks ended and the other's began.

I am awaiting Emma's return with great curiosity; she has said she will tell me as much as she dares about what it is like to go 'all the way', now she is a married woman. I know it has happened to her before, but in such different circumstances. I could never ask exactly what happened between her and Mr N, and I am sure she will never talk of it to a living soul, even her husband. I wish Mr and Mrs Henry Tinker all the best for their married life and we are all hoping for a more cheerful and perhaps peaceful 1943.

The tide of the war is turning. Douglas and HMS Furious were indeed heading for North Africa, in support of the huge task force led by General Eisenhower. His Eighth Army offensive at El Alamein has won a great victory, breaking through Rommel's line and getting him and his Nazis on the run. Douglas's Seafires were first into action and he himself shot down at least one of their planes. Mr Churchill said they had won 'The Battle of Egypt' and made a marvellous speech about it which we all listened to on the wireless in the sitting room. He said "I have never promised anything but blood, tears, toil, and sweat. Now, however, the bright gleam has caught the helmets of our soldiers, and warmed and cheered all our hearts," as indeed it had. He said it was not the end, it was not even the beginning of the end but perhaps it was the end of the beginning. It was a rousing speech and Archie stood at the end and sang 'God Save the King', which we all joined in. As well as the Germans, we are smashing the Italians and pushing back the Japanese in Burma, and the Russians are fighting them off in Stalingrad.

Aunt Philly and Anne are more excited about Sir William Beveridge's Report recommending that we have a 'Welfare State' after the war. I do not like to talk about such matters with Archie as he could not agree less with them, but things cannot continue as they are after the war. He is one of the few people whose existence has gone on much the same, but most of us women, and the men who will return from fighting, have had our lives quite changed. Some, like me, have had change for the better and we will not want to return to the old way. Even Archie, though, will feel lost without his Home Guard duties and the links it gives him to Lord Buxton and Haddeston Hall. He gets very angry if anyone suggests that we will not need the Home Guard for much longer, which is what more people think as the threat of an invasion becomes less and less. My poor Archie's rages against things he does not agree with, rarely bring him any satisfaction.

―――

I surprised both myself and Venetia by flinging my arms around her skinny shoulders the minute she extracted herself from Nick's brand new Alfa Romeo GT.

Never one to be demonstrative, she gave me a brief and bony squeeze in return.

"Missed me, then?" she asked coolly, and looked pleased

despite herself when I agreed wholeheartedly that I had.

Nick engulfed me in an altogether warmer and softer embrace; he had lost weight since I'd last seen him, but his tall and solid frame appeared massive in comparison with his girlfriend's boyish figure, now crouching to greet Lily, who was equally excited to see her Not-Godmother, as Venetia liked to style herself.

"How's things?" I asked quietly when Nick released me. He raised an eyebrow.

"Who knows? We had fun on the drive, despite her appalling map reading skills. I'm hoping you'll talk some sense into her this weekend, Mo."

"What's that about my map reading?" called Venetia over her shoulder, as Lily pulled her by the hand to see her newly built climbing frame. "How can you follow directions when you're driving so fast in that environmentally hostile, macho monster machine, that the road signs are nothing but a blur?"

"It's reassuring to see that Venetia hasn't changed," smiled Jack, who had come out with Felix and was shaking Nick's hand. "Good to see you. Can we go for a spin in the macho monster machine sometime this weekend? How was her performance on the way up – the car's, I mean?"

"She loves you," I reassured Nick before he was sucked into a male bonding marathon on the minutiae of sports car mechanics. "She's always rudest to her nearest and dearest – just in case you start to notice that she has a soft and vulnerable underbelly beneath the spiny shell!"

He shrugged his shoulders and released the bonnet catch. The lid rose elegantly into the air and Nick, Jack and Felix bent their heads over the shining, immaculate engine, now revealed in all its glory, and worshipped.

———

Venetia and I had managed to have the nearest we ever came to a heart-to-heart discussion while watching Lily's new DVD of *Black Beauty* that evening.

Her horse mania had evolved just as I had feared, thanks to Kathleen's encouragement, though at least she took Lily to and from, and paid for, her weekly riding lessons on a Saturday morning. I was genuinely grateful for this as the first stables visit, the one I had missed, had proved once and for all that Felix was seriously allergic to hay. Jack had been close to taking him to Accident and Emergency, but his breathing had eased by the time the four of them returned home and the crisis had been averted.

While we had watched the equestrian melodrama unfold on screen, Venetia had given me to understand that she was seriously considering marriage to Nick, but, though he was happy for her to continue in her high ranking Civil Service job and would live wherever she wanted, she couldn't quite bring herself to utter the Yes word and watch herself *'dwindle into a wife'*.

"Congreve wrote *The Way Of The World* three hundred years ago now; 'dwindling' is hardly required of wives these days," I had told her, laughing, "especially at your age. It's not like you're going to be confined to domestic duties or mother a brood of children. Nick's the only person you're ever likely to meet who'll put up with your evil temper and wicked tongue, he's a great companion and just happens to be loaded. So what's the problem?"

"His only condition is a Catholic wedding – and you know I don't do church, don't believe in anything, let alone that mumbo jumbo. Though I might enjoy shocking the faithful with my choice of dress." Venetia's eyes had glazed over as she reconsidered the wedding as a golden opportunity for outrageous behaviour.

"Shush, Mummy and Venetia," Lily had broken in at that point. "This is the sad bit where Black Beauty's being taken away. When can I have a pony? Kathleen will buy me one if I ask her."

And the subject had changed from Venetia's marital problems to mine. I had summarised my mother's explanation of Jack's and Kathleen's relationship in cryptic language augmented by mime, so it would pass over Lily's all too perceptive little head. Then, despite her reservations in London, it had been Venetia's turn to dismiss my fears and ask what the problem was with the children acquiring a fairy godmother who bought them ponies, taught them Wordsworth and took them off my hands on a regular basis? And as for she and Jack having some kind of affair – her derision had only been muted by Lily asking whether it would be a fair with rides and a big dipper.

"Anyway, Maxwell Robards is pretty straight laced by all accounts. He'd have something to say if he thought his wife was playing away with a man young enough to be her son – sorry, who actually *is* her son," she teased me.

———

This morning, though, I could see Venetia was taken aback by the slightly over long hug Jack gave Kathleen when she stepped out of her BMW in elegantly tight black jodhpurs and knee-length riding boots, her emerald green polo shirt setting off her still long, strawberry blonde hair to perfection.

I regretted the baggy tracksuit I had chosen for comfort and fumed inwardly as Jack put his arm lightly round Kathleen's slim shoulders. They walked together to the front door and came through to my study where we had been drinking our coffee and watching them through the bow window.

"You know my mother, Kathleen, don't you?" Jack asked Venetia and Nick rhetorically and the three of them shook hands.

"Of course we know each other, darling," said Kathleen. "We occasionally bump into each other around Westminster when Max is in the Commons. He'd love to see you both; why don't you all come over to us for dinner tonight? It would save you cooking, Mo."

I was aware of Jack's face and the body language of both our guests conveying interest in this offer, but swiftly told Kathleen we had already asked some neighbours over for dinner. She looked at Jack as if to say 'I tried my best', but smiled brightly.

"How nice. Have fun. I'm sure you'll enjoy meeting Mo's local friends," she told Venetia, pointedly I thought, before calling Lily by Jack's pet name for her.

"Come on, Li'l Girl – time to go riding! We've got to get your rising trot sorted out this morning and then we might be really naughty and go for a McDonalds – if Mummy'll let us."

I smiled weakly, knowing I had been put on the spot and could only lose by demanding Lily's return for the family pub lunch I had planned. I watched helplessly as Kathleen kissed my husband goodbye, brushing his lips with hers as if accidentally, and carried off my adoring daughter for a morning of fun and freedom.

"My god, she looks good for sixty!" exclaimed Venetia as we watched the BMW glide out of the drive. Nick shook his head at her tactlessness and gave me a sympathetic look while Jack enthusiastically agreed and went on waving after the car had disappeared from view.

———

The minute Laura and Pete arrived I regretted not remembering to ask Venetia to go easy on them.

Jess had joined us for lunch and we had sat out in the pretty pub garden with spritzers, starters and salads so as not to spoil our appetites for the evening. Although Felix took up more adult attention than he would have with Lily there to play with him, we relaxed and reminisced about friends, families and familiar places. We revisited old times when Mark and Jess had been Lily and Felix' ages and Aurora their surrogate older sister.

"And now my role model's settling down with her man. Are you cool with that?" Jess probed Venetia in a way that only she could get away with. Venetia composed her features into a non committal expression and remained silent.

"Oh, face it. You're going to love being Granny and Grandad when they have a sprog in year or two, aren't you?" Jess eyeballed Venetia and Nick and waited for the response to her challenge. Venetia looked sideways at Nick's impassive face and held the moment for dramatic effect.

"Granny and Grandad? You must be joking!" she cried angrily.

Then her lips twitched. "We'll be Vee and Nick, the coolest grandparents in the world, won't we?" She turned smiling to face Nick full on, and put her hand over his. An involuntary grin spread across his face as the import of her words sank in, but he said nothing as if fearful that any response on his part might change her mind.

I grabbed my glass and raised it towards the two of them.

"Here's to dwindling," I toasted their union.

"To dwindling, by degrees!" Venetia clinked her glass on mine.

The others shrugged, uncomprehending.

"Whatever," said Jess and she, Jack and Nick joined the toast.

"Wha'ever," piped up Felix in her exact intonation, slurping his apple juice and making us all laugh.

And so we had whiled the afternoon away, pottering around the fields near the church and school before returning to Stargate Farm in time for Lily to be dropped off by Kathleen. Jack alone went out to see her as she pulled into the drive, but even he didn't extend an invitation to stay, so we remained a comfortably united group, sharing references and recollections that, for me and Venetia at least, reached back over more than thirty years.

It was only when Laura, Pete and Grace knocked on the

front door that evening that I realised I had still told Venetia nothing about them and issued no warnings. As they entered, dressed up to the nines, and saw us still dressed down in what we had worn all day, the clash of cultures between my town and country, old and new lives was palpable and horribly discordant.

Chapter Five

Laura was deep in conversation with Normal-for-Norfolk Nina as I delivered Lily to school on Monday morning.

I tried but failed to catch her eye. After the children had disappeared into school I walked disconsolately back to the car and was strapping Felix into his seat when Laura clacked past on stiletto heels.

"Thanks for a lovely evening Saturday. Busy day today, Gracie's having tea with Kimberley so I can work late. Must catch up sometime," she called over her shoulder, not stopping for an answer as she headed for her car.

"Laura, I'm so sorry...".

If she heard me she pretended not to, but flashed an artificially bright smile and wave through her windscreen as she drove past us.

Since when did she need to ask Charlotte to help with Grace, I fretted. Laura and I had acted as a mutual support group to manage the girls and our respective work commitments from the very start of our friendship. What must she think, then – that I'd set her up to amuse my London friends? Or, equally bad, that I'd over estimated her and Pete and they had somehow failed the coded intelligence test concealed in our dinner party?

I cringed as I remembered their faces as they walked in and saw Nick and Jack lounging in front of the tv sports news, while in the kitchen Venetia and I were slurping wine as she chopped a messy pile of salad ingredients and the roasting duck spat grease over my t-shirt as I opened the oven to baste it. Lily wasn't even in her pyjamas, unlike Grace who was ready for bed, the sitting room was a mess and the dining room table as yet unlaid.

"Overdressed, or what? It's because I'm in retail fashion, don't ya know," Laura had laughed bravely, divesting herself of her chic black velvet jacket in an effort to look less formal. She searched for a vase to hold the stiff bouquet of dahlias they had brought me while Jack thanked Pete for the bottle of Le Piat d'Or and thoughtlessly plonked it down next to Nick's obviously exclusive bottles of Michel Niellon Chardonnay.

"Lovely to meet you at last," Laura had gushed, kissing an unresponsive Venetia, "I've heard so much about you – all good of course!"

"I wish I could say the same," Venetia had replied sweetly, rubbing lipstick from her cheek. "Mo, you haven't told me a thing about - "

"Laura, meet Venetia, my oldest best friend; Venetia, meet Laura, my newest best friend," I said, trying to ignore the glint of rivalry I had inadvertently struck in the oldest best friend's eye.

Luckily Jess had appeared downstairs at that stage, in clean jeans and a floaty top that emphasized her slender curves, her long hair wet from the shower. She instantly understood the situation and my dilemma, gave Laura a big hug, wetting her silky camisole but breaking the ice, and took the blame for my appearance.

"Sorry, Mumma, you can go and change now I'm out of the shower. We had lunch up the road and we've been running late ever since," she told Laura, while her eyes told me to get upstairs and get into something more appropriate to the dinner party our guests were clearly expecting. By the time I came down, my daughter had found a topic that both Venetia and Laura could contribute to – me.

"Mo's a Londoner, always has been, always will be," Venetia was saying in response to Laura's effusions about my arrival in the village. "She'll be back, she's wasted in the country, if you ask me."

"But I love it here," I protested as I walked into the kitchen. "I feel like I've lived here forever and we've had such a warm welcome in the community." I smiled affectionately at Laura, but she seemed anxious to placate Venetia.

"You must miss London, though, Mo. You can take the girl out of the city, but you can't take the city out of the girl. What do you miss most, your friends, your work, or the shops?" she asked me intently.

"Honestly, there's not much I really pine for. Friends, of course, our weekly coffee mornings, but other than that.... not being able to get a takeaway delivered, and never seeing any black or brown faces."

Laura laughed uproariously. "Yeah, right!" she said, and looked round at us to share the joke. I tried to pass off her politically incorrect faux pas lightly.

"No, really, Laura. When you're used to London's multiculturalism, it feels weird to live in such a homogenous community as Norfolk."

"Homojo what? Don't go using those long words on me, you know I'm not clever like you! No, of course there's nothing wrong with coloured people, we've got a lovely girl working with us in Jarrolds at the moment. We just quite like Norfolk the way it is," said Laura uneasily.

"Jesus Christ!" muttered Venetia audibly and, picking up the salad bowl, stalked out to the dining room from where we could hear the sound of crashing cutlery as she ferociously laid the table.

For once I was grateful for male machine mania.

Pete was thrilled by Nick's Alfa, which he'd seen in the drive, and a mine of inside information about Lotus cars and their engineering plant up the road where he worked. The guys chatted happily through dinner, oblivious to social or geographical differences and the undercurrents that were swirling around their other halves. Laura's wifely interest in and support for Pete's work rubbed Venetia's already raised hackles still further the wrong way, so she counter-pointed the entire conversation about cars and motor racing with snide remarks to everyone in general, and withering put downs of Nick in particular.

The boys had laughed these off good-naturedly, but after hoovering up my home made rhubarb crumble they decamped to the drive, armed with torches, to check a fault in the engine of Jack's Landrover and listen to the purr of the Alfa in action. Before I could open my mouth to start a more inclusive, girly conversation, Venetia leaned across the table to me and Jess, cutting right across Laura.

"And do you remember Mrs Thorne?" she asked us, as if continuing a discussion from earlier. "She was still going at the school in your day, wasn't she, Jess? I still think she was one of the most inspiring English teachers you could ever hope for. Do you remember how she made *The Way of the World,* come alive, Mo? We did it for 'A' level – that's what your mum was quoting at lunch about dwindling into a wife," she explained disingenuously to Jess. "Such a brilliant play, all about the problems of marriage and the clash of cultures between town and country. Congreve set it in all the places of iconic importance to Restoration London society, which is 'the world' to the insiders; while the country visitor, Sir Wilful Witwoud, finds them as strange as an alien planet."

"I wish I'd had a good education," sighed Laura to Jess. "I'm hoping Gracie does well at school and makes it to college."

"I never got my head round English literature," agreed Jess

comfortingly. "Figures were always my thing, though I don't know where I get that from!"

"Oh, it's having a stimulating home environment and intelligent parental input, as much as good teachers that enables children to develop their natural talents," said Venetia smoothly. "Don't you agree, Laura?"

It was at this point that Laura had refilled her glass and knocked back the contents in a few large gulps. She followed it up with several more in short order and then started on the Cointreau that Jess had found in Jack's 'cellar'. By the time the three men came in from the cool evening air, rubbing their hands and asking if there was coffee, Laura was leaning at a dangerous angle in her chair, her eyes somewhat glazed, and had given up trying to contribute to the bantering debate about relative levels of student debauchery now and in the seventies, that Venetia was conducting with Jess.

When I had come back in with the coffee, Pete was helping Laura to her feet and apologising for breaking up the party.

"You work too hard, you do." he told her. "You do get too tired to enjoy yourself and all we do of a Sunday is household chores and catching up. If you didn't have to work every Saturday, we could have had a relaxing pub lunch too. We've got to make some changes, my woman." And he had bundled first his wife, then his sleeping daughter into the car and driven off into the night.

I had remonstrated with Venetia the next day about her treatment of Laura, but she denied any malice on her part.

"I thought she was very sweet, really," she told me. "but I didn't think I had to make allowances. Why should I waste the little time I have with you making polite conversation about high street fashion?"

"Laura doesn't just talk about that kind of thing. She's really sensitive and empathetic – and usually a great laugh as well," I insisted, but I could tell Venetia felt she'd scored a victory for both the primacy of her friendship with me, and the city as my natural habitat.

And of course she had, for now Laura felt alienated, I was doubting my own judgment of someone I had thought a kindred spirit, and wondering once more whether I would ever really fit in amongst the school gate mums I was just getting to know.

So when I stopped off at the village shop after dropping Felix, and saw a poster advertising auditions for a production of *Hamlet* by the Haddeston Players, which just happened to be taking place this evening, I decided to go along. Amateur theatre was a very sociable activity; I might meet people who shared other interests of mine and would prove Venetia wrong about the limitations of country life.

———

April 1943

It is spring again and the end of my second year at Jackson's Farm.

How things have changed since I first arrived: I am stepping out with Archie; Emma and Tink are married and Maudie is now officially their daughter and quite a grown up young lady. She will go to Gt H School after the summer and be taught by Aunt Philly in the junior class. And now Emma has just discovered she is pregnant again! Only Tink and I have been told so far, but her morning sickness will soon alert Mrs J, if no one else. They are so delighted, the two of them, and I am pleased too, though I think it may mean Emma moving out of the farm when the baby is born. It is a tight enough squeeze when Tink is on leave and able to stay over, and Archie makes it very clear he does not enjoy his brother-in-law's company.

He does not like the Yanks, either, who are everywhere now, and more coming over all the time. They drop into the 'Trowel and Hammer' for a drink or two and Archie is happy to play Crown and Anchor with them and take their money when they lose, but behind their backs he complains that they are a rum lot and too interested in Norfolk women for his liking.

"Overpaid, over-sexed and over here," he says.

Tink has taken Emma, me and Heather to some dances at Coltishall airbase where we find plenty of them. They are all very agreeable and seem to us like film stars, with their funny accents and charming manners. There are always more men than women at the dances, and we Land Girls have an advantage, for those in the forces have nothing to wear but their uniforms, whilst we can dress up in civvies, paint our legs with Silktona and wear our high heels. Heather wears new frocks and fancies herself a cut above, but I am lucky to have Mrs J to 'make do and mend' my dresses and occasionally run me up something special if a piece of fabric comes her way. Emma will be first in line for new clothes now, though, as she starts to get bigger.

This year the Ministry of Agriculture has told us we must grow more potatoes, so Archie has ordered in Majestics, which are cut in half before planting to double the yield. We also have to grow flax, as it is needed for parachute harnesses and military webbing, and this week I have been sowing the seed by hand in the lower fields. As the weather is warm, I find it quite a pleasant activity. It is something Heather could easily have managed, but she has now entrenched herself in work which keeps her near the house – tending the poultry, churning butter in the dairy and doing odd jobs for Mrs J. She may have originally done this because it kept her nearer to Archie, as he spends a good deal of time in the farm office, but he is still devoted to me in his own way and she has other fish to fry.

He has finally persuaded Mr J to buy a new tractor, an Allis Chalmers Model B, which is much more modern than the Fordsons. It is a small, high tractor with good clearance, and I use it for light work and carting on the roads. It is fortunate that I enjoy my own company, as this modernisation means I spend a good deal of time on my own.

I fear that Archie may be considering proposing marriage, from some hints he has been giving. He said he had bought the Allis for me because I will soon be the mistress of all I survey and now I can survey it from on high. I am fond of him, though he is no romantic, but I do not know whether I want to be his wife. The Yanks have *shown us how gentlemen can behave towards ladies, without losing a jot of manliness. They have quite converted Heather, who has lost all interest in Archie and flirts like mad with the 'fly boys'. She says she will find a husband among them and go to America when the war is over, because it is the most glamorous place in the world. I do not want glamour, or to travel that far, but I would like to see more of the world than Gt H, and I suspect I will not get much further if I settle down with Archie.*

He is preparing for the Home Guard's third birthday celebrations next month, and drilling his men for parades and demonstrations that will be taking place. As he is taken up with this and Emma spends Sundays with Tink and Maudie when she can, I usually have Sunday lunch with Aunt Philly and Anne. Aunt Philly makes all sorts of clever dishes with the ingredients she can get hold of. Today she cooked us game pie, with two pigeons Archie had shot, her home grown onions, carrots and potato pastry, followed by apricot crumble. She made me and Anne guess what went into the crumble – no apricots, of course, but grated carrot, Mrs J's plum jam and almond essence all boiled up. I had brought over a jug of cream from the farm, carefully balanced in my bicycle basket, even though we are not allowed to sell it and are supposed to use it for nothing but churning butter.

I asked them what they thought I should do if Archie proposed and they looked at each other before answering me.

Aunt Philly said I was too young and that I should not make any decisions before the war was over. Anne said I should see more of life and love before I settled down and there were plenty more fish in the sea. I believe she would have said more, but Aunt Philly gave her a look.

"If he loves you, he will be happy to wait until you are ready," she told me. I could not tell her that I do not think I can make Archie wait much longer for what he really wants. Emma says going all the way with the man you love is a wonderful thing and something she cannot describe in words, but quite unbearably horrible with someone you do not have feelings for or who forces you into it. I am scared to

let Archie go all the way in case it turns out I am not in love with him and I feel I have been forced into it.

———

Miss Oldroyd hung onto Lily and beckoned me over for "a word" when all the other children had been collected and Grace had run out of the school gates hand in hand with Kimberley.

She asked Lily to go and pick up some playground equipment for her and, when she was out of earshot, looked me in the eye.

"I'm afraid we've had another incident today, Mrs Patterson. Lily appears to have an imaginary friend who she insists has to join in with skipping games and hopscotch, which annoys the other girls. She had quite an argument with Grace at playtime and I had to take her back into the classroom. Lily did eventually apologise, but not very nicely and she will insist her friend is real. She wanted a chair next to her so she could work with Lily. She's a little old for those sorts of games and I really can't allow that sort of behaviour. Perhaps you could have a word this evening?"

I sighed and said of course I would talk to my daughter and that I didn't know where this nonsense was coming from. She had never been the sort of child to have make believe friends, so I could only believe it was some reaction to problems with real friends. Privately I wondered if this was Lily's way of getting back at Grace for going off to tea with Kimberley, though it seemed a little extreme. Perhaps I would give Ros a call and pick her child psychotherapist brains this evening – after the auditions, if that wasn't too late.

Things didn't improve when we arrived at Ruth, the child-minder's: Felix had had a severe bout of wheezing this morning and his ventolin inhaler had made him hyper without having the desired effect on his asthma – though Ruth had coped and eventually the attack had died down of its own accord.

"I don't know if I can really be responsible for him when he gets bad like that, Mo," she told me. "He's a lovely little boy and he's settled in very well, but what if he had a bad attack and I couldn't reach you or Jack? I can't cart all the children off to hospital and look after them in A and E while Felix is being treated. It's not fair on the other parents to have that hanging over them."

I saw her point and told her I had a new treatment that I would start using from tonight.

"Please don't give up on him just yet," I pleaded. "It's just the time of year. We can put him onto a steroid inhaler, but I'm not very keen to do that because of the side effects, which could be worse than the hyper activity and palpitations he gets on the ventolin. I'll talk to Jack and see if there's anything else we can give him, but it's just possible this infusion might do the trick, it is supposed to work as a preventative if you give it every day."

I didn't want to appear callous, but I was silently panicking about how I would deal with the work I had to do on *Time Crunch* if I had Felix to look after; wondering what other childcare options there were within the village, or whether I would have to consider the expense of a full time nanny, if such a person even existed around The Haddestons. But Ruth agreed to keep Felix on if I promised that Jack or I would always be contactable and available, at least until he had another serious attack.

Nonetheless, I was feeling somewhat jittery by the time we got home and possibly not in the best of humours for discussing Lily's imaginary friend with her. Like a good mother, I gave both children a drink and some fruit and sat down with them at the kitchen table to talk over their respective days. She must have sensed impending confrontation, though, as before I even had a chance to raise the subject, Lily jumped up, knocked over her juice and ran out of the kitchen shouting "Miss Oldroyd's a liar, she is, she's a liar, liar, pants on fire!"

"Well, that went well," I told Felix, who was muttering "Pants and fire, pants and fire" as he chomped his apple. "Shall we try your inhalation? I'm sure that'll go down just as well." And I went to turn on the kettle, leaving Lily to calm down in her own time.

I wanted to ring Laura, tell her what had happened and get her sympathy; hear how Gracie had thought Miss Oldroyd was being unfair on Lily and laugh at the joke she would have cracked to diffuse my tension and make me feel a trouble shared really was a trouble halved.

But I couldn't.

Venetia, however unintentionally, had soured a friendship I had come to value even more than I'd realised.

———

To be fair to Felix, the bottled brew that Charlotte had given me did smell rank, which was why I didn't think I'd get any down him by mouth.

Pungent fumes filled the kitchen when I poured the required amount of brown liquid into a bowl of boiling water and Felix was most unwilling to put his face in the eye watering vapour; even less to have his head covered with a towel so there was no escape from the swirling steam. I put my head under the toweling tent with him.

"Come on, sweetheart, just take a few deep breaths and you'll feel much better," I gasped at him, and held his little auburn haired head even when he began to cry. "We have to do this, otherwise you won't be able to go to Ruth's any more.

"Stop, Mummy, don' like the smelly stuff. It's too hot!" he screamed, but at least he was breathing in the healing infusion. I managed to keep his head in place for a couple of ear splitting minutes, when suddenly the towel was pulled from our heads to reveal Jack standing over us with a furious look on his face.

"What the hell's going on, Mo? Lily's upstairs throwing toys around in her bedroom and you're down here torturing Felix. This is a madhouse! Go and sort your daughter out. Please. I'll look after this one." And Jack picked up his son and took him out into the garden, doubtless undoing all the good Charlotte's infusion had done with a fresh dose of pollen.

Lily remained intransigent on the subject of her make believe friend, though she agreed to help me clear up the mess in her bedroom.

"I'm not making anything up, my friends are just people at school. Miss Oldroyd's blind if she can't see... "

"Can't see what, or who?" I asked casually, as Lily broke off in mid-sentence.

"Anyone!" she shouted back, ready to reignite her fury if I overstepped the mark.

I tried a change of tack. "Did you mind that Grace went to tea with Kimberley today?"

"No. Why should I? I can play with... other people, not just Grace. Anyway, she was being a dummy today, she said your friends had been mean to her mum. I said Laura was stupid to think that and they didn't like her anyway, so there."

My heart sank.

Lily would have inadvertently tangled the web of already crossed wires even tighter with Laura, as Grace always shared these sorts of conversations with her mother.

"And I don't care if Elfrida didn't ask me to her birthday party. She thinks she's so clever because she lives in a big house, and she's not."

My heart sank further down into my stomach.

"Well, she's probably just having a small party, darling, and you can't always ask everyone," I suggested comfortingly.

"It's a disco party and a sleepover and I'm the only girl in the class she didn't give an invitation to. Grace said she wouldn't go without me, but then we had a fight and now she says she wants to go. I don't care, my best friend's... " and once again Lily broke off in mid-sentence.

Something was clearly going on with Lily's 'friends' at school, real or imaginary, but I wasn't going to get any more information out of her in this mood.

"Shall we decorate your bedroom, Lils?" I asked her, changing to a more innocuous subject. "We could go and choose some new wallpaper and material together, then send it to Nanny to make into curtains for next time she comes up."

"No way!" Lily turned to me with a look of horror on her face. "I don't ever want this room to change. And don't do anything to it when I'm at school!"

"Alright, Lily, I won't. There's no need to get so upset." As I spoke, I felt a familiar lurch and sense of dizziness. Lily's face seemed to melt and reform and when I could focus again, it was on the face of a blonder, slighter girl with large blue eyes.

"I do love it, I do love my new room, I do. Thank you, Em!" she said, flinging herself at me and throwing her arms around my neck. As she reached across my distended belly to do so, I realised that I was heavily pregnant.

A quick glance showed me the faded pink and yellow floral wallpaper was now bright and must have been recently applied; the ceiling, door and window freshly whitewashed; and the curtains a uniform bright yellow edged with pink braid, no longer faded by the light to strips of cream and primrose. I hugged the child to me, but corrected her gently.

"You now do call me Ma, not Em. And do you thank your Pa for the matchly cloth when he comes, and your gran'ma for making it up to beautiful curtains."

"I will, Ma," she said. As she jumped up my vision pixilated like the start of a migraine and my own world reformed quickly about me. Lily's deep brown eyes peered into mine from her cross and anxious little face.

"What's the matter, Mummy? You looked funny then. I'm sorry I was grumpy. I just like my room, and I won't be rude to Miss Oldroyd again, OK?" Another daughter's arms went round my neck.

Again I had the urge to phone Laura, the only person I had confided my bizarre experiences to. Venetia's friendship did not extend to sympathising with anything she herself could not believe in and she was as sceptical as Jack when it came to matters spiritual. I could share our children's problems with him tonight, but I was alone with my other worldly encounters.

I heard the sound of the old taps squeaking open, then water running and Jack came in to ask Lily if she wanted to join Felix for an early bath.

"Are you OK to do tea and the bedtime run?" I asked him. "It's great you're back early, there are auditions at the village hall for a production of *Hamlet* and I thought I might go along. See if I can get myself a walk on role, take part in a community event, meet some different people. Why are you home so soon, by the way?"

He sighed and I noticed that his face wore a strained look I hadn't seen since we'd moved out of London.

"I'll tell you why later. Of course I'll do tea and bed, but you won't be late, will you? We need to talk."

I grimaced inwardly, anticipating a lecture on the foolhardiness of using quack, alternative cures for Felix's asthma.

"No, I'll come straight home after my turn. But we're about to lose Ruth as a child minder if he has another attack, so we've got to do something and you know I don't want to go down the steroid route. There's cold duck in the fridge, I'll just grab a sandwich and see you later."

I kissed the children goodbye and went off to shore up my sense of belonging in Great Haddeston.

———

November 1943

I am writing tonight to while away the time of Emma's labour.

Her waters broke four hours ago while we were clearing away tea in the kitchen. Now she is lying in her bed with Mrs J and old Nanny

Barham, the midnight woman, as they call a midwife here, in attendance and the rest of us are left to wait. Doctor Coleman has been in once and pronounced everything to be going well; Mr J is pacing about downstairs and smoking endless pipes; Archie has been sent off to H. Hall to telephone through to Coltishall and let Tink know his wife is in labour, from whence he has not yet returned. I do not think he would do anything foolish, such as not passing on the message to upset his brother-in-law, but these days I would not put it past him.

Maudie is lying asleep in my bed while I write at the dressing table. She woke up with all the commotion and came into my room like a little ghost in her white nightdress. She did not want to be on her own, even though she adores her newly decorated, pink and yellow bedroom. Emma finished it only last week and it was a sight to see her on a step-ladder, pasting up wallpaper with her enormous belly. Mrs J was loath to be diverted from knitting and sewing baby garments, but ran up some lovely curtains from a bolt of yellow chintz which Tink procured from somewhere, to hide the blackout blind.

Emma was most anxious that Maudie should not feel neglected when the baby came, nor jealous of it sleeping in with Emma. I did not think this likely, for she has grown up so much since the start of the school term. She cycles off quite happily down the lane every morning with her dinner box over one shoulder and the cardboard box with her blue and orange Mickey Mouse gas mask in it over the other. Aunt Philly says she is a pleasure to teach and her reading and writing are coming on well. She seems to have inherited Emma's love of literature, as well as of the countryside. Emma and Tink took her to visit The Rectory at Forncett St Peter last Sunday, where the poet William Wordsworth used to stay with his sister, Dorothy. Now she repeats incessantly a poem of his that begins: 'I wandered lonely as a cloud, that floats on high o'er vales and hills, when all at once I saw a crowd, a host of golden daffodils.' It sounds like doggerel to me, but Aunt Philly says it is an important work of the Romantic Movement and clever of Maudie to have memorised it.

I hear Emma groaning a little from next door, but now she is quiet again. Well in advance of her due date, she had prepared bottles of infusions and jars of creams and jellies to ease the baby's passage and her pain..Mrs J has brought some up to her room, along with endless kettles of hot water and towels, and made tisanes and poultices downstairs in the pantry with others. If the peaceful nature of the labour so far is anything to go by, they have been most efficacious.

Mr and Mrs J have made no secret of the fact that they are hoping for a boy with a view to him taking a role in the farm, which puts Archie's nose out of joint. He has told me that Tink only married Emma to get his hands on the family money and now he wants to get a son into the line of inheritance, which will only happen over his, Archie's, dead body. He seems to forget that it is only because of his own efforts to turn Tink against Emma, and Tink's resulting generosity to her and Maudie, that he has become part of the family. But I have little patience with him these days, despite the fact that everyone believes we are about to become engaged. I could not agree to become his wife, though, because I now know I am not in love with Archie.

Strangely enough, it is Heather, and her obsession with the Yanks, that I have to thank for this realisation. She has continued her search for an American husband all through the summer and autumn, batting her eyelashes at one GI after another and claiming to have found her soul mate on a couple of occasions. Now the 445th Bomb Group has taken up residence at the new Tibenham Airfield a few miles away from us, and before a single one of them arrived, rumours had started to circulate that their squadron commander was a famous actor who had joined the US Army Air Force. They gave an inaugural dance there last weekend, and even though Emma was feeling too big and uncomfortable to join us, Heather insisted that Tink took her and me along to meet the new crowd. Heather was dressed up to the nines and as soon we arrived I could see she had only one thing in mind.

The minute she laid eyes on him, his tall, thin frame leaning against the bar, Heather grabbed me by the hand and made a beeline for Lieutenant Colonel James Stewart, the Hollywood film star. Although he seems unassuming and even shy, his long face is quite recognisable and at least as handsome as it appears on the screen. At first I was flattered that Heather wanted to take me with her to meet him, and then I realised she would only have done so if she did not think I was any kind of competition for his attention. Indeed, she had clearly planned to use me as an excuse to introduce herself to whatever famous person turned out to be there. She shamelessly interrupted Lt Col Stewart's conversation with another airman, to announce that I was his greatest admirer and simply desperate to have his autograph. I was most embarrassed at this lie, and even more so when he wrote 'Best wishes, James Stewart' in the little notebook she produced from her handbag, and handed it to me with that familiar smile. I hardly had time to thank him before Heather managed to step between him and me and begin an animated conversation about his acting, leaving me no option but to talk to his friend.

I was somewhat annoyed by this, for at first glance I saw Crew Chief Jackie Warzynski as just a small, foreign looking man with a large nose. But I soon began to find his warm dark eyes and twinkling crooked smile increasingly attractive. He told me about their flight over from America in the 'Gremlins Roost', one of the six B-24s the squadron traveled in. He was most amusing about how, half way to Florida after leaving Lincoln, Nebraska, they heard the familiar voice of Lt Col Stewart singing "Oh, how I love the kisses of Dolores", because just before leaving, one of the crew had married his sweetheart of that name.

He said they were still getting used to the flat, wet countryside they have found themselves stationed in, and the austere accommodation, which is apparently a far cry from the comforts of their training base in Iowa. Then he looked at me and said, "But do you know what? It is growing on me all the time." He asked me about myself and whether I had always lived in this part of the world, and listened with such interest while I told him the story of my life and about Mother and Father and growing up with Douglas in Raynes Park, that I poured out my heart to him.

When he asked me to dance, they were playing American jazz music and I was reluctant as I did not know the steps, but Jackie can do wonderful swing dancing and he was so masterful. He twirled me round, pulled me back to him and whispered the moves to me. It felt as though we had always danced together. By the time we sat down again I was quite breathless, but perhaps as much at the excitement of my feelings as from the exertion of the dancing.

We went outside to smoke a cigarette and Jackie did not try to roughly kiss and fondle me as Archie does, but held my hand and told me about himself and his life in the US of A. His real name is Jacek and his family is Polish; his parents emigrated when they were young to find work and he and his sisters grew up in New York, more American than Polish though he can speak both languages. He said in Polish my name would be Dorota, which I think is prettier than either Dorothea or Dottie. He told me how beautiful he found me, complimented me on my hair and skin and my velvet brown eyes, and eventually asked me softly if he might kiss me. I had no thoughts of Archie when I told him yes, and melted into his arms as if I belonged there.

He is a perfect gentleman.

While we rode home, squeezed in the front seat of Tink's RAF Bedford, Heather prattled on about 'Jimmy' and how many times she had danced with him and when she was going to see him again – though it was not clear whether this was at his request or her insistence! He has apparently already asked her to visit him in Hollywood after the war, but in the mean time she plans to invite him to luncheon at her parents' house, with some 'suitable' friends. She did eventually ask me if I had enjoyed the evening and whether I had danced with anyone nice. I simply replied "Yes, thank you for asking, Heather, I did." She enquired no further, but Tink shot me an inquisitive glance and winked.

Unfortunately, Archie was waiting up for me when we got home and was most put out that we were back so late. He wanted to blame

Tink, but I said it was Heather's fault as she had been so entranced with James Stewart. Archie, who had obviously drunk a good deal during his evening up at H. Hall, was infuriated by talk of not only Yanks, but film star Yanks to boot, and said he forbade me to go to Tibenham again. He made me feel quite anxious and I feared he would guess that I had been in another man's arms, so I forced myself to be affectionate to him, feeling all the while disloyal to Jackie.

I have just heard Tink arrive downstairs, so Archie did telephone through to Coltishall. He is talking to Mr J and I will leave the expectant father and grandfather to their own company. I can hear Mrs J and Nanny Barham through the wall and all sounds well so I will not worry about Emma, who only cries out occasionally. Heather is down at the T&H where the Tibenham boys, including Jimmy Stewart and Jackie, are having drinks tonight. Of course I would love to be there, but Emma, her baby and Maudie are more important.

It is not as if I have not seen Jackie since the dance. I was working in one of the lower fields on the Allis two days later when I heard a tooting from the lane, and there was Chief Engineer Warzynski in a USAAF jeep. I climbed down from the tractor and he from his vehicle; as he came towards me I could feel my heart beating fit to burst and felt myself falling into his deep, dark eyes. I had been thinking about him ever since Saturday, but it was beginning to feel like a wonderful dream and I did not know if he felt the same.

Then there he was.

He told me I had been constantly in his thoughts too, and while the crews had been out on their practice training flights he had been driving the lanes around the Hs in the hope of finding me out working. I sat in his jeep for a while and we shared my sandwiches and some kisses. His surname is pronounced "Vah-<u>zhin</u>-skee" and probably means his family originally came from Warzno in Gdansk province (wherever that is). Jackie says the Germans are doing terrible things to his country and people, but when the war is over he would like to take me to see it. I explained my position with Archie and that I am not only a little scared of him, but also in a difficult position as he is my employer. Although we have only known each other a week, and *seen each other twice, Jackie and I have a perfect understanding and I would trust him with my life.*

I shall have to disentangle myself from Archie.

I hear Emma crying out. There is a flurry of movement next door. Maudie is stirring.

Oh, a baby's little cry – it brings a lump to my own throat.

Tink is running upstairs. I must wait until the family has met their new member and not intrude on their happiness. One day Jackie might be running to hear my baby's first cry. I never thought that about me and Archie.

Mrs J is weeping. Emma is laughing.

"It's a boy, Elijah!" calls Tink to Mr J. And now he has put his head round my door.

"Come on, Dottie, come and meet my son, Samuel," he says, looking proud as Punch.

Archie will not be pleased.

———

I checked the *Dramatis Personae* in my school copy of *Hamlet* as I munched a cold duck and salad sandwich in the kitchen, and found I'd remembered correctly that there were only two possible speaking parts for a woman of forty eight.

I'd played Ophelia nearly thirty years (three decades!) ago in a university production, but now it was either Gertrude, Hamlet's twice married mother, or her alter ego and bit part, the Player Queen. Otherwise there were various non speaking Ladies and Attendants in the big, set pieces. The local am dram stars were bound to get the plum roles, I reflected, and I wasn't sure I could remember lines any more anyway, so standing around for a couple of scenes in a pretty Elizabethan dress and giving a bit of help backstage would do me fine.

But the director, pink cheeked with graying hair and a somewhat camp manner, sitting on the little stage in the village hall, introduced himself to those who didn't know him as Ian Hammond, Professor of Drama at the University of East

Anglia, and outlined his very different vision of the production. The Haddeston *Hamlet* was to be set in 1940s rural Norfolk, perhaps in this very village, as it would have been at the start of the Second World War.

"What's that got to do with the Prince of Denmark?" someone shouted out.

"Well you see, Tony, I don't read *Hamlet* as a play about just one man," replied Ian. "Shakespeare shows us 'the time is out of joint' in a global sense and right at the start he makes it clear that Denmark is in a frenzy of preparation for war. Hamlet's indecision is not just about how to right the injustice done to his father, but also about him taking part in the conflict. From the first act to the final curtain we hear the tramp of armies off stage, so the little court of Elsinore is just a microcosm of a world in which greater upheavals, plots, and power struggles are going on. It could be any small community caught up in any big conflict, so why not Haddeston in World War Two?"

He thought Claudius and Gertrude would be the local squire and his wife, landowners and farmers; Hamlet would be reluctantly in the Home Guard, not yet signed up to the proper military. Ophelia would be a land girl, her brother Laertes an RAF pilot and their father, Polonius, a retired RAF Wing Commander. The Players would be a troupe of entertainers from ENSA.

"What's ENSA?" asked a spiky haired youth.

"Entertainment's National Service Association, and a very fine organisation it was too, entertained the troops all over the world," growled an elderly, bearded man.

"Whatever," shrugged the lad and turned back to his mates.

A buzz of discussion broke out and a couple of people, who had doubtless anticipated a classic costume drama, stood up and walked out, but the rest looked interested and the chat sounded positive.

Ian walked around handing out sheets of audition readings: for the men it was Hamlet's Act 2 soliloquy, '*I have of late, but wherefore I know not, lost all my mirth*'. I mused briefly that, as a baby boomer, I would always mentally hear those lines sung to the melody in *Hair* – before taking the piece of paper he handed to me with the women's reading: Ophelia's speech on Hamlet's madness: '*O! what a noble mind is here o'erthrown*'.

Ian told us that he was not looking for classical Shakespearean acting, but a natural delivery that made sense of the words and conveyed the emotions contained in them. It wouldn't matter if we didn't completely understand the language at this point, and we shouldn't try for any particular accent, our own was fine. He would not be making any final decisions tonight, but would post the cast list and back stage roles on the notice board within a couple of days.

With these guidelines set, the auditions began.

As with any amateur production, the standard of acting in Great Haddeston spanned the embarrassingly dreadful to the impressively professional, but the director made notes, thanked each contender for their reading and gave nothing away. I whiled away the time until my turn by picking my own cast: a beautiful young man with soulful eyes, glossy gelled hair and a dancer's body was my choice for Hamlet; Ophelia was either a tall blonde girl with wide, high cheekbones, or Charlotte's daughter Kylie – I suspected there was a really pretty face under the Goth mask; Clive the butcher's *basso profundo* voice would provide an ideal rumble for the Ghost's lines; the bearded man might make a suitably pompous Polonius; and Mr Chatham the Head Teacher could carry off an oily, smooth talking Claudius, I thought resentfully. I supposed I was in competition with Charlotte, who delivered Ophelia's lines with sensitivity, and Lady Janet, who was nothing if not regal, for the role of Queen Gertrude. I didn't feel I'd outshone either of them when it came to my turn, although Ian smiled as

I finished and I could see him scribbling something beside my name.

As I left the village hall I said goodnight to Charlotte and Janet who were standing in the foyer, but they were deep in conversation and didn't appear to notice my departure.

———

December 1943

My Dearest Jackie,

I hope you will receive this note from Henry Tinker, who I will ask to deliver it to you at Tibenham as soon as possible. I am in a terrible quandary. Archie formally asked me to marry him today. He wants to announce it to the family on Christmas Day – which is to be the day of Samuel's christening. He wants to get married as soon as possible – he will even go down to London to ask my father for my hand in marriage. He wants us to have children as soon as we are married. I do not believe Archie loves me any more than I love him – and you know I do not. He is so jealous of Emma and Henry and terrified that Sam will grow up and take his place on the farm. He only wants me to produce a son for him in order to secure his inheritance.

Of course I should just say no, but I feel that there are also other matters, probably to do with money, that are making Archie quite unhinged and I am very afraid of crossing him. I have told him I will give him his answer before Christmas, but how can I refuse him and keep my job? Mr and Mrs Jackson would feel I had betrayed them if I appear to have led Archie on and would surely ask me to leave. It would break my heart to return to London and not be able to see you. I cannot burden Emma with my problems, she is still regaining her strength after the birth, feeding Sam and looking after Maudie.

You are the only person who can help me.

We cannot meet at the Trowel and Hammer as Archie is always there and does not want me to socialise with Americans. Will you come to lunch this Sunday at my Aunt Philly and her friend Miss Pringle's cottage – Ivy Cottage on Church Lane, Haddeston Rode?

Archie will be training with the Home Guard and I will send a note with Maudie to Aunt Philly at school to let her know. Do not tell a soul where you are going. Archie will kill me, or worse, you, if he finds out about us.

I hope with all my heart to see you on Sunday.
I.T.A.L.Y.,
Your Dottie
S.W.A.L.K.

———

Jack was up in his study when I got home, so I decided to put in a quick call to Ros about Lily before going to talk to him. She picked up almost immediately and I pictured her working late at her elegant roll top desk, waiting for Joe to return from the long running West End show he was starring in.

"Hello, Mo! It's so good to hear from you – you're much missed at the French café, you know, we were saying so only this morning."

The soothing power of Ros's dark chocolate voice had doubtless been developed as a professional tool over years of psychotherapy. I may not have been one of her young patients – or were they called clients these days? – but it worked for me.

"I miss you too," I replied, "but it's been the right move for us. Joe would be proud of me: I've just auditioned for a local production of *Hamlet*, though I'll probably only get a walk on part."

"Good for you, Mo. I'll tell him, and if it coincides with one of his days off we'll come up and see a performance. Can we stay? Venetia obviously enjoyed her weekend with you."

I'm sure she did, I thought to myself. She'd be enjoying it even more if she knew the extent to which she had undermined the foundations of the life I had been so painstakingly building in Great Haddeston. But I wouldn't risk a sniff of success getting back to her through Ros.

"Yes, we had a great time and of course come and stay.

You'll love it here. Did Venetia tell you that I've got a few concerns about Lily and school, though? I wondered if I could pick your professional brains about her."

I outlined the problems that had developed in Lily's relationships with the other girls and teachers at school, including the imaginary friend who appeared in the classroom, but whose existence she wouldn't admit to me.

"How interesting," Ros exclaimed. "I've just been reading some recent studies on ICs – Imaginary Characters, we call them – and I wouldn't think there's any need to worry about Lily having one."

She explained that although having an 'IC' used to be considered the preserve of pre school children, new research showed that almost half of children between up to the age of twelve had them. Far from being a sign of emotional disturbance, they could be useful ways of understanding relationships, working out problems and expressing creativity. I would have to bring Miss Oldroyd's disapproving attitude up to date.

I could hear Ros clicking on her keyboard as she searched for the information on her PC.

"Ah, here it is," she said. "You typically get two kinds of IC: either one that presents as less competent than the child, who then enjoys bossing it about and feeling comparatively powerful; or an imaginary friend that represents the child's projected desires of being more competent – a kind of wish fulfillment character. Of course both kinds can provide companionship and alleviate loneliness, which may be what Lily needs at the moment if she's having trouble adjusting to a new peer group. She might also be using her as an emotional outlet, or someone to take the blame for her, a tool for creative fantasy or a source of advice – which is of course coming from her own subconscious."

"OK, thanks, that's really helpful, Ros. So if it's not a major problem, how should I deal with it?"

Ros gave me some links to articles on the net I could show to the teachers. I hoped this wouldn't make them view me as an interfering, know-it-all parent, but decided I would give it a try anyway.

"And what should I do with Lily at home?" I asked her.

"Perhaps it would be best to try and bring it out in the open, but not by asking direct questions or being confrontational. Lay a place at table for the friend, ask what she likes to eat; suggest Lily draws a picture, or writes something about her. You only need to worry, Mo, if Lily starts saying the friend is making her do things she doesn't want to do, or act inappropriately. If that happens, let me know and we'll think again."

I thanked Ros for her comforting and sensible advice and chatted on for a while about our friends and Venetia's impending wedding to Nick.

I heard Jack coming down from the attic and remembered *we need to talk*, so I said a fond farewell to Ros and turned to face my husband as he ducked his head under the low door to the kitchen.

I didn't like what I saw.

Had getting Felix to inhale a herbal brew really been so stupid as to make Jack look grey with worry?

I decided sorry might not be the hardest word to say.

"Look, I'm really sorry if I've made Felix worse with that herbal stuff. I just didn't think it could do any real harm. I mean I know he didn't like it, but steam's good for him anyway, isn't it?"

"Yes, of course it is," replied Jack wearily. "That's why I gave him a bath."

"So, is he OK?"

"Yep. They both went off to sleep really quickly. I've checked on Felix a couple of times, and he's breathing more easily than usual. Who knows why? Coincidence I expect."

Jack got out a bottle of brandy from which he poured

himself an uncharacteristically large slug. I looked questioningly at him.

"Want some?" he asked. I shook my head. "You might need it," I thought he muttered. I ignored the provocation.

"Look, I don't want to have an argument, and we can't afford to lose Ruth as a child minder," I started. "If you won't let me try the herbal remedy and there's nothing else you can suggest, I suppose I'll just have to go with a steroid inhaler. I'm just worried that it will stunt Felix's growth – he's smaller than Lily was at his age anyway – and give him brittle bones. I know you say it won't make him put on weight or become more aggressive, but pharmaceutical companies always deny side effects until parents or patients throw the evidence in their faces."

Jack shook his head and shrugged.

"Try the herbs if it makes you happy. You're not going to believe me until you do. Can you sit down, please, Mo. That wasn't what I wanted to talk to you about."

I felt my hands and face go cold at the seriousness of Jack's tone. He wasn't given to dramatic pronouncements and I couldn't even make a guess at what was coming. I pulled out a chair and sat awkwardly on it.

"The Clinic received a complaint today."

"What on earth about?" I asked, confused. Was my behaviour in the village not appropriate for a doctor's wife?

Jack gulped the last of the brandy from his glass.

"Elizabeth got a letter from the father of a seventeen year old, female patient. It claimed that his daughter had been sexually abused by a doctor while she was being examined."

"Oh my god, how terrible! Who was it, one the locums?"

"I wish. No, no such luck. The doctor the girl accused of molesting her was me."

———

December 1943

I see my letter to Jackie is still in my journal for, as things have turned out, I have had no need to tear it out and send it. I have not even had the chance to ask Tink if he would deliver it.

This morning, Mr Baines, the Haddestons' postman, cycled out to Jackson's Farm with a telegram addressed to me. The first I knew of it was when Archie appeared in the top field where I was working this morning and handed me the little yellow Post Office envelope. I feared the worst and my heart leapt into my mouth. When I read it, though, I almost laughed in sheer relief. I will paste in Father's telegram.

DOUGLAS WOUNDED. ARRIVED HOME YESTERDAY. MOTHER
REQUIRES YR HELP. PLEASE RETURN SOONEST POSSIBLE.
YR LOVING FATHER.

For Archie's benefit I forced tears to my eyes and clapped my hand to my mouth.

"I shall have to go home instantly," I told him. "My poor brother has been wounded in action and I must help care for him. I cannot possibly think of engagements or weddings when my family is in such distress."

I knew that Douglas could not be seriously injured or Father would have said so, and at any rate he would not be allowed out of hospital if he was in mortal danger. I could also envisage the funk Mother must be in at having to nurse anyone, even Father with a cold is too much for her, and hence his urgent request for my return. But on the face of it, it looked severe enough and Archie was almost touching in his concern for me.

When we returned to the farm, Mr J said I must get the train that day and they would manage without me for as long as I was needed at home. Mrs J has packed me a hamper of provisions and Emma has given me some of her herbal palliative for Douglas. I have just taken the time to write this before packing my diary, and while I try to think of a way I can let Jackie know that I am going to be in London for some days, at least, perhaps longer.

Chapter Six

Jack told me the letter had been hand-delivered – by whom, Sarah, the Haddeston Health Centre receptionist, could not say – after the end of morning surgery. She had found it on the counter, addressed to Dr Gidney herself rather than the Practice Manager and there had been no prior request for the Centre's complaints procedure.

By the time Elizabeth had opened it, it was early afternoon when everyone was catching up on their admin between surgeries. She had taken the letter straight to Jack, asked for his response and requested to see his written notes of the appointment in question.

Shocked to the core, he had absolutely denied any impropriety of any kind with the young woman who had booked an emergency appointment yesterday and been assigned to him at the end of afternoon surgery. He had handed over his notes and a practice meeting had been quickly convened so the complaint could be discussed under 'clinical governance'.

Jack repeated what he had, rather shakily, explained to the meeting.

"The girl, and she was a girl – seventeen, so still a minor – seemed quite agitated when she came in. I'd never seen her before, she's not one of my patients, but I don't even know all of them yet. She told me she was pregnant before she even sat down. Obviously it's a frightening situation for a young woman to find herself in, but she knew what she'd come for. She said she wanted to be examined so I could book her in for an abortion. Well of course I can't do that, and what's more I'd just read her patient notes which said she had a history of depression and drug abuse, though apparently not current.

"I thought I'd defuse the situation and offer her a pregnancy test to take to the toilet and bring back the results to me. But she point blank refused. She said she'd already done one and it had been positive.

"So then I suggested that the best course of action was for her to go to the Family Planning Clinic at the hospital – and I gave her the brochure with the opening times – where she would be offered counselling and advice about unwanted pregnancy. I told her it wasn't in my power to organise a termination myself and she might, in any case, want to consider her options. I said she should come back and see her regular GP at any time to discuss what the Clinic had advised. I really thought I'd been soothing and supportive and done my best for her."

Jack put his head in his hands.

I had a flash of telepathic understanding.

This girl was only a little younger than his own mother had been when she discovered she was pregnant with Jack and Julia. If Kathleen hadn't been a Catholic and in the very different Britain of four decades ago, the twins might never have been born. Could this have unconsciously affected his attitude to the young woman he had seen yesterday, I could sense him wondering, to the detriment of his patient care? To speak the thought would have been to assign it an untimely reality, so I stayed silent.

"But she didn't seem happy with my suggestions," Jack continued. "She asked me if I'd at least check her out to see how far along the pregnancy was; she claimed she didn't know exactly when she'd conceived and wanted to be sure she wasn't too late for a termination."

Jack said he had, quite properly, asked her to wait a couple of minutes, so he could get the Practice Nurse to step in and act as a chaperone while he performed the examination. But at this point the girl had become quite angry and said she didn't want a bloody chaperone; if he wasn't going to sort out an abortion she just wanted him to check her out *now* so she could go and meet her friends for a drink.

"She started taking her top off and unzipping her trousers, so I quickly told her that wouldn't be necessary, to keep all her clothes on, lie on the examination table and just lift her top above her stomach. I gave her a reasonably thorough exterior abdominal examination without removal of clothes – but I couldn't feel any sign of pregnancy whatsoever. When I told her this and offered the test again, she was furious, jumped off the table shouting that I was totally incompetent and not fit to be a doctor, and then she stormed out."

"Oh god," I said, putting my hand on his arm. "Did you go after her?"

"No, I didn't want to inflame the situation. And OK, it wasn't very pleasant, but we saw a lot worse than that in Crystal Palace, so I didn't think that much of it. She was my last appointment of the day, I wrote up my notes, including that she'd refused the offer of a chaperone, and came home. She didn't say anything to Sarah on her way out and I didn't consider I needed to inform anyone else as a matter of urgency. It was Elizabeth's half-day so she wasn't in yesterday afternoon or I might just have mentioned it to her before I left, and this morning's surgery was hectic. The fact is it slipped my mind, though I had made a note in my diary to mention it at the next partners' meeting, which would have been quite soon enough in London."

But Elizabeth, with her determination to treat patients as if they were family, had been a little tight lipped about Jack's more relaxed attitude, though she admitted that even if he had told her they couldn't have anticipated a complaint about something that had never happened.

Jack had had the meeting's full support and the complaint would now be taken through the Health Centre's official procedure. Mick, the Practice Manager, would write back to acknowledge it immediately. In another couple of days he would write again to the girl's father to say his complaint had been investigated and that the GP in question had not acted inappropriately and the man and/or his daughter would be offered an appointment to discuss the matter with Mick and another partner. Hopefully the girl, when challenged, wouldn't want to pursue her story any further and that would be an end to it. But if she did, they would be advised of where they could take their complaint next.

"Oh, darling, what a horrible experience. I know there were some difficult patients in London, but you've never had anything like that before. You poor old thing," I told Jack when he'd finished, and was pouring himself another brandy. "But you did nothing wrong; you told her what her options were if she was pregnant and that, as far as you could see, she didn't seem to be. If she wasn't relieved to hear that, she must be seriously mixed up."

Jack looked unhappy.

"Whether she's pregnant or not, she's accusing me of assault. And with a father like that behind her, they could make things unpleasant for me – us – you know," he muttered. "Mud sticks and if it gets out in this small community, people are bound to say 'there's no smoke without fire', and all that. If it came to it, the village would probably support its own against a newcomer." He looked up at me, a little glazed from the brandy.

"You do know I didn't touch her, hon, wouldn't ever do anything like that, don't you?" he asked, pleadingly.

"Well of course I know you didn't, wouldn't!" I was surprised he'd even asked – my honourable, sensible, cautious husband. So why did a little voice in my head whisper, he "doth protest too much, methinks" and nudge me to wonder whether it was possible that Jack had subconsciously linked this young woman to a younger Kathleen and offered some instinctively tender gesture during his examination of her?

I ignored it.

"Are you going to tell me who she is?" I asked. "If it's someone I'm likely to come into contact with, I really need to know."

Jack didn't seem to hear my question, but answered it nonetheless.

"And what made the whole thing even more weird was I don't know what she actually looked like. Her face was covered in that ridiculous black and white vampire make-up – perhaps she's simply out for my blood!" He laughed mirthlessly at his own joke.

Kylie.

She had been suspicious of me when Charlotte invited me to their house to get the herbal medicine for Felix. As a Goth teenager of course she wouldn't want to appear in *Time Crunch*; the sub culture identity was in total conflict with the balanced normality the programme would be promoting. Her family hated mainstream doctors and Kylie had "a problem with authority". Charlotte had obviously underplayed the extent of her elder daughter's instability, though she had admitted she had been excluded from school.

Between us, Jack and I had pushed all the wrong buttons for this child-woman, with an explosive result.

"Come on, darling, let's go to bed. There's nothing more we can do, it's all got to go through procedure now. No one's going to believe her story, so stop worrying. I know we're in the right place for us at the right time, even if it doesn't feel like that to you at the moment."

But Jack didn't respond to my affectionate support.

He stayed sitting at the kitchen table staring into space and, despite an anxious half hour in the dark, I was asleep when he eventually joined me in bed.

——

I made my encounters at the school gate as brief as I could over the next few days, dropping Lily off at the last minute in the morning and arriving to pick her up as everyone else was straggling off to their cars or the park and she was the last child left in the playground. I always seemed to miss Laura and no one else made any effort to speak to me – which was, on balance, a relief. For the moment Lily was as good as her word, and Miss Oldroyd only smiled wanly when my all but late appearances finally released her from duty at the end of the school day.

I managed to get Felix to drink Charlotte's syrup in his fruit juice and dosed him three times a day. What I would do when the bottle ran out I didn't know. Especially as, although I dreaded picking him up from Ruth's every afternoon, his asthma seemed to subside and remain stable. Thankfully, Ruth didn't ask whether this was the result of steroids in his inhaler, but just accepted the improved situation.

Charlotte herself hadn't contacted me about pulling out of *Time Crunch* and I wondered whether she believed Kylie and supported her father, whoever he was, in the complaint he had made against Jack. I decided to let sleeping dogs lie and say nothing yet to Jane or Tamara, just in case there was the ghost of a chance of keeping the Tinkers in the programme. From a production point of view, after all, Kylie's instability would make the family even better material to work with. But I would ask Miranda whether she, with Si and the girls, would act as a substitute 'sandwich generation woman' if I got desperate.

"Sure, Mo," she agreed when I rang her at work. "Naomi's starting to look at a career in the media so she'll be happy, and if it makes Simon engage in a little self analysis about his contribution to family life, the time will have been well spent. My own time management has always been excellent, as you know, but who knows what tips I might learn from an expert? And how about you all? You're sounding a little stressed yourself, Mo."

"Oh, we're all fine – " I started, but a lump came to my throat and I couldn't go on.

Miranda would normally have been the last person I would have confided Jack's problems to, but I was reminded that life gives you the people you need at the time you need them. It was only as I haltingly described how my poor husband had been accused of sexually interfering with a young girl patient that I appreciated how upset I was myself at the slur on his character and the implicit questions I suspected it had raised in his mind and, I had to admit, my own.

"That is the most outrageous allegation I have ever heard!" Miranda responded unhesitatingly, making me feel remorseful about my own misgivings. "If there's one person whose professional behaviour and personal ethics are above reproach, it's Jack. Tell him if he wants a reference from me and my daughters – he was our GP for eight years – he has only to ask."

"Thanks, Miranda, but I shouldn't have told you so don't mention it to him unless he puts you in the picture himself. And please, don't say anything even to Si, and certainly not Venetia and the gang. Hopefully it'll all be sorted out very soon and then we can all laugh about it in retrospect."

"You got it, Mo," she agreed, and I knew she could be relied upon for absolute discretion.

"Supporting Jack through this is going to be hard for you, too. Call me any time, at home or at work. You two have seen me through some testing times and I'll be real happy to repay the favour. Come spend a night if you need to get away, or would you like us to visit with you?"

I was grateful for Miranda's reinforcement, but took a rain check on another weekend invasion of Londoners. I could do without any more collateral damage – or Jack finding out that I had divulged classified information.

At home alone with the children after school, there being no tea time swaps with Laura and Grace or any of the other friends Lily had slowly been making, I tried to use the time positively. We worked through her school reading books and learned the weekly spellings Miss Oldroyd gave out. Lily patiently helped Felix with his chunky jigsaw puzzles and colouring-in books, and we went for walks through the lanes around the fields in the lengthening, early summer evenings. It was on one of these, while I was pushing Felix on his toddler trike down the bumpy dirt track and Lily sped ahead on her purple chopper, that her cheerful chatter drifted back to us on the still air.

"Don't you know what pitta bread is? It's kind of flat bread you can put fillings in, like chicken and mayo, or hummus and salad.... I don't 'zackly know what hummus is, it's kind of a dip. What did you have in your packed lunch then?"

I listened curiously, wondering what Lily would have her imaginary and apparently ignorant friend eat at school dinnertime. This IC must be one of the less competent variety Ros had described, I concluded, until I heard Lily speak again.

"Buttermilk scones! They sound yummy.... With cream cheese and plum jam mmmm.... Yeah, our school dinners look yuck too, but we don't have chocolate concrete or pink custard.... Oh, we don't do that – what is an air raid practice? Hey, watch out with your great big handlebars!" And I saw her swerve almost into the hedge.

Then, as she righted her bike and rode along the lane, she started to sing something I remembered hearing as a child, but didn't recall the full lyrics that Lily knew:

"On the farm every Friday,

On the farm, it's rabbit pie day,
So every Friday, that ever comes along,
I get up early, and sing this little song.
Run, rabbit, run, rabbit, run, run, run.
Run, rabbit, run, rabbit, run, run, run.
Bang, bang, bang, bang, goes the farmer's gun
Run, rabbit, run, rabbit, run, run, run."

She must have sung it before, because Felix joined in the next refrain:

"Run, rabbit, run, rabbit, run, run, run.
Don't give the farmer his fun, fun, fun.
He'll get by without his rabbit pie...."

Lily was waiting for us to catch up before venturing onto the tarmac of Buxton Lane. As we approached I sang along with the last line.

"So run, rabbit, run, rabbit, run, run, run!

"That's an old song, Lils, I used to sing it when I was small. Did you learn it at school?" I asked her.

"Maybe," was her enigmatic reply.

"It's Maudie's song," piped up Felix. *"Bang, bang, bang – "*

"Shut up, Felix, you idiot!" shouted his sister, pedalling furiously off. "You don't know Maudie or anything, stupid!"

But he clearly did know something to have annoyed her that much, and now I knew the name, at least, of her imaginary friend. I wondered fleetingly why 'Maudie' and how she had merged her into the 'Past, Present and Future' curriculum area they were covering at school.

Before I could come up with any answers I was distracted by a screech of tyres and Lily's scream; and watched helplessly as she swerved her purple chopper sideways and tipped off it into the ditch.

———

December 1943

As luck would have it, Tink was on leave, turned up at the farm just as I had finished packing and offered me a lift to Attleborough Station. Once we were on the Turnpike, though, I asked him to take the turn off to Tibenham Airbase, where I went in search of Jackie to tell him my news.

My dear boy went straight to Lt Col Stewart, requested emergency leave then and there, requisitioned a jeep and drove me all the way down to Raynes Park himself. I swore Tink to secrecy that he had not in fact taken me to the station, but I do not mind if he has told Emma.

It was sheer bliss to be alone and unwatched with my dearest love for nearly five hours. We had never had so long to talk before and, although it was cold, we even stopped in a field in Essex to picnic on some of Emma's soda bread, apples and cheese, which we washed down with some fizzy pop that the Yanks have so much of.

Jackie called me "Baby" and told me he had never met anyone like me. I have never met anyone like him either; he is so well mannered and thoughtful and tender as well as being clever and funny. Although he trained as an engineer, he wanted to be a doctor but his family did not have enough money. He is fascinated by Emma's herbalism and would like to find out more about her cures. His grandmother in Poland was considered the wise woman of her village as she used to make potions and medicines from plants and flowers as well. He believes we are losing such traditional knowledge and crafts and that after the war is over, people should think about this and not insist on more and more modernisation. Jackie is such an interesting man and talks about things I have never thought about before. I am sure Aunt Philly and Anne will take to him when they meet him, and he to them.

Mother and Father did not seem particularly impressed when he dropped me at Raynes Park and Jackie instinctively knew it was not the time to talk of our attachment. He came in briefly for a cup of tea – which I had to offer, as they did not – and Douglas, who is on crutches, hauled himself up and chatted affably to him. You would *have thought Mother was the invalid, lying on the sofa and fanning herself, rather than her son, and Father simply looked relieved to see me. He had taken leave from the War Office and been caring for both of them. He does not look in the pink himself.*

I could not kiss Jackie goodbye even outside the house as Mrs Watson next door and her gormless son Bertie were peering through their net curtains. He promised to come down on his next leave and take me out if I am still here, which I hope not to be.

After all his bravery and the danger he has faced, Douglas has been invalided out of the Fleet Air Arm because he missed his footing climbing out of his Seafire, landed awkwardly on deck and broke his left ankle and right shin. He was shipped back to Blighty and the Naval Hospital where his legs were set in plaster casts, then as soon as he could manage to get about on crutches, was turned out to make room for more serious casualties of war. He wired Father to let him know he would be home for indefinite R&R, whereupon Mother had one of her turns and insisted Father get me home to help. He has been most apologetic about taking me away from my war work, but, as I explained to him, he has saved my bacon with Archie.

However, if I am not to be stuck here skivvying for my family indefinitely, I must get Douglas out of here and I think I know how to do this.

I shall write to Aunt Philly and ask if her friend Mrs Mortimer at Black Carr House in H. St Michael will take in Douglas as a paying guest. She is a good housekeeper and her daughter a trained nurse and they have had a number of wounded service men convalescing with them to help pay for the upkeep of their rambling old home. If he is there, Aunt Philly and I can keep an eye on him, he will be out of danger and able to recuperate in fresh country air – and I will have a reason to leave the farm on my own.

By the time Douglas' legs have healed, the war may even have ended and then everything will change. Even after twenty four hours at home, he too is desperate to get out of Raynes Park and excited by the idea of coming to Norfolk with me and meeting all the people he has heard about in my letters. I have confided to him my situation with Jackie and Archie and he will be a splendid ally for me to have nearby. I am hoping that I will hear from Aunt Philly by return post, and that I can take my brother home (as I now think of it) for a jolly H. Christmas.

———

The high octane, dark silver, four wheel drive was skewed across the lane. The driver, a late middle aged man in a well cut suit, was bending over Lily when I got to her, panting from pushing Felix in front of me on his trike. Having established that there was nothing seriously wrong, the man lifted Lily and her bike out of the ditch, set them both upright, then turned to me with fury on his face.

"Jesus Christ, woman, you should keep your children under control! That kid nearly caused a serious accident riding down the middle of the road unattended like that. She's bloody well scratched my new car." He bent over to examine a nasty looking gash in the paintwork above the front wheel.

Trembling with combined relief that Lily was unhurt and rage at his aggressive attitude, I tried to answer with a steady tone, but heard my voice come out shrill and shaky.

"My daughter's bike didn't even touch your car. She was perfectly 'under control', as you put it. She was riding carefully along a quiet country lane within my sight, and luckily for you she swerved before your ridiculously over-sized vehicle, which you were driving far too fast, actually hit her. If she had been hurt I'd be calling the police now," I blustered.

"Oh would you indeed? Who the hell do you think you are and where do you come from? You're not from round here," the man sneered, checking his ostentatious gold watch, and starting to climb back into his car.

"Actually, I am very much from round here," I retorted, aware that discretion would probably have been the better part of valour. "That's my house," I pointed to our roof across the field, "and my husband is the local doctor, so he'll be checking our daughter when we get home. It's me who should be asking for your details! "

I broke off as the man snorted derisively out of the window.

"I don't have time for this! Make no mistake, your husband will be hearing from me."

He drove off as fast as he had appeared, leaving behind a stink of diesel fumes and the diminishing roar of his powerful engine.

I put my arm round Lily, who seemed as shaken by the exchange as by her fall.

"Don't worry, darling. He was a very rude man and a dangerous driver and it wasn't your fault at all. Let's go home and tell Daddy all about it, see if you've got any bumps or bruises."

But she didn't seem to be bothered on her own account.

"I'm fine, Mummy. It wasn't me he hit, it was Maudie. He didn't see her, but her big old handlebars went into his car. I hope she's not hurt. She's gone now and I don't know when she'll come back."

I didn't know which to be more concerned about: Lily's near accident with the belligerent businessman or her involvement with her fantasy friend.

Jack was definitely more troubled by the former.

"Sounds to me as if word's got out already and this guy wants to put the boot in too. I wish you hadn't mentioned me," he worried. "Are you sure Lily didn't damage his car?"

I assured him that her bike hadn't touched it – though there had been a fresh looking scrape on the shiny new wing that I couldn't account for – and we heard no more about the incident.

The surgery, though, received a swift response from Kylie's father, who informed them, again by hand delivered letter, that he was not satisfied with their handling of his complaint. He did not want to meet with Mick and Elizabeth but would be pursuing the matter with the Norfolk Primary Care Trust – in effect Jack and the Health Centre's employer; and the General Medical Council – the regulatory body for all UK doctors and in charge of their 'fitness to practice'. Just for good measure, he would be writing to his local MP to complain about the low standards of small, country GP practices.

Jack returned home on the day this had arrived even more dejected than before.

"What does it all mean?" I asked him. "Will there be some kind of investigation? You're completely in the clear so there's nothing to worry about, surely?"

"The PCT will have to investigate the complaint," he explained, "and, depending on how seriously they take the accusation, it's possible the GMC will run their own investigation as well. It could all be quite long drawn out and it'll cause problems for the whole Health Centre, not just me, to have this hanging over us, especially if the family decides to go public on it at any point."

As it was simply the girl's word against his, though they would have to look for other witnesses and the result would be down to whose evidence was the more credible.

"But of course that will be you, Jack," I told him. "Apart from being innocent, you're obviously honest and reliable. And Miranda – I mean, I'm sure people like Miranda and her girls would give you character references if it helped."

He remained uncharacteristically down, though, and was certainly not cheered up by my news, after I'd popped into the village hall to check the notice board, that I had been cast as Gertrude in the Haddeston *Hamlet*.

"It would be better not to draw attention to ourselves at the moment," he grumbled. "We've already got a few problems with Lily at school; we don't want to make the family look any worse."

"Thanks for the vote of confidence in my acting abilities," I threw back at him. "This is about getting us involved in the community, and to turn down the part after auditioning for it would look churlish. I'm really chuffed to have been picked and I'm going to do it. I hope you'll support me, just like I'm supporting you. Anyway, by the time *Hamlet's* ready to perform, the complaint will have all been sorted out."

———

January 1944

I do believe this has been the best Christmas of my life.

Douglas and I came back to the Haddestons on Wed 22ⁿᵈ Dec,
which was when Mrs Mortimer said she could accommodate him. He
is now happily ensconced on the ground floor of Black Carr House in
a study she has turned into a bedroom so he will not have to negotiate
the stairs on crutches. Mrs M is putting up several American officers
as well as some convalescent airmen and it is turning out to be a
convivial place for my brother to recuperate. Her daughter is a trained
nurse and has returned home to help her mother with the invalids. Dr
Coleman came out very promptly to examine his legs and declared his
progress satisfactory. Whether he will ever fly again is another
matter.

Mother and Father seemed almost relieved to see us leave before
Christmas, so I shall not feel guilty about them being alone for
another year. I left them with enough provisions to have a decent
Christmas dinner and most people (except the Yanks) are not
exchanging gifts this year as there is almost nothing to be had. Aunt
Philly tells me Mother is having the change of life and suffering from
fevers and aching joints, which combined with her agoraphobia makes
her most miserable. I feel sorry for Father, but he does not do much to
help himself, except drink brandy when he can get his hands on it.

There was a big celebration in the T&H on Christmas Eve, to
which all the Tibenham boys came, bringing gifts of nylons, cigarettes
and chewing gum to their favourite girls. Heather delayed going
home to Norwich to be there, and spent the evening batting her
eyelashes at Jimmy S, who gave her two pairs of nylons and some
tinned fruit. I am still not convinced he is as smitten with her as she

claims.

Jackie managed to come down for a day in London before I returned.

I left the family and we went to a matinée of 'Watch on the Rhine' with Bette Davis, but did not see a great deal of the film as we were sitting in the back row and more interested in each other! Darling Jackie had bought me a little antique silver locket for Christmas, which I am wearing as I have said it was a gift from my parents. One day I will be able to put his picture in it. I found an old photograph of myself in my room at Raynes Park, taken when I started at Mayfield Secretarial College. In it I have permed hair, rouge, powder and lipstick on and look quite glam, though younger and plumper than I do now. I brought it back with me and asked Billy Stonepicker to make me a wooden frame, which he did very nicely. I wrapped it in newspaper and managed to slip it into the pocket of Jackie's new leather flying jacket – which the Yanks have all been issued with – at the T&H, without anyone else seeing. He was very touched when he found it, but we could not manage to steal so much as kiss with Archie hovering over me.

I did not see him again until New Year's Eve, when there was a great dance at Tibenham. But Christmas Day at the farm was still enjoyable. Samuel was christened at the morning service and I, as the only Godmother (he has two Godfathers), held the darling boy at the font. Afterwards we had turkey, pheasant and sausage, sprouts straight from the field, crisp roast potatoes, artichokes baked with tomatoes both grown by Emma, bread sauce and redcurrant jelly. This was followed by Christmas pudding with brandy butter, after which the men all snoozed in the sitting room while we washed up.

Baby Sam is a happy, chubby fellow and much fussed over by Emma, Tink, Maudie and Mr and Mrs J. Archie ignores his existence and, thank goodness, nothing has yet been said about the Tinker family moving out of the farmhouse. There were no presents other than a few home made toys for the two children and Mrs J had refashioned some blouses for Emma and me. I had some weeks ago sent away for a one-handed, storm-proof cigarette lighter for Archie, which I had seen advertised in the Eastern Daily Press. As he had bought me nothing, I was even more resentful of the 6/6d plus 6d postage and packing I had spent on him and wished I had kept it for Jackie.

Heather and her family paid the farm a visit on Boxing Day, as they did last year.

Mr Newling dandled Sam on his knee and tried to engage Maudie in a game of Beggar My Neighbour, but, unusually for her, she was reticent with him. Emma looked most uncomfortable, especially when he enquired about Maudie's asthma, and went out to busy herself in the dairy. Tink told him it was much better since Emma had been dosing her with a new herbal remedy, and Mr Newling looked directly at him and said "I too suffer with asthma. I believe these things are hereditary. Perhaps your wife would be so kind as to let me try a bottle of your daughter's medicine."

Tink went out to the pantry and came back with a bottle. "With our compliments," he said to Mr Newling. "But the fact is, blood is not always thicker than water in these matters." The Newlings got up and left shortly after this, and I saw Archie having an earnest conversation with Mr N in the yard, while Heather and her mother waited in the car.

Archie has not pressed me again about becoming engaged and I have made much of my worries about Douglas, and Mother and Father in London. He is still very possessive, and I keep telling him I have headaches or am tired when he gets amorous. It is easier, now, to see Jackie without Archie getting suspicious. Sometimes I spend a little time with Douglas at Black Carr House and then cycle on to Tibenham; sometimes Jackie comes out to visit Douglas when I am there, and then my dear brother discreetly goes for a smoke, leaving us alone in his bedroom and knocking on his own door when he returns. I would prefer to be honest with Archie, but he is so moody and often angry for no reason that I can see.

He has had a couple of arguments with Mr J about which of them should be controlling the estate and deciding what money should be spent. They continue these discussions over the tea table, to Mrs J's annoyance. When he is rude to his father she tells Archie to "Hold you hard, bor, and stop acting like you were brought up on a hog line"! Mr J is looking tired and worried, older than his fifty four years. I wonder if the farm has real problems.

There are even more Yanks in the H's to annoy Archie, as the USAAF 453ʳᵈ Bombardment Group has now taken up residence at Old Buckenham Airbase. Lt Col James Stewart is to be promoted and transferred there as their Operations Officer. Heather is over the moon, but could not give a fig that he is taking Chief Engineer Jackie Warzynski with him. It is a little closer to Gt H than Tibenham, though there is not much in it. When he heard this, Tink said he would try to get transferred there from Coltishall as there are jobs at all the US bases for some RAF ground crew. It would make a great difference to Emma, as it takes him a good hour to drive to the farm from North Norfolk and it is hard to 'pop over' if he has only a little time off.

I was allowed to go to the Tibenham New Year's Eve Dance as Archie decided to come too. He will not even try swing dancing, but could not force me to refuse requests to dance with others. I made sure to dance with a lot of the Yanks so I could have one or two with Jackie. He has a friend, Staff Sgt Walter M, whose family is not Polish but Russian, and knows Jackie from New York. He told me his family's apartment on the Lower East Side, was very poor and had no hot water, which is unusual for a big city but not out here in the country. He is a radioman and gunner – very comical and likes play acting and making people laugh. Jackie has told him a little about me, him and Archie, and he said it sounded like a "mighty SNAFU". When I did not understand, he told me it meant "Situation Normal: All F***** Up"! That's the Yanks for you!

———

I had a number of reasons to be nervous about my first rehearsal for the Haddeston *Hamlet*.

I had made a start on learning Gertrude's comparatively small part in the play and found that my memory was much less able to retain lines of dialogue than when I had last acted. Added to which, Jack, who had never even seen me on stage, had unconsciously undermined my confidence in whatever ability I might once have had; and his situation could have meant this new group of people might have heard gossip about my family. But if they had, no one showed it when I walked into village hall.

Ian had convened a meeting of the main 'family' characters, as he called them. The dark eyed boy I had selected was playing Hamlet, whose name I now discovered was Tom, an English student at the University of East Anglia. The role of Ophelia had been given to Rachel, the tall blonde girl doing A levels at a private school in Norwich and apparently on the way to a top modelling career. My stage husband, Claudius, was not, to my relief, Mr Chatham, but Graham, a thickset, forty-something man with a strong Norfolk accent. Polonius, though, was my casting choice of bearded, ex-army Norman; and his stage son, Laertes, a beefy, posh-sounding lad named Eddie, who worked on his father's farm.

Ian introduced each of us, and I was glad that I had only described myself on my audition form as a researcher who had recently moved to the village. My fellow cast members would doubtless discover soon enough that I was the doctor's wife and had children at the school. He then told us more about his vision of the play and the setting of his production in World War Two.

"Elsinore, or Haddeston in our case, just happens to be where the spotlight is shining, but we're continually made aware of Poland to the east, Paris and Wittenburg to the south, England to the west and the fever of activity there, as well as in Denmark and Norway, as they all prepare for war. There's a constant duality of the personal and political intrigues in a small community, playing out against a vast, restless background of the struggle for supremacy amongst nations."

"Excellent. Bang on target for a modern Shakespeare

production. Resonates with today as well. Jolly good show," enthused Norman. "How about getting the locals involved by putting out a request for 1940s props, memorabilia etcetera? Might be able to provide one or two items myself."

We all agreed that this could boost interest and audiences, though Ian pointed out that he wouldn't be going for complex sets, but planned to use just a few iconic props, such as an RAF Bedford truck, or a spigot mortar (whatever that was), sound effects and atmospheric lighting.

"But we could have an exhibition in the lobby," suggested Rachel excitedly. "My dad's got loads of family stuff from the war in the attic. I bet lots of people would be interested, maybe it would help get local media coverage."

"Yes, it's a great idea to get community involvement," Ian agreed. "Perhaps you'd like to coordinate it, Norman, with Rachel's help? Thanks. Now, what I wanted to start working on with you this evening was your characters and how they relate to each other. All the main roles in the play, except King Claudius if we accept that he did indeed murder his brother and usurp the throne, start off 'in the light', with the right moral intentions. But they're dragged into the darkness by their own egocentric needs and views; all the men by various kinds of self-seeking machismo and both the women by apathetic weakness.

"That may sound a little stereotypical and, as we all know, Shakespeare rises above such clichés, but to get this across to a modern audience we have to work from recognisable, emotional truth. So I want each of you to tell us all something about your character that you can relate to in yourself."

There was a tense silence as we contemplated the complexity of what we were being asked to do, and the candour with which we were prepared to do it. Ian gave us a few minutes to ponder and then picked off his first victim – me.

Nothing ventured, nothing gained, I thought, and made

ready to bare my soul.

"I've got to say, I do think the women in *Hamlet* are a little sketchily drawn," I started out contentiously, hoping I didn't sound too much of a know all. Ian raised his eyebrows and there was no discernible response from the other actors.

"But from the little she actually says," I continued, "Gertrude comes across to me as a languid, sensual woman, almost like a cat, who likes an easy life and her place in the sun. She only wants to please others, especially men, and avoid conflict at all costs. I feel she's probably charming, fun loving, a good people person. She must be attractive and I don't think she's immoral, she just prefers not to question people – until in the end she's forced to."

I could feel everyone's eyes boring into me. Ian nodded and waited for me to go on.

"I don't relate to all of that," I admitted. "I'm a doer and a thinker – well, perhaps a worrier is a better description. I don't let things lie and I need to know why I'm doing what I'm doing. But..." and here I could feel the interest level in the room rise, "I don't like conflict around me, my family or close friends not getting on, or people feeling bad. I understand how you can get stuck in the middle between a child and a stepfather. That's happened to me once or twice, and I would lie a little to protect my child like she does. And I think we can all relate – "

"Please don't generalise, Mo," interjected Ian quietly, "this has to be about you."

"OK, *I*, can relate to loving or needing someone who you know isn't exactly squeaky clean or as morally perfect as you'd like." In my mind I saw Paul, my first husband and father of Mark and Jess, as the gorgeous art student I had fallen for and whose emotional instability and flawed character had almost destroyed me as well as our marriage.

Ian nodded again, but didn't comment, and the rest took their cue from him. Norman went next.

"In my view, Polonius is basically a good chap. Upright, honest, he gives his children good advice: *'To thine own self be true'*, and all that. He's good at his job, especially to begin with, but the fact is, he's getting on a bit, losing his grip as the play runs its course, and so he starts to look a bit pompous and foolish. Doesn't deserve what he gets, but there you are."

Norman paused, as I had, before admitting to which aspects of his character he related to. Ian smiled encouragingly.

"Well, now, let's see," Norman started up again. "I was a military man, and good at my job before I retired, and that might make me seem a little starchy to some. Don't think I'm losing the old marbles, but my children and grandchildren take the mickey, even when I'm talking damned good sense. No doubt I seem a *'tedious old fool'* to them, and others, so, yes, I can relate to Polonius. Hmmm."

He cleared his throat and blew his nose into a large, clean white handkerchief, which had been neatly folded into the breast pocket of his tweed jacket.

Ian turned the spotlight on his leading man.

"I know it's impossible to sum Hamlet himself up in a few sentences, but have a try, Tom. Tell us the character traits you see in him that you most identify with."

Tom, though no more than twenty one, I guessed, looked composed and confident. To be as beautiful and presumably intelligent as he was probably did wonders for the self esteem, I thought, appreciating the graceful pose of his long limbs in the hard, plastic chair. But apparently there was more to him than met the eye.

"So much has been written about Hamlet, that I can hardly come up with anything original," he said, smiling in a charmingly self-deprecatory way. "But here are some random thoughts: he's contradictory, confused, a 'divided self'. He cares about other people, like his mother and his dead father, but he's been hurt so he can't trust, either her or the ghost. He really loves Horatio because he's cool and maybe more than a friend, but he fancies the arse off Ophelia even though he doesn't think much of women. He wants to do the right thing, take action, be a hero, but he's not like that and he doesn't think anyone likes the person he really is, inside. So he acts mean and bad anyway, because it can't make people like him any less.

"He's self-obsessed because he's depressed. Clinically depressed, I mean. If he was around today the play wouldn't have been a tragedy. His mum would have sent him down the surgery for some Prozac and he'd have been sorted; turned into a geezer, pulled Ophelia and gone down the pub with Claudius. I've been there, been in that head. Now it's all good, but I know some parts of Hamlet from the inside."

It was a virtuoso performance, which boded well for the production. I saw both Ian and Rachel gazing at Tom with something akin to adoration and remembered his guarded allusion to Hamlet's sexual confusion – an original take on the character despite his modest opening remarks. And he had known what was coming; this speech was prepared, which indicated a close relationship with the director. But something in his eyes belied Tom's upbeat finish about his personal life. This young man was not "sorted", I'd stake my life, and my woman's intuition, on it.

Ian was kind enough not to let beefy Eddie's contribution contrast directly with Tom's intellectual analysis, and Graham was asked to talk next about the play's incontrovertible baddie, Claudius.

"If you together do think I'm going to say he's a good sort and I know just what that feel like to want to kill my brother to get the top job – hold you hard!" He grinned, making his weathered face instantly attractive, and we all laughed with him. "Nay, being as Claudius do love power and money more than his own family, and I'm a working man and always have been, I've a job of acting ahead of me."

Graham stopped and looked at us, as if deciding whether to

say more. He did.

"I'll give you this, though. I know what 'tis to love another man's wife. There, that be your lot."

"Eddie," said Ian, swiftly ending the moment where none of us knew quite where to look. "Any thoughts on Laertes?"

"Ah, yes. Well, you know, he seems like a good man to me," said Eddie, flushing up to his straw blonde hair. "I'm not super-bright like Tommo, so I might have got it all wrong. But as far as I can see, he's pretty straight, even if he's a bit fruity with his sister and over keen to defend her virtue. His father gives him a lot of advice and doesn't trust his judgement, which is, you know, a bit close to the mark for me. And clever dick Prince Hamlet makes him look a bit of a prat – yeah, well, you know, that's real life for you."

He stopped abruptly, leaving Rachel, who had just returned from the Ladies, to complete the exercise. She looked relaxed, with wide, sparkling eyes and a more engaged manner now she was the centre of attention.

"Ophelia is, like, Hamlet's 'anima', his muse – although he doesn't recognise it until it's too late," she said, fixing her eyes on Tom, and twisting a pretty pearl and garnet ring round and round her finger. "She may seem to be just an innocent young girl, but she's, like, the one true voice in the play. She's misunderstood and mistreated by Hamlet, who she loves; she's treated like an idiot by her father and brother who insist on controlling her, but she's, like, the only one who stays in touch with her inner reality. No one takes her seriously, she doesn't get the attention she needs to show what she really is and blossom, so she, like, has to go off into her own world. Then she does things that other people think are mad, and it actually kills her in the end!"

Rachel's words became almost accusatory; her personal involvement and identification with the character were self evident, and Ian sensibly didn't ask her to explain this any further. Instead he thanked us all for our perceptive comments and frankness, which, he said, would stand us in good stead as we worked together on the production.

"I'm sorry if you've felt under pressure this evening, but I wanted to fast track a sense of mutual dependability. In the seventies we'd get actors to play trust games like falling backwards into each other's arms, relying on the person behind not to let them crash to the floor, but that's a bit old hat. I find this works better in terms of getting to grips with the play at the same time as giving a bit of personal exposure. Now we can get on with rehearsing knowing something about where each of you is coming from and how you're approaching your roles."

He handed out a rehearsal schedule with the requests that we start learning lines immediately, and that if any of us couldn't make the designated time for our scenes, we should let him know as soon as possible.

We stood around, checking our timetables and congratulating each other on the insights of the evening. Rachel said goodnight to everyone individually, pointedly missing out Tom and kissing Eddie fulsomely on both cheeks. He flushed again and looked delighted by her attentions. I wanted to warn him not to take the gesture at face value, but realised I was making assumptions about the younger cast members who probably already knew each other well. When she came to me, Rachel put her hand on my arm and turned her wide eyed gaze on me.

"It was great to meet you, Mo, you were wonderful tonight, starting us all off like that. I do so get what you were saying about loving people who aren't morally strong, and it not being a reflection on you," she said, looking at me significantly. I guessed this was an allusion to Tom, and made a mental note not to get involved in any real life relationships amongst the cast. "I'm really looking forward to working with you – I think we should stick together as the only two females."

"Thanks, you were great too, really impressive," I replied,

flattered by her words and as sucked in by her manner as young Eddie. It was going to be good, this production, I felt, and I was already meeting a new social circle who saw beyond the small world of the school gate and the internal politics of Haddeston Health Centre.

———

"How did it go?" asked Jack, without real interest, when I got home.

"Good, I think. It was a bit like an AA meeting: 'I'm Gertrude and I love my son. We think incest's fun – it's a game all the family can play," I quipped, then fell silent as I caught sight of Jack's stony face.

"Did anyone say anything? About me, or the Health Centre?" he asked.

"No, not a word. I doubt anyone even knows I'm married to you. Actually they're a nice bunch, a real mixed bag, but interesting. Ian, the director's very bright; Tom, who's playing Hamlet, is presumably one of his students at UEA. I must get him and Jess together, he's very attractive, although he may have a thing going with the girl playing Ophelia. She was very friendly – and she might be interested in babysitting… hmm, there's a thought. Maybe we could go out to dinner or see a film one night."

"Maybe," Jack replied unenthusiastically. "But I'm not going to be very good company while I have the complaint hanging over me. It's probably a good thing that you've got this play on; it'll give you something to take your mind off the problem.

"Don't be so negative," I told him. "You have to visualise positive outcomes, write them down as affirmations and make them happen."

"Oh, that's how I fix the PCT investigation, is it? And where did this gem of self help jargon come from?"

"From Tamara, actually. It's part of her strategy for helping people set and achieve life goals, but it works for anything you want to happen. If you think about anything often enough, your subconscious brain starts to try and make it a reality. So if you always think of negative things, they're more likely to come about. Doesn't that make a kind of sense?" I asked Jack.

"It could do," he responded. "OK, I'll try to be more positive, but it really is getting me down, Mo. I keep asking myself 'why?' Was it me, something I said, the way I treated her? Or would she have done the same to anyone who told her what I did? It's more that I can't make sense of it, than the thing itself. But it makes me wonder, is Venetia right? Has it all been a big mistake, forcing you to come here when you wanted to stay in London? Making Lily change schools, lose her friends? I don't know if I was right any more, hon."

I put my arms around him and reassured him that Stargate Farm was the place we were meant to be; that he hadn't forced me into moving, just shown me that it was time to make changes; and that I had no regrets, nor had the children and nor should he. This was no time to give in to Venetia's damaging mind set. Tomorrow I would get my own goal setting back into action. I would talk to Laura and make things right with her, see if with her help I couldn't get to the bottom of Kylie's grievance against Jack.

Chapter Seven

I left a couple of messages on Laura's phone and texted her mobile, but she didn't return my calls.

I didn't see her at school either and wondered whether she was making other arrangements for Grace specifically so as not to come into contact with me. Don't be so paranoid, I told myself briskly. You're not that important to her, she's just gone back to how things were before we turned up in Great Haddeston.

Then driving home after one of my almost late pick-ups of Lily from school, I spotted Nanny Babs teetering along Church Lane on her circa 1980s court pumps with Grace scuffing her black, shiny school shoes behind her. I drew in beside them, wound down the window and took a chance.

"Hello Babs, can I give you a lift home? Grace looks a bit done in."

I hoped she couldn't hear Lily in the back seat hissing "No, Mummy, don't stop. I don't want to play with Grace."

"My dear, you're a lifesaver, thank you so much!"

There was no visible hesitation or animosity in her response, although Grace seemed torn between the two evils of walking home and sharing a car ride with Lily, whom she glared at. She had no choice, though, as Babs opened the back door for her granddaughter and clamped her in a seatbelt before settling herself into the front seat next to me. Before I even had time to ask how she was, Nanny Babs launched into a tirade about Laura.

"Well she's still ill, you know. She hasn't been right since that weekend they came round to dinner with you, but she soldiered on, going into work – well, she can't get the cover, shop girls these days are so unreliable, won't put themselves out to help in an emergency, but they expect time off whenever they want it, of course. But this week she's almost collapsed; had to go to the doctor and get a prescription, though she's hardly even been able to get out of bed. Pete's had to take time off work and I've been staying with them to help out. Of course I'm always happy to look after Gracie, but I can't go on forever. I do have commitments too: other grandchildren, my charity work and my flat to look after. She'll have to pull herself together and get on with things."

I felt a paroxysm of guilt. Perhaps Laura hadn't been avoiding me at all. On the contrary, my friend had been ill and in need of support and I had been too busy nursing my own obsessions to even check that she was all right.

"Come in and have a cup of tea, my dear," offered Babs when I drew up outside Laura and Pete's neat, new build cottage. "It might perk her up to have someone to talk to."

I still wasn't sure that Laura would be at all pleased to see me, but I couldn't let the opportunity of making contact slip by. I coaxed a reluctant Lily from the car with a whispered bribe of sweets for a quick five minutes play with Grace, and followed Nanny Babs through the teak front door into their bright and perfectly tidy hall.

Laura's appearance, though, as she came down the stairs to greet Grace, shocked me. Above the fluffy pink dressing gown, her face was pasty and, devoid of makeup, her eyes looked puffy with dark rings below them. Her lips were dry and cracked and her usually glossy, swinging bob hung flat and lustreless around her face.

Grace and Lily appeared to forget their differences by mutual consent and ran out into the garden. Nanny Babs bustled into the kitchen to make tea. Laura and I stood looking at each other in the hall. We both opened our mouths to speak, but I got in first.

"I'm so sorry, Laura. I had no idea you were ill. I thought you were upset with me about the dinner. I thought you were avoiding me. Some friend I've been."

Laura shook her head. Her voice came out in a throaty croak.

"It's me should be apologising, Mo. I did avoid you. I ruined your evening with your nice friends by being stupid and getting drunk, then I was so disgusted with myself for that, and not being able to face you, that I got a bad dose of the black dog. Went into a real downer. The tonsillitis is nothing compared to that. The antibiotics are starting to work; I'll be OK in a day or two."

We looked at each other for another moment, unsure what to say next. Then Laura put her arms out and I hugged her hard, with a simultaneous rush of affection and desire not to catch whatever she had. She pushed me away, choking and laughing.

"Thanks, mate, but no need to asphyxiate me. I'm still delicate. Oh dear, must sit down!"

We moved through to join Nanny Babs in the small but immaculate kitchen, where a floral teapot with matching cups and saucers and a plate of home made biscuits sat waiting for us on the table. Laura took a handful of pills with her tea and, unlike me, refused a biscuit. Ignoring Babs, I spoke quietly to Laura.

"You weren't stupid and I don't blame you for getting drunk. Venetia was in one of her evil moods; she really gets quite jealous of other friends of mine and she's secretly furious that I've left London. We've been best friends since we were at school and she's always been like this. Her father died when she was young and her mother disappeared off to live in Spain with a boyfriend and I kind of became her family. She can be vile to all our gang – I probably get off lightest – but it's just defensive. We've learned to take no notice and for some reason we all love her. She said she liked you and I think it's true. She tests everyone to breaking point, just to see if they can really hack her. Nick's the only man who's stuck around, and if she's not careful he'll disappear too. She's more or less in the last chance saloon there, but she doesn't see it.

"Oh, poor thing," rasped Laura, instantly sympathetic. "I'm so stupid, I can't see past my own paranoia sometimes."

"Please stop saying you're stupid, you're really not at all. And I'm the one who's been paranoid. It feels like the whole village is against us." I stopped as Laura looked at me curiously, realising I'd said more than I should have. We were diverted by Nanny Babs, who had swirled the dregs of her tea around the cup, upended the teacup onto the saucer into which the remaining liquid ran, and was now staring into the empty cup.

"Scrying," said Laura. And in response to my puzzled face, "She's reading the leaves. Uncanny, what she comes up with sometimes. What do you see, Mother? Is there a new boyfriend on the horizon? Better watch out if there is."

Babs turned her teacup round and examined the contents, then looked up and gave us a satisfied smile.

"Possibly, dear. You're so sceptical, Laura, you always see the negatives. I'm bored with being on my own," she said to me, "so I've taken out a personal advertisement in the *Eastern Daily Press*. Just a light-hearted caper. I put 'Essex girl of seventy plus looking for fun, willing to dust off white stilettos and dance round her handbag for the right man'. Can't do any harm, can it? See, here's an egg, which is a good omen and suggests new beginnings; hmm, this looks like a fork to me – false flattery, I'll have to be wary of that one. But here we are: a parasol – a new lover, although it could just be something hidden. Ah, and a heart – love, of course, and a harp for harmony. Would you like me to do yours, dear?"

I passed over my almost empty teacup, visualising Jack shaking his head in disbelief at my willingness to participate in such irrational nonsense. Babs repeated the swilling and spilling and peered into my cup.

She frowned.

"What's up, Mother?" croaked Laura. "Has Mo won the lottery or is Jack off with a floozie?" She laughed, setting off a hacking cough, and I tried to smile. Nanny Babs was still looking puzzled.

"Would you know what I mean, my dear, if I said I can see two readings here?"

I shook my head.

"As if there are two lives in one. One has been and one's to come, but they cut across each other."

Laura looked at me significantly.

"Tell her, Mo. If anyone can help, Mother can." I said nothing, so she continued. "She's been having flashbacks; snatches of a past life that happened round here. Seems like it was in the 1940s, or some time like that."

"I see, that makes sense," Babs nodded sagely, as if what Laura had just said was nothing out of the ordinary. "In that case, I think this line is you, now… do you see there?"

I peered where she was pointing into my teacup and saw nothing but randomly distributed tea leaves around the sides.

"It's a book, which would mean good news if it was open, but it's closed. You will have to investigate something, my dear, but here's a candle, so there will be help from others and… I think this could be an elephant: strength, wisdom – you're going to need both. This is definitely a house – yours, I feel, where you have security, and a fence which indicates you will have setbacks, perhaps in your investigations, but they won't be permanent. Here's a mask – someone is not what they

169

seem, or something is hidden. But you will arrive at this circle, so success, completion even, is waiting for you."

I shrugged, relieved that nothing Nanny Babs had said struck any chords, and I could dismiss the 'reading' as without significance. But she went on.

"Now this line runs across yours, as it were, with the house in both as a centre point. This reading is almost the opposite to yours; it starts with the circle – this time with dots, so happiness, a baby or two. But then a cap, which means trouble. And there – very clearly - is a nail: injustice. In fact, like the house I see now that it falls into both readings. Are you battling against injustice, my dear?"

Babs didn't seem to require an answer as she concentrated, but tears started to my eyes.

Injustice? Of course: Jack had been wrongly, horribly accused and there was an investigation underway, but I had no part in it. Unnoticeably, I hoped, I put up a finger to catch a tear at the corner of my eye.

"Here's a cabbage, which indicates jealousy, and a dagger – danger. I'm afraid this line ends in disappointment; a broken wheel."

"Oh, Mother, you can't see all that in one cup! There aren't even enough leaves," Laura protested, laughing croakily, and then observed my continued attempts to avoid crying. "Hey, Mo. What is it? Did she hit that nail on the head? Tell us. We can help you sort things out if something's wrong."

———

February 1944

All the news from the front is good, these days, though the Luftwaffe are bombing London heavily again.

The war will soon be over, so everyone believes.

The Allies have landed at Anzio, though they have a fight on their hands still. Leningrad was relieved from the German siege a few weeks ago. How the inhabitants survived after nine hundred days is anyone's guess. And we in Norfolk are in the thick of the bombing of Europe. There are now thirty Yank airbases in Norfolk and hardly a minute of the day when there are not planes buzzing overhead, as if an invasion were permanently underway.

The boys at Old Buckenham have just joined the fray in their B-24 Liberators. There are some sixty of the big beasts at the new air base with the 453rd's black and white tail fin markings. That and their flat tops and curved undersides make them easy to recognise from the ground. Sometimes you can even make out the decorations the nose artists have painted on the planes to illustrate their names. I have definitely identified 'El Flako', with its big shark mouth, and the glamour girl on the side of 'Blondes Away' from the top field near the H. Stores, which they use as a turning point to fly into the airbase.

The first mission that the 453rd Bomb. Group flew out of Old Buck was on the 5th of this month, against the airfield at Tours, France. Everyone was on tenterhooks, but the crews came back in one piece and they have flown several missions into France since then. The last few days, Jackie tells me, they have been flying into Germany to bomb aircraft factories (though I am not supposed to know this).

It is a freezing winter, and the Yanks feel the cold dreadfully. But Jackie and I get quite steamed up in the little hut he has made into a cozy den on the airfield. We cuddle up in the old armchair that Tink – who has his transfer to Old Buck – found him from somewhere, or sometimes in the bunk Jackie has fitted up. We make the most of the short times we can snatch together away from Archie's prying eyes. Jackie makes me fried egg sandwiches he calls Egg Banjo on his little primus stove and we talk about the life we will have in the US of A after the war.

Until then, though, I have to deal with Archie, who has again started pressing me to become engaged to him. The more I compare him to Jackie, with his generous, gentlemanly ways, the more I see what an ill-mannered brute Archie is. The other day he took out the Allis, against my advice, and drove it too fast down Buxton Lane, which was slippery with ice. He swerved round the corner by Primrose Farm and knocked Maudie, who was pedalling home from school with her friend Lily, right off her bicycle. He did not seem at all sorry, indeed he blamed the children for the accident, and now the poor little mite is covered in bruises. Emma was furious. She is treating Maudie with hot poultices and a cream made from marigold, comfrey, speedwell and Anne's clover honey.

While Archie was out with the Home Guard last week, Tink brought Jackie to the farm on the pretext, although it was true enough, that he wanted to talk to Emma about herbalism and see how she produces her recipes. He and I pretended we hardly knew each other, as much for Heather's benefit as anything, as she also frequents Old Buck Airbase, and I would not trust her not to give me away to Archie.

Jackie was very charming to Mr and Mrs J. He told everyone about his grandmother, her farm in Poland and her healing gifts and explained how after the war he wants to set up a business in America, growing herbs and producing these traditional medicines commercially. He would like Emma to become involved and Tink is most excited at the prospect of such a business venture. I believe he would be happy to emigrate, but to leave Gt H might break Emma's heart, and certainly would Maudie's.

Heather has become a frequent companion of Jimmy Stewart, and puts it about that she and he are all but engaged to be married. Jackie, who is close to him, says this is not true at all, that Jimmy simply enjoys her attentions and is happy enough for her to be one of his popsies while he is here. She has bleached her once pretty, golden hair an unnaturally bright blonde and when she goes to see him in the evening, does herself up like a film star – as if to show that she is a cut above the rest of us and ready for the new life in Hollywood she dreams of.

She heard a rumour (which Jackie says is quite untrue) that Jimmy asked the actress Carole Lombard to marry him when she and he were making the film 'Made For Each Other', and she turned him down. Now Heather has a photo of Carole Lombard pinned up by her looking glass and I believe she tries to look as much like her as she can. Certainly one night at the T&H, when the Old Buck boys were *in for a drink, she was done up to the nines and kept repeating to poor Jimmy, "Don't we make a handsome couple? We were <u>made for each other</u>!" He looked quite embarrassed and pulled one of his comical faces at me over her head.*

Archie has bought a new threshing machine for the farm from Ransom's of Ipswich, against Mr J's wishes as the old one was still serviceable. There is more and more need for straw on the smaller farms, so we must bail up some of our great corn stacks to transport the stuff to where it is wanted. We have some Italian prisoners of war helping on the farm, and Mr J has consigned them to the threshing gang with me in charge. They are mainly quiet, nice men who do what I tell them, but Flavio, who is very handsome, smiles and flashes his beautiful dark eyes meaningfully at me. Archie once saw this and called him a "greasy Eyetie".

I was able to protest my innocence quite truthfully and hoped it at least kept him from suspecting me of anything else, but Flavio had some terrible bruises the next day. He explained, through mime, that he had tripped and fallen, but he has kept his distance from me since then and I cannot help wondering whether Archie had anything to do with it. The threshing is cold work in this weather, and the wind whistles through me when I am standing on top of the stack, forking corn into the hungry machine. If it gets too wet, though, we have to stop or the straw will rot. We have had to get the dogs in to chase the rats out of the corn stack, where hordes of them have nested for the winter. When I see the Italians learning the ropes, I realise how experienced a farm hand I am now, coming up to my fourth Spring at J's Farm.

Today, Sunday, has been a lovely day. Archie was on parade with the Home Guard, Tink was at home on the farm with Emma, Maudie and Baby Sam, and Mr and Mrs J were doting on their family. Heather had invited Jimmy home to meet her parents in Norwich, so I cycled over to lunch with Aunt Philly and Anne. I told everyone that Douglas was going to be there, but not that I had also invited Jackie. As it turned out, he was not the only guest as Douglas, too, had brought someone with him – Miss Yvette Mortimer, his landlady's daughter and nurse!

She is homely looking, but something of a wag and I believe my brother has quite fallen for her. He laughed heartily at everything she said and could hardly take his eyes off her. And I am certain Douglas did not need as much assistance with his crutches as Yvette thought it necessary to give him! It is a pleasure to see him so happy and I am sure her ministrations are speeding his recovery. Yvette endeared herself to Aunt Philly by praising the mutton stew, which was indeed tender having been cooked through for several hours in the hay box as there is so little fuel to be had. Yvette also noted down the recipe for the 'mashed bananas' which she served us for pudding: boiled parsnips mashed with three drops of banana flavouring and a little sugar. With some of Anne's honey and a coating of custard, I could almost believe it really was banana.

The six of us had a delightful time; it was such relaxed company compared with the tension that is often present at farm meals these days, between Archie and Mr J, Archie and Emma, Archie and Tink if he is there. Archie even resents Billy Stonepicker and accuses him of stealing from the Jackson family. I could not bear to be married to someone who is constantly at loggerheads with all around him. Aunt Philly and Anne took to Jackie immediately and they discussed all manner of books, socialism, feminism and the war. I did not mind that I could not join in with all of this, and chatted with Douglas and Yvette about our parents, as I was most anxious that the three of them should make friends..

After we had drunk our coffee (if you can call Camp Coffee that), Douglas tactfully took Yvette for a walk so that I could explain to Aunt Philly and Anne that Jackie and I wanted to marry and live in the USA after the war; but that we did not want to cause trouble at the Js by letting Archie know this before my work there is done. My aunt and her friend took this surprising news well. They congratulated me and Jackie and said they were happy for us, accepting without question that our affection for each other was heartfelt and serious.

Aunt Philly asked if I had told Mother and Father. I said I had not as I did not believe that Mother, especially, would have the same even handed view of my best interests and I could not be sure they would not make trouble with Mr and Mrs J. I believe she agreed with me, as Douglas does, though she would not say so in as many words. Anne was more worried about our position with Archie, as she has heard rumours about his gambling habits up at H. Hall and his quarrelsome behaviour in the village and with the Home Guard. When Aunt Philly suggested we should be open with him, Anne disagreed.

"The man is dangerous," she said. "Although it goes quite against my principles, I suggest you agree to become engaged if that is what he demands, then as soon as the war is won, leave the farm, write to the Jacksons to explain you cannot go through with the marriage, and do not let him know where you are. I believe if he finds out you have betrayed him, both you and Jackie will be in danger. His violent temper is well known around here."

This made me more nervous than I had been before, as I had not thought that Archie's angry disposition was either known outside the farm, or considered truly dangerous. Jackie and I have agreed we will be even more careful and, when it comes to the time, tell no one else about my plans to escape. I do not relish the pretence I will have to undergo in the meantime, but there seems to be no alternative.

———

My feelings of relief at having reconnected with Laura, and the support she and Babs offered, were dashed when I got home.

Jack was there already, with more bad news.

The General Medical Council was taking the complaint very seriously and had initiated an investigation. As the matter was one of sexual advances towards a patient, the first step they had taken was to refer the matter to the Interim Orders Panel. This committee had directed an interim suspension with immediate effect: Jack could not practice as a GP until he was cleared of the accusation, and if he was not cleared, that would be the end of his career.

"Oh my god!" I hadn't expected that.

At this moment, Jack was technically no longer a doctor, banned from the profession he loved and the role he felt defined by. How was he dealing with this body blow?

"Are you OK? What will you do? How will they manage at the Health Centre?"

Jack's almost cheerful response told me that the reality had not yet hit home.

"I'm fine, hon. Don't worry about me. I'll still get paid, so long as the investigation doesn't take too long, and we've organised temporary locum cover for the Health Centre. Elizabeth's completely behind me so there's no problem there. I've decided that I'm going to make the best use of this unexpected free time and start decorating the house. That'll keep me busy, give me goals to work towards and I'll be around to see more of you and the children."

"Well, that's great. I'm glad you're being so positive," I said uncertainly, a further barrage of questions forming in my mind. "But what do we say to the children? And do we tell other people – in the village, your parents, Kathleen and Max, other friends? Are you still alright with me acting in *Hamlet*?"

These details had clearly not yet occurred to Jack in his drive to remain optimistic, so I suggested we told the children he was having a break to work on the house, and that he should phone his mother and adoptive parents to alert, but not alarm, them to the situation. His preference was not to talk to anyone else about it. I insisted, though, that I would have to tell my family too – Mark, Jess and my mother – but refrained from admitting I had just revealed all to Laura and Babs and that Miranda already knew.

Each of the latter had told me I would need support myself in sustaining him through what would be a time of high stress and anxiety, however certain we were of his innocence and exoneration. And unlike Jack, whose coping mechanisms involved internalising problems until he arrived at a solution, I had to talk, listen and evolve strategies with others in order to stay sane under pressure.

"Hello, Daddy. Why are you home early again? Don't they like you at work any more?" Lily came straight to the point as usual and forced Jack to put his just formulated plan into practice.

"Come here, Li'l Girl," he told her, lifting her onto his knee. "Guess what? Daddy's decided to take some time off work so he can be at home with you and Felix and Mummy, and start decorating the house. Would you like me to give your room a new coat of paint first? It could be pink, or purple – "

I had forgotten Lily's antipathy to change in her bedroom, and not thought to warn Jack. Now she jumped off his lap and stood, hands on hips, her face contorted with emotion.

"No! No, no, no, no, no! Don't change anything in my room and don't go in and paint it gross colours when I'm at school. I like my room how it is, so there!"

"No, no, no! Paint my room gwoss colours!" shouted Felix in imitation of his sister, and followed her on his chunky little legs as she stalked out of the sitting room and upstairs to guard whatever secrets inhabited her precious, faded bedroom.

"Let's hope your parents and Kathleen take the news a little better," I tried to joke, but Jack's face had dropped and I realised the shock was starting to take effect. "Look, I'll ring Ian and say I can't make tonight's rehearsal so I can stay in with you."

Jack shook his head and insisted I should go; he'd make things up with the children by putting them to bed and put in the calls to his family while I was out of the house. It sounded as though that was what he really wanted, so I swiftly multi-tasked, ringing first Mark and then Jess to fill them in on Jack's situation while I cooked the children's tea and served it up to them.

Mark took the news in his stride and said he and Zoe would come up whenever we needed them, but of course Jack would be cleared of the charge. So concerned, though, was my eldest daughter at the news that she wanted to get the bus in from Norwich immediately. I explained that Jack had chosen to be left alone to ring his parents and I was rehearsing for the Haddeston *Hamlet*. She asked what time I would be finishing, so I took a guess.

"OK, Mumma," said Jess. "I'll meet you at the village hall. The 10A goes straight past it, I'm sure the driver'll let me off. If you're still rehearsing I'll sneak in and sit at the back. You can introduce me to that fit guy, Tom, and if it's too early to disturb Jack we can go for a drink at the 'Trowel and Hammer' afterwards. In fact that would be cool anyway, yeah?"

I told Jack I was meeting Jess after rehearsal, but I wasn't sure he had taken it in.

Outwardly his entire attention was taken up with a conciliatory game of Happy Families with Lily; inwardly I felt his mind swirling around the events of the day and the ever expanding repercussions of his desire to move to the country and live in close proximity to his biological mother.

———

Ian had scheduled the second and third scenes of the play for rehearsal this evening; I was in the earlier but not the later one, but Ian felt the two were strongly related thematically.

"The motif of incest runs throughout the play," he told us, "and Hamlet frequently alludes to it, most obviously in conversations about Gertrude and her husband Claudius, who were formerly brother- and sister-in-law. Then there's a subtle element of incestuous desire in the relationship of Laertes and Ophelia, as Laertes speaks to his sister in suggestively sexual terms when he's warning her against Hamlet's advances in Scene Three. However, the strongest overtones of sexual connection are between Hamlet and his mother Gertrude. Hamlet is fixated on Gertrude's sex life with Claudius and preoccupied with her in general. I want to see you play this up as much as possible," Ian instructed us.

So I found myself up close and very personal with my stage son whilst trying to persuade him to get over his father's death and my hasty marriage to his uncle. By the time I was begging him:

"Let not thy mother lose her prayers, Hamlet:
I pray thee, stay with us; go not to Wittenberg,"

I was oblivious to the others on stage and watching us, as I stared into the depths of Tom's cavernous brown eyes. His face was only inches from mine and I was conscious of the heat from his muscular body as he replied slowly and intensely:

"I shall in all my best obey you, madam."

We held the moment instinctively, and when Graham, as King Claudius, eventually broke it with appropriately false jocularity –

"Why, 'tis a loving and a fair reply" – Ian jumped to his feet and applauded.

"Perfect! Exactly what I meant when I spoke before about finding the emotional truth behind the words. You took the loving mother-son relationship to a slightly unhealthy extreme just through tone and body language. Please hold that in mind and play the scene like that every time."

Tom seemed relaxed about the plaudits for our performance, but I felt both elated and disturbed. Could this moment of stagecraft have emulated the electrical charge that would arc between Jack and Kathleen if, or when, they allowed it free rein? How could I blame them for struggling with such powerful sensations when I had been momentarily captivated by an unknown young man whose mother I was only pretending to be?

But before I could dwell on this disquieting insight, Ian had moved onto Hamlet's first soliloquy:

"O! that this too too solid flesh would melt,
Thaw and resolve itself into a dew..."

Tom seemed to have no trouble projecting the emotional truth behind this escapist yearning, until he got to the part about Gertrude's swift transfer of affection from her dead husband to his brother, Claudius. From the misogynist cry of *"Frailty, thy name is woman!"* to the culmination of the tortured speech – *"But break my heart, for I must hold my tongue"* – Tom appeared uncomfortable, and unwilling to invest any of himself in Hamlet's disgust with his mother and her sexuality. Ian addressed him gently.

"OK, Tom, you got nicely into Hamlet's general melancholy and discontent with the political and family state of affairs. But I didn't really feel you identified with his specific disappointment at his mother marrying his uncle so quickly. His words indicate a deep distaste and distrust of women in general, which you may not go along with personally, but you have to find a way of getting inside his head at that point. I'm going to set you an exercise: I want you – in fact why don't you all do this, not just Tom? Take this speech and write your own modern translation of it – I don't want poetry, I just want the emotions behind the words. We'll compare everyone's efforts at the next rehearsal."

I noted down the task and we ran through to the end of the scene, during which I observed Jess come in with Rachel, who was joining Eddie and Norman to rehearse the next scene between Ophelia, Laertes and their father Polonius. When Ian had finished giving us his notes, I went over and took the opportunity to introduce Tom to Jess. They looked at each other with something more than passing politeness, but not instant attraction, I thought, a little disappointed.

"Do you want to join us for a drink at the 'Trowel and Hammer'?" I asked Tom, but he declined saying he had to get off home to his mum. Ian said he'd pop in later and might see us if we were still there, so Jess and I left with Graham, who turned off in his battered pick-up truck, up the long drive to Haddeston Hall.

"He's Lady Janet's estate manager and lover, so Laura says," I told Jess. "Which makes sense of the confession he made about loving another man's wife. Nice man, though. Perhaps she would have married him if they hadn't needed the money to keep the Hall."

But Jess wasn't interested in my speculation and questioned me intensively about Jack, the young woman who'd accused him and the GMC investigation until I had told her all I could, and had finished the one glass of wine I was going to allow myself before driving home.

"There's something wrong with all this, but I just can't put my finger on it," she finally announced. "I don't think this whole thing's about Jack, it's bigger than that. There have to be other reasons for this happening, to him, right here, right now."

"*Something is rotten in the state of Denmark,*" I muttered, recalling how Ian had compared that small country with the community of Haddeston.

"You know Tom's gay, by the way," Jess broke into my musing. "I've seen him on campus with his friends and he certainly goes to all the gay and lesbian parties." So that explained the look between them; they already knew each other and perhaps he didn't want his sexuality made general knowledge in the village.

"I thought he might be – and he seems close to Ian, although Rachel appears to think he's her boyfriend. I suppose that would explain why she thinks he's messing her around, even if she doesn't realise why," I commented.

"And you know she's doing coke, don't you?"

My eyes opened wide.

"Yeah, Mumma. Don't stress, it's available in all the best schools in Norwich. No big deal, but I found her snorting up in the Ladies when I came in. Couldn't you tell she was wired by that big eyed, 'wow, you're *so* interesting' attitude? It can really suck you in. And I'm sure I've seen her somewhere before...

just can't quite work out where."

As we were preparing to leave, Ian breezed into the pub, ordered a double whisky just before last orders were called and kissed his fingers at me from the bar.

" *'How does the queen?'* " he called, "My lovely Gertrude!"

"Good rehearsal?" I wandered over to ask him, pleased to be complimented and to have a chance for more than a business exchange with him.

"Yes, I'm happy with the way things are going. The younger members of the cast might need a little extra help, though Rachel was on top form tonight and she fired old Eddie up. Nice boy. Hope he doesn't take her too seriously – all that stuff about a modeling career, all in her mind, you know. Norman's a love, too, isn't he? He's getting ever so eager beaver about the exhibition of 1940s memorabilia."

I laughed at the thought of Norman's reaction to being called 'a love' and an 'eager beaver', and asked something I'd had on my mind for a while. "What made you decide on the World War Two setting, Ian? I understand all the historic comparisons between Elsinore and Haddeston, but was there something specific that started you down that track? It seems almost personal to you."

"I had you down as the intuitive kind, Mo," he replied with a little satisfied smile, and patted my hand. "You're quite right, of course. I had an aunt who worked round here during the war. When she died, I ended up with all her family papers, including a sort of diary she kept of those years, and as I was trying to come up with a local twist for this *Hamlet*, her situation came back to me. You can read it if you're interested. I'll dig it out and drop it in to you."

———

May 1944

I have agreed to become engaged to Archie.

He has been so unreasonably possessive of me lately that I have hardly seen anything of Jackie. He was coming to meet me at Black Carr House last week, when Archie turned up out of the blue, I can only believe to check up on me. I did not think he suspected anything but now I do not know. Luckily Yvette was able to warn Jackie when he arrived and he drove straight away again, so Archie simply added his awkward presence to an innocent visit by a sister to her brother.

Flavio no longer comes to the farm and the other POWs tell me he has disappeared. I do not know what to think and do not dare to ask. I can only hope that the engagement will soothe Archie and make him less angry and difficult to deal with. I have told him that I want no more underhand fumblings at Lovers Leap and we will wait for everything now until we are properly married. Of course this is unfair, as Jackie and I have been all the way in his hut, which was quite wonderful and has only made me more certain that he is my one true love.

Archie has told his parents we are to be married, though I have not told mine. I have said Mother and Father are happy for us and will come and meet him when the war is over. He will not think of going to London any more than they would think of coming here, so I am safe on that score. Mr and Mrs J are so pleased to welcome me into the family that I feel doubly guilty. I believe Mrs J is worried about whether I will be happy with Archie, and has asked me if I am sure I want to be the mistress of the farm when the time comes, with all the work it entails. I found it hard to tell her I did.

Archie has given me a gold ring with a pearl set in garnets. It belonged to his grandmother and is luckily too big for me so I cannot wear it. I have said I do not want anyone else to know or any fuss made, and I will certainly not contemplate marriage until the war is won. Emma understands why I have to do this and is angry with her brother for forcing me into this situation, but she feels badly about dissembling to her mother and father. There have already been too many lies in her family.

I pray the war cannot last for much longer now. The Allies are starting to win against the Japanese. The Russians have got the Hun to surrender in the Crimea. Polish squadrons have arrived at

Coltishall and are flying their de Havilland Mosquitoes. The bomber boys at Old Buck and other airbases have dropped tons of bombs, some in broad daylight, on Berlin and Hamburg, and Cassino has been taken. Jimmy has flown in some of these dangerous raids from which not all crews have returned and Heather, of course, has her heart in her mouth every time she knows he is flying. Emma and I count ourselves lucky that our men remain on English soil (though no one but she and Tink know that for me the man in question is not Archie, but Jackie who, as Chief Engineer looks after the planes but does not fly them). Tibenham has lost far more men than Old Buck. They lost one hundred and twenty two crew in their 'Big Week' back in February, and just yesterday suffered one of the most disastrous missions of the whole war. They are saying at least twenty five B-24s went down and up to four hundred and fifty men were killed. One of their planes crash landed at Old Buck on its return home.

It is a tragedy that men are dying all over the world for the cause, but it brings it home when you know the chaps who were only drinking at the T&H a few days ago may be nothing but charred remains in their burned out planes.

Douglas was excited to hear that his old squadron on HMS Furious had taken part in the attacks on the Tirpitz in Kaa Fjord, at the top of Norway, but it has also provoked in him a deep sorrow that neither I nor Yvette can relieve him from. He feels he should be there, especially as his wounds are neither life-threatening nor even acquired in action. Although his legs are healing and the plaster casts have come off, he is limping severely and needs his crutches for anything more than a few steps. Yvette says the bones were not set properly in the Naval Hospital and he was allowed to walk on them too soon. She does not think he will ever be walking freely, let alone running, again, though we do not say this to Douglas. She has him working on the accounts and other administrative tasks at Black Carr House to keep him occupied, and I believe she would be happy to care for him for the rest of his life, even if he does not completely recover.

Archie has been engrossed with the fourth birthday of the Home Guard and 'Salute the Soldier' week, which has taken his mind off me a little. He takes personal credit for bringing down several enemy aircraft on the recent night time attack over East Anglia because some of his men were operating the AckAck rocket battery that night, but I suspect it was not they who actually hit the planes. He tries to lord it over Tink with such successes, and quotes Stafford Cripps, who said in the Eastern Daily Press that the Home Guard is as important to the country now as it ever was. He tells Emma that Tink is still shirking because he is only a base wallah and not in the line of fire. In return Tink calls him a half pint hero.

Tink got his own back the other day when he drew up outside the farm, not in his usual Bedford, but a great big, military green Humber Snipe – which even Archie had to admit would only be used by top brass. He had even borrowed a Kodak camera from Walter M. and got Emma to take a photograph of him leaning on the car outside the farm gates, as if both belonged to him! Tink would not say where he was going or who he was to drive in the Humber. "Can't give you the low down on this op, all very hush hush," he said, tapping his nose in a way he knew would make Archie still more brassed off. Emma and I tried not to laugh, but it turned out to be true. Tink told Emma later he had driven Air Chief Marshall Sir Arthur Tedder, second in command to General Eisenhower, to a top secret meeting about the invasion of Europe.

Emma is worried because Mr Newling has paid Heather a number of visits at the farm lately, and makes a point of seeing Maudie if she is home from school. He brought her a pretty little china tea set with roses on it last time, which he said she could use as a plaything with her friends and her dollies. Emma hates it and will find an excuse to break it if she can, but cannot forbid Maudie from accepting presents from Mr N as that would rouse more suspicion.

There is some business, too, going on between him and Archie. The Home Guard boys whisper that Archie is badly in debt to Lord Buxton from the gambling parties at H. Hall and is borrowing money to pay it back. I wonder if he could be borrowing from Mr N, who is also part of the H. Hall circle. There are also more arguments between Archie and Mr J, which can be overheard in the yard if they are shouting at each other in the office and generally seem to be about money and the estate. Money is on everyone's mind: Jackie is looking for investors for his new herbalism business so he can start up as soon as he goes home to the US of A, and Tink very much wants to be one of these, but other than his pay has not two beans to rub together. Even Billy Stonepicker has lately asked to for a wage for his work on the farm and a labourers' cottage to live in. I cannot see that this is unreasonable, for he works hard at whatever he is put to, is very loyal and in this day and age should not be sleeping in a stable and living upon charity. Mr and Mrs J would happily agree to this, but I believe even they are frightened of Archie's temper.

———

Jack had the brandy out again when Jess and I got back.

His phone calls had not been received as he expected. Betty and Colin had been unpredictably supportive and not at all offended by his news, when usually they were fundamentally shaken by anything that nudged them even a little out of their conservative comfort zone. They planned to come and stay next weekend to demonstrate their solidarity and help in any way they could. He didn't offer any information, though, about his biological mother's response.

"What did Kathleen say when you rang her?" I asked, tentatively.

"She said it wasn't appropriate to talk to her about the matter, I couldn't tell her any details, she couldn't get involved, it would compromise Max's position. I'd forgotten the constituency boundaries cut right through the Haddestons. He's the girl's father's MP and he's already received a letter of complaint. For the moment he's just said he'll wait to hear the outcome of the GMC investigation, but if it's bad, he may have to look into the Health Centre in the context of small rural GP practices and their limitations. It could be really bad news for Elizabeth. And if the Haddeston Health Centre closes, the whole village will suffer."

"You mean Kathleen isn't going to support you through this?" I asked.

"She not only won't support me, she can't be in contact with us at all until it's cleared up. So we're going to have to explain to Lily that riding lessons are on hold, as are any other treats from and visits to Kathleen and Max."

So much for blood being thicker than water, I thought to myself, but withheld the comment. Jess, though, was less restrained.

"Bitch!" she spat. "How could she do that to Lily – and to you, Jack? You're her son. Can't she see that you're not guilty, that this is some kind of beat up by a neurotic kid?"

"It's not her fault, sweetie, it's Max," replied Jack, pouring himself another brandy. "He's a friend of Elizabeth's, but that wouldn't stop him getting the Health Centre closed if it was expedient to his career. Kathleen's his wife; she has to go along with him. Things would have been different if my father had lived."

This maudlin talk from Jack was so uncharacteristic as to be worrying. Kathleen had been tragically 'widowed' before she'd had the chance to marry Jack and Julia's father, and had only found she was pregnant, at a very young age, after his death. Whilst this had clearly had a major and traumatic effect on her, none of the rest of us had known the young man whose genes Jack carried, so assumptions that his integrity was superior to that of Max, were unwarranted and possibly unfair.

I exchanged a glance with Jess, who looked shocked. She and Mark had learned to rely on Jack's dependable, grounded sanity while he had stepfathered them through adolescence, and I could see that his display of unbalanced behaviour was undermining her world too. For the first time in our marriage I would have to take over the role of rock; central pillar of strength on which the family could rely absolutely, and renounce my inclination to indulge my emotions and flights of fancy.

Suddenly Nanny Babs' scrying of the tea leaves made total sense.

I would have to rely on my own resources – strength and whatever wisdom I had accrued over nearly fifty years – and draw on the support of friends and family to overcome this setback, if I wanted to arrive at the circle of completion she had seen in my empty cup.

———

Despite the need to be there for them, I was going to have to desert my family for a couple of days for meetings in London about finalising *Time Crunch*.

These had been scheduled for ages and were unavoidable, and there was nothing to be gained from me losing my job as well. Jack was at home, of course, so child minding would be no problem. I would take the opportunity to see my Crystal Palace girlfriends between work commitments and stay the night at my mother's house in Pimlico.

But in order to prepare for the production meetings at Generation Films, I had to finalise the subjects participating in *Time Crunch*. The trial bottle of herbal remedy had run out and Felix' asthma was definitely getting worse again – proof to me, if not to Jack who blamed it on the early barley harvest, that the alternative treatment was having a positive effect. I would put in an ongoing order with Charlotte and hope that this would enable us to agree in a civilised manner that her family would not want to take part in the television series given the complaint they were pursuing against my husband.

Dreading the encounter, though, I left it till the last minute and called into the Post Office on my way to catch the train to London from Diss. As she had before, Charlotte closed the shop and took me to her bungalow.

Kylie, to my relief, was not in evidence so I didn't have to confront Jack's antagonist face to face while I sat in Charlotte Tinker's lounge. As neither of us had yet done so, I was left wondering how best to raise the subject while she went out to her conservatory laboratory to prepare the asthma remedies I had requested. To occupy my nervous hands, I picked up a couple of worn volumes lying amongst the women's magazines on the coffee table.

One was *Culpepper's Herbal*, annotated throughout with old-fashioned, copperplate hand writing. It fell open at a page on 'Nettle (Common)' and I read with interest, 'The roots or leaves, or the juice of them, boiled and made into an electuary with honey and sugar, is a safe and sure medicine to open the passages of the lungs, which is the cause of wheezing and shortness of the breath.' There was a penciled heading in the margin:

Asthma – children, under which was listed *Nettle, Wild Thyme, Mullein, Plantain, Elecampane, Primula – infuse with clover honey (Anne) and water for syrup. Teaspoons hourly while symptoms persist, 3 x daily for prevention. Attacks – add, Lavender, Pine Resin, Lungwort, Mallow and inhale. Saturate in hot lard for chest rub. Coughing fits: equal quantities of Alehoof, Horehound, Coltsfoot.*

I turned to the fly leaf to see who the writer might be. Inscribed in faded purple ink and a flowing, flamboyant script, were the words,

'There's rosemary, that's for remembrance; pray, love, remember: and there is pansies, that's for thoughts.'
For Emma, who is always in my thoughts.
Hoping you remember your devoted
Henry Tinker, at Christmas 1941

As I read them, for a moment Charlotte's lounge slipped away and I seemed to be in a busy room full of chatter and good cheer: the bar at the 'Trowel and Hammer', I realised. As I re-read the words, now freshly etched on bright paper, I became aware of a length of purple cloth lying under the book on my knee, of the comfortably familiar seat in which I sat, warmed by a blazing fire, and the pleasant tang of beer in my mouth. I looked up into the expectant face of the handsome man I had bantered with on Buxton Lane in my first flashback. My heart melted at the tenderness I saw there, and then tightened with pain as I knew that he could not be mine.

"My grandmother's," said Charlotte proudly, dissolving the Christmas revelry I had fallen into by returning with a large bottle full of the brackish fluid, a plastic bag of dried herbs and a glass jar containing a pasty ointment.

"I learned everything I know about herbal remedies from her. You can ask her anything about them and she still remembers, even though she doesn't know what year it is, or sometimes even who I am these days. She's stuck in the past now, like it only happened yesterday. When she goes, a whole world in her head will be buried with her. The present's just a fleeting dream – or nightmare, I think sometimes – though they're good to her at Black Carr House."

"It must be very hard to see someone you love deteriorate like that," I offered, affected by the sense of loss I had briefly felt as well as that which her words conveyed.

Charlotte took the thicker tome from me.

I saw it was a battered, leather-bound *Complete Works of Shakespeare*.

"This was hers too. It's where I got my love of Shakespeare, and reading in general – though don't think I begrudge you getting Gertrude over me," a smile lit up her face briefly and faded again. "Gran brought me up when my mother, her daughter, did a runner. Got pregnant with me and couldn't face the responsibility. Haven't seen her since I was a few weeks old. No idea what happened to her, she never got back in touch."

"I'm so sorry," I murmured. "That must be painful to live with." I almost opened my mouth to tell her Jack had found a long lost mother, but remembered that he was the reason I was here.

"That's why I'm so careful with my two girls," Charlotte continued. "They mean the world to me and I won't have them hurt, not by anyone." She looked me in the eye, defiantly.

"I can totally understand that," I replied, seizing an opening for the subject I needed to tackle, "even if you'll have to allow me to take a different view of the complaint you've made. I presume it means that you and your girls won't want to take part in *Time Crunch* while it's being resolved. Sorry to bring it up, but I have to be absolutely certain that you're out."

"What?" Charlotte's blue eyes opened wide in genuine disbelief. "You mean you don't want us in the programme just because – "

"*Just* because of your complaint?" I broke in angrily. "This is extremely serious for Jack. Do you realise he's been suspended from his job, he's being investigated by the General Medical Council and he could be put on the Sex Offenders Register because of your daughter?"

"But I don't understand how what she said happened could possibly have had that affect on him!" Charlotte looked completely astounded. "We were only drawing attention to what could have been the start of something unpleasant."

"Well if an under age, female patient accuses a male doctor of making sexual advances to her during an unchaperoned consultation, it's hardly going to be passed off as a trivial issue! If you're telling me Kylie is not serious about what she's said happened – "

"Kylie? What's Kylie got to do with this?" Charlotte's voice rose in pitch to match mine. "I'm talking about your Lily picking a fight with my Kimberley. I went to Mr Chatham because I thought it was better to nip that sort of thing in the bud before it got into the realms of bullying, and I didn't want to make it personal. My Kylie's never been near your husband. We don't go to doctors in this family, you must know that!"

My hand flew to my mouth. I'd got the wrong end of the stick on two counts. Kylie was not Jack's accuser – and nor had he ever said she was, I realised now. And Lady Janet was not the mother who had complained about Lily insulting her family. The few solid facts I thought I had about the problems we were facing danced away like dust mites in a bright shaft of insight.

I was still trying to make sense of all this as the train pulled out of Diss.

Gazing into the distance beyond the abundant green and gold fields racing past the carriage window, I was jerked out of my reverie by the bleeping of my mobile. Jess had texted me.

hi mumma. Just seen rachel in norwich hanging at forum with goth gang. knew had seen her b4. only 1 with blonde hair! Have fun in london, luv to v. will check on jack 4 u x

Chapter Eight

December 1944

S.N.A.F.U., as the Yanks say.

This may be the last chance I have to write about my life as a Land Girl on Jackson's Farm. Archie is down at the T&H with Heather and anything may happen when they return. Heather was in a vile temper tonight and I suspect she will take her chance to spill the beans on me.

After D-Day in June and all the celebrations and parties, the liberation of France in August and the advance into Belgium in September, we thought the war must soon be won. The blackout was over and the call up to the Home Guard stopped, even though the V-2 rockets were raining down on London and the doodlebugs kept coming. Then last month the whole of Belgium was freed, the first big German town, Aachen, fell and we read headlines saying 'British bite into the Siegfried backbone'. But now Germany is fighting back again.

Last month 'El Flako' was shot down over Germany and all ten of the crew killed. The pilot, Isaacson, was a good pal of Jackie's and had only ever been on one bombing raid before taking up his own crew. There have been two raids on Coltishall, the last of which damaged the watch tower. Then we had the mid air collision over H. Rode and lost two crews from the 389th Bombardment Group at Hethel. The shattered planes were scattered all over the fields.

General Patton has just said we could still lose the war if we do not win what they are calling The Battle of the Bulge in the Ardennes, and yet the Yanks are starting to leave our shores, and amongst them my darling Jackie. He has been recalled to Utah – his overseas tour to Britain will end just after Christmas. No matter how desperately I would have missed him, I was prepared to sit it out, working here for King and Country until the bitter end, before joining him in the US of A. But now I suspect Heather has put paid to that.

Last week, Archie was driven down to London for the day with Lord Buxton, to take part in the big 'Stand Down' parade marking the end of the Home Guard. I took the opportunity to escape from the farm and have 'chow' with Jackie at the Old Buck Mess Hall – he soft-soaped the MPs on duty to let me in, even though I could not get a Mess Hall ticket for that day. We were sitting together eating our lunch, when suddenly a rumpus broke out at the other end of the hall. I was facing that way and, to my dismay, saw Heather, who I did not know was there, stand up suddenly from where she too had been having chow with a group of the bomber boys and stalk out of the hall, passing me and Jackie on her way. He was sitting with his back to her, so did not see her approaching as I did, and just as she reached us, he put his hand out to affectionately brush some crumbs from my cheek, leaned over and kissed me. She stopped in her tracks, gave me a meaningful look and continued, her high heels clacking on the hard floor, until she flounced out of the big doors.

I rushed out after her, and found her in tears of fury. She told me she had been eating with the boys while Jimmy had been briefing a crew for a mission, and they had started teasing her about him. One of them had foolishly repeated a risqué story Jimmy had told them about when he had begun acting in Hollywood a few years before the war broke out. Apparently he had been a shy and inexperienced young man and his studio bosses had feared he was 'not the marrying kind'. To make sure he was leading man material, they had sent him out, one night, to a house of ill repute with orders to go all the way with at least two of the ladies working there, in the presence of witnesses! Since then, he told the boys with relish, he has never looked back. Heather did not find this at all amusing – indeed she was mortified by the revelation and said she could never associate with a man who had behaved like such a cad. She is more unworldly than she makes herself out to be, unlike her father.

"I can never look him in the eye again," she wept, and then turned on me. "It is all your fault," she spat. "If you had not enticed my Archie away from me with your fast London ways, I should never have looked at another man. Well, we shall see what your fiancé thinks of you carrying on with a Yank!" I tried to calm her down, persuade her that the story about Jimmy was probably untrue (though I think not), and that Jackie and I were just friends, but she would have none of it. I could tell she wanted to blame someone for her disillusionment, and I was in the firing line. She flounced off and I ran back into the Mess Hall to tell Jackie that Heather might betray us to Archie. My sweet love was so concerned for my safety that he could not eat another mouthful. We went to his hut, where he racked his brains to come up with a plan for me to escape from H, and with his quick mind he eventually did so.

If possible, I will keep Archie at bay till Christmas Eve, when I am to take part in Old Buck's 'Operation Santa' to fly a consignment of Christmas presents to liberated French children. I have been recruited as a French-speaking 'Mother Christmas', or 'Mere Noel', to T/Sgt Reuben Brockway's Father Christmas. (For the first time I am grateful to Mother for forcing me to take conversation classes with Mademoiselle Joubert, Raynes Park's most tedious French teacher.) But our secret plan is that I will not return to Old Buck with the rest of the crew that night for what will probably be their last English Christmas. Jackie has some cousins who escaped to France before the Nazis invaded Poland, and are now living in bombed out Paris. He has managed to contact them and they will meet me wherever we are to drop the cargo of Christmas, and take me to stay with them. Once he is home and the war is over, Jackie will make arrangements for all of us to join him in Utah.

In the meantime, I shall stay at the farm as long as it is safe to do so, and so far Heather has confined herself to telling everyone what an immoral heel Jimmy is, and making snide comments about me which Archie has not yet understood the gist of. She is unpredictable, though, so I have a bag packed and hidden in Douglas' room at Black Carr House in case the worst happens. If Archie finds out I have betrayed him, I will escape there and Douglas and Yvette will hide me in one of the attic rooms until Christmas Eve. Then, whether from Black Carr or the farm, I will make my way to the Old Buckenham Airbase with all the local children and their presents for the war orphans of Paris and fly out on the 'Liberty Run' with Major O'Dwyer and his crew – the few French-speakers amongst the Yanks.

I determined, when I left Raynes Park for Jackson's Farm, that it would be the start of a different life for me and it has certainly turned out that way. This Christmas I shall miss the festivities I have grown so used to, and spend it with a group of Polish people who may not even speak English. But the Warzynskis are to be my family now, and no matter how strange and awkward, it will be the beginning of my brand new life with my beloved Jacek. If I take nothing else, I will keep his locket around my neck until we are reunited in America.

Now that my time here is so short, I feel quite sentimental about Gt H and J's farm. I shall miss my dearest friends Emma and Tink so very much and hope to coax them out to the USA to join us in the herbalism business at the earliest opportunity. I have been saving my sweet coupons so I can get a good bagful from Swords in Wymondham to leave for Maudie and Sam. I hope I have time to do this before I leave, though they are sick of the liquorice root and locust beans that pass for sweets these days. Perhaps I will have one more Sunday lunch with Aunt Philly and Anne, who know my plans and wish me well. They say that they, perhaps with Douglas and Yvette, will come to visit me and Jackie one summer holidays when the war is well and truly over.

We agree that I will never be able to entice Mother and Father out of Raynes Park, so I do not know if I will ever see my parents again. I cannot trust them with my plans and I do not know if or when I shall return to Blighty, so I am leaving a letter and a photo of me and Jackie for Douglas to give them when I am safely out of the country. I shall write to Mr and Mrs J from Paris to explain why I cannot marry their son and hope that they – and Archie too – can forgive me in the fullness of time.

I hear voices.

Heather and Archie have returned from the T&H. He is shouting in the yard. Oh no – she has told him, I am sure.

Mr J is going downstairs to see what the row is about.

Emma is coming into my little maid's room. She has embraced me and told me to go, she will keep Archie out the front for as long as possible. I must slip out through the wash house door, to where, as every night now, I have hidden my bicycle in the orchard hedge, and pedal to Black Carr House when the coast is clear. God be with

————

I closed the worn notebook on its final, unfinished entry as the train pulled into Liverpool Street Station.

My disappointment at the untimely departure of Ian's Aunt Dottie was dulled by the synapses in my brain snapping like firecrackers as they made connections between her account of wartime Great Haddeston and my experience of the present day village. Was Jackson's Farm, with its new star-patterned gate, my Stargate Farm?

In all her descriptions of the old farmhouse I had visualised my new home – and if nothing else, surely Emma Tinker's decoration of her daughter's pink and yellow bedroom must bear out my theory. If it did, though, how had Lily discovered that it had once belonged to a little girl called Maudie?

I made my way off the train, tripping onto the platform from the carriage step, treading on the heels of the passenger ahead of me and trapping my suitcase in the exit gate as I headed for the Underground station. My mind remained stubbornly in Haddeston, refusing to focus on my physical progress through London to the key meeting at Generation

Films about *Time Crunch*.

Was herbalist Emma Tinker of the diary the gaga grandmother of Charlotte Tinker, Great Haddeston's Sub Postmaster and alternative healer?

Were my strange episodes of time travel snatches of her life I was somehow tapping into?

What other explanation could there be for my recognition of the photograph in the Trowel and Hammer? If the handsome man who quoted Shakespeare at me in some unknown time on Buxton Lane had been Henry Tinker, it was also him hanging on the wall of the bar.

"Find tinker and tailor, find soldier and sailor; of rich man, poor man and beggar man, which is the thief?"

The riddle of Nanny Babs' ghost came into my head as if suddenly placed there by an outside force. "A wrong to be righted…. you are the person who can do it, who will make things right at last," her voice repeated to me.

I stood up to get off the crowded tube train at Warren Street station, my head still spinning with unanswerable questions as I rode up the escalators and was ejected onto the Tottenham Court Road.

Enough, I told myself sternly. This is hysterical nonsense. You're over-reacting to the diary story – which could possibly have taken place in our house, but has no other relevance to you. The rest is a trick of the imagination triggered by the stress of moving, the Kathleen situation and now the complaint against Jack. What happened before when you were searching for Kathleen was a one off.

Get real. Get a grip.

I was still belabouring myself when I arrived at the basement offices of Generation Films. Ellie, the receptionist, buzzed me in through the front door while continuing to file her long, jewel-encrusted nails, and gave me no warmer greeting than if she had seen me only yesterday.

"Hi, Ellie. Long time no see. Like the hair. How's it going

in media land?" I asked pleasantly.

She tossed her new, waist length extensions, chomped on her gum and replied indistinctly.

"Same old. You know. David's grumpy, Jane's snotty – and as for that Tamara woman! She seems to think I'm here to do whatever she wants, whenever!"

I refrained from remarking that Ellie was indeed there to do whatever the programme makers wanted, and tried to look bright, business-like and focused as David, MD of Generation Films, came up and air kissed me on both cheeks.

"Mo, darling, great to see you! Jane says you've been working wonders from your country mansion. *Time Crunch* could be a landmark series if we get it right, peak viewing figures, international format sales – the making of Tamara. She and Jane are waiting for you in the goldfish bowl. Have a good meeting!"

I walked down to the glass walled board room and saw my series producer and the balance expert deep in stacks of documents and serious discussion within. I shook off my country concerns and stepped back into the hectic, hermetic world of television production.

"Ah, Mo – just the person!" Jane's husky tones greeted me. Tamara's more grating voice followed it; dispensing with any greeting she got straight to the point:

"Charlotte Tinker's grandmother, the one with dementia. Can we get some footage in the care home of interaction between the old lady and her family? Sensitively, of course. I just want to make sure the viewers understand the very real stress that long term caring for a degenerating family member can cause. Oh, and Ellie – " she pressed the intercom through to reception. "Can we have three coffees and a jug of water, now, please?"

———

My mother listened intently as I outlined how the complaint

against Jack had progressed.

Sitting in her faded velvet wingback chair, her feet on the little footstool with its almost threadbare tapestry cover, she sipped her Lapsang Souchong tea and made no comment till I had brought her up to date.

"The latest blow is that Sarah, the receptionist, has been asked to give a witness statement on what happened while the girl was in the surgery. She told Jack she didn't want to, but she'd have to say that she heard the girl shout, 'Get your hands off me, you filthy perv'."

"I see," responded my mother quietly.

I let the silence hang between us and noted how noisy I now found the traffic rushing past the tall, thin terraced house in Pimlico where I'd been brought up. I poured myself another cup of weak tea from the tarnished silver pot and took a stale Amaretto biscuit from the chipped antique plate.

"You don't think he did anything, do you, Mum?" I asked suddenly, unable to bear the suspense any longer, and surprising myself as well as her by the strident tone of my voice.

"No, no I don't think he did anything at all improper to that girl," she replied quickly. "And I don't think she did what she did to get Jack into trouble either. Jess is right, it's unlikely to be a personal vendetta, especially as she hadn't even seen him before."

"Why, then? Why is she doing this if it's all lies? What does she want from Jack? Is there something he can do to make her stop it all?"

She peered at me over the top of her half moon spectacles and prepared to give her professional opinion.

"Women make false accusations of rape, or sexual assault, for a variety of different reasons. Most frequently these include revenge – but not necessarily on the accused; guilt – for instance about an affair; shame about their own sexual feelings; or to test the love of a husband, boyfriend, father even.

Sometimes, of course, it's simply a desperate attempt to win sympathy and attention. On the whole, though, women tend to make false allegations to get themselves out of trouble rather than to get men into trouble. They lie when they feel cornered, put in a tight spot. The whole thing can get out of hand and then there's no way of stopping the process they've accidentally set in motion."

"OK. I can understand that, but how could it work in this case?"

"Let's assume for a minute that this girl Rachel, who Jess says is taking cocaine and dresses in gothic costume, is Jack's accuser. She came into the surgery saying she was pregnant and had taken a test, but that clearly can't have been true. She was either consciously lying or fantasising about the pregnancy; either way it was serving her emotional needs," my mother theorised. "She told Jack she wanted the pregnancy terminated. Knowing her a little, at least, can you imagine how that could benefit her – to be thought distraught at finding herself in such a position?"

I hardly had to think before the answer came to me.

"Tom!"

My mother raised her eyebrows.

"She's obviously infatuated by Tom – he's playing Hamlet to her Ophelia – and she seems to think he's her boyfriend, but he's almost certainly not even interested because Jess says he's gay. My guess is she doesn't know that and he doesn't want it to be public knowledge. So perhaps he's fooled about with her a bit to please her and cover himself, and now she wants more than he's prepared to give. But if she said she was pregnant by him, perhaps she thinks he'd have to – I don't know, look after her, be involved with her, support her through the fake abortion process? That makes her pretty nutty, though, and she's really sweet and charming."

"Research also suggests that about seventy percent of false allegers have a psychiatric history," added my mother. "You said Jack saw from her notes that the girl had a history of drug abuse and depression."

"God, yes. That's right. And Ian said her modeling career was a total fantasy as well.... And then there was all that stuff she said about Ophelia."

"What on earth do you mean, Mary?" My mother appeared thrown by the reference to Shakespeare. I'd forgotten that my artist father had been the one to encourage my interest in drama and theatre, while my mother's passion was always for facts, not fiction.

"Ian made us all analyse the characters we're playing in *Hamlet* and say how we personally related to them. Rachel got quite agitated when it was her turn, she talked about Ophelia being misunderstood and mistreated, controlled by her father and not taken seriously. Then she said some weird stuff about not getting the attention she needs and having to do things that other people thought were mad – till it kills her. Oh god!"

Concern ravelled the fine lines that traversed my mother's forehead.

"I think you should find out from Jack, now, whether this girl is the one alleging the assault. If she is then you have information that no General Medical Council investigation is going to uncover. And there could be more implications for the child even, than for Jack himself. He may have inadvertently shattered an emotional construct that this girl was using as a lifeline to manage her delicate mental stability. Go and ring him in the study, darling. And give him all my love and encouragement."

———

"So was it mad Ophelia?" asked Venetia, voicing the curiosity manifest on all four of my friends' faces.

We were sitting in the mid morning sun outside Café St Germain while the buses rumbled in and out of the bus station opposite, spewing passengers and exhaust fumes onto Crystal

Palace Parade.

"Rachel Jackson is the patient's name, and Jack says she had long fair hair, so I guess that's pretty conclusive. I never checked her surname on the *Hamlet* cast list, but I'll ask Ian as soon as I get back."

There was no way, I had realised, that I was going to be able to get through a coffee morning with the girls and not tell them about the most significant issue in our lives, so on the phone from my mother's I had asked Jack's permission to share his predicament with them.

He had agreed, reluctantly at first, then admitting that he could have no stronger group of supporters.

"What sort of legal counsel is Jack getting?" asked Suzy, whose husband, Duncan, was a senior partner in one of the top solicitors firms. "The Health Centre must have its own legal representatives."

"He's rung his medical defence organisation," I assured her. "They would pay for the costs of an appeal if he's found guilty by the GMC investigation, but so far they've just advised him to cooperate. When he asked whether he could speak to Alison Wood at Newling and Wood – she's the Health Centre's solicitor – Elizabeth was quite sharp and said it wasn't appropriate in this situation because there could be a conflict of interest."

Suzy shrugged, but looked unsatisfied with this answer. It was Ros's turn to offer her expert advice.

"You know, Mo, you have to consider that this Rachel may have convinced herself that she's telling the truth. Emotionally troubled teenagers can get into situations they don't understand and then try and make sense of it by creating a story to explain it to themselves as well as the outside world," she suggested. "Then the more they're questioned, the more detail they produce to fit the fabrication and they can become increasingly persuaded that this is what really happened. Sometimes even hard evidence to the contrary only bolsters their false belief. Some can become very paranoid and start to believe that they're the only sane person in a mad world."

"Just how Rachel described Ophelia," I muttered, beginning to feel defeated by this depressing information.

"So how do you break into that cycle?" asked Miranda. "It seems to me that Mo is the one who's going to have to take action here. Jack can only cooperate with the GMC investigation, or he will be seen to be trying to influence or undermine the patient. His boss seems unwilling to take a stand and the investigators may not get below the surface, especially if this girl comes over as credibly as Mo suggests."

"Maybe drama is the level you can reach her on," interjected Venetia, surprisingly.

Ros smiled approvingly and waited for Venetia to continue.

"She identifies with Ophelia – her feelings for Hamlet and his treatment of her; how her father controls her, lack of attention and all that. Couldn't you have a girly chat after your next rehearsal, talk about the characters in the play and get her to open up that way. It's a good way to make a point."

"What, like when you were talking to Laura about *The Way of the World* the other weekend?" I asked, meanly perhaps. Venetia had the good grace to look embarrassed. "Mrs Thorne would be delighted to know that her drama lessons made such an impact on you – considering what a hard time you gave her in class."

"Just a thought. Obviously a bad one," Venetia retorted huffily, and turning to Suzy, began a conversation with her about an exhibition at the Dulwich Picture Gallery they had both seen. Miranda got up and went to the ladies, giving me an opportunity to talk quietly to Ros about another worry.

"The weird thing is," I whispered to her, "it seems there was a little girl called Maudie who used to live in our house, and Lily sleeps in what was her bedroom – but there's no way Lily could possibly know anything about that. This girl was about her age in the war, and Lily keeps coming out with these wartime songs and –" my brain made another connection – "even a poem that this child apparently memorised and we certainly never taught Lily. I know this sounds really bizarre, but..." I tailed off and scrutinised Ros' face for signs of scepticism.

" *'There are more things in heaven and earth, Horatio, than are dreamed of in your philosophy'*?" she quoted, looking quizzically at me.

"I can't help wondering if there's something other than her imagination involved here. Have you ever worked with any children like that?" I asked. Ros turned in her chair so the others didn't catch what she was about to tell me, and spoke softly.

"One of my clients was a boy whose mother brought him to me because he kept talking about his past life experiences. I did a lot of research into the phenomenon, which is well documented and for which there is some pretty compelling evidence. The mother also checked out the information the boy gave us and discovered there really was such a person who had lived exactly where the boy said, and that other details he had given were absolutely accurate. There was no way he could have found them out and there was nothing else mentally wrong with the child. I don't think I believe in reincarnation, but there was certainly something outside the realms of clinical psychiatry going on there. Lily's a very sensitive child; perhaps she's tapping into some similar source, some emotional echoes in your house."

Miranda returned from the loo and asked me whether her family was going to be needed for *Time Crunch*.

"At the moment we seem to have our seven subjects signed up and ready to shoot," I told her. "Production starts next week, so fingers crossed that no one will pull out, but I'd be really grateful if you and Si would hang in there as reserves just in case anyone does get cold feet."

"Sure, Mo. We were quite looking forward to it and the

girls will certainly be disappointed if you don't want us. Simon sends his love, of course, and wants to come visit for a weekend as soon as – well, as soon as you feel it's appropriate. I think you have to intervene, Mo, on Jack's behalf. I think we all do, don't we girls?"

I looked around the table at the faces of my oldest friends. It was apparent they all agreed with Miranda.

"You're going to have to do your own investigation into why the girl has behaved like this," said Ros. "The only thing that will clear Jack, as it's pretty much her word against his, is uncovering her motivation for lying."

"That's right," Suzy concurred. "You have to be both detective and lawyer: find the facts and present the case for the defence."

I sighed. "I don't know if I can get her to talk to me."

Venetia looked at me and shrugged. "*'The play's the thing…'*"

'*…wherein I'll catch the conscience of the King*', I mentally finished the quote. I wondered whether, if Rachel was capable of such acts, she had a conscience in the normal sense of the word.

"But Jack won't let me interfere in the General Medical Council investigation," I protested lamely. "He'll be furious at the very idea that I could uncover something that they couldn't."

"Then you might have to keep it a very private investigation," Suzy smiled, though her eyes had never looked more serious.

———

I tried to psych myself into a positive frame of mind about Jack and his problems as I drove home from Diss Station.

After spending longer than I'd meant to with the girls in Crystal Palace, I'd missed the train which would just have allowed me to collect Lily and Grace from school. Jack hadn't sounded thrilled about having to pick them up when I'd rung to let him know, but that was nothing to his views on the school gate experience when I did arrive home.

"Bloody, hell, Mo!" He'd hardly let me pick up Felix, hug Lily and say hello to Grace before his resentment overflowed. "I'm not doing that again. Those women, they all stand in their little cliques, talking about god knows what, eyeing up the other groups. Not one of them gave me so much as a smile, even the ones who I've seen as patients. And the teacher looked very suspicious when I said I was collecting Grace as well. But then I suppose they've all heard that I'm some kind of –"

He stopped, seeing Lily was following every word of his outburst, a curious expression on her face.

"Some kind of what, Daddy?" she asked, inevitably.

"Some kind of idiot," I jumped in irritably. "You do know you're talking rubbish, don't you? They're all perfectly nice, they just don't know you and you don't know them. If you went there looking as grumpy as you do now, I'm not surprised no one smiled at you or talked to you."

"Well, one mum did talk," he admitted. "She was nice – Nina Stone, she said her name was. Four kids and a baby, but she seems to cope well. She told me her grandfather used to live and work up at our house as a farm labourer, then they kicked him out at the end of the war. But he had a lucky break, married a local woman, had some children and ended up quite comfortable. She still lives in his old place; a beautiful old house, but very tumble-down now. Lavender Farm, it's called."

"Normal-for-Norfolk Nina lives in Lavender Farm?" I queried.

"Yes, I told you she's called Nina. She's a real villager. This grandfather of hers couldn't even write his name, but apparently he could make anything with wood."

"Billy Stonepicker," I thought I heard Lily say under her breath, but must have misheard. Jack had more complaints.

"And I got virtually no sleep last night, what with Felix's asthma and Lily's nightmares. You really picked a good night to go off having fun!"

I wanted to defend my working trip to London, but with immaculate self control I stalked outside and took some calming breaths as I took the bag of herbal cures from the car, walked back indoors and gave Felix a dose of Charlotte's tincture.

Only then did I trust myself to speak reasonably.

"Jack, you know perfectly well I had an important meeting to go to and I stayed overnight with my mother, who I don't get to see very often any more. Lily, darling, what did you dream about last night that upset you?"

"Nothing! Can't remember," she shrugged. "Come on Grace, let's go and play Black Beauty."

"She was shouting at someone to stop fighting Grandaddy," said Jack, holding Felix on his knee while I rubbed some of the piquant fatty ointment on his little chest, "which is odd, because she's never called my father that. She must have been sleep walking, because I woke up to find her standing beside our bed, shouting at this imaginary person to let Grandaddy go, but I it took me a minute or two to work out what was happening. I admit I'd had a couple of brandies to help me sleep. By the time I got the light on, she'd gone and when I went into her room she was back in bed. As I went out I could have sworn I heard her say, 'Are you alright, Maudie?', but I must have imagined it. I don't know what's happening to me, hon. I feel like I'm losing it. I hope this investigation's over quickly, because hanging around here doing nothing is doing my head in."

I looked at the state of the kitchen and wondered why men thought that running a house constituted 'doing nothing'. Why he didn't feel the need, nor consider that it was his responsibility, to wash up and clean the kitchen after meals; or pick up dirty clothes and put them in the washing machine?

Why, equally, could I not stand to live with the mess and felt, resentfully, that somehow it was always my duty to deal with it? Still, Jack was a very good and responsible dad, I told myself as he took Felix off to play football in the garden; and the only husband I would want to be married to, even if he had his share of male blind spots and unreconstructed sexism.

I swept the piles of colouring books, pens and pencils, puzzles and newspapers into a pile and prepared to attack the sticky kitchen table top with a wet cloth. As I scrubbed at some dried-on strawberry jam mixed with yoghurt, the edge of a piece of paper sticking out of my copy of *Hamlet* suddenly caught my eye. I pulled it out and looked at the scrappy sheet covered with lines of neat writing. Jack, it seemed, had done my rehearsal homework for me. What had he written?

I discarded the cloth, sat down and read his version of Hamlet's nihilistic soliloquy.

I wish I could just stop existing, or that suicide wasn't such a wrong, cowardly choice. Life has lost all its joy, its interest, its meaning to me. Like our garden, the wild, uncivilized elements have taken hold and it has run to seed – the bad is suckering out all that's good, and life seems gross, as Lily would say. I can't believe it's come to this for me.

Then there's my mother, once so in love with my father, who must have been an exceptional man and adored her. But she has no moral strength, perhaps women don't (how can that girl lie about me like that?). She talks about how she mourned his death, what a tragedy it was for her, but then she married a man nowhere near his equal and look at the result. She's less of a mother than the beasts in the field; she takes his side against mine when I most need her.

No good has come of this move and it breaks my heart. But there's nothing I can say to put things right.

I put the torn page of the exercise book back where I had found it and mechanically started to swab at the table again. It wasn't a very accurate translation of Shakespeare, but it told me clearly enough that Jack was at the end of his tether, had probably contemplated suicide, felt Kathleen's lack of support like a dagger in the heart and believed that our move, and the investigation, would end in tears. And that there was nothing he could do about it.

Well, if he felt powerless to act, it was, as the girls had urged, down to me.

I would take on Rachel at our next rehearsal tomorrow night.

———

I arrived early at the village hall guessing, rightly, that Ian would arrive in advance of the actors. He greeted me from the stage, where he was pacing about, making chalk marks on the floor.

"Greetings, Mo. I'm just marking out the set – we'll play the interiors up here and the exteriors down in the auditorium. I'm having a scrim made, a sort of netting blind that we can have front and back projection on, and some other exciting effects which you'll see in due course. Did you read Aunt Dottie's diary?"

"Straight through, on the train. It was fascinating," I told him. "I can see why it's inspired you with *Hamlet*, but what happened to her and the other people she wrote about?"

"Oh, Aunt Dottie and Uncle Jackie made a reasonable living out of their herbal cures business – and her agricultural experience was put to good use growing their crops. He died before the alternative therapy boom started, but eventually Aunt Dottie was able to sell off the company at a huge profit. They never had any children, which was sad for them I think, so all her money came to me when she died a few years ago. My father, who was her brother Douglas, and my mother Yvette, had long since passed away by then. They never got out to the States to see her, but I did. I got quite close to her – though she was a funny old stick and would never talk much about her life in England before the war. The first I knew of these goings on was when I found the diary among her papers."

Ian surveyed his designs on the stage, rubbed a chalk line out with his foot, and started again in a different place.

"After the war ended my parents built up Black Carr House into a proper care home, mainly for war veterans at first, but then for the local elderly. Dad never recovered the full use of his legs and he died when I was in my twenties. Mother soldiered on alone, but she finally sold the house and the business and ended her days as a resident herself. Now it's part of a chain of residential homes, but it's still Black Carr House and serving the Haddeston community, which is what they would have wanted. And I use some of Aunt Dottie's money to finance the Haddeston Players, and other local projects from time to time."

I took a moment to digest this information.

"And what about the other people in the diary? What happened to them – the Jackson family, and their farm? And the Newlings? Newling and Wood did our conveyancing and they're the Health Centre's solicitors...." I faltered, realising I'd never said anything to Ian about Jack and the Health Centre and probably shouldn't raise it now. But he didn't notice my slip and talked on as he re-drew his ground plan.

"Well, James Stewart's career is history, but did you realise that Uncle Jackie's comical Russian friend, Walter M, went on to become the actor Walter Matthau? Yes, the 453rd was quite a star-studded unit!

"And the family? My Great Aunt Philly and her friend Anne Pringle – they were a sweet old lesbian couple, devoted to each other – lived in Haddeston Rode and died within weeks of each other at a ripe old age. They understood when I came out – about the only members of my family who did.

"Then poor Granny, Dottie and Douglas's agoraphobic mother, stuck her head in the gas oven a couple of years after the end of the war, and my parents brought my grandfather to live at Black Carr House. He was a dear old chap and I was fond of him. He had a lot more to him than Aunt Dottie gives him credit for in her diary.

"But as for the Jacksons, I've no idea what happened to them. Aunt Dottie said none of them ever contacted her again, which she felt badly about. I left the Haddestons when I went to university and came back as rarely as I could for a good many years. Then I got my job at the University of East Anglia, inherited Aunt Dottie's money and felt it was time for me to come home. I don't think I'll be moving away again."

Ian finished marking out, pocketed the chalk and jumped down off the stage.

"So you don't know where Jackson's Farm is, or was?" I asked. Ian shook his head dismissively.

"No idea. It's all water under the bridge and although it makes a good setting for *Hamlet*, Aunt Dottie was always a bit melodramatic and you have to take what she said with a large pinch of salt. I should think they're all long gone by now."

"But isn't Rachel's surname Jackson?" I pushed. Ian nodded. "She could be related to the people in the diary, couldn't she?"

"It's a pretty common name, Mo. And what difference would it make if she was? The poor girl's got quite enough problems with her own parents, without looking for more mad relations – '*How now, Ophelia! What's the matter?*' " he called across the hall, as Rachel herself pulled open the door and walked over to us, carrying a large cardboard box in her arms.

" '*O! my lord, my lord, I have been so affrighted!*' " she laughed back, pleasing Ian with her command of the text.

Wearing a pretty floral dress in a retro style with her blonde hair tumbling round her shoulders, she looked wholesome and uncomplicated; far from the psychotic, junkie goth I had been building her into in my mind.

"You're going to love what I've got for the exhibition," she told us excitedly. "And have a look at this, it's my grandad's Home Guard uniform. Tom could actually wear it as his costume!"

———

Jacksons Farm
The Street
Great Haddeston
Norfolk

Friday, February 15th 1946

My dearest Dottie,

I trust this letter finds you in America, safely settled with Jackie now the war has ended, even though we have not heard from you all this time. I hope we will see you in your new home for ourselves one of these fine days.

Sad to say, things are not so good with us. I know, Dottie, that it will give you clawth to learn the reason for our troubles is my dear Pa's sudden death just afore Christmas last. Elijah Archibald Jackson, which was his full name, was found dead of a heart attack in the farm office on Wednesday December 19th 1945. The safe was open and papers and bank notes scattered around. A deal of money and the deeds to the farm were gone missing. Poor little Maudie was the one to find her Grandaddy, and has been in a misery ever since. I do not know if she saw anything of what happened to cause his passing, but she cannot speak of it at all. Pa did always have a soft spot for you, Dot, and I recall you once saying he was 'a big pussycat'.

Archie first blamed Billy Stonepicker, as I do still, for attacking Pa and thieving from him when he was at the weekly accounting. Archie threw him out, and Billy was lucky to be taken in by Henry's uncle at Lavender Farm, though I did warn them off him. But then my brother found the receipt for the £60 that Pa gave me and Henry as a wedding gift, so we could invest in Jackie's herbalist company. Archie has accused Henry of stealing the missing assets and causing

Pa's death (though he stopped short of calling him a murderer).

But worse did follow. It seemed that Pa had made no will – for there was no sign of one in the office or the house, and Mr Newling swears he had not lodged one with him, though it was not like Pa to be so remiss. So he was declared intestate by His Majesty's High Court of Justice at the Principal Probate Registry, and in accordance with law, Ma and Archie were named his representatives and given joint charge of his estate. But my poor Ma was quite crazed by your disappearance, Dottie, and Pa's death has just about done her in. She has lost all heed of life and become quite buffle-headed, which means Archie has sole care of the farm, or what is left of it. The way he is selling off livestock and land would make poor Pa spin in his grave.

I'll not mardle to you on the brangling between him and my Henry, but just tell you we must leave the village as soon as we are able. Archie is demanding repayment of 'stolen' funds, and refusing me any legacy from Pa. He is backed up by Mr Newling who now says we do have no claim on the estate, nor any rights to be living here at all. When Archie bezzles down the Trowel and Hammer he is ready to lam into whomever he comes across and I fear for our lives, just as you did. To make matters worse, I am expecting again in June and we must find a place to call home before the baby is born.

Henry has laboured on the farm without payment since he was demobbed, so we have no money at all. When it came clear that we would have no part of the family business, he tried his hand at selling country produce down in London again, but he stopped over at your parents' house one night and Mrs Watson next door reported him to the Ministry of Food. He was lucky to get away with no more than a warning.

This will make you laugh, though, Dottie. Your father told Henry that when there was a rations issue of bananas, Mrs Watson's Bertie managed to get a hold of a great bunch. He took his young lady to the cinema and in the middle of 'Brief Encounter' thought he would surprise her with one of his precious fruit. Well, in the dark she thought he was curling her hand around something quite other and shruck the place down! Bertie has not shewn his face at the

Wimbledon Odeon since.

But Dottie, in all truth, we are desperate. Archie has turned the village against us, or if not they are too afeared of him to speak up for me and Henry. And now all the men have returned from war there are no jobs to be had round here, in Norwich, nor in London. Henry thinks he can get work with an old friend in Birmingham, but we have not even money enough for the train fare, let alone to take lodgings there. I would not ask unless I had to, but if Jackie's business is in good kelter, could you send back the £60 to me and Henry by return, or I do not know what we shall do. If you do desire us to join you in America that would be still better, but you would be obliged to forward us the boat fare until we can repay you. Dearest Dottie, I beg you to help us get away from my brother's madness, just as I did assist you.

Your affectionate friend,
Emma.

———

I slid the flimsy sheets of paper, covered with the same copperplate hand-writing as I'd seen in Charlotte's *Culpepper's Herbal*, back into their yellowing envelope, which I turned over and examined carefully. The address in Utah, United States of America, was clearly written, but there was no post mark across the threepenny 'Victory' stamps bearing the profile of King George VI. This letter had never been posted to its intended recipient, despite the urgent request it contained.

I looked up, saw the other cast members were absorbed in picking over the items of Home Guard uniform and paraphernalia which Rachel had unpacked and, without quite knowing why, slid Emma Tinker's letter into my pocket. I closed the lid of the tin tea caddy in which I had found it, replaced it in the cardboard box amongst the other period trinkets and took a sip of the gin and tonic that Ian had bought me when we had come into the 'Trowel and Hammer' for a post rehearsal drink.

"Look, Mo, doesn't Tom look handsome in this?" Rachel called to me across the bar.

She was flushed and excited by the attention her box of memorabilia had produced, especially, no doubt, because Tom had allowed her to dress him in the faded khaki Home Guard forage cap and epauletted shirt with its stripes sewn neatly across the right sleeve. He was parading around the pub with a military air and did indeed look the part, even with his faded denims tucked into the heavy boots and puttees.

I felt a sudden rush of fury that this girl could be enjoying herself without an apparent care in the world, when because of her thoughtless, treacherous accusation, Jack was sitting at home fighting depression.

"Very handsome!" I agreed. "You want to be careful dressed up like that, you'll have all the gays in the village after you." I attempted a smile to suggest I was joking, but Tom, Rachel and Ian all stared at me with varying expressions of surprise on their faces.

I shrugged and stood to leave.

"I need to get home to my husband, Jack. He's a GP at the Health Centre – I don't know if I ever said so before." I saw a shadow flicker across Rachel's glowing face, and hoped I had hit another nerve. "Oh, and Rachel, why don't we have that girly chat about Gertrude and Ophelia, you suggested before? Shall I come over to your place when you're back from school tomorrow? Your address must be on the cast sheet. I think there are some scenes we could usefully work through. See you then – night, all!"

I swept out of the door without giving her a chance to refuse me and found my heart beating painfully fast with the hostility I felt, as I walked home. My sudden rage had made me give too much away, and the subtle use of drama to engage Rachel in personal discussion, as Venetia had suggested, was probably impossible now. I might have no choice but to confront her directly.

I breathed in deeply to calm myself and tried to turn my thoughts elsewhere. Where was the glade they called Lovers Leap that Dottie and Archie, Emma and Henry had stopped off in for their illicit trysts, I wondered? Probably long covered by the post war council houses and modern bungalows which interspersed the older dwellings along The Street. Yet as if in answer, my eyes seemed drawn down a dirt path beside the last cottage in the row, behind which a stand of trees surrounded by a tangle of hedgerow was silhouetted against the evening sky.

And where had the farm office in which Elijah Jackson suffered his fatal heart attack stood? The question seemed to present itself to me, as I crossed the road into our drive, rather than formulate itself from my own thoughts. Once again I felt my eyes directed, this time to our dilapidated barn, the lower end of which housed chopped wood, bikes and outdoor toys, and along to the higher end in which the Landrover and ride-on tractor were garaged. Its stepped roof of moonlit pantiles started to pixilate, and I felt an uncomfortably familiar lurch behind my eyes.

But I fought, and won, the battle to stay in the present.

As I pushed the front door open I was surprised to find our ground floor in darkness. I switched on the lights as I walked through the sitting room into the kitchen.

Jack was slumped over the kitchen table, the drained bottle of brandy stood next to his tousled head and in his hand was an open, and almost empty, bottle of pills.

———

The Manor House, Haddeston Rode, was an imposing, eighteenth century brick building with a well kept, gravel sweep leading up to the porticoed front door.

My mud spattered car looked out of place parked outside the carport in which nestled a classic Bentley, immaculate E-type Jaguar and an angular car which I thought might be a

Maseratti. As I walked towards the house, I noted beyond the expanse of lawn on the far side a swimming pool, tennis court and what might be a stable block – until a movement in a ground floor window diverted my attention. The front door flew open before I had reached the doorstep.

"Nice cars," I said to Rachel, with a friendly smile.

"My dad collects them," she said with an anxious look. "He'll be back soon. What do you want to talk about, Mo? I've got an essay to write and – "

"Nice house, too," I continued breezily. "Must have been a great place to grow up in. Bet you had everything a little girl could dream of, swimming pool, tennis court – did you have your own pony too?"

Rachel stood back as I strode determinedly past her into the large hall, watching me uneasily. In contrast to last night her face was pasty and there were dark circles under her eyes. She looked younger in her private school uniform with her hair tied back, and far more vulnerable.

"Yes, I did. Rosie's still in the stables. She was my best friend. I wouldn't let them sell her even though I grew out of her years ago."

"So the world was your oyster, just like Ophelia, privileged daughter of the Principal Secretary of State, at the court in Elsinore," I pressed on, walking uninvited into the massive kitchen whose open door I spied at the back of the hall. "I could murder a coffee, OK if I put the kettle on?"

Rachel had no choice but to follow me, and took down mugs and instant coffee from the custom built, weathered pine cupboards while I filled the old style, designer kettle and put it on the Raeburn to heat.

"I suppose that's how you can identify with her so well, but why do you think she loses it, goes crazy and kills herself? Is it all for love of Prince Hamlet?"

"*No!*" Rachel's face contorted as she almost shouted the word at me. "No it's not all for that – that's just the last fucking straw! I thought you might understand, but you don't get it, do you? Nobody understands! No one understands anything about my life!"

Her furious outburst was so startling that I spilled coffee granules over the marble worktop. I had hit the nerve I was aiming for, but apparently harder, and certainly sooner, than I'd expected.

"Hey, Rachel. It's OK. Calm down. Tell me what it is I don't get..." The kettle came to the boil in sympathy with Rachel's emotions and I lifted it off the stove to silence the piercing whistle it was emitting. I filled the mugs and took mine to the huge table where I sat nervously, hoping I hadn't unleashed something I couldn't handle.

She paced the kitchen like a neurotic tiger, back and forth between the island unit and the American fridge-freezer, as she struggled to enlighten me.

"Look, Mo. You don't know this place, you've only just moved here. I grew up in this village, with all the gossip and the feuds and the history. My dad's family used to be big in the Haddestons, then they lost all their money and land because some loser married into the family and sold them down the river. My grandad got rid of them, but he had to sell of most of the land and the villagers turned against him. He never really recovered and growing up with that hanging over him made my dad obsessed with getting the family money back and being an important figure in the village again, so he's just always been a complete workaholic. And yeah, I've always had everything I could ask for and more – you probably think I'm really spoiled! But I never had what I really wanted. *Ever!*" she cried shrilly at me.

"And what was that, Rachel?" I asked quietly.

"Love of course!" she shouted. "Just love, that's all. Not that much to ask, is it? My parents don't love me – I reckon I was probably a mistake in the first place. Now they want me to be some kind of trophy daughter: clever, pretty, talented –

whatever, and I'm none of those things. I can't keep up at school, but they just tell me to work harder. I'm not the right shape to be a model and they don't like me acting. They never spent any time with me, never played with me, never read me stories, helped me with my homework. Family holidays were just about being dragged along on business trips and at home it was always nannies and housekeepers looking after me. And I never had proper friends in the village because the other kids all thought I was this snotty, rich bitch. They liked the pool and the pony, but they never liked me. Except Eddie." Her voice softened. "He was always a good friend."

"But you've got friends at school, in Norwich now, haven't you?" I asked.

"Other weirdos like me," she agreed sulkily. "But at least they understand. If my dad knew who I was hanging out with and what I was doing, he'd kill me – and I'm not joking."

"And what about Tom?" I asked. Rachel stiffened.

"He's a bastard, just like all the rest. I met him at a student gig we blagged our way into and he was quite sweet to me at first. But I love him, Mo. I adore him and – swear you won't say anything, because I haven't even told him yet – I'm going to have his baby, so he'll have to love me and look after me, and our baby."

Rachel's eyes had fixed in an intense stare, and the smile playing round her lips was starting to worry me. She had veered off from deeply held belief – though how factually accurate I couldn't tell – into twisted fantasy.

"I see," I smiled back at her, hoping I looked calmer than I felt. "Rachel, have you and Tom ever had sexual intercourse?"

She bridled like a nervous pony.

"What's that got to do with it? It's none of your business." Her features took on a dreamy expression. "What we've done is special. It might not be what *you* call 'intercourse', but I know he loves me and he's given me his baby and that's all that matters."

I gritted my teeth and went in for the kill.

"So, when the doctor told you you weren't pregnant, you must have been pretty angry with him, I guess?"

Rachel's face suffused with colour.

"What doctor? Your husband? He's just a filthy old pervert and you know it! You said so at the first rehearsal, about loving people who weren't morally strong and I knew exactly what you meant. You didn't tell anyone you were married to that ginger" (she pronounced it to rhyme with 'singer', the ultimate insult), "but I'd seen you together in The Close, outside Newling and Wood so I knew who you were."

"But Rachel," I tried not to show any of the fury that was bubbling up in me again. "Why would he lie? He was a doctor just doing his best for a patient and I certainly didn't mean *he* wasn't morally strong. You must know at your age that you can't get pregnant without having sex."

Rachel picked up the cup of coffee I had made for her and hurled it to the ground, where it smashed on the grey slate tiles. As a stream of coffee snaked across the floor, she began stamping on the fragments and screaming in a high pitched voice, "Pervert! Pervert! Pervert!"

Before I could reach Rachel to restrain and calm her, a voice from the hall shouted,

"What the bloody hell's going on in here? Rachel, get to your room right now!"

As Rachel slunk silently out of the kitchen, I turned to the doorway and came face to face, to my horror, with the obnoxious businessman who had knocked Lily off her bike.

"Oh, so it's you causing trouble again," he sneered. "Come to try and get my daughter off your husband's back, did you? She may have her problems, but she's not backing down on that. I'm not having a paedophile in my village, make no mistake!"

"You don't have to - my husband was never a paedophile, and he didn't do anything wrong towards Rachel," I retorted shakily, wrong-footed again by being found in such circumstances and his hostile approach. "And it's not *your* village; we have as much right to be here as – "

"Get out of *my* house and stay away from *my* daughter," he responded grimly, standing back so I could walk past him into the hall. "You can tell your arty farty friends she won't be playing any more of your theatre games, she's got far too much school work to waste time with a bunch of losers on that nonsense."

He stood on the doorstep, hands on hips, and watched me walk ignominiously across the gravel to my dirty little car as if to ensure that I actually left the premises. As I fumbled with my keys, a smart Japanese sports car drove in through the gates and drew up next to the silver four wheel drive which was now sitting on the drive. Out of it stepped Alison Wood, in a black tailored suit with black leather briefcase in hand. She nodded at me across the drive, with an expression that gave nothing away.

"Ah, here's my legal representative," called Mr Jackson. "I hope your husband's got a good lawyer to defend his interests."

I slammed my door, started the engine and manoeuvred my way out of The Manor House, wishing with all my heart I had never entered its grounds.

———

While Colin was taking Lily to school and Felix to the child minder, Betty bustled around, bringing order and hygiene to my kitchen. We had decided that life should continue with as much normality as possible for the children.

Despite the lateness of the hour, they had responded to my frantic phone call with uncharacteristic calm and driven swiftly from Surrey to Norfolk.

By the time they had arrived, though, Elizabeth had been assured by a slurry-voiced Jack and her own examination of him, that he had taken only a couple of Diazepam, along with most of a bottle of brandy, to help him calm down. He had stayed in bed for last twenty four hours, throwing up and sleeping off the after effects of this noxious, but not fatal combination. When he came round properly, I would no doubt have to face his fury at being embarrassed in front of his partner and employer in this way, but the searing shock and freezing fear at finding my husband apparently comatose, or worse, had still not completely worn off.

"Are you sure you couldn't manage some nice scrambled eggs?" asked Betty solicitously. "You need to keep your strength up, Mo, dear."

I shook my head, grateful for her concern, and poured myself another black coffee from the pot.

"I'm so grateful for you being here, Betty," I told her. "Jack's usually so strong. I just haven't known how to help him – although I never realised he felt this bad until the last couple of days."

"He was always the strong one, even as a little boy. Perhaps it's our turn to show him that he can depend on us, dear."

"Even if he won't like the way I go about it?" I asked my mother-in-law, who liked everything to be done properly.

"I know I haven't always agreed with your methods, dear," she replied. "But I've learned my lesson and you must do what you think best now. There's something I have to do, too, and he may not like that either. I don't want to, it goes right against the grain, but it's the right thing – " Betty turned guiltily as we heard a noise in the sitting room next door.

"Is that you, Colin, love?" she called.

"No, it's me, Mum."

Jack shuffled slowly into the kitchen, his face nearly as white as the toweling dressing gown he was wearing, framed by a disheveled halo of auburn hair. His diminutive mother put out her arms and her son walked into them and bent to bury his head in her shoulder.

"I'm sorry. Sorry about all of this," he said indistinctly.

"There, there, shush now, dear," Betty comforted him, gently patting his wide back.

Jack straightened up and turned to me. I braced myself for his annoyance at my over-reaction, calling out Elizabeth and summoning his parents to an emergency that had never existed.

He held out his arms to me.

"Mo. Darling Mo, I'm so very sorry. I didn't mean to scare you, hon. I've been such an idiot. Please don't be angry with me – at least not till I feel a bit better."

As if.

Chapter Nine

Ian's reaction to the loss of his Ophelia was phlegmatic.

I had half expected a theatrical tantrum in response to my doorstep confession, and to be expelled from the production myself. But on the contrary, seeing that I was upset he invited me into his double fronted, bay windowed Victorian home on the border of Haddeston St Michael for a reviving drink.

Relaxing into the soft leather Chesterfield sofa in his academic's study – tastefully decorated in muted warm shades and lined from floor to ceiling with books – I inhaled slowly and deeply and willed myself to be calm and in control. Ian poured two generous glasses of rich, red claret

"You don't need to apologise for this, Mo," he told me, raising his glass to the light before quaffing deeply from it. "I knew Rachel would be a risk when I cast her, but I was just hoping we'd be able to channel her unpredictability into the role, and make her a wonderfully edgy Ophelia while keeping her a bit more balanced in real life. I thought it might be Tom, though, rather than you, who could send her over the edge."

"It was," I told him as the vintage wine flooded my body with warmth and my mind with relief. "And then my poor husband stepped right onto the landmine of Rachel's volatile emotions and they blew up in his face."

I explained about her outburst at the surgery, her father's complaint and the General Medical Council enquiry that was now underway; and how that had led me to go round and confront her under the guise of talking about *Hamlet*.

"I'm even more impressed with your performance as Gertrude," said Ian sympathetically, "when you've got all this going on in your life as well. Don't worry about the play, I think I can fill the role and probably should have gone that way in the first place. But Mo, m'dear, could we have no more gay remarks about Tom, please?"

"I'm sorry," I muttered, embarrassed. "I was trying to see if Rachel had any idea. My daughter, Jess, she knows Tom from university and she said... I really didn't mean to upset him. Or you," I added, suddenly thinking I might have been even more insensitive than I'd realised.

Ian laughed, a little regretfully.

"Me and Tom? Oh no. I've taken him under my wing in terms of his studies, and I'm not saying I'm not fond of the boy. But although he's got over his depression, he's still not sure about his sexuality and the last thing he needs is to think an older man's genuine friendship has to be repaid in any way. He also has a devout Italian family to deal with; they'd love to see him settle down with a nice girl and have lots of babies rather than go into the theatre, which is what he really wants to do, so he has a lot of difficult decisions – just like Hamlet."

"You say he's not sure about his sexuality," I questioned Ian. "Do you think he and Rachel could have slept together – there's no chance Jack was wrong and she actually is pregnant, is there?"

He shook his head.

"I shouldn't be telling you this, and it mustn't go any further, but it might ease your mind if I tell you that Tom's mixed emotions mean he, er, has problems doing the business with either girls or boys at the moment. He has confided in me that much – and I'm sure he would have told me if he'd had a relationship with anyone. And Rachel's a lot more innocent than she makes out, not to mention scared of that father of hers. She's been acting in my productions since she was about twelve. She could be a good little actress, but she's got progressively more unstable and I'd be happy to tell the GMC that, if it helps your husband."

"Thanks, Ian. I'll suggest it," I told him, touched by his support.

He opened a drawer of his leather topped, walnut desk, and pulled out an envelope.

"I found another letter of Aunt Dottie's about how she escaped from Haddeston – I thought you might like to read it as it completes her story. It might take your mind off present day problems for a minute."

I thanked him, put the envelope in my bag, then asked him, as an afterthought, if I could show it and the diary to someone else.

"Of course," he agreed easily. "Just don't let it get lost or damaged, I might do something with it some day. Now don't worry any more about Rachel or *Hamlet.* You get home and sort out that poor husband of yours. I hope to meet him at the first night, if not before."

———

I had pleasurably anticipated a one-to-one catch-up session with Laura when she invited me to bring Lily to play with Grace after school, but Nanny Babs was there, with the kettle on the boil when we arrived.

Then the doorbell rang and Laura went to answer it.

"Oh, I know," I heard Charlotte Tinker's Birmingham twang, and caught sight of Kimberley's blonde mop vanishing up the stairs in pursuit of Grace's dark head and Lily's coffee coloured curls.

"Now girls," smiled Laura, seeing Charlotte's curt nod and my tight smile as we acknowledged each other's presence in the little kitchen. "I thought it would be good to clear the air about any falling out between the little girls at school, but I'm sure that you two need to talk, as well."

Charlotte looked no more enthusiastic about this invitation than I felt. Nanny Babs enticed us to the table with a laden tea tray and words of enlightenment.

"Laura's right, my dears. There are forces and faces from the other side who are willing you together. Shared knowledge can bring release to those who have passed but are not at peace; and relief to those in this world whose lives are blighted by lies and misunderstanding."

Seemingly this struck a chord with both of us.

We sat down mechanically on opposite sides of the table, with Laura between us at the head, as if to arbitrate. For me, Babs' words had alluded to Lily's imaginary friend Maudie, and Jack's situation; she must have hit a reflex in Charlotte's mind too, as her large blue eyes, which had been avoiding mine, flicked sharply towards me with a questioning look.

It was down to me to play the opening move in this game. I felt on safest ground talking about the living rather than the dead.

"Charlotte, I don't know exactly what Laura and Babs expect from getting us together like this, but it's true, I do want to apologise for suspecting that you and Kylie had made an unfair complaint about Jack. I know now who it actually was, and I can explain why I confused her with Kylie," I faltered uneasily, not knowing how my contrition would be received.

Charlotte's pursed lips gave a slight twitch, and then a surprisingly sweet smile illuminated her thin face. She tucked a heavy strand of dark hair behind her ear and leaned across the table towards me.

"Oh, I know. All these goth girls look the same in their makeup, don't they? All hiding from something behind the war paint."

"You know, then?" I asked, astounded.

Charlotte smiled again, with a satisfied air.

"Oh, I know! Not much gets past me in this village, does it?" she said, looking to Laura for confirmation. Laura shook her head, her plum rinsed bob now shiny and swinging again.

"And anyway, Rachel's my cousin, though her lot don't admit to being related to the Tinkers, and she's no better than the rest of them. You wouldn't be the first family the Jacksons have ruined and driven out of the village. They'd get rid of me again if they could, but they know there'd be an outcry if the Post Office closed down and it was their doing. Cowards and hypocrites they are, it runs all through their side of the family."

Two pink spots had appeared on Charlotte's cheekbones during this diatribe, making her look pretty as well as animated. I could feel data shooting down the neural pathways in my brain, but knew I didn't have all the information to connect it together into a coherent configuration. I needed Charlotte to supply the extra links in the chain.

"So your grandmother was, is, Emma Jackson whose family lived at Stargate Farm?"

Charlotte took a gulp of the tea Nanny Babs had poured us, and a bite of home made plum cake to fortify her during the explanation I hoped was finally coming.

"My Gran's parents lived in your house. It used to be a huge farm – they owned most of the land in Great Haddeston, as well as the mill that stood where the Health Centre is now. Their children were my Gran, Emma, and her older brother, Archie. Gran met Grandpa, Henry Tinker, during the war and they got married and had my Auntie Maudie and Uncle Sam and they all lived on the farm together. Then just after the war ended, Great Grandaddy died and it turned out he hadn't made a will, and that money had gone missing.

"Great Uncle Archie blamed Grandpa – Henry – because he was what they called a spiv, and had already borrowed some money off Gran's parents to invest in some American business. But Grandpa always swore it was never him. He said it was

Archie covering his own tracks because he was a mad gambler. Grandpa said he was always placing bets for him on dogs and horses. He said Uncle Archie lost loads that way and he didn't have any money outside the family business so where else could it have come from? But Gran thought it must have been one of the men who worked on the farm that she didn't like. Someone called Billy."

Billy Stonepicker: my mind filled in the missing name. Charlotte drained her cooling cup of tea and continued.

"Anyway, Great Uncle Archie inherited the estate, cut Gran and Grandpa out completely and forced them out of the village, more or less penniless. They went to Birmingham where they just about made ends meet with Grandpa doing this and that over the years. I suppose you'd have to call him a failed businessman; Henry Tinker always had great plans that never came to anything. He ended up as a driving instructor – he'd been a driver in the RAF during the war.

"My mother, Dorothea, was born there. Then not long after that, my Auntie Maudie, who I never knew of course, died. She was the child who had terrible asthma and Gran couldn't get the plants she needed for her herbal remedies in the city. One time Maudie had an attack and they couldn't get her to hospital in time. Gran blamed her brother Archie for Maudie's death, but she also used to say that Maudie died from a broken heart – she loved the farm and the village so much, and hated Birmingham and the school she went to there.

"So then they just had the two kids, Sam and Dorothea. Apparently my mother always felt second best to her dead sister – perhaps that's why she ran away. She was only eighteen when she got pregnant with me, then legged it a couple of weeks after I was born and never came back. So it was my Gran and Grandpa brought me up and were like parents to me.

"Grandpa – Henry – died ten years ago and after that Gran started to get the Alzheimers. After a bit all she could talk about was the farm and Haddeston and wanting to go home and be with Maudie. It was as if she thought Maudie was still alive, still a little girl living here. My Kimberley was born around then – I can't pretend she was planned, and her father was giving me grief, so I thought a move to Norfolk would suit everyone.

"I just wish I could bring some peace to Gran before she dies. "There's things troubling her, even though she's home now, and well looked after at Black Carr House."

So many bells were jangling in my head, I had difficulty deciding which of my many questions to fire at Charlotte first. It was Laura who asked what was perhaps the most pressing.

"So, Charlotte, this Rachel girl who says Dr Jack was feeling her up, how come she's your cousin and nobody knows it?"

"Rachel is my Great Uncle Archie's granddaughter. Archie married Great Aunt Heather after my parents had left the village. We heard tell that he let Jackson's Farm go to rack and ruin, sold off the land bit by bit and ended up with just the house. Archie and Heather were quite old when they had Nigel, Rachel's dad. He took after his father – nasty piece of work, kept up the feud against the Tinker family and all he cares about is money and status."

So… aggressive Archie Jackson had ended up marrying haughty Heather Newling and they had, eventually, produced the nauseating Nigel Jackson. Poor Rachel hadn't stood a chance of normality with those characters setting the scene for the action of her life. But there was one other leading player who had not yet been introduced.

"So who was Rachel's mother, Charlotte? I presume she's not around any more, for whatever reason."

"Oh, she's around alright," Charlotte replied dismissively, "but not for Rachel. Alison and Nigel are both complete workaholics. Alison Wood Jackson is the managing partner of Newling and Wood solicitors. She works under her maiden name because she belongs to one of the founding families. That bloody firm is her life, which suits Nigel because he's completely self-obsessed too. I'd feel sorry for Rachel if I could bring myself to."

"Oh, I see!"

What I saw with sudden clarity was that Alison Wood Jackson did indeed have a major conflict of interest with Rachel's complaint against the Health Centre – daughter v client – which Elizabeth had not seen fit to tell Jack about. And that perhaps Nigel Jackson had been trying to hide their relationship, as well as unnerve me, when he called his wife "my legal representative". I wondered whether there was husband v wife conflict in the handling of this case, and whether it could be used to our advantage.

But it was Nanny Babs' turn to channel the discourse that she and Laura had set in motion.

"And now, my dear," she looked intently at Charlotte, "perhaps you should tell Mo how little Lily managed to upset young Kimberley at school. Tell her what you told me."

Charlotte looked sour at this reminder, and the good will I had sensed growing between us seemed to evaporate.

"I won't be telling you anything you don't already know, will I?" she scowled. "Your daughter saw fit to try and scare mine with ghost stories and insults, when Kimberley was just trying to be her buddy like she was told. It went on for days and Kimmie was having nightmares and all sorts, which is why I went to the Head. I thought it was better that school dealt with it rather than start an argument with you when you'd only just moved here."

"Even Gracie got fed up with the invisible friend who had to have a chair and work next to Lily," Laura chipped in. "But look how well they're all playing together now, good as gold. You should never fall out over your children, they all go through their good and bad phases, and don't forget Lily had just been through a humungous change in her little life."

"That doesn't explain why she picked on Kimmie,"

snapped Charlotte. "Lily said this imaginary child had a secret to tell Kimberley about her grandfather. Then there were all those lurid details about a man being beaten and robbed; quite horrific, really, coming from a child of that age. And of course Kimmie doesn't know either of her grandfathers and nor do I, so that put me in difficult position, I can tell you. Not to mention Lily calling her a little bastard – which is not a word I allow in our house."

I am so sorry," I apologised to Charlotte, shocked by this revelation myself. "That must have been awful for both of you, and I didn't know Lily even knew that word – she's never used it at home."

Nanny Babs fixed me with a piercing look and, as if she was silently communicating with me, an explanation for Lily's uncharacteristic behaviour and language began to crystallise. I wondered if Charlotte would have any sympathy with it.

"I'm not trying to make excuses for her, but it could be that Lily wasn't trying to frighten or upset Kimberley at all. It's pretty bizarre, and I don't know if you'll believe it, but I do have something that might just convince you that Lily wasn't inventing gory tales or name-calling. You see I eventually got her to tell me that her invisible friend is a little girl who seems to live in her bedroom and whose name is Maudie."

———

Colin and Betty were poring over a map of Norfolk spread out on the kitchen table when I arrived home after dropping the children off the next morning. They started guiltily as I came in and Betty began folding the chart along its grid of creases.

"I thought I'd take myself off on a little trip today, if that's alright with you, dear," she smiled brightly at me. "Jack seems much more himself now and Colin's here to help with the children or shopping, or anything else you need."

"Jeeves at your service, ma'am!" Colin clicked his heels and hung one of my scruffy tea towels over his arm in butler fashion.

"We're fine today, honestly. I'm going to be working on *Time Crunch* and Jack's clearing out the sheds, so why don't you both go off and have a day out?"

My parents-in-law exchanged a glance, then Betty replied for both of them.

"Thank you, Mo, but I'm going off on my own today. It's time I stopped being scared of driving in strange places, and I've got an errand or two I need to run. I'll be back in time for tea and then you can get off to your rehearsal, dear. See you later!" And Betty gathered up the map, her neatly packed shoulder bag and waterproof jacket and headed for the front door.

Colin stood at the kitchen window, watching as she got into the car, started the ignition after a couple of false tries and backed carefully out of the drive.

"She's one in a million, is Betty," he said to me with more feeling than I had possibly ever heard in his voice. "I'm a lucky man, and so have the children been, finding a mother like her."

"I know that, Colin," I replied. "When I first met you both I made the mistake of thinking that what you saw was what you got with Betty. But she's full of surprises."

"Well, if all goes to plan she might surprise you again today," he said, tailing off as Jack came into the room and changing the subject abruptly. "Want a hand with the sheds, son?"

Jack looked pleased at the offer and I left them devising a plan of attack on the rubble, rats' nests and spiders' webs they would have to clear out to see what lay beneath.

I took my coffee through to my study to check the shooting schedule that Jane had emailed. The 'Sandwich Generation Woman' programme started filming tomorrow, I realised with a shock, and the first location was listed as Black Carr House, Haddeston St Michael, where Jane and Tamara hoped to get some affecting footage of the confused old lady with dementia, her carer granddaughter and two great granddaughters.

As I worked through the rest of the schedule, I kept turning to look over my shoulder, so strongly did I feel the presence of someone standing behind me. Jack and Colin were out in the barn and I was alone in the house. Or was I? I found myself typing, as if from dictation,

Find tinker and tailor, find soldier and sailor; of rich man, poor man and beggar man, which is the thief?

Was he there, my handsome ghost whose riddle Babs had interpreted to me?

Was it Henry Tinker asking me to put right the wrong that Archie Jackson had done to him and his family? Or could it be the other way round? The twenty first century Jacksons were obviously convinced that it was their branch of the family which had suffered the injustice.

Henry must surely be the tinker of the riddle, and his mother-in-law, Charlotte Jackson, was an impressive tailor according to Dottie's descriptions. Archie was a soldier, and Douglas a sailor. I had found them all, and their descendants, but only through the accident of auditioning for the Haddeston *Hamlet*, no initiative of my own. Or had the spirit of Stargate Farm, or fate, taken a hand in leading me there?

From the various viewpoints, past and present, I had heard in recent days, rich Archie Jackson, poor Henry Tinker and beggar man Billy Stonepicker were the three suspects in the unsolved mystery of Elijah Jackson's missing will and money, and his untimely death.

Nanny Babs had seen in the tea leaves two lives crossing through one house, and an injustice. I had experienced snatches of what seemed like Emma Jackson Tinker's life in Stargate Farm, read about the death of her father and was now embroiled in the ensuing feud that had continued down the generations. Perhaps there was a way that could be resolved, but how would it help Jack in his representations to the General Medical Council? My brain whirred into overdrive and

I realised I was getting nowhere with the work I was supposed to be doing.

———

"Over here, Mo!" called Laura as I arrived at the playground with Lily, who instantly disappeared into the after-school throng of children. She was sitting at one of the tables with Nina, enthusing about the latter's youngest child snoozing in the buggy.

"Alright, mate?" she asked solicitously. "Have you heard anything about anything?"

"Jack's working on his statement for the GMC, in between clearing out the sheds in the barn, and I haven't seen Charlotte since we were at your place. I want to know if she's read the diary before I show her something else."

Laura pointed to the table at the other end of the playground where Charlotte was sitting, talking to Janet Morton.

"Your husband's a nice man," Nina smiled up at me. "I had a good old mardle with him at the school gate the other day. He looked right lost, he did."

"Dr Jack? He's a bit gorgeous, isn't he?" laughed Laura, lasciviously.

"I told him my grandad used to work up at yours in the war when it were Jackson's Farm."

"He wasn't, by any chance, known as Billy Stonepicker, was he?" I asked.

"That's the one. How in heck did you know that?"

I explained briefly about Dottie's diary and then decided I might as well ask what I needed to know without beating about the bush.

"It seems that some people suspected Billy of stealing money from old Mr Jackson, and even having something to do with his death. I suppose it looked odd that he went from sleeping in the stables to owning Lavender Farm," I put to

Nina.

"That was a lucky old devil, but Billy weren't no thief," she told me. "He went to work at Lavender Farm and a few years down the line he got the girl of the house in the family way, so they made him marry her. From what my family do say, I don't reckon old Billy was as simple as he made out. His wife, my gran, was an only child and when her parents died she inherited the farm – and so did he, of course. They must have been at it like rabbits, them two – they had fourteen children and let the farm go to harriage. Now the house is falling down around us, but we got all the beautiful wood furniture Grandad Billy made – beds, chairs, tables, cupboards, and all our Christmas decorations...."

I told her I'd love to come and have a look at Billy Stonepicker's handiwork one day, but was, in truth, far more interested in the explanation for his rise in fortune. Emma Tinker may have suffered from his predilection for farmers' daughters, but it didn't sound to me as if Billy was likely to have attacked and burgled his employer.

"Go and have a word with Charlotte," advised Laura. "Might as well get it over with."

I walked over as nonchalantly as I could to the other table. Charlotte and Janet both stared up at me and I couldn't tell whether the severity of their expressions was due to the sun in their eyes or their attitude to me. I sat down beside Charlotte, feeling like an intruder.

"I read the diary," she said abruptly. "I was just telling Janet about it. I never knew that Maudie wasn't Grandpa's daughter, but Maurice Newling's. Or, of course, that Gran had been raped by that evil old – there's no word bad enough for him! They never spoke about that, nor told me how romantic their courtship was, although they adored each other right up to the end."

"I'm sorry if it came as a shock," I offered feebly. Charlotte ignored my excuse for an apology.

"So what you're saying, Mo, is that you believe my Auntie Maudie is your Lily's imaginary friend?"

I shrugged.

"I'm not saying it's not possible," she continued, "but I don't see what Maudie could possibly have to say about either of Kimmie's grandfathers."

"But that's just it," I said. "If any of this is true, it wasn't about Kimberley's grandfather, but Maudie's. She was apparently the only witness to his death – although she could never speak about it while she was alive. Look at this." I fumbled in my bag and handed her the letter I had failed to replace in Rachel's box of memorabilia. "I didn't want to give this to you before, in case you didn't, well, make the same connections I did."

"But this is Gran's writing!" Charlotte looked shocked as she unfolded the letter and started to read. As she fell silent, Janet spoke quietly to me.

"I hope you don't mind, but Charlotte let me have a look at that old diary, as it had references to my family in it. I can tell you that there was gambling for very high stakes going on at the Hall during the war years and immediately after. It's one of the reasons I had to, to make the arrangements I have in order to hang on to the estate. Buxton family lore has it that we lost half our land, and Archie Jackson lost considerably more than half his farm, playing poker when they were supposed to be running the Home Guard. And it all went into one person's pocket: Maurice Newling's."

"But his daughter married Archie Jackson," I challenged her. "Surely he wouldn't have taken money off his own daughter and son-in-law?"

"That man was an absolute snake, according to my family," she replied with venom. "He probably cheated at cards, but no one could ever work out how, built up a fortune by selling off the land he won and kept expensive mistresses all over Norwich. Then he left his money in complicated trusts so

Heather and Archie couldn't get hold of it even when he died. But by then Archie Jackson was a desperate, alcoholic gambling addict, so perhaps it was no bad thing. It wasn't until Alison Wood married their son Nigel that she untied all the legal knots and got the capital released. Nigel bought The Manor House with the trust fund money, but Alison's insisted on putting a lot of it back into the community."

The evidence was definitely panning out in favour of Henry Tinker and against Archie Jackson, if the reminiscences of present day Haddeston families were to be believed. But how was I supposed to put right the injustice that underlay all the rancour and infighting in our outwardly tranquil village?

Charlotte finished reading and replaced the letter in its envelope, which she handed to me. I shook my head, seeing unshed tears sparkling in her large eyes.

"It's your grandmother's letter. You should keep it. I don't know how it got into Rachel's family's possessions – it was obviously never posted."

"It's typical of Gran, just the way she speaks, and to be telling rude banana jokes even when she's in such a terrible pickle." Her smile made the tears overflow the crows' feet at the corners of her eyes, but then an expression of pure anger overtook Charlotte's face. "There's only one explanation – Archie got hold of the letter before it was posted, and Gran would never even have known. No wonder her friend Dottie never answered her; Gran was always sad about that. What happened to this Dottie, does Ian know?"

I suddenly remembered the other letter he had given me lurking, unread, in my bag.

"Hang on – " I rummaged among the other detritus of my life and pulled out the envelope with its American stamps. Charlotte and Janet moved in close, either side of me.

"Not known at this address. Return to sender," I read. The words were written in laboured handwriting over Dottie's neat script which had originally addressed the envelope to Mrs H.

Tinker at Jackson's Farm. I extracted the letter and spread it on the picnic table. The three of us read:

156 Duck Spring Drive,
Mount Pleasant,
Utah, USA.

February 15th 1946

Dearest Emma,
I am afraid you did not receive any of my letters from war-torn France, as I had no reply from you whilst I was in Paris, but I trust this will reach you safely at the farm through the United States Postal Service. The most important things to say are that Jackie and I are married and we have incorporated T W Herbal Remedies (the T is for Tinker and the W for Warzynski, but we thought the two names in full too much of a mouthful!) and business is booming, as they say out here. I have sent, under separate cover, the certificate of incorporation and shareholders' register, which shows you and Tink to own 25% of the shares, Jackie and I 51%, and the remaining 24% held in small denominations by other friends and relatives of Jackie's who have each invested a few dollars. We are keeping our fingers crossed that in a few years' time we shall all be drawing substantial dividends from the profits, if not living in the lap of luxury!

The remedies, and other products, based on your recipes and those of Jackie's grandmother, have found great favour with the folks who have purchased them. Our market is a local one so far, but we have high hopes of extending sales across the US of A over the next few years. I know, Emma, how wedded you and Maudie, especially, are to Jackson's Farm and Gt Haddeston, but if you would like to join me and Jackie in TWHR and Utah, there is a place for you, Tink and the family here. I believe you would enjoy this life: you could devote yourself to herbalism, Tink would make an excellent salesman for our products and the children would soon make friends. You have only to say the word and Jackie will wire the money for your journey here to a bank in Attleborough. Do come, Emma. I am very happy with my darling Jackie and have grown close to his family, but I miss you, Tink, Maudie and Sam and we could once again be best pals and kindred spirits if you lived nearby.

I hope Archie and Mr and Mrs J have found it in their hearts to forgive me for my disappearance. Douglas and Yvette who, as you may know, are now engaged, tell me they stay well away from the farm in case Archie's rage has not yet subsided and he may have realised that they concealed me at Black Carr House until my escape on the Liberty Run. Aunt Philly and Anne have likewise kept their distance, but only for the same reasons and would, I am sure, welcome a visit from you.

It is nearly a year ago since that fateful journey, but it still seems like yesterday that I said my last goodbye to you at Old Buck. Since I presume you never received my letters from Paris in which I told you what had happened to me, I will quickly outline the events again.

After the children had finished eating in the Mess Hall, I slipped off to Jackie's hut while they were watching Walter M perform his conjuring tricks. There we said a fond farewell and I dressed in my Land Girl's uniform for warmth and Jackie's leather flying jacket, with my red Mere Noel costume on top. I joined Reuben B (resplendent as Pere Noel), Major Tom O'D, the crew, journalist and photographer, and we climbed through the bottom hatch into the belly of the Liberty Run. I had never been inside a B-24 Liberator before and was amazed at the size of its interior and all the equipment it contained – not just the cockpit with its two steering wheels, and green bank of dials, buttons and handles, but running back from that, on both sides of the plane, the mass of radio and radar equipment, oxygen cylinders, gun turrets, ammunition, wiring, tubes etc. There is only just room for the normal ten man crew and we were an extra three on that flight. Because of that, and as we were on a peace mission and in no danger, they put me up in the top gunner's seat, where I sat under the glass dome on a swivel stool and had a three hundred and sixty degree view of our journey over the Channel and Northern France.

But I am getting ahead of myself, as this did not take place until early on Christmas Morning, not Christmas Eve as intended. I do not know if you and Maudie stayed to see the Liberty Run take off, but half way down the runway, the wet conditions made the plane slew off course and into the mud, where it ignominiously stuck! We had to disembark and I ended up staying the night, most illegally, in Jackie's hut (which was not such a tragedy!), then we took off again early the following morning, after a large breakfast and a humorous briefing session from Jimmy S. ('Life' Magazine here devoted its front cover and a long article to his home-coming in its September issue last year. It was strange to see him fêted as such a star, when we had known him so well in the' Trowel and Hammer', and seen him as a pawn in Heather's clutches!)

We arrived at Paris in just over two hours, and distributed all the home made presents to the three hundred or so French children selected by the American Red Cross, who were grateful, if somewhat bemused, by this offering. At the end of the ceremony, to my relief, Jackie's cousins, Valentyna and Andrzej, turned up to take me back to their small appartment in Montmartre, where I lived with them and the rest of their family until August 1945. I helped Valentyna look after the appartment and children, and with the sewing, washing and ironing she took in to make ends meet, while Andrzej, who is a talented musician, earned money by playing piano in cafés and clubs.

They are now living down the road from us and back in the bosom of the American Warzynski family. During the months in Paris, which I thought would never end, my French improved no end and I picked up some basic Polish so I can now converse a little with my mother-in-law in her native tongue. Then finally Jackie was able to arrange tickets for us and we made the long boat trip to America. Imagine my joy at seeing my beloved waving on the quay as we docked, after a separation of nine months!

Once home in Utah, we were married within four weeks and the whole Warzynski family has taken me to their hearts. We are working hard on providing a grandchild for 'Mama', which is what I too call Jackie's mother, and hope to be able to write you soon with the news that I am pregnant!!

Oh, Emma, do come and join us out here – this relaxed, American way of life with all its freedom and convenience would suit you down to the ground, and Tink would get on famously. I have asked Douglas and Yvette to come out, but they are making Black Carr House into a business and cannot leave her old mother. Please write by return to tell us where to wire the money for your fares – and give Archie my best regards, if you dare!

With much love,

From Mr and Mrs Jackie Warzynski! (Dottie xxxx)

"Look!" cried Charlotte, pointing to the date on the other letter. "They were such friends, they even wrote to each other on the same day, Gran asking for the fare out to the States, and Dottie begging her to come. Archie stole one letter, I'm absolutely certain, and I bet this is his writing on the other: 'Return to sender. Not known at this address'. That's why Gran thought Dottie never wrote to her, when she says she did, even from Paris. He stuffed up everything for Gran and Grandpa, when they could have had a wonderful life out there and Auntie Maudie would still be alive. Bastard, bastard!"

I put my arm around Charlotte' shoulder as her rage produced more tears, but Lady Janet looked pensive and turned back to the first page of Dottie's letter.

"Listen, Charlotte," she said briskly. "Save the waterworks till later, we've got work to do. You and I are going to an emergency meeting. I'm sure Mo will have Kimberley for tea and keep an eye on my lot until Graham can come and pick them up. Oh, hello sweetie pie," she said into the chunky old mobile phone she had pulled out of her pocket. "Yes, it's little old me. Something's come up, urgent business. Can you bring the truck and run the children home? Yes, now, never mind the pheasants. I'll explain later. Kiss, kiss."

And with this unlikely conversation completed, she and a bemused looking Charlotte climbed into her khaki green landrover and roared off up the Turnpike towards Norwich.

———

Lily and Kimberley were in an affable mood by the time we arrived home, and took Felix upstairs to play without being asked.

I had handed over care of the Morton tribe to Graham, we had stopped off at Ruth's to collect Felix and I was glad the children weren't around when Jack asked me to look at some of the items he and Colin had found behind the junk they had cleared out of the sheds. The first was a rusty, but nicely fashioned iron door plate, with E. A. JACKSON HADDESTON cast in relief on it.

"So we know for sure that this was Jackson's Farm before it became known as Stargate Farm," I murmured.

"Yes, but look, I think this explains the name change," Jack told me with some excitement in his voice. He held a wooden structure away from the barn wall it was leaning against and I saw it was an old gate: a once sturdy five bar gate with an unusual star shaped design in the centre, now full of woodworm and with a couple of the struts hanging limply where they had become detached from the main structure. I put my hand out to the top rail and felt a pull towards the past, and those who had opened and closed this gate when it had hung, newly made, between our brick and flint gateposts.

But I had learned to resist, and did so now – even when Jack wheeled his last exhibit out of the shed with an apprehensive look on his face.

"I don't quite know what to make of this, or whether to show it to Lily," he said, leaning the ancient child's bicycle against the gate. Its upright frame was rusting under the bubbling black paint, the narrow tyres were flat and the basket attached to the big old handlebars was rotting. But we both knew, without a shadow of a doubt, who the bike had belonged to.

"Here she comes! Betty's home!" Colin came running out of the house from where he had evidently been scanning The Street for the return of his wife. Seconds later, Betty swung their car into the drive and pulled up within inches of Jack's Landrover before stalling the engine and stepping out triumphantly.

"All sorted, love?" asked Colin, embracing her fondly.

"I think so, dear," she replied with a satisfied look. At that moment, Kathleen's sporty BMW pulled through the gateposts and parked in the last remaining space on the drive.

———

There was a knock at the front door as the children were eating their tea and Betty, Colin and I were trying not to refer to what might be passing between Jack and Kathleen in his attic study.

I went to answer it, and was surprised to find a distraught looking Nina Stone on the doorstep with all five children in tow. I invited them in, but was relieved when she refused and instead handed me a large, yellowed envelope with a broken seal on the back flap.

"After we were talking, I went back to ours and had a gander in Grandad Billy's old chest where we do keep all the papers – certificates and that. I didn't think I'd find nothing out of the ordinary, but I then caught sight of this at the bottom and I had a look inside. Oh, Mo, he didn't mean nothing bad, wouldn't have knowed what it was. He couldn't read a word, used to make his mark, couldn't even write his own name. Will we be in trouble?"

I gingerly opened the dusty packet and pulled out an ancient, but official-looking document of thick paper bound with ribbon. The heading read, 'The Last Will and Testament of Elijah Archibald Jackson, Farmer, of Jackson's Farm, The Street, Great Haddeston, Norfolk, this nineteenth day of December in the Year of our Lord nineteen hundred and forty two'.

"Don't worry, Nina," I told her reassuringly, though I had

no idea what the implications of her find might be. "Leave it with me and I'll make sure it gets into the right hands. Of course you're not in trouble – it's nothing to do with you. In fact no one needs to know where it came from, and they won't hear it from me. Go home and forget you ever saw this envelope. I'll sort it, OK?"

Nina nodded, sniffing, and managed a small smile.

"Thank you. We've only got the house and that won't be worth much in the state it's in."

I assured her again that neither she nor her family would be in trouble for her grandfather's misdemeanour, and that Lavender Farm wasn't at risk. I was longing to read the old will and see what Elijah Jackson's true intentions for his property had been, but as I closed the front door on Nina and the little Stones, Jack and Kathleen came down the stairs, smiling and animated. Jack went through into the kitchen, but his mother laid a hand on my arm and drew me the other way into the dining room, where we sat awkwardly facing each other across our big pine table.

"I don't quite know what to say to you, Mo," she began, and I sensed she was pleading for empathy and understanding. "Jack has been very generous and forgiven me for my appalling behaviour of the last few weeks. But he is my son and, luckily for me, he still wants to have a relationship with me."

I couldn't stop a ripple of anxious nausea sweeping through me at the words she had chosen to use, but I tried to smile encouragingly.

"It's taken Betty to make me see a lot of things," Kathleen continued uncertainly, "and some of the things she's told me today have been hard to take, but quite right. I had no idea Jack had been so upset by this complaint, or that my support mattered so much to him. You must understand, I've never been a mother in the true sense, not like you and Betty. Having the twins and their adoption when I was so young shook me to the core, and I never really recovered emotionally. Maxwell has looked after me, like a father in some ways, ever since we were married, and I generally accept that what he does is right. But of course he isn't a parent either. When he told me I had to stay away from Jack while the investigation took place, it didn't feel good to me, but I thought he knew best. He apologises, too, for what it's worth."

"That's OK, Kathleen. As long as you've made it up with Jack and he knows you're there for him, he'll be fine. We'll be fine." I forced the words out, although it didn't feel fine to me at all. Kathleen, to her credit, knew this.

"Thanks, Mo, but we're not fine, you and I, are we? Betty made me see this afternoon – though she was kind and didn't put it in so many words – that I've been very insensitive in the way I've tried to make myself part of the family. Your family. I realise I've gone overboard with Jack, assumed a kind of closeness because of our blood relationship that I now see takes time to build up. And I was so thrilled that Lily liked me that I'd probably pushed the horse riding more than you were comfortable with. Are you very angry with me? I hope you can – " Kathleen pulled a tissue out of her pocket and dabbed her eyes. "I hope you can let me try to do it better from now on."

The angst and jealousy I had harboured for so long, melted away with her tears; I stood and held out my arms. She felt softer and more fragile as I hugged her, than the strong, slim, athletic woman I had imagined my husband to be attracted to. And I remembered that my first experience of the telepathic gift (if that was what it was) which had opened up Emma Jackson's life to me, had been triggered by the search for Jack and Julia's birth mother.

"Kathleen, I don't know if this can possibly make any sense to you, but I do actually understand some of what you've been through. It's like sometimes I can actually get into someone else's head – or rather someone gets into my head – shows me their memories as if it's happening to me. You did that to me when I was trying to find you for Julia. It was as if you were calling me. I had flashbacks of your life, of when the twins' father died. It was scary, but I really do know how you felt."

She looked taken aback by my revelation, and I couldn't tell whether Kathleen had any real conception of what I was telling her, or simply appreciated that I was sharing something very personal with her.

"That sounds quite extraordinary, Mo," she said slowly, processing the information. "I don't know that I believe in that sort of thing, but I'm sure your experiences are very real to you. I don't think you could quite know how I felt, however hard you tried. But perhaps I should take a leaf out of your book and make more effort to put myself in other people's shoes. In fact I promise you I will, if you will work with me. If I'm doing it wrong, causing you or Jack problems or treading on your toes, would you please help me by telling me? Think of me as a mother and grandmother with L-plates on, and not a very promising pupil at that. I could do with advice from more experienced drivers like you and Betty."

We laughed at the image she had drawn, and agreed to be more open with each other, in the interests of our own relationship and our various complicated family bonds, as we went to join the others in the kitchen.

———

As it was a warm and sunny day, Mrs Furness, the pleasantly efficient Director of Black Carr House, decreed that the shoot should take place outdoors in the Rose Garden.

So as to cause the least disturbance, Jane suggested Tamara might interview Charlotte while most of the residents were taking their early afternoon nap, after which old Mrs Tinker could be brought down to sit with her family while the camera rolled quietly in the background.

After Jane had directed the crew about what she wanted, and placed Tamara and Charlotte on a pretty bench near a sundial, I held the clapper board in front of the lens and read out the scene number, time and date.

Tamara was impressive, there was no doubt. She was not only an expert in the subject of balancing life and time, but knew exactly how to encourage her interviewee to reveal the imbalance of their life in a meaningful and moving way. Charlotte, who I had not spoken to since her disappearance with Janet, opened up spontaneously and gave a genuine insight into the stresses generated by being responsible for an adult with dementia while parenting two children; managing the demands of her job at the Post Office and making time for her own interests such as her herbal remedies.

Then Mrs Emma Tinker was wheeled through from her room to join her granddaughter in the Rose Garden. I was apprehensive about seeing what remained of the spirited young woman whose mind I had occasionally inhabited. The frail old lady, with rugs tucked around her legs despite the summer warmth, appeared confused by all the people waiting for her and I wished I could reassure her. Her long, grey hair was loosely pinned in a bun, with one heavy hank at the front hanging loose over her still large, but rheumy eyes. Her resemblance to Charlotte was obvious through the sagging and wrinkled skin, which didn't completely hide the fine contours beneath.

"Hello Gran, it's me!" Charlotte approached her and took the handles of the wheelchair from the nurse. "It's lovely out in the garden today, isn't it? Come and tell me what you've been up to."

Emma's face lit up with recognition.

"Is that you Dorothea? Where's Maudie? Where's Sam?" she asked in a reedy voice. "They mayn't go out playing on the road, not like at home. Too many cars here in Brum."

Jane indicated that the camera man should catch this interaction. Tamara brought over Kylie and Kimberley from where they had been amusing themselves and they joined their mother on the bench next to which she had parked the wheelchair. Charlotte started to explain to her grandmother where and who they were, but Emma couldn't seem to grasp her meaning. She caught sight of Kimberley and stretched out her long, thin hand to the little girl's golden curls.

"Maudie, there you be, little maw," she said tenderly. "Have you took your tincture today, else you'll be gasping again in this weather."

"Say yes," whispered Charlotte, and Kimberley sighed, obviously used to submitting to her great grandmother's whimsical world view.

"Yes Gran, I took it. Mum, can't I bike home now, I'm bored?"

Charlotte shook her head, but this reference seemed to open another window in Emma's befuddled mind, and she addressed Kimberley again.

"That's right. You get off on your bicycle now. Me and Pa will get Dottie hidden in the Bedford; she's waiting for us here in the Rose Garden. Nobody will be looking out for her with the roads packed all the way to Old Buckenham. Where is she, now? Dottie, we've come for you..." Emma called in a whisper, and searched around for someone, apparently oblivious to the people surrounding her. Her old eyes lit on me and relief flooded her face.

"There you be, Dot. We're ready for you, Henry's got the motor running outside. Last trip in the old Bedford."

She stared at me with affection and regret and I couldn't but look back into her deep eyes, which dragged me helplessly, with a sickening lurch, into her world of memory. Now I saw what she saw: the same rose garden, but in winter and empty of care staff and television crew. The girl with the chestnut curls and freckled face ran towards me, wearing a military style greatcoat and carrying a battered hold all.

"Are you sure he has not guessed where you've come, has not followed you, Em?" she asked, and I knew she meant my brother, Archie.

"He's no concern for little children, neither here nor in Paris," I told her. "He won't be joining the jollifications today. Here, pull on this balaclava, wrap the rug around you and we'll pack you round with littl'uns in the back so no one will see you."

Dottie did as I told her and we walked together to the front of the house where the man I knew to be my husband, Henry Tinker, was waiting in the olive green RAF Bedford truck. He winked at my friend and while she quickly climbed into the canvas covered rear, I got back into the front seat next to him, squeezing up close for warmth and comfort.

We set off and turned right from the Turnpike, where we picked up some children walking down the road, into Great Haddeston's The Street.

There an extraordinary sight met our eyes.

We had joined a convoy of green RAF and USAAF vehicles, into which as many small children as could fit were packed and, between them, older children, some with adults, walking and cycling down the village as far as the eye could see. They seemed to be dressed in their best clothes, covered by old-fashioned, ungainly overcoats and jackets, hand knitted scarves and gloves, with peaked caps, bobble hats, woollen berets, felt bonnets and balaclavas to keep out the cold. The noise of their chatter and singing filled the air.

I caught a glimpse of Maudie on her shiny black bike, her blonde curls flying out from under her dark beret. I looked once, and then again, at the girl riding next to her. She wore an incongruous pink quilted nylon jacket and her bike was a modern purple chopper.

"*Bang, bang, bang, bang! goes the farmer's gun.*

Run, rabbit, run, rabbit, run, run, run."

Their voices sang in unison, and as we passed them the two girls turned to wave. I waved back in confusion to my daughter Maudie and my daughter Lily.

I had no time, though, to ponder this apparently impossible trick of time. Behind us, and from all the lanes we passed, came more cars filled with more children from all the local primary schools: Tibenham, Tacolneston, Bunwell, Forncett, Ashwellthorpe, Carlton Rode. They followed us left down Upgate Street, right into Old Buckenham Road, and round the corner of Abbey Road. There we met more vehicles and children heading from the opposite direction of the Old Buckenham and Attleborough schools, and all converged into one steady stream, flowing steadily up the drive and into the Airbase itself.

A jumble of images superseded the clarity of the journey. I guessed the dementia had temporarily disrupted Emma's capacity to retrieve memories, but the flickering collage gave me an idea of what had happened next.

I briefly saw children tucking into a Christmas meal, exclaiming at the ice cream served up to them by khaki clad US Airmen in what I assumed was their mess hall; in a club room, bedecked with red and silver paper chains and a decorated Christmas tree, kids gawped at a scratchy Mickey Mouse cartoon – only Lily looked bored – until the film ended and a man and boy stepped onto the little stage.

I tried to use my own mind to still Emma's jumping thoughts, and felt I had gained some influence over the surge of her memories as she allowed me to focus on the magic show that was now in progress.

"Your wand's broke, Cornelius," shouted a group of kids to the boy who was playing his hapless assistant, but I was trying to see the face of the amateur conjourer. It was, I was sure, a young, black haired Walter Matthau, his baggy features unmistakable even before fame had made him a public figure. His trademark (to me) grimaces and pretend grumpiness were keeping his young audience in stitches.

But now Emma's recollection seemed to move into fast forward and suddenly we were standing outside on a windswept airfield. Some fifteen hundred children, I estimated, were gathered around a big World War Two bomber parked on the runway. A dais had been erected beside one of its huge metal propellers and against the plane's nose, on which had been expertly painted the name 'Liberty Run' and a fat cartoon Santa holding British, American and French flags.

"Welcome, to Old Buckenham Airbase and the 453rd Bomb Group," cried the MC Airman into the old-fashioned ribbon microphone. "Have y'all had a good time?"

The children yelled their ear-splitting appreciation.

"Did Santa bring y'all a stocking?"

"Yes!" they yelled.

I realised I was standing behind Maudie and Lily with a hand on each of their shoulders. Maudie turned and showed me the bar of Sunlight soap, the packet of Wrigley's chewing gum and the shiny shilling piece that Father Christmas had presented her with. I wondered which generous US airman had donated his PX rations to fill my daughter's stocking.

"Now we wanna thank y'all for all the wonderful Christmas presents you've made and donated to the children of Paris. Their great city has been liberated by the Allied Forces, but they're still having a pretty tough time over there, and they sure will appreciate your work and your good wishes to them this Christmas."

There were more cheers from the crowd. Flashlights popped as reporters took shots of the momentous event for their local newspapers. The MC grinned widely and continued.

"All the gifts that we've collected this week from all your schools are safely stowed in the hold of this old flyer, the Liberty Run. You know what? She's flown seventy four successful missions and this will be her seventy fifth. Very shortly the crew, including Santa and Mrs Claus, are going inside her and they'll be flying that precious cargo right across the Channel to Paris, France, so all those kiddies will have a gift tomorrow on Christmas morning. Now, before she takes off, who'd like to write their name and a greeting to our little French friends on the side of the 'Liberty Run'?"

There was a rush forward as all the children pressed to make their contribution to the plane's artwork. Pens and pencils were passed around and the smaller children lifted onto airmen's shoulders to write their autographs on the metal bodywork. The crew walked onto the runway and prepared to board. Father Christmas and Dottie, swathed in a long, hooded red cloak, were hoisted onto the dais to wave to the crowd.

"Maudie, Lily, let's be off," I told my daughter and her friend. "We'll see Dottie again before too long, you'll see. Remember, not a word to your Uncle Archie, else there'll be trouble." We pushed our way out through the crowd and went in search of their bicycles before the whole throng headed in the same direction. I heard the engines rev and looked back one more time. I thought I could see a flash of red and a waving hand in the plane's transparent top gun turret, but I couldn't be sure.

The girls were riding ahead of me down Abbey Road when I heard the familiar howling of B-24 brakes in the distance – but the countryside around me faded and I was back in the Rose Garden, looking at Charlotte holding Emma Tinker's bony old hands and trying to coax her back into the present day.

Some of the other residents had tottered out into the garden to see what was going on, and one shriveled old lady with bouffant, bright blonde hair and erratically applied red lipstick wandered over to the camera crew.

"You're very late," she admonished Jane. "Where's Jimmy? James Stewart, the film star. We're engaged, you know. I wrote and told him only last week that I'd forgiven him and that we were still *made for each other*. He's coming to take me back to Hollywood with him."

Chapter Ten

The dressing rooms at the back of the village hall were crowded with cast members and extras struggling into RAF, Home Guard and Women's Land Army uniforms, labourers' smocks, double-breasted suits, knee-length skirts and dresses, seamed stockings and period shoes and boots.

The women were styling their hair into side partings and rolled bobs, the men combing theirs back with Brylcreem or water. We hummed along to the wartime songs that were playing on a real His Master's Voice gramophone as part of the exhibition of memorabilia.

The dress rehearsal had not gone as smoothly as Ian would have liked so there was apprehension in the air as he came backstage to give us a final pep talk.

"Don't worry, there's a fantastic crowd out there, we're packed to the gunnels and they loved the exhibition," he told us reassuringly. "They're all on your side and it was a great idea, Norman, to open with a matinée and have a traditional village fête afterwards. You're all going to be stars! Break a leg and I'll see you at interval. Last call for scene one actors. Places, please."

We fell silent backstage, as the opening sound effects started: the roar of fighter plane engines overhead; the whine of bombs dropping and exploding; the clatter of AckAck guns; screams and the crackle of flames; distant sirens. Then the first lines of the play, delivered in an almost totally dark auditorium, lit only by flickering orange lights like faraway fires, throwing the spigot mortar on stage into occasional relief:

"*Who's there?*"

"*Nay, answer me. Stand and unfold yourself.*"

"*Long live the king!*"

The exchange could have been written for a 1940s Norfolk scenario, and I envisaged the actors in their Home Guard uniforms, clicking on their heavy, wartime torches to light each other's faces as they continued the dialogue. They were not on the stage but the floor below it, beside the classic RAF, olive green Bedford truck that Ian had, with some difficulty, parked there. Despite his first night nerves, Clive the butcher's resonant voice made the Ghost's first appearance, backlit behind the scrim, a hair-raising moment, and the audience gave an audible gasp.

As the first scene drew to a close, I stood in the wings with Graham, Norman, Eddie and Tom, waiting for our first entrance. I was delighted with the fitted dress, jacket and matching hat and shoes that Janet had found in a trunk of old clothes at Haddeston Hall, and not too nervous about forgetting my lines. She had invited me round on the pretext of a rummage for costumes, and Lily had been excited by her first chance to explore the rambling old house. One real reason for our invitation, I suspected, was to make amends for Lily not being invited to Elfrida's birthday sleepover, which, Janet explained, had been motivated by Kimberley's very real upset at the time.

"It's not a problem, I quite understand how it must have looked," I had told her, hoping she would explain where she had taken Charlotte off to after reading Dottie's last letter. As it turned out she was dying to tell me of her success.

"It's lucky I know Alison Wood Jackson as well as I do, and

the truth about Maurice Newling," Janet had started, "or I might never have got her to admit there was an embargoed safe with all his papers in it at Newling and Wood."

Charlotte had been distressed that Archie had concealed Dottie's letter offering the Tinkers a fare to the States, but Janet had been more struck by the mention of another letter containing their share certificates for the original herbal remedies business; the company that Dottie had later sold, according to Ian, for a considerable sum.

As well as more discreditable information about Maurice Newling and a bundle of Archie Jackson's gambling IOUs, the secret safe had yielded a certificate for twenty five original shares in Tinker Warzynski Herbal Remedies in the names of Henry and Emma Tinker. There were also years of notifications of the company's Annual General Meetings, all addressed to the couple c/o Newling and Wood – no doubt fraudulently requested by Maurice Newling.

The most recent communications had been information about the takeover of TY Herbal Remedies, requests to vote on the matter, and finally an announcement that in their absence the buyout had taken place on a majority vote, with an offer to purchase their automatically awarded shares in the new, international parent company.

Alison Wood had been so horrified by the dishonest behaviour of her husband's grandfather and founding partner of her legal firm, that she took responsibility for recouping all unclaimed dividends and selling the now valuable shares on behalf of the Tinker heirs.

The stage lightened, Graham nudged me to take his arm and we strolled on set, every inch the wartime squire and his lady, surrounded by members of their family and household. He was word perfect in his long, opening speech, delivered with a compelling mixture of ingratiation and gallantry which I found easy, in my cat-like Gertrude character, to be utterly charmed by. Eddie had finally found a plausible persona for his patriotic young soldier Laertes, and Norman had nicely escalated his natural tendency towards pomposity and fussiness to present an equitable but exasperating Polonius.

But it was Tom whose acting took the production to a higher level. He looked for all the world like a '40s film star in Archie Jackson's full Home Guard kit, his hair slicked back and sporting a newly grown pencil moustache. For the first time, real charisma radiated from him as he parried the King's blandishments and sneered at the Queen's platitudes. We all raised our game to meet his high-powered performance and by the time he was left alone on stage to deliver his first soliloquy, *"O! that this too too solid flesh would melt..."* the audience was putty in his hands.

I liked to think that Jack's heartfelt translation, which I had passed off as my own in rehearsal, had had some impact on Tom's insight into Hamlet's state of mind, but tonight he made the emotions his own. I stood in the wings and watched the rest of the scene, until I felt something fluttering beside me. It was the sleeve of Ophelia's Land Girl Aertex t-shirt; she was shivering with stage fright.

"Deep breath, you'll be fine," I whispered, as Eddie took her hand and led her on stage for scene three. And indeed she was – sweet, innocent and out of her depth as the role required – but it was not until the start of the third act that she too really came into her own. After another intensely moving speech from Tom, the famous *"To be, or not to be: that is the question..."* Kylie sauntered on stage looking luminous, despite the unflattering uniform, her dark hair dramatically framing her pale face and deep blue eyes, and was every inch *"The fair Ophelia!"*

"Nymph in thy orisons Be all my sins remember'd," Tom greeted her seductively. For a split second my head spun as I remembered another handsome, moustachioed man in uniform uttering those words to me in another life, but I was held in the moment by amazement at the evident sexual provocation with

which Kylie imbued her simple response:

"*Good my lord,*

How does your honour for this many a day?"

I saw in a flash that the electricity that sparked on stage between her and Tom went beyond acting. They lit each other up like lightening in a dark sky and sent shock waves into the audience. There was nothing confused about his response to her, and Kylie was light years from the shadowy teenager in monochrome makeup I had first met. Their dialogue crackled with energy and intensity and Ophelia's final speech, the one I had auditioned with, lamenting Hamlet's state of mind – "*O! what a noble mind is here o'erthrown*" – had the audience on the edge of their seats with empathy and compassion for the rejected girl.

As she came off stage, I went to congratulate Kylie on her performance, but Tom reached her first and within seconds the two of them were entwined in a clinch, their lips crushed together, their hands glued to one another's bodies. I had to tap Tom on the shoulder to get him back on stage for his next scene with the ENSA Players. Those of us listening to the action off stage couldn't help smiling as we heard him deliver his instructions to the acting troupe in an all too accurate imitation of Ian's directions to us. I crossed my fingers that Ian would also find it funny, especially when taken in conjunction with Tom's evident heterosexual feelings for Kylie.

The two of them made even greater play of this while watching the 'play within the play'.

When Tom asked suggestively, "*Lady, shall I lie in your lap?*" I felt Kylie might just grab him again, instead of responding with Ophelia's modest "*No, my lord.*" It wasn't original, but Tom's emphasis produced a ripple through the Haddeston audience when he asked her "*Do you think I meant country matters?*"

Despite the pace and power the cast was achieving, and the positive response from the audience, I became increasingly nervous waiting for my big scene with Hamlet in 'the Queen's Apartment' – a chaise longue to one side of the stage, lit in subtle shades of pink. Norman led me on, his fussing as Polonius giving me a chance to steady myself, till Tom's call, *"Mother, mother, mother!"*

My thoughts went out for an instant to Kathleen and Jack, both watching the play, but focused back immediately at Tom's appearance and question: *"Now, mother, what's the matter?"*

So sure was this young actor tonight, and immersed in his role, that he carried me with him and I didn't even worry about forgetting the lines that had kept eluding me in rehearsals. He enabled me to feel genuinely abject when I told him:

"Thou turn'st mine eyes into my very soul;
And there I see such black and grained spots
As will not leave their tinct."

I had felt much like this when I had finally admitted my jealousy of Kathleen and suspicions of their relationship, to Jack. He had been horrified by the idea that I had believed even a latent sexual attraction could have flickered between him and his birth mother, and I felt foolish and small.

"Being suspected of being a parentophile, whatever the word is, by you is worse than being thought a paedophile by the GMC," he had told me. "If *you* don't trust me, who on earth else would?"

"I'm sorry," I muttered. "I'm just insecure sometimes. I'm older than you and Kathleen's very attractive."

"She's sixty and the mother who gave me away as a baby! You're my wife, the mother of my children and the centre of my world. There's no contest there."

"But you seemed to want to spend more time with her than with me. I felt pushed out, unwanted, and what with Lily and the riding stuff…"

Jack told me that whatever my mother's academic research showed, he had not fallen in either love or lust with his birth mother when she appeared in his life.

"You know how careful I am with my emotions, hon," he said. "I don't do falling in love at first sight, except perhaps with you, though I admit I was confused. I'd refused to think about it at all for so many years, pushed it away. I didn't know what I felt about having another mother and I needed time to work it out, to see who she was, to see who I was in relation to that. And it was something I had to do alone."

I looked puzzled. Why could he not have shared his feelings with me if I was the centre of his world? Again, his explanation was honest and poignant.

"You're very strong, Mo. I felt I'd just end up taking on your views of Kathleen when I needed to form my own. And to be truthful, I also felt for Kathleen – there you were, a mother four times over, and totally comfortable with it. She didn't know how to be with me, with the children: she needed time too. I didn't not want you around, but I couldn't find the words to explain, without hurting you."

"You idiot! You only had to say and I would have understood," I had assured him, though not entirely honestly, as I put my arms around his neck.

"I felt I'd done everything wrong by dragging you to the country and stuffing up with a patient," Jack had replied, holding me close. "But then you sorted a life for yourself here and I was just bringing you down. I felt useless, hopeless, and that perhaps the adoption had screwed me up after all. It all came together at the wrong time and for a bit, I just didn't know who I was any more. I'm sorry for being an idiot and so weak. But I did do your positive goal setting, affirmations thing."

And Jack had grinned as he pulled a worn sheet of paper from his pocket, unfolded it and handed it to me to read.

I am the husband Mo wants me to be and she loves me as much as I love her

I am making a good life for my family in the best place for us to be

I am a good son to all my parents, who all get on well together

I am cleared of all charges by the GMC and the Health Centre

I am Managing Partner of the Haddeston Health Centre

I had raised my eyebrows at the last one.

"Great, that's very positive goal setting. You will be, too. I have every confidence in you, Dr Patterson and you are everything I want you to be. But no more brandy, OK?"

"Not a drop, ever again," he had murmured as he put his lips on mine and we had kissed as we had not for a long time...

"Good night, mother." Tom's closing words vibrated with tenderness, even though he was dragging Norman's prostrate body along the stage. The audience applauded long and loud as the interval lights came up and there was a moment of stillness before people started to rise from their seats and head towards the cups of tea and home made cakes the Haddeston Women's Institute had laid on.

I caught Tom having a smoke outside the back door, this time on his own.

"I just wanted to say congratulations, you're amazing today. And sorry about the uncalled for remark in the pub."

He smiled, put his arm round my shoulder, gave me a cuddle, which I didn't find at all unpleasant, and blew smoke peaceably towards the blue sky.

"Kylie's a lovely girl," I ventured.

"My mum and dad'll love her, too." He suddenly looked young and vulnerable again. "They're still very Italian even though we've been here since the '40s. My *grande nonno* was a prisoner of war from Sardinia. He got beaten up by the farmer he was working for and escaped, hid out till the war ended and then married into the Italian community here."

"What was he called, your great grandfather?" I asked. Tom looked surprised.

"Flavio Orru – why?"

I shrugged. "Let's go back inside. Come and meet a friend of mine who's watching the show, he said he'd pop back stage in the interval."

———

Joe and Ros had already made their way to the dressing room and she was standing at the door watching in amusement the effect her partner was having on the female cast members.

Joe's intermittent role in a nightly soap opera had made him a minor celebrity over the last couple of years and now he was playing his on screen, lovable rogue character for all he was worth. He looked up from signing autographs when he saw me and came over to embrace me.

"Great Gertrude, babe. You should be on the stage, Mrs Patterson."

"Not me, Joe, I'm only just managing to remember the few lines I've got. But… ?" And I jerked my head at Tom who was standing, awestruck, behind me.

"Yes, indeed," said Joe quickly. "That is some performance you're giving out there, mate. And I'm not just saying that. I'd like you to come and audition for a small, but professional, role in a new play I'm directing next month. If you don't have other plans, that is?"

Tom's face lit up.

Kylie's dropped.

Ros, ever the psychotherapist, noticed.

"You'll need an assistant stage manager and an understudy for all the girl's parts, too, won't you, darling?" She asked Joe, indicating Kylie with her eyes. He caught on immediately and included her in the possible plans.

Ian came in and shook hands with Ros and Joe, trying to hide his delight at both the success of his production and the congratulations of a well known actor.

"Act two beginners," called the stage manager.

Our guests slipped out and we were back into role.

The second half, shorter than the first, picked up even more pace. The audience lapped up the fights and death scenes. Some cheered Eddie's RAF uniformed Laertes in his quest to avenge his dead father; others cried at Kylie's mad, sad Ophelia. But Tom held all their attention with his very sane, totally single minded and blisteringly angry Hamlet, intent on razing the evil around him to clear the way for a fresh beginning.

For the first time, too, I understood how his aunt's chronicle of death and destruction, even in one small corner of England, had fired Ian's desire to expose the futility of war.

Tom, as he had been directed, made Hamlet's attempt to galvanise himself to action after being told of a war over a territory not big enough to bury the casualties, a lacklustre effort. His

"O! from this time forth
My thoughts be bloody, or be nothing worth!"

was intentionally unconvincing. His ultimate revenge, and its unintended carnage, was a strong anti-war image for those who could, or would, see its significance.

The parallels were not one to one, but Ian's visionary Second World War background for Shakespeare's masterpiece made perfect sense in this village setting. His final scene, in which all the bodies, including mine, were laid in the canvas covered back of the Bedford truck and driven out of the double doors in the side of the auditorium to strains of The Last Post, achieved an emotional climax that was almost tangible. The applause was long, loud and heartfelt, especially for Tom who we pushed forward again and again to receive the adulation he so well deserved.

———

As I changed out of my formal costume into jeans and t-shirt, wiped off my penciled eyebrows, thick foundation and dark lipstick and reapplied lip gloss and mascara, a steady stream of family and friends came backstage to say hello and congratulate the cast.

Jess hugged me and whispered that she'd seen a whole new side of Tom on stage. I showed her my good luck cards from my mother, Mark and Zoe, Suzy and Duncan, Miranda and Simon, who were all coming to next week's performances.

Betty and Colin, Kathleen and Max, an unlikely foursome, had sat together and seemed to have unexpectedly bonded.

Venetia's praise was fulsome for her and I was touched when she said Kylie's Ophelia had been only a bit better than my student performance. Nick looked proud when she waved her left hand at me to show off the flashing diamond engagement ring, and whispered thanks in my ear as he kissed me. I only felt slightly apprehensive when Venetia told me she was going to look for Laura, as they went back out onto the playing field.

Eventually Jack appeared, having rushed off at curtain call to collect Felix and Lily, who had both been at Ruth's during the performance.

"I'm so proud of you, hon," he told me as Lily half dragged me outside to watch the maypole dancing that the school had organised as their contribution to the festivities. "I didn't know you could act, or that there was so much talent in one village."

"So where was your faith in me, then?" I teased him gently.

"Come on, hurry up, Mum," nagged Lily. "We're about to begin. And Maudie's mum's come to watch as well."

I wondered if she was once again crossing between two worlds, but realised, when I emerged into the sunlight, that Black Carr House had ferried a minibus full of residents to enjoy the fete, of which Emma Tinker, in her wheelchair, was one.

We joined her, Charlotte, Laura and Nanny Babs to watch our three young daughters in their white dresses with coloured sashes as they each took hold of a streamer attached to the wheel on top of the maypole.

"I knew you'd be good, mate, but you were fan-bloody-tastic!" Laura enthused, planting a kiss and a lipstick stain on my cheek. "Mrs Talented, or what? Course I didn't understand half of what you were all on about, but that Tom's a bit of alright."

"Thanks, but what about Kylie?" I addressed both her and Charlotte, who was looking pleased and proud. "She was stunning, especially when she only stepped in at the last minute. Tom obviously thinks so too." I gestured to the far end of the playing field where the two were strolling, heads together, arms around each other.

"Damn," joked Laura, "missed my chance! Here they go."

The irresistible beat of the recorded country music got us all clapping along as the girls began their circular dance, weaving their coloured ribbons in and out, back and forth, forming complicated plaits and cat's cradles. I noticed that one streamer was flying loose, as if they were a dancer short, but somehow the wind wove it within the patterns they created. We applauded loudly when they finished, and old Mrs Tinker joined in. As I turned to look at her, I had the hazy impression that a man in a pinstripe suit and a trilby hat was standing behind her wheelchair and Hamlet's dying words came suddenly into my mind:

"*Horatio, I am dead;*
Thou liv'st; report me and my cause aright
To the unsatisfied."

But it must have been a trick of the light, for when I blinked the shadowy figure had gone.

Lily, Grace and Kimberley came running across the field to us, their white dresses flying.

"Did you see Maudie?" asked Lily. "She was dancing with us. She was the Queen of the May!"

"I saw her, dear," said Nanny Babs kindly. "It's nearly time for her to go. But you must help her, Lily. Tell us what she told you, then she's free."

I could see annoyance on Jack's face and wondered what on earth Babs was playing at in this incongruous situation, and how Charlotte and Emma Tinker would react to her bizarre suggestion. But Lily nodded and stood in front of the old lady, who seemed to understand what was happening and smiled encouragingly.

"Maudie says," Lily began, and paused, cocking her head in just the way Nanny Babs had the first time she had sat in our kitchen. "She was putting her bicycle away after school when she heard a noise in Grandaddy's office. She looked round the door and saw Uncle Archie. He looked like a robber, pulling out all the papers in the safe. He saw Maudie and she thought he was going to hit her."

She stopped and looked at me, then Jack. I smiled and nudged him. He looked uncertain, then nodded at Lily.

"It's alright. Go on Li'l Girl."

"Maudie's running into the house," she continued, as if she was now seeing the action of her story as it took place, "and she's pulling Grandaddy to come and see what's going on. He's shouting at Uncle Archie and they're both shouting and fighting. Stop it! Stop, Uncle Archie! You're hurting Grandaddy."

Lily's face crumpled with fear and concern. I put my arm around her, but she pushed me away and seemed to pull back from experiencing to observing what was happening in her head.

"Uncle Archie's pushing papers and money into his pockets. He says Maudie's a bloody little bastard. Now he's running off... Grandaddy? Grandaddy, what's wrong, do your chest be paining you?"

Lily was back in the thick of it. She reached out as if to touch someone. Old Emma Tinker took her little soft hand in her arthritic fingers.

"That be alright, little mawther. Don't you be frit. Tha's when you come running for me, in't it, Maudie?"

Lily nodded. "And Billy Stonepicker did come in, but he didn't help Grandaddy. He pick some money and a packet and stuff them in his pocket, then run off again."

"Thank you Maudie, thank you Lily," Babs cut in. "It's over now. You can leave the grown ups to sort it all out."

Emma Tinker sat back with a smile on her face that could have been peaceful, but might have been simply vacant. Lily shook herself as if emerging from a daydream.

"She's gone," she said with a look of surprise. "Gone to join her Pa. Daddy, can you come and do the coconut shy with me?"

Jack stood up and with Lily and Felix headed off to the stands of traditional games. Laura, Charlotte and I looked at each other. Did we believe that Lily had been speaking for the spirit of Maudie Tinker?

Apparently we did.

"She can't have been making it up," said Charlotte. "As far as I'm concerned that's all the proof I need. I agree that Lily probably doesn't even know what 'little bastard' means and wasn't name-calling Kimmie. Well, it's all in the past, there's nothing to be done, but at least I'm satisfied I know the truth. Henry Tinker was no thief."

"But you should get a decent payout from the shares when Alison sorts it out for you. You could send Kylie to drama college and buy a bigger house with more room for your herbs." I turned to Nanny Babs. "Was Henry Tinker my ghost?" I asked.

"Was there truth in the tea leaves?" she asked, sidestepping the question. "I told you when I first met you, my dear, that you had psychic gifts, but yours are with the living. I didn't feel it my place to tell you that your daughter had a more powerful gifting, more like my own. Maudie's been with her ever since you moved into Stargate Farm, I've seen her with Lily on many occasions. But now she's free to pass, and she will."

"Lily may miss her, I suppose," I reflected aloud.

"What, when she's got Gracie and Kimmie to play with? I don't think so." Laura intentionally brought us down to earth. "Time to leave the twilight zone and tell you my exciting news. Your lovely friend Venetia has just asked me – top secret, I'm not supposed to tell you, so don't say anything – to help her choose a tasteful wedding dress, and..." She paused for dramatic effect. "Bridesmaids dresses for you, Jess, Lily and her daughter! I thought maybe shocking pink polyester with lots of nylon lace?"

We laughed and I marveled how marriage, or the prospect of it, had finally mellowed my oldest best friend. She was doing her best to make amends for her destructive behaviour, and seemed to have accepted that my life in the country was what I wanted and where I wanted to be.

———

Betty and Colin set off for home the next morning, with plans to visit again soon and take up Kathleen and Max's invitation to lunch or dinner at their place.

We weren't left alone for long, however.

Our first visitor was Charlotte, who came to let us know that her grandmother, Emma Tinker had passed away tranquilly last night in her bed at Black Carr House.

"I'm so sorry," I commiserated with Charlotte. "You'll miss her."

"Oh, I know. I will. But she was ready to go. After yesterday afternoon she was completely at peace, and when we said goodbye last night, I sort of knew it was for the last time."

"Maudie's taken her to be with Pa," shouted Lily casually from Charlotte's car, where she was chatting through the window to Kimberley.

"I should tell you, Mo, that I'm resigning from the Post Office. I've been offered – something better and I'll be moving house, like you suggested, as well."

"Oh, no, Charlotte," I said, alarmed that my village community was starting to crumble. "Does this mean you're moving away, and that the Post Office will be closing?"

"Oh dear, no," she replied, cheerfully. "My cousin Nina's going to become the Sub Postmaster. She's been looking for work locally for ages; it'll suit her down to the ground. And I'll be staying in the Haddestons, don't worry. I was wondering if you'd help me try and track down my mother, but with Gran gone, Kylie off to London and my new work, I don't think we can be in *Time Crunch* after all. Sorry Mo."

I was still wondering how I could break this bad news to Jane and Tamara, when a smart little Japanese sports car arrived and Alison Wood stepped out, in tailored slacks and a fitted shirt – probably as casual as she ever gets, I thought, opening the front door with some apprehension.

"I'm sorry to disturb you on a Sunday morning, but it's rather urgent. May I come in?"

I ushered her through to the sitting room, wishing it was not awash with toys, Sunday papers and general disorder, and called Jack in from the garden.

Alison refused a cup of coffee and looked immensely uncomfortable as she faced us, side by side on the sofa, from her armchair.

"I wanted to be the first to inform you," she began in her legal style, "that my husband and daughter have written to the General Medical Council to withdraw the allegation of sexual impropriety against Dr Patterson. We all accept that it was a flight of fancy and never in fact took place."

Jack and I stayed silent.

I imagined he must feel the same mixture of incredulity, relief and fury that I did.

Alison leaned forward and we saw emotion flood her face for the first time.

"I am so sorry that it happened at all. My daughter's not well, but we didn't realise how – how really very ill she had become. Nigel and I both work very hard, too hard, and we weren't paying enough attention. He genuinely believed her story. I think she probably believed it herself. I... well, I admit I tried to stop him filing the complaint. It put me in a very awkward position with the Health Centre, of course, and from our brief business dealings, I didn't believe you would have done such a thing."

"I see. Thank you," Jack answered charitably. "That's a huge relief and I look forward to returning to work."

"I thought perhaps you would like to know that we are paying for Rachel to attend a private drug rehabilitation clinic and taking her out of the high pressured, academic school environment she has been unhappy in. She thinks she might like to train as a riding instructor and I wondered whether your daughter might want to come and ride our pony, Rosie, and provide her with some work experience?"

"I'm sure Lily would love to do that," I replied, warming to Alison Wood more than I had ever thought possible.

She tried a small smile. It seemed to work.

"Thank you, you're being very generous. Could I ask you a personal favour, Mrs Patterson?"

"I'm Mo," I said. "Ask away."

"Mo. I've heard through the village grapevine that you are working on something to do with time and life balance. Nigel and I desperately need some help in that area, we are both self-confessed workaholics, he has an elderly mother in care locally who takes some managing, and I feel sure this time pressure is part of Rachel's problem. There may be some hereditary factors we can't alter, but we need to do some work on how we operate as a family. Is there anyone with the appropriate expertise you could put us in touch with, or a therapy programme we could enroll in?"

I tried to repress the grin that was attempting to spread across my face.

"Funny you should say that," I told her. "I think I can help you there."

———

On the doorstep, as she was leaving, clutching my press release and other material about *Time Crunch*, I asked her for some professional advice in return.

"Alison, if someone died without leaving a will and everything was sold off, then sixty years later a will turned up, what would happen?"

She looked shocked for a minute, before resuming her composure and answering in her legal voice.

"If the estate had been disposed of, the will would have no validity whatsoever. Fighting a court case over property that no longer exists would be a complete waste of time and money."

"OK, that's what I thought. Thanks, Alison. Give my love to Rachel and tell her to ring when she's ready for Lily to come round."

———

We were all up in Lily's bedroom, discussing her choice of new colour scheme, when Elizabeth Gidney called up the stairs.

"Yoo hoo, Jack, Mo! The door was open, just like it always was in my day, so I've let myself in. May I join you?" and we heard her footsteps coming up the stairs.

"Daddy's going to decorate my bedroom," Lily told her importantly. "I want it bright purple and pink, but Mummy says it would be prettier in pale colours. What do you think?"

"Well now," said Elizabeth. "Perhaps somewhere in between would be nice. When my daughter slept in this room she would never have it painted. It's the only room in the house we didn't touch. I'm glad it's getting a makeover at last. Jack, I have some wonderful news. Look, I've brought a bottle of champagne to celebrate with!"

Our spirits were as effervescent as the bubbly after she had informed us that the Assistant Registrar of the General Medical Council had closed the case against Jack without further process. He could start work again immediately, but if he wanted to take some time off to recover from his ordeal, that would of course be his prerogative as the new Managing Partner of the Haddeston Health Centre.

Jack and I looked at each other, and back to Elizabeth.

"Yes, Managing Partner, that's what I said. It's high time I retired, though I hope you'll let me continue to work as a part time GP. I'd hate to lose contact with the patients and what would I do with myself? And then of course you might need some support with setting up the new Emma Tinker Alternative Healing Foundation."

We exchanged another incredulous glance.

What neither Charlotte nor Alison had told us this morning, thinking it best left to Elizabeth Gidney, was that the two of them had come to an agreement on a way of righting the injustice between their two families. The Jacksons, out of the capital they had inherited from Maurice Newling, would found a charity, to be based in an entirely new wing of the Health Centre. Its main work would be to develop Emma and Charlotte's herbal treatments but would include other alternative therapies such as osteopathy, shiatsu, acupuncture and aromatherapy. Charlotte Tinker would be the charity's director, but Jack, as Managing Partner of the Health Centre, would be in overall charge of its work as well as the mainstream medical practice.

———

We stood between the gate posts, Jack, Lily, Felix and I, to wave Elizabeth off down The Street.

My head was spinning a little from the champagne, but I felt an overwhelming sense of being in the right place at the right time. Lily climbed astride the old-fashioned child's bicycle that was still leaning against the wall.

"Can you mend this for me, Dad? I've nearly grown out of my chopper and this one's a bit bigger."

"Yes, we can make it all new and shiny again for you, if that's what you want, Li'l Girl," said Jack fondly.

"Well Maudie won't want it any more, she's gone for good now. They've all gone. I miss her a bit, but it's our house now."

Jack and I exchanged a glance. He would never admit to believing what Lily's words implied, but he wouldn't dismiss them quite so lightly any more.

"And can we restore Billy Stonepicker's star gates – or get some new ones made in the same pattern?" I asked.

"We can do whatever you like, hon," replied my husband, grinning happily. "I am, after all, the Managing Partner of the Haddeston Health Centre."

I beamed back at him.

"And you are exactly the husband I want you to be and I love you at least as much as you love me."

We turned together to look up at the high, pantiled roof of our house, its two tall chimneys lit from the west by golden rays of the descending summer sun. The primrose yellow walls glowed with a warmth that seemed to envelope the four of us standing in their lengthening shadow.

Was it fanciful of me to feel that the ancient building was extending a new welcome to its most recent inhabitants; that Stargate Farm, released from the hostility and injustice its walls had harboured, offered us afresh its shelter and protection?

"You know what?" said Jack. "It really was a very good idea of mine to move to the country."

Bibliography

A Land Girl's War – Joan Snelling, Old Pond Publishing, Ipswich 2004

A Wartime Winter, A Wartime Summer – Great Takes Television Ltd for Anglia Television Ltd 2006

Betty's Wartime Diary 1939–1945 – Ed, Nicholas Webley, Thorogood, London, 2002

The Blue-Eyed Son, The Story of an Adoption – Nicky Campbell, Macmillan, London 2004

Favourite War-time Recipes By Housewives of Leigh – assembled by members of the Surrey 272 Red Cross Detachment, December 1943

Larn Yarself Norfolk, A comprehensive guide to the Norfolk dialect – Keith Skipper, Nostalgia Publications, Dereham, 1996

Literary Norfolk, An Illustrated Companion – Julian Earwaker and Kathleen Becker, Aurum Press, London, 2003

Norfolk Airfields in the Second World War – Graham Smith, Countryside Books, Newbury, 1994

Primal Wound, Understanding the Adopted Child – Nancy Newton Verrier, Gateway Press, Baltimore 1993

Standing Up to Hitler, The Story of Norfolk's Home Guard and "Secret Army" 1940–1944 – Adrian Hoare, Countryside Books, Newbury 2002

The Home Front in the Second World War – Paul Fincham, Longman, Harlow 1986

The Seven Basic Plots, Why we tell stories – Christopher Booker, Continuum, London 2004

More by the same author:

BLOOD AND WATER

Mo Mozart feels she's at last getting the balance of her life right as a professional researcher, **wife and** mother. Until, that is, her husband's twin sister asks Mo to help find their birth mother…

MR MIKEY'S LADIES

Mr Mikey is middle-aged, gay – and sick of being a hairdresser. He married his Aussie lover's sister to gain residency Down Under, but then lover Bryan died and wife Dolly got pregnant. His Ladies sustain him with their friendship and confidences. As he listens to their scurrilous tales of love and loss, Mr Mikey decides to weave them into a Mega Musical – his escape route to fame and fortune!

THE BOOK OF BALANCED LIVING

Under pressure at work and at home? No time to get organised, to meet commitments, to get the balance right? This is a book for people who want to take back control of their life - but who don't know where to start or which way to turn…

About the Author

 Lucy McCarraher has written three novels, two self-help books, scripts for television, and numerous articles and reviews for newspapers, magazines and journals. She is an expert in work-life balance, has been a consultant to a range of organisations and advised many individuals on the subject.

She has also worked as a tv script-editor, concept developer, researcher, producer and presenter; as a magazine publisher, book editor, writer's agent, ghost writer and theatre critic; and as a conductor on the Blackpool trams.

Lucy was born and has lived most of her life in London. She was brought up in Chelsea and, after spending nearly a decade in Australia, gradually moved south through London via Stockwell, Kennington, Peckham and Crystal Palace.

She has two adult sons and now lives in rural South Norfolk with her husband and two young daughters.

Printed in the United Kingdom by
Lightning Source UK Ltd., Milton Keynes
137206UK00001BA/1-24/P